SPIN

Also by the author

The Colors of Infinity   (North Star Line/Blue Moon Books)
Against Gravity   (Grove Press)
The Hawk's Dream and Other Poems   (Grove Press)
Sliding down the Wind   (Swallow Press)

SPIN

Donald Everett Axinn

Station Hill

Published by Station Hill Literary Editions, a project of the Institute for
Publishing Arts, Barrytown, New York 12507. Station Hill Literary Edi-
tions are supported in part by grants from the National Endowment for the
Arts, a Federal Agency in Washington, D.C., and by the New York State
Council on the Arts.

Front cover photos copyright © Michael K. Nichols and Elliott Erwitt,
Magnum Flash. Back cover photo by Tom Jenkins.

Text and cover design by Susan Quasha.

Typeset by Delmas Typesetting.

Distributed by The Talman Company, 1509 Fifth Avenue, New York, New
York 10011.

Library of Congress Cataloging-in-Publication Data
Axinn, Donald E.
    Spin / Donald Everett Axinn.
        p. cm.
    ISBN 0-88268-125-7 : $19.95
    I. Title.
    PS3551.X5S65   1990   90-23530
    813'.54—dc20   CIP

Author's Acknowledgments

For their encouragement and help, I am deeply grateful to Frances Jalet,
Devon Jersild, Sara Blackburn, Roger Straus III, Jonathan Galassi, Leon
Friedman, and Dianne Francis. And to my wife, Joan, for her support and
comments as the work progressed.

Manufactured in the United States of America.

For Morgan, Lucien and Zahra

Who is the slayer, who the victim?
Speak.

Sophocles

ONE

This was very good, what was happening. The terrible past stuff would be over forever. The ache and longing he couldn't keep away would be smashed by his father, beaten, vanquished, never to confront and frighten him again.

Certain memories were branded onto him, scar tissue he had run his fingers over so often it was as though they had always been there: his mother not letting him keep his light on when he heard scary noises; once telling her he never knew what would happen next and that in the pitch black something might get him—but she just smiled and said it was silly; his mother and even sometimes his father yelling at him when he never expected it. But other memories: when she washed and dried his hair slowly and nice; how good it felt when she touched his neck and ears; when his father tossed him up and they both hugged him at the same time.

He was almost seven in 1945 when his father was finally released from the Air Force and started flying again with United Airlines. Thinking about his father coming home for good was as terrific as if his mother told him there would be a crackerjack birthday party for him that would last for days and days.

It was wonderful fun the way he and his mother prepared for the event: hanging red, white and blue streamers across the living room from corner to corner and side to side. They taped a batch along the front entrance. Candies and nuts brimmed to the top of the cut-glass dishes used for company. Edward took a long time selecting which "penny" candies he wanted but finally settled on coconut chocolate Mounds, Jujubes licorice and six boxes of Crackerjacks. His mother made him give up half of them. (But then she always would spoil things a little.) They made the "Welcome Home" sign together: "WELCOME HOME" was painted on the first line, and then, underneath, "MAJOR SAM SLAVIN." Smaller, on the third, was "Five L-O-N-G Years in the Service of His Country." His mother went back and underlined the "L-O-N-G."

"You do the inside of the letters, sugar-lamb. Whatever colors you like. You don't have to ask me," she said beaming as she hugged him. She hummed continuously and every so often she sang, "Mairzy dotes and dozey dotes and little lambsey divey." She was happy like that sometimes when they walked the baby in her carriage or when she had received a letter from his father. His baby sister looked weird and runty when his mother first brought her home, like a scrawny puppy he once saw. Except the dog's face was sort of cute, so you could like it if you wanted. This thing couldn't play, and besides it wasn't even a boy.

"Oh, Edward, everything is finally going to be the way it should. We won't ever be split up again. Daddy will be home *every night,*" she told him. "Well, not *every.* He won't be when he's on a trip, will he?" (Edward agreed by shaking his head back and forth.) "But that's only one or two nights, not whole weeks and months."

Edward remembered the beginning when all the fathers wore khaki uniforms. That's when everything was khaki, khaki and brown, every base, all the buildings and the rooms, all the blankets and all the bathrooms and the plates and even the food. It was all like some punishment.

All the khakis and brown stunk, but nice colors, they were good: the ribbons on the fathers' chests, all the little bands of green and blue and red and yellow; the fat red, yellow and blue balls he bounced in the playground or off the walls in his room when his mother wasn't around. And the pictures he made with his crayons, his own pictures. He could use whatever colors he wanted. Besides, nobody cared anyway.

It was always better when he could decide what *he* wanted. That was swell, when his mother didn't tell him what to do. He felt different with his father. He'd do anything his father told him, except he was away so much. He hated his not being around. Edward felt a kind of hard pressing in his chest when he saw a father hold hands with his son or run along next to him when the son rode a new bike. And if they whispered he wanted badly to know what they were saying.

At this one particular base he and his mother had moved to it was real cold. The wind howled a lot, like some monster out to get you. Edward looked across the flats during the day. They seemed endless and forever. He shivered no matter how tight his coat was buttoned. He felt like the wind monster was grabbing at his skin with all its ugly fingers. He'd look straight into the howl just to prove to himself that it couldn't get him. But at night he'd have to remind himself again. Nights were dark and bad. He got all kinds of thoughts, weird ones about his father not coming home because something terrible had happened to him. Sometimes that made him mad, and then afterward he'd feel he was bad because he'd been angry. His father couldn't help it, could he? But Edward knew he was angry when he'd spank his teddy bear. And he loved Teddy. It wasn't Teddy's fault, was it? Once in a while his mother sat with him and tried to answer

3

his questions. He sure did have a lot of them. And problems, too. But usually she was too busy, or she would say, "later on, dear." So how could he tell her at bedtime about the howls?

"It wouldn't be this way if it wasn't for this stupid war, Edward. Daddy has to fly his plane to show the Germans and Japs they can't just take over the world. You know, tell us how to live. God knows I need your father back with us. Raising you alone is very difficult." She sighed when she said that.

Sometimes she'd get real cranky and scream at him. Edward could see she was right that he was a problem. He decided he'd better try to do what she said. Maybe then she wouldn't be so mad.

They moved all the time, and he never knew when it was going to happen. If his father was going to be at the new base, that was okay, but Edward hated always having to make friends all over again.

His mother taught him about the states. Nevada and California had mountains called the Rockies. Georgia had lots of farms, fruit ones. Florida was hot, but the ocean was there. Arizona was the real West, with huge ranches and horses that turned on a dime when the cowboys roped the baby cattle. The desert didn't have water and was tough to live in, but it was beautiful, with cacti that looked like people with their arms sticking out. Also mountains with snow on them and a great big giant split she said was the Grand Canyon. Texas had lots of bases but everything was flat. The wind howled the most in Oklahoma, and there were no cities near the bases.

Oh, but the cities! Cities had wonderful stores and huge parks with all kinds of animals and lots of movies. The people sometimes weren't friendly—they didn't seem to want to do much talking and weren't very interested except in their own stuff. He wondered why. How else could he find out about things unless everyone talked to everyone else? At least maybe the kids. He sure would have liked to know them. He'd see them and he'd want to speak to them, but they were always with their mothers or their brothers or sisters. Edward

4

didn't have anyone like an older brother to play with. He once asked his mother how come he didn't have one. Everyone else did.

"No, *not* everyone does. Your father doesn't. I'm kind of thinking that you might one day, but I am certainly not promising." She laughed when she said that.

At one base in Texas, they had stayed a very long time. His father was stationed there, at least most of the time. Some weekends were especially great then because he did things with Edward. And there were lots of other kids his age, and older ones too. Three brothers lived in the very next building, one his age and two older. They were friendly, but sometimes they could be mean.

They had a game called "Salouji." It always started out with the two older brothers throwing the ball and Edward and their little brother in the middle, trying to catch it.

"I caught it!" Edward shouted. "Now it's my turn, and you're in the middle!"

"No it isn't," one yelled. "You have to get it three times."

"But that's not the way you said it."

The older kid, Richard, pulled his knit hat off his head and using one hand, tossed the ball to himself—up in the air, not high, just right above his head. "If you want to play with us, that's the rule." He kept tossing and catching the ball. And he whistled too. It was lousy of him to change the rules.

"I'm getting tired of this," the oldest one said. "Let's do 'The Lone Ranger.'"

Edward knew they listened to it every night because all the kids did. "Jack Armstrong, The All-American Boy," too. Also "The Green Hornet." That always was the best part of the day, because he didn't have to worry about anything. He wanted badly to play this new game.

They made faces like maybe. "See, we can use these sticks as guns unless you want me to get mine from inside," Edward said. "You thought I was the louse who plugged your father, but I'm not. And when you shoot me I fall off Silver, but I'm not really dead, just pretending. And then we team up together and go off after the real bad guys, okay? Your little brother can be Tonto's brother."

They nodded. Edward was relieved. He always liked games when they ran around better than he liked the throwing ones.

"You're a Ichabod Crane," one of them once said. He had to ask his mother what that was because he didn't want them to find out he didn't know. Anyway, he was taller and decided that meant he was sort of ahead.

"And what's that *thing* on your face?" they'd demand. His birthmark. He'd do anything to make it disappear. He tried to turn away slightly and also not show any feelings when the kids teased him. He never wanted them to have something on him. More than anything, he wanted to feel he belonged and that people liked him. He hated having to explain this stupid red birthmark on his forehead. Once he even tried to scrub it off with a washcloth.

One morning, watching his father get dressed in his uniform, Edward asked, "Daddy, how come I have this real dumb *thing* on my face?" Sam Slavin had lifted him onto the bureau and with an elaborate, sweeping gesture placed his officer's hat on his head. Of all the things he wanted, none made him feel better than when his father was pleased with him. He stood in front of Edward with a wide grin; his teeth were perfectly white except for the tobacco stains in a few places. (Edward didn't know why, but he thought perhaps there was a place in the world where people's teeth were some other color than white, like maybe orange or red, even blue. But it'd sound crazy to ask about that.)

"Hey, that's nothing, Eddie! This one character I knew had a huge one smack on his rear end. You can imagine what kind of trouble *that* gave him." His father adjusted the hat so Edward could see better from beneath the polished brim. Edward couldn't figure out why having a birthmark there was worse than on your face, where everyone could see it.

How he admired his father's muscles, the way they indented and moved. His pectorals and biceps and shoulders looked a little like water pouring from the kettle because there were grooves in the stream of them. His father was very strong. He lifted chairs and tables and his mother as if they were small toys.

"I wish mine was there. The kids tease me."

Most of his father's assignments were at bases where he couldn't obtain leave, and now he was departing again—after just two days, and the first time he had been back in three months. Edward didn't like his parents going out at night and leaving him alone with a baby sitter.

"Hey, Butch," his father said, "I have an idea that'll fix them. Tell 'em you were in a plane crash with me after we shot down ten Nazis. Five more finally got us. You were grazed on the forehead by a bullet." He pushed Edward with his finger until he giggled. "And you have to limp, it's because you were also hit in the leg. Six times!" He exaggerated his walk, almost falling down, which made Edward shriek with pleasure.

"Like this?" Edward asked, laughing as he copied his father's movements until he fell over. Later, he would always associate his birthmark with this incident.

"Couldn't have done it better myself. And listen, don't you want to be different from the other kids? Besides, who wants to be perfect? That can be a real pain in the birthmark, believe me."

Edward was aware how very handsome and graceful his father was. He had a clean, firm line from the back of his jawbone to his chin, smoothed-out hollows under his cheekbones, and light brown hair with a large, sweeping wave on the wide side of the part. Even his electric eyes were an unusual color, somewhere between blue and green. They pushed you until you agreed on whatever it was he wanted. He also liked to stare at you to see who could keep a straight face the longest. But how did his father always know just what to say and do? It was great the way he figured things out and took charge, and he almost always could find something funny or amusing in every situation.

Edward observed every move his father made buttoning his shirt. He pulled it down tight and fitted his pants over so that it looked perfectly neat. He talked as he performed each detailed part of the process, not needing to concentrate at all on moving his fingers in complicated ways to slip buttons into their holes or on making sure the shirt was just right. No matter how he scrutinized the way his father tied his tie, he knew he could never imitate that intricate procedure. One day soon, he'd ask him to teach him how he did it.

"Oh, yes, and you can tell them about the medals we were awarded. Too heavy to wear them all. Besides, we're not show-offs, are we?" He pulled Edward off the bureau and crouched down until they were face to face: "As a matter of fact, I think you're an all-around terrific boy. Like—who is it? Yeah, Jack Armstrong." He grinned, lifted him straight up above his head, let go, and then caught him. Then he squeezed him and kissed him. "I love you, son. But now I have to leave. Take-off's in forty-five minutes. I can't be late."

"Why do you have to go again? I want you to come back right away, Daddy. Please?" His father raised his arms straight out, started to move as if he were an airplane, and made sputtering noises that sounded exactly like an engine warming up. Then he smiled and saluted. Edward watched and raced after him into the living room. "Here, son," his father said, hugging his mother, "hold my hat. I'll see you by the car." Edward made a face. His father pointed a finger at him. Edward saluted and bolted out the front door.

§

TWO

His mother. She warned him all the time that everything had to be kept very neat because the rooms they lived in were not theirs. Would they ever have their own rooms? "Yes, when this stupid, stupid war is over. Then we'll have our own home, and we won't have to leave it. But right now we're in The Military. And you can't let anyone know how you really feel." But when no one else could hear, she sure did say exactly how she really felt about the people and the things she didn't like.

One afternoon, at Fort Sill in Arkansas, she told him, "You'll have to say good-bye to everyone, Edward." He looked at her flatly, instinctively trying not to show how he felt at hearing this dreaded pronouncement once again. "I'll be back in a little while. Don't look at me that way, darling. We leave first thing tomorrow morning." She grabbed both his hands. "You want to see Daddy again, I know you do. So go and play nicely with your friends out back. I have to go to the hairdresser, I really must. It's important I look my best, not like this." She kissed him on the forehead. "If you get sleepy, take a nice nap. And be a good boy."

I hate moving all the time, he said to himself. And I *won't* be a good boy. She can't make me! After she left, he went over to his bed and lay down next to his teddy bear to think about how terrible everything was. He slid the furry animal under his quilt with only its head protruding, and after a few minutes, without realizing it, he closed his eyes.

§

On the train from Fort Sill, they sat with another woman from the base and her baby. It was a boy. Edward settled himself on the seat next to the window and took out his crayons and coloring book. His coat, with his cap tucked in a pocket, rocked on the hook the same as the train. His mittens were pinned to the ends of the sleeves so he wouldn't lose them any more. They were hard to get off that way and he had to use his teeth, but he was glad because now at least his mother had one less thing to be annoyed about.

The train was brown, but that was okay because the letters and numbers were nice and white. The contrast made the brown different, not ugly and just brown, the way khaki looked. The conductor wore a blue uniform with silver buttons that were also sewed in a line on the ends of his sleeves. He clicked his ticket puncher and had all sorts of stuff hanging down from his belt. Long, important-looking cards stuck out of his pockets. He knew how to walk straight even though the train bounced side to side as it raced to wherever they were going. That came from practicing, Edward supposed.

Bright red signal lights blinked at the road crossings. On, off. When one went on, the other went off. Blinking, switching, taking turns. It was wonderful how it did that! He closed one eye and tried keeping the other open, then closed the open one and reopened the other, switching, but he couldn't do it right. They'd either both stay open, closed or part-way. But the signal lights worked so perfectly, the way they did it. How could the machine be timed so that it was exactly smooth, and one was all the way on when the other was all the way off? Why couldn't you work your eyes that way? I'll practice so I can. Daddy said you have to practice real hard if you want to get good at something. ("You have to remember, kiddo, that machines don't get born. They're made by people. If you're patient and learn how to work them," he would say, "they'll be your friends for life. And having friends counts.")

"I'm so glad we're together, Diane," his mother was saying. "I wouldn't have had anyone to talk to." She smiled sweetly when she said it. The lady named Diane had hair that hung down straight and curled in at the bottom in a line. It looked like all the wigs Edward had seen on plastic ladies in department stores. His mother's hair was fixed exactly the same, except the color of the lady's was like the shiney yellow of corn. They both wore bangs that were straight and stopped just above their eyebrows. The baby didn't have any hair at all and made noises when he squirmed. And he gassed stinky. Mostly he sucked on his fingers.

"I was only a sophomore when we met," Edward's mother was saying. "My cousin Carole had a party, and Sam wouldn't let anyone dance with me except him. It was very embarrassing. He's still so possessive!"

Edward tried to concentrate on his coloring book. Pinks and purples, maybe light blues and nice greens. Yes, lots of greens, for leaves and grass. Why not for clothes, too, hats and dresses and pants? The others can be blues and purples. Mix all the colors together for neckties.

Another stupid train to another stupid base. Maybe Daddy won't let them make us move to any more stupid forts. I won't even think about him because maybe he won't be there. Last time we moved, he wasn't there because he had to fly somewhere and didn't tell us so we didn't know. Do you like me, Daddy? I love you so much. He felt the tingle in his arm, like he did sometimes when something important happened. He'd better close his eyes. He did, trying to think about something different. Signal lights.

Pretend I work them perfectly, each one on then off, switching, a great giant signal-light everyone saw when there was danger. There they are, cars coming fast, but they stop in time because they see my lights. I'm the lights. Me.

"Yes," his mother was saying, "he started because he was a line-boy or something on Long Island when Lindbergh was getting ready to fly to Paris. He didn't have any money, so he ran away and joined the Army Air Force. Isn't that romantic? He was commissioned a second lieutenant and flew those old Martin bombers."

"That *is* interesting, Edith," the lady said. "I knew your Sam was older than most of the other men." She leaned down and kissed her baby. "I suppose you've heard Vance is also going to make Captain."

"They all wanted Sam to stay in," his mother said, smoothing her hair. "But he accepted an offer from United Airlines." She turned to Edward and stroked the hair from his forehead and eyes. "Actually, there was another reason too."

The train lurched, and Edward's crayon box slid off the seat, fell to the carpeted floor and spilled like spaghetti sticks from a box. He surveyed his mother's face. "The train banged, Mommy, and ..."

"Edward! You're so careless! Now, pick them all up immediately." She turned back to the other woman and said quietly, "We're Jewish. You knew that, didn't you?"

His mother had told him they were Jewish. Why did she need to tell it to this lady? Was it so important?

"Now with the war and all, it doesn't make much difference, but in those years, well, officers who were Jewish didn't go very far." She smiled and smoothed her bangs nervously. "But Sam worked hard and did well." The other woman didn't answer, but she kept talking. "You know, Diane, I wouldn't tell him he was the only one when we first got together. I didn't want him to take me for granted. Wasn't that smart?"

"Yes, I suppose so," the woman said, "but it doesn't matter any more. We're all in this together." It sounded like they were having two different conversations. She touched his mother's arm.

His mother glanced out the window onto the undulating flatlands. Edward looked out too and noticed how the grasses bunched in brown clumps and rose through patches of the March snow. Gusts of wind bent them and made them look like people swaying and moaning. He felt his mother shiver.

He turned to a new page of his coloring book. Grays and blacks. Naw, he decided. Mix the blacks and browns together. Browns look like doody.

"Don't you love to see your husband in his uniform?" his mother asked. "I love how Sam looks in his. On our honeymoon at this fabulous resort on Mackinac Island, I made him wear his uniform with his new fourth stripe when we went to dinner. He didn't want to, but he had to if he wanted to please me."

The woman's baby began to cry. "Sometimes having children . . ." she said, lifting her son up and nuzzling him. "Teething. And he dribbles so much." Edward put his hand on his mother's lap and slowly rubbed his fingers against the material of her dress. He looked up at her.

"My Edward was hardly any trouble at all. He was a very good baby." She stroked his head and smiled at Diane. "Do you think they'll tell us when we can have lunch? I might even have a teeny drink."

Edward peered out the window. The flats were long, rolled a little and seemed to be without an end. He couldn't hear the howl, but he knew it was there.

"Diane, I'm going to confide something, but don't tell, okay?" She giggled like a teenager. "When Sam went to fly for United, I made him promise he would never talk to any of the stewardesses. And I also told him the war in Europe wasn't our war; besides, he had a wife and a little son to take care of. But Sam said Hitler and the Nazis were doing horrible things to the Jews. We have relatives there. And I knew then that no matter what I said he was going back in. He wanted so much to get into the fighting."

His mother took one of his crayons and colored in one of the figures. She smiled at him and continued. "Sam promised that even though he wanted to enlist, he'd always take care of me and our children. So I talked to Daddy. He called someone, because he said fathers weren't supposed to be in combat. And as soon as he enlisted, Sam was assigned to teach flying. I never, never told him about Daddy. Please don't ever mention it to anyone." His mother kept talking. Edward leaned his head back to rest. The rocking motion of the train felt nice. Even though it was morning, he fell asleep.

§

One evening after dinner, at the new base, when he was playing with his friends, his mother came outside. "Okay, young man, right to bed. Lights out at seven-thirty."

He flinched. Everyone had heard her. "But Mommy," he whispered, "all the other kids are still playing. Why do I always have to go to bed before they do?"

"Because I said so. Now inside!" She gave him a little shove.

I wish you were dead, really dead, he thought. He slammed the door to his room, grabbed the neat line of pressed shirts and pants from his closet, and flung them to the floor. Then he pulled his underwear and socks from his drawers. He kicked the clothes into the air, tripped on them, fell down, and screamed. His mother opened the door.

"Just what is going on in here? You stop that this minute!" She held him firmly. "I will not stand for any more of your temper tantrums. It's time you outgrew them." Edward tried to turn away, but she made him face her. "What will people say about how I'm raising you?" He struggled for another moment or two, but then he calmed down. He didn't want her to say he was a bad boy. He couldn't stand it when she did that.

The temper tantrums never made him feel better; they just seemed to happen. He'd thrash around, throw himself on the floor, and kick and shriek. At those times everyone was his enemy, everything became crazy. In his room, even the brass knob sticking out of the closet door glared at him, his books on the shelves were ugly, and the floor lamp with its stupid head looked like a weird animal with a gigantic round, open mouth. The toys in his toy box and even his stuffed animals all seemed to be against him. None of them understood or helped, and they could have. Now they were only mean and nasty. He'd lose himself in a frenzy until he was dizzy.

Now, in a calmer voice, his mother was telling him, "None of us can have what we want all the time, Edward. You must learn you're no different."

Bad mother, saying that, not knowing he couldn't help it! Edward slipped from her grasp and stood in the middle of the room, his hands clenched. "Nothing ever happens the way I want!" he shouted. He spun around and glared at her. "Not anything!" he yelled, smacking his clenched fists against his thighs. His mother started to laugh.

"You're making fun of me," he sobbed. "You're a terrible Mommy! I hate you!" He stomped toward the door. She grabbed his arm and pulled him onto the bed and put her arm around him. He noticed that her legs and feet were exactly the same shape as his—funny thick calves and skinny, long feet.

"I'm not laughing at you, darling. Sometimes you're adorable, but I do want you to grow up." She held his hand, and he could smell something sort of summery. Perfume stuff. His knew his father had brought it back for her from one of his trips. "What about putting these clothes back?" she suggested.

"Mommy," he asked slowly, "why isn't Daddy home? All my friends' fathers live at the base."

"Not all, by any means. He'll come home as soon as he can." She stroked his forehead. Her fingers felt soft and cooling. "I've told you it's not up to him. Just believe he will, and soon—God willing—he'll be back with us for good. Now, Edward, please get ready for bed."

He took his second favorite pajamas from the drawer. They were his "Dr. Denton's," which had gotten pretty small. When he had complained to his father that the "feet" they'd had originally were too hot, his father had cut them off. Then his father and he had brought the woollen feet with the pads on the bottom and put them ceremonially on the dinner table. "Edith, Edward's asked two of his friends over. Hope you don't mind," his father had said solemnly. They had all laughed together for a long time.

"Mommy," he asked, "can I have a cookie? And some water?"

She brought in a glass of water and sat down on the edge of his bed. "It's way past your bedtime. You've had a long day, so close your eyes," she ordered impatiently.

"Sometimes I'm scared," he said. He knew the last word was hardly audible. "I try to sleep, but I keep seeing other fathers and not Daddy. I'm scared he's not coming back." He turned away quickly and clasped his teddy bear.

His mother said, "I've told you, Edward: soon he'll come back to us for good. You have to believe that. *I* have to. There's nothing more I can say to you." She bent over, kissed him on the forehead and left the room.

He was in the dark again with the ugly, terrible creatures looking at him. He would have the dreams again and not be able to run away—from the pale things that chased him, or the big, fiendish kids who pinned him down and let their saliva slowly drop on his face.

Slimey, cold and horrible-looking, kids with strange eyes, weird ears, misshapen noses and mouths. When he dreamed that he was lost and shouted for his parents, they didn't come—even his father. What came instead were parts of people: faces, hands.

He woke from a half-sleep, from the terrible images, and hugged his teddy bear. "Daddy's a bad boy because he's away," he said out loud. "Mommy doesn't help me, but you're my best friend. You always will be, I know you will." He patted the bear. "Don't cry, Teddy, you can't cry. You're too old to cry."

He felt burning in his stomach and had to sit up. His mother always told him it was indigestion and not to eat too fast. But one day it might not stop and maybe he'd die. "Teddy, I don't want you to be bad, but if you are, you're going to get spanked. That's what has to happen, you know. Now, no more talking."

A tremor passed through him, as if he were cold. Maybe he could picture his father in the dark. The dark didn't frighten *him*, he knew how to deal with scary things. Sometimes he explained to Edward that the things weren't real, even though at night they seemed to be; you just get scared when bad ideas happen, he said. His father had asked him if he ever met a person who had been hurt or even touched by a monster. Now Edward tried again to remember what his father had said. Something about . . . . He slept.

§

THREE

That morning, Edward waited for his father endlessly. Finally he saw that certain walk a block away and raced down the street. His father dropped his khaki canvas valise and swept him up, hugged him and swung him around onto his back. Holding his valise in one hand, he ambled up to their front door, which was wide open, stopped a few feet in front of where his mother was holding the new baby, and asked, "Could you possibly be Mrs. Sam Slavin, wife of the famous aviator?" His father *would* say that, make a joke even though he knew how important this moment was for his mother.

But she was ready for him. "Major, oh, my goodness, no! She's in the next building, but you can visit with us awhile if you want. My husband likes the war, I guess, because he said he wants to be the last one discharged." He just stared at her, and for the first time Edward could remember, his father didn't have any retort.

"You get in here this minute," she commanded in measured cadence, "before I don't let you in at all." Edward laughed with them.

Only the baby, Susie, didn't laugh. Her white bonnet with the pink trim had slipped over her eyes. What could she know about how special this moment was?

His father flicked off his officer's dress hat and handed it to Edward. "Yours, son, from now on," he said with a grin. Edward put it on and hugged his father's leg. Then his father held his hand and they moved toward the front door. Edward whooped and skipped alongside his father's large steps.

His mother pressed her lips tightly together, hesitated, then said softly, "We have you home for good, darling." His parents embraced for what seemed to him a very long time and then they kissed. Then his mother said, "The war and this whole damn screwed-up period is finally over." She enunciated "over" with deliberate slowness. "Take your daughter, Major. The three of you, into the living room," she ordered. She darted toward the kitchen and returned with a bottle of champagne and two glasses.

"You drink early, Mrs. Slavin. This part of your normal ten-o'clock routine?"

"Yes, you big boob, every morning. I get drunk with this little boy here. It helps the days pass when there's no man around. Of course, there have been men who've tried to spend time with me." Then she slipped into a southern accent and said, "But mah man, Mistah Rhett, he told me ah has to stay away from the othahs. Have you seen him, suh? It's been so many, many long yeahs, ah don't really know whethah ah would remembah how to behave with a *real* man." She fluttered her eyelashes, and his father laughed. Intensely excited, Edward laughed too.

"Suppose I show you," his father said, putting his mouth a few inches from hers. Then he popped the cork, and it hit the ceiling with a clunk. The champagne foamed, and his father quickly poured some of the bubbling liquid into the two glasses. "Just one minute," he said. "There's a special *man* here who doesn't have any of this holy

20

water." He rose and brought back a small juice glass, grinned at Edward and then filled it half-full. "Special occasion, Butch, but drink it very slowly. Then he said, "One second, everyone." His father brought a chair from the dining area. While he was straightening his uniform and adjusting his tie, Edward shifted the chair closer. His father didn't notice, and as he went to sit down, he stumbled. "For Christ's sake, Edward, you trying to be funny?"

"I wanted to help you." Tears filled his eyes.

"Sorry to yell at you, Buddy. Okay, let's get on with the hero's welcome." He patted Edward on the head and jumped up on the chair. "Honored guests, Commanding General Edward—keep your hat on straight, General—Mrs. Slavin, wife of the famous aviator and national hero. This indeed is a splendiferous day in the history of our glorious nation. I had planned to speak to you for several hours, but just let me end by saying that it was a marvelous five years." He made the noise of a Bronx cheer. "We saved the world from evil and those infamous dictators—which of course I did single-handedly." He bowed to his audience. "In closing I'd like to say that the one 'snafu' the service didn't commit was making sure my orders for discharge had my name, rank and serial number spelled correctly on them." He took a sip. "Oh, yes, one last request: if you do this again, my family and I would appreciate it if you would first lose all my records. I'm sure you will. You're good at that. And thank you again for a most stimulating vacation."

He and his mother applauded. Edward watched them chatter and hold each other's hands. "I've got a special present for you, Major," his mother said. "In a little while, Edward is going to the movies with one of my friends and her son." (She hadn't told Edward this. He wondered why she didn't give his father the present now.) "Help me put Susie to sleep, and then you can tell me war stories. And whatever else you can think of," she finished, slightly raising her eyebrows and fluttering her eyelashes.

21

"Your orders will be obeyed, Your Royal Underwear. Inside and to the very depths."

"I'm so glad we understand each other, Major. And I don't plan to disappoint you." They both smiled in that silly way they did sometimes.

"Daddy, you said you'd do stuff with me."

"Yes, I will. Later. I told you, there are things that sometimes come first." There was a brief silence, and then he said sternly, "Your mother tells me you don't listen, so go into your room until I tell you you can come out." Edward stood, motionless and surprised. "I said, inside your room until you go to the movies. Now scram! I'm home and there's going to be a little more discipline around here."

Edward turned and shuffled toward his bedroom door, went in, grabbed his teddy bear, closed the door and sat on the floor. "Boy oh boy, Teddy," he muttered, "Daddy is very mean to me. It's just as bad as when he's away. Nobody cares about us. Right now I wish he would just *stay away*." He felt hot juices pouring around in his stomach.

§

They moved to Highland Park, a small suburb not far from Midway Airport in Chicago, where his father flew for United. Croydon Road had rows of small homes that were set back from the concrete sidewalk on small lawns, with driveways on one side and entrance walks in the center of each plot. The architectural designs differed, but every house was two stories high with an attic, a basement and a one- or two-car garage in the rear. After Edward met the other children on the block, he settled in to a new and secure routine. He often lost himself in the fun and games he played with his new friends.

He loved the new bike that his parents gave him as a surprise. And it was a Schwinn! His mother and father were both in the living room when he came in from playing, and there it was, a big two-wheeler that had silver-chromed fenders with neat blue stripes. And it even had a horn and a light on the handlebars! Not many of the other kids' bikes had those. There was also a rack behind the seat to put books or other stuff on. "How come, Daddy, it's not even my birthday?" he burst out.

"Well, kiddo, because now you're in school full-time. Besides, our son gets the best, especially when he behaves and does what he's supposed to." His mother nodded and smiled. "You were kind of outgrowing that kid's bike, weren't you?" his father asked quizzically.

They really understood! He had been thinking of mentioning it for his next birthday. They knew how important a new bike was after all.

"I'm so happy you got it for me! Thanks, Daddy. Thanks, Mom. I promise I'll try to deserve it and do everything you want me to." He put out his arms and buried his face in his father's neck when he bent to sweep him up. His mother hugged them both. It was as wonderful a moment as he ever remembered.

"Okay, tell you what, old sport. I know you want to go for a test flight in your new machine. Your mother and I are shooting over to Matt Spenadel's for a drink. He's my new boss. We'll take Susie with us. You and I'll play some ball when I come back. I want you to become the best clean-up hitter on the Croydon Alligators, or whatever you call that rinky-dink team of yours."

"It's a good team, Dad. We won our last game. What time will you be back, so I make sure I'm here?"

"Oh, an hour or so. Before dark. We'll have plenty of time." His father went to the bicycle and tapped out V for Victory, dot, dot, dot, dash, on the horn, saluted and winked. Edward ran and hugged his leg, and then gave his mother a kiss.

Boy, was it fast! Racing up the street, around corners, everything a blur. Then over the top, downhill, his arms straight out like wings. Edward imagined he was flying, the wind against his face, his open hands and his whole body. He was taking off, rising above everything, streets, houses, garages, trees, people. This was being free. Now he knew what his father meant about how it felt to be off the ground, in that invisible ocean of air you swam in with your plane enclosed around you, like a colossal bathtub you could float in. Or through cloud-mountains that would sprout up like mushrooms or giant ice cream cones. He said in the sky you were in charge of everything, particularly when you were the pilot flying people to cities they wanted to get to. But when you flew alone, he said, it was like nothing else. Sliding down the wind and soaring, defeating all the laws of gravity. Even to places where you could see the colors of infinity. You could dream anything, be a great bird and part of a hawk's dream.

Now, on his wonderful new bike, he was the pilot of a sleek, fast Corsair fighter, and then he was an adventurer like Lindbergh or Floyd Bennett, exploring places men had never been to. Like in China or Alaska or the Amazon, seeing amazing people and places, carrying special medicines they had to have. All kinds of momentous and noble missions.

He knew this wonderful bike his parents gave him was the vehicle to his imagination, transporting him into dreams and attainments he could never realize without it. He had the best Dad and Mom anybody ever had. He was sure God was very good to him. He decided to stop off at his friend Leo Guthart's house to show it to him.

"What do you think of it, Leo? My parents just gave it to me as a surprise!" He was going to say something about his bike being just as large as Leo's, but he decided not to. Leo said it looked really great, a response Edward hadn't expected. He decided Leo was his best friend. "I'd stay and we could go biking together, but my Dad said he'd play ball with me so I gotta be home in time. See you tomorrow, okay?"

He got off to a running start alongside his bike, putting one foot on a pedal and then hurling himself onto the seat, like the Lone Ranger did on Silver. He knew he was showing off, but he raced all the way home. The Buick wasn't in the driveway. They'll be home right away, he thought, because it's going to get dark soon. Dad promised.

Much later, Edward was listening to the radio when the car swung into the driveway. He ran to the side door, saw the headlights go off in the garage and heard his parents in animated conversation. His father stopped talking when he saw Edward at the top of the steps.

He snapped his fingers. "Oh, Jesus, Eddie, I'm sorry about the time. I just clean forgot. Matt's my new boss—remember?—and he wanted to get to know us. You know, sit down with the wives, have a drink and schmooze. He's actually checking me over. We couldn't just run out. It's connected to my work." Seeing the forlorn expression on Edward's face, he let out a sigh. "I guess you don't understand."

"You promised you'd play ball with me, Dad. I waited. Susie was at least *with* you." He turned to walk away.

"Hey, wait a second. These things happen. I didn't plan to disappoint you. There's always another day." Edward faced around, looked at him and nodded.

Late the next day, Edward was playing in the backyard. He had placed the hose in the dirt gutter between the lawn and the flower bed, letting the water run slowly, simulating a river. The rocks he had located at certain points were dams, and he was on a mission to bomb them so the river would flood the factory where the Nazis were making bombs and poison gas.

His father pulled the Buick into the garage, and Edward went over to greet him. "Here, Eddie, this model is for you. The guy in the store said it was perfect for a boy your age. Sorry about yesterday. If you have any trouble, I'll help you with it." Edward wished he had said he'd work on the model plane with him, but he was glad his father had brought him the present. He loved building model planes down in the basement. He had his own area there, a bench with all his special stuff, including a knife for cutting, which he used carefully because his father always advised him to. This new kit was for a Mustang fighter, a P-51. It sure looked great in the picture on the box. After he finished it, he'd hang it from a string over his bed so he could see it all the time.

His mother told him he could work on his new model, but that dinner would be ready soon. His father played with Susie, swinging her around and around. Why was he doing that with *her*? Rough stuff was for boys, not girls. He emptied the contents of the box carefully, and placed the boards with the printed parts on them in sequence so he could follow the instructions. The bottle of dope was on the shelf, where he also put the tissue paper that would be used to cover the plane after it was assembled. He opened the instructions. They were printed in small letters. Maybe he'd ask his father to help him.

"Dad," he yelled upstairs, "these instructions are hard to understand. Come show me how I should do it." He didn't get an answer, but he could hear Susie giggling and his father saying something to his mother about her. He climbed the steps to the landing next to the kitchen. The smell of chicken cooking wafted through to his nostrils. His mother was humming. "Daddy, would you?"

"I'm trying to teach this little imp to do loops and rolls. She's starting to get the hang of it. I'm the plane, she's the pilot."

"You've played with her enough. It's my turn."

"You're much better off figuring out those instructions by yourself," his father responded. "They can't be that hard. Show me you can stick with it." His voice had a hard edge to it. "Once you've learned what it says, you . . ." Edward ran down the stairs and went back to his bench; he didn't hear him finish.

There's always some reason, Edward began to think. I wish I was more important to him. He's more interested in her than me. Susie has Mommy. I wish she'd never been born.

He decided to skip the instructions and placed the top balsa wood board in front of him. He grabbed the knife and swiftly began to cut along the line which delineated one of the wings. In his rush he pushed too hard and plunged the knife into his hand, in the soft area between his thumb and second finger. The blood spouted as the point of the knife penetrated through.

"Ouch! Mom, Dad!" he screamed.

His mother reached him first. "Oh, my God! Sam, Sam!" His father was right behind her. Edward was crying and holding out his arm. It was shaking. Blood covered the whole side of his hand.

His father took his handkerchief, wound it around the wound, and said calmly, "Take it easy, kiddo. It looks worse than it is. Here, come with me upstairs and I'll fix it up. I know it hurts, but it'll stop." He led Edward up the stairs. "Edith, call Doctor Herschkowitz. If he's already gone, telephone him at his house. I think he'll have to stitch this."

"What! What'll he do to me?" Edward asked, fearfully. "I don't want him to hurt me. Don't let him."

"Now listen to me," his father said in a measured voice. "It's a puncture, and if we don't get it stitched, it'll take too long to heal. Hell," he consoled, "everybody gets something like this when they're young. I had lots of them. Besides, you're lucky it wasn't your right hand. When you go to school tomorrow, you can tell the kids they should see the other guy." He gently swatted Edward on his rear end.

When the doctor sewed a single stitch to close the wound, Edward began to cry, but he stopped when his father told him to "act like a man." "He handled it very well, Edith," his father told his mother later. "You can be proud of him." Edward wallowed in the approval, but he didn't make the connection between the attention he was receiving and what he may have unconsciously done to achieve it.

§

He'd been dreaming of watching himself in a contest involving a large ball that could be thrown or kicked. There were two teams, the Reds and Blues. He was the captain of the Blues. The score was tied, and someone threw him the ball. It somehow became larger and larger, like he was a circus clown who was suddenly faced with an expanding sphere so large he couldn't move it. Then he saw that the clown looked a little like his father. Edward struggled fiercely to help the clown push or pull the ball any way at all, but it had become too gigantic.

"Eddie," his father said quietly as he leaned over him, "wake up. You were having a nightmare." He brushed the hair from his forehead. "I have something to tell you."

"Daddy? I was having this terrible dream, and we couldn't do something with this huge ball." He sat up, pleased to get away from the frustration and hugged his father, whose face was rough and darkened with a day's growth of beard.

"We're going on vacation, the whole family. I have a week off. How would you like to go to southern Arizona, away from all this slush and freezing weather?" He grazed his face lightly against Edward's.

"Like at a base?" He rubbed an eye, pushing the dream further behind.

"Hell no, much better. A cattle ranch that's owned by Major Healey and his wife, in an area where I was once stationed. Near Fort Huachuca."

Edward looked at him wide-eyed. "Cowboys and Indians?"

28

His father nodded. "Absolutely, but not the kind in the Lone Ranger. Hey, what do you see in that masked man anyway, an invincible guardian of the righteous?"

"What?" Edward didn't understand those last words. "He's really terrific. And the stories about him are really terrific and exciting." He knew his father was teasing him. He did that a lot, except when he was angry, but that never lasted. Not nearly as long as when his mother was. It could be all day with her.

The next day his mother packed the clothes he had put on his bed, but only a few of his toys and games. "How come?" he asked. "You're bringing all *her* things."

"For goodness sake, I expect you to understand better, young man. Can't you see I have my hands full, especially now your father's home full time? You're supposed to help me, not be a problem! There's not enough room to take all your toys. Why do you think I didn't pack them, because I want to make you unhappy?"

This was different, her talking grown-up to him, really explaining to him with a tone in her voice that was only a fraction short of pleading. At least that's how it sounded to him. A disgusting noise emanated from Susie's bottom. His mother shook her head and closed her eyes.

Edward took his mother's hand and kissed it. "I'm sorry, Mommy. I'll understand from now on, I promise." He'd remember the baby was tiny and needed help. He'd be good to her even when his mother wasn't looking, even though Susie never did anything good in return.

"Yes, that's fine," she said. "You'll be my special helper." She bent over and nuzzled Edward's ear with her nose. He began to imagine the ranch his father was taking them to, and all the fun they'd have. The best thing of all was knowing they'd all be together, the whole family, the way it was supposed to be, the way people *should* live, children with both parents around, and for boys, especially their fathers when they had been away flying in the war to save their country. His father was really back with him. Nothing could take him away again.

§

FOUR

The Huachuca mountains bunched up out of the high desert, as if the largest arms of a great earth giant had broken through by lifting himself from underneath the floor of the land. The huge crevasses which split through the bulging protruberances were the canyons, where streams slithered down and vegetation gathered in profusion at their edges. Every change in elevation, from the fifty-two hundred feet at the base to heights that reached more than ten thousand feet at the peaks, offered its own varieties of hard and softwood trees, bushes and wildflowers. To the east, across the broad expanse of the plains, some fifty miles away, were the Mule and Dragoon mountains. Bisbee and Tombstone waited there, mantled inside their histories of copper and violence.

What a place! Edward was amazed when he saw it. Immense mountains God must have decided should be located there, some pointed and sheer, and some smoothed as if they'd been whittled, like the way he fashioned certain kinds of model airplanes from balsam wood. The mountains were dark at night, but in the morning

31

when the light began to appear, they changed from gray to shades of purple and tan. In front of them, the land seemed to glide across the enormous plains.

Part of the Healey ranch was high up Carr Canyon Road, where the ranchhouse, the stable and other small buildings were situated. The bulk of the ranch was below on the prairie where the Healey's pastures extended for miles; the far-off specks were cattle, and the few distant sticks were windmills that Edward's father said were the only way water could be obtained because it rained so seldom. Edward didn't understand the connection and regretted he didn't ask.

Everybody dressed in cowboy pants called Levis. They wore either denim blue work shirts or fancy dress ones with stitching around the pockets, the collars and even on the cuffs. The real surprise for Edward was the boots, because the only high heels he had ever seen before were on women's shoes. The cowboy hats the men wore varied in the size of the brims. Colors ranged from tan and brown to black. Edward decided on the spot that one day he'd own a pure white one, like the Lone Ranger's.

"Daddy, Daddy! My horse Nellie—in the corral—she did just what I told her to. Ernesto showed me how to turn and stop her, and I did it by myself!" He adjusted his tan hat to angle it at the same tilt as his father's. "All the cows and calves. And lots of turkeys jump on top of each other and make funny noises. Why do they jump on each other? They look so silly."

His father examined his son's curious face, smiled and then laughed. "They get tired of standing on their own feet and want to let somebody else carry 'em around for a while." He brushed the dirt from his chaps. "Hey, cowboy, too bad you're having such a terrible time." He swung Edward up on his back, holding his two hands around his neck. "Look out there at that desert and those mountain ranges. Isn't it spectacular? We're sure going to have one helluva good vacation."

"Does *spectacular* mean 'specially different?'"

His father nodded. "You should ask your mother when you're not sure what a word means. She studied to be a teacher, you know."

"I do, only she always tells me she's busy or has to finish something or go somewhere. She says I should find out things in my books."

"She's right, you should. You know she has a lot going on. I'm sure she answers your important questions."

First he distracted Edward by pointing toward the horizon, then he grabbed his hand and ran like a blue streak to the corral. Inside, the horse he rode was bridled to a post, without a saddle strapped onto its back. His father looked at him. "I'm going to take you on White Sock the way the Indians rode." Edward yipped with pleasure. His father flung him onto the horse, motioned him to hold onto the long hair from his mane and then mounted behind him. "Ready, cowboy?"

He untied the reins, leaned down and pulled the latch up on the gate. "Hang on!" He urged the horse into a gallop and yelled, "Hiyo Silver! Away!" They shot forward, and in Edward's ecstatic mind, he was Tonto, and they were after robbers who had stolen gold from a stagecoach. They raced down the dirt road, his father's arm tightly around him. Then without warning, he reigned in sharply. "Nobody out West can get away from those cool, fast-shooting Slavins. Watch out, all you bad guys!"

"Right, right! They'd better, because we rode faster than anyone ever did without a saddle. Let's do it again, okay?"

§

Early the next morning after breakfast, Edward watched intently as his mother and father were preparing to leave. "Where 'ya going?" he asked. "Can I come?"

"Flying. With another couple," his mother responded. "The man owns a beautiful plane. Your father is going to fly us to Nogales. We'll be back by dinnertime."

He turned to his father. "I want to go with you."

There was a pause. "No, not today." His father finished pulling his boots on, and stood up and eyed his mother, who nodded in agreement. "Look, son, there are times children don't do the same things as adults. This is one of them."

Edward made protesting sounds and turned away. "You never take me with you," he said.

"I certainly do. You're acting like a baby. Just get used to the idea that when I say 'no', it's 'no.' That's it. Besides, it's up to you to look after your sister," he said. Edward slouched forward with his hands thrust into his pockets. His father said, "All right, tell you what. I'll take you for a short ride."

"Sam," his mother interjected, "there isn't time." She stopped applying lipstick and faced him, her stare unwavering. "This is *our* day. Besides, we'll be late." His father brushed his hand across Edward's face. She continued, "He can have you all day tomorrow."

"A few minutes, that's all. A father and his son have to do certain things together. Just men. Right, Edward?"

Edward turned around, the sulkiness on his face transformed into a grin. His father held his arms out, and he ran into them. He was lifted up, whirled and thrown gently onto the bed. He got ready in a flash.

How pretty it was outside! It didn't matter that the sky was soggy and grayed like at home, because he was with his father. "Okay, cowboy, let's go!" Edward brushed off his chaps the same way he had seen his father do, and his father reached down and lifted him up onto White Sock's saddle, in front of him.

Oh, up here, alone with Daddy, riding like this, Edward thought. Nothing could be better. He leaned back against the strength and protection of his father's body, the world exactly the way he wanted it. He placed both his arms over the one his father held him with and squeezed it against himself. He turned around and gazed at him, wanting to make sure he would remember this wonderful occasion.

They galloped a short distance away from the buildings to a spot that overlooked the plains and distant mountains. What they viewed was somber-colored, but that was okay. There were no howls out there. His father reined in, jumped off, tied the horse to a branch. "Daddy, I missed you, all the time you were away fighting," Edward blurted. He choked on the words, trying to control the tears he knew were about to come.

"I missed you, too, but no more my being away like that." His father patted Edward's thigh, and motioned to him to slip off the horse and into his arms. Edward hugged him tightly. They stayed like that for a few minutes. "Here's something special I want you to have. My wings from the Air Force." He pinned them on Edward's jacket. "Take care of them."

"I will," Edward exclaimed. "It'll be the most special of all my things. Always and always, I promise." He threw his arms around his father again. "You're the best of all daddies. Ever."

His father nodded. "And you're the best son a man could have. I mean that. You're a sweet boy. And even though you're not grown up yet, I'm very proud of you, what you are. I can see how you're going to turn out. Now, we've got to get back. We'll do more of this, Eddie, and other things together."

A short time later, Edward watched his parents drive off down the roadway from the ranch house. He ran a short distance after them, and then returned to the porch. Mrs. Healey was there and said to him, "I've brought the baby outside. You can play, Edward, but I want you to listen and tell me if she cries. Your mother showed me about her bottle and all." As she was about to walk away, she told him, "You're supposed to be a good boy today. Oh, I mean, I'm sure you're good every day." She smiled but it didn't seem she was happy about anything. "Everything is run on schedule around here. You'll learn how we do things. I told Ernesto to take you riding this afternoon when the baby naps. I'll watch her then. But remember, no galloping. It gets the horses all sweated up. You ride hard only when it's necessary." She smiled again, sort of, and gave him a little wave. She seemed a little angry, he thought, but he wasn't going to worry about why.

§

FIVE

S am Slavin attentively inspected the four-passenger Fairchild 24 monoplane that had been rolled out of its hangar at the Fort Huachuca airport. Wisps of wind, like miniature tornados, carved the soil into sculptured patterns. He concentrated deeply, unaware of his sigh, and barely aware of what was being said to him.

At six thousand feet, the airfield was unobstructed and exposed to the desert prairie in every direction. To the east, the valley, scarred by ancient floods, was bordered with distant mountains that were sharply visible in good weather and darkened by the colors of the San Pedro River valley: umbered tans, nut browns, lead and smokey grays mixed into tones and shades in accordance with the changing light.

Crouching, Slavin lifted his face into the pewter sky. He looked toward the western horizon, then rose to study the map he had laid across the airplane's stabilizer. He drew his fingers across his mouth as if to keep his thoughts from being uttered. Images of flying jostled for attention and position. Some seemed perpetual, and some were like the quick flashes and surprise of lightning during summer storms.

Finally the tall pilot glanced up from the map. Edith Slavin caught his eye, waved a hand and smiled. He shifted his eyes from hers to the bunching grays above them, then once again to the Huachucas they would have to cross on the flight to Nogales. The ceiling cut across the mountains, lopping off the peaks.

"Listen to me, everyone. It's really not the best of days to fly. We'll have to get over those ranges, and this plane has very few instruments. The weather service advised there'll be snow showers and lousy visibility. I could fly around them, but that would take extra time." He surveyed the frowns and scowls of his passengers. "Say, ah, how about a nice trip to Tucson, or maybe Douglas? No mountains. We can stay lower, turn around if we have to. That'd be much smarter. I really think . . ."

"Sam," Edith interrupted, "since when does United's best captain let some clouds stop him? You've flown everywhere! Pat's just been telling me about the wonderful turquoise jewelry and beautiful linens in Nogales. We planned this day so carefully—we all trust you to handle any situation."

He laughed and shook his head. Edith squeezed his arm. "And if we don't leave right away, it'll be very late by the time we get back. I don't want to be away from the children any longer than necessary. You saw the way Edward was acting."

Slavin turned to the plane's owner, Bob Johnson. Johnson shrugged. "Well, it's really up to you, Sam. You know I just started flying."

Edith appealed to him again. "Pat agrees with me, Sam."

"Sam, I've lived in this region since I was a little girl," Pat Johnson added, her pleasant moonface dashed with false eyelashes. "The weather changes all the time, and more often than not, the clouds simply disappear."

"She's usually right, Sam," Bob said with a grin. "What do you say? Shouldn't be a problem." There was something a bit too cavalier about the manner with which he conducted himself that reminded Sam of many of the inexperienced pilots he had instructed—the bravado masked an unsettling feeling of vulnerability.

Sam peered up again at the thickening blanket. "I don't make the weather, and the sky looks crummy." The other three moaned. "All right, you malcontents, but remember who's in charge. If I don't like what I see, it's a fast one-eighty and no complaints. Understand?"

The Fairchild-24 that Bob Johnson had purchased had been built ten years earlier. It had not been flown very often by its original owner and was in superb condition, a real "cream puff," Sam thought. Its Ranger in-line engine made the portion in front of the cabin appear longer and more rectangular than the round, stubby look that radial engines gave to planes. Wheel pants enclosed the front wheels, and instead of the standard tail skid, the Fairchild utilized a small wheel. The fabric was taut and glazed. The exterior's basic color was cream, and there were two smart brown stripes along the fuselage that separated at the end and curved gracefully into the chocolate-colored cowling of the engine.

Pat Johnson sidled over to Sam as he was opening the cowling and was about to inspect the engine. "Are you worried about something?" she asked quietly.

"No, not at all. Just routine checking," he said, looking directly into her green eyes. "The only reason there are accidents is because people haven't been thorough enough. By doing this I can catch anything I don't like the looks of." He saw that his explanation didn't seem to satisfy her. "Pat, you don't just get in a plane and go like you do in a car. And pilots are trained for all kinds of emergencies. That's why there's absolutely no need to be concerned. We're taught to check everything we can think of. What I'm doing is routine. All right?" She nodded. He was aware he had used the words "check" and "routine" more than once.

Sam settled the two women in the rear and Johnson on his right in the co-pilot's seat. The interior was plush, with the seats, ceiling and side panels upholstered with tan leather. Everything was immaculate, and the polish that had been applied to the leather made it smell brand-new. Sam opened the map and handed it to Johnson to hold on his lap. He had already walked around the plane, checking its fabric, moving parts and connections, and noting the level of oil and fuel. He also drained the bottom sump to purge any water that might have been in the gas. Now he examined the instruments, pressed his feet on the top of the rudder pedals which functioned as the braking mechanism, and yelled to the mechanic standing in front of the propeller, "Off and closed!"

A voice called back, "Off and closed!," and the man pulled the propeller through twice.

"Braked and contact!"

"Contact!" was the reply, and the attendant pulled the prop through again with a hard swing. The engine came alive, coughing blue smoke into the crisp air as the gas was ignited in the cylinders. Sam waved and began a slow taxi to the take-off position.

"What the blazes are those long red hairs stuck along the side window, Bob?" Sam asked. He had just brought the plane to a stop before advancing the throttle to check the magnetoes and carburetor heat.

"Oh, those. My Irish setter's. He thinks he owns this plane. I keep telling him it's mine and the pick-up is his. He's pushing for flying lessons, but I told him only after he graduates from high school." Johnson was obviously pleased with himself.

"Maybe I should have checked with him about the weather," Sam said. "He seems to be in charge of everything around here."

"Now *that* I wouldn't do," Johnson answered. "He's really a complete jerk and 4-F, besides. If it wasn't for me, he'd starve for sure."

Sam swung the aircraft in a circle in order to observe any planes that might be in the traffic pattern. Then he turned around to the women. "Seat belts secured? Okay, everyone, here we go," he said matter-of-factly.

He released the brakes, and the four-passenger monoplane began its roll. At a certain speed, he pushed the wheel forward, and the tail lifted. Four hundred or so feet later, he gently pulled back on the wheel, allowing the flow of the wind to push the tail down. That plus the power of the fully energized engine lifted the airplane from the runway, through and past the force of gravity. No matter how many times he had flown, Sam was struck with an enormous pleasure by that first moment of being airborne without anything between him and the ground. It seemed almost spiritual.

He circled the airport and rocked the wings in the traditional gesture of farewell, gaining the precious altitude he would need to cross the mountains. The plane will do its part, he decided. All he had to do was to navigate through the Huachucas, between the peaks that were cut off on this day by an overcast of gathered grays. Then they'd simply proceed across the rubbled desert that was snaked with smaller mountains. He understood it was not always possible to have unlimited ceilings and visibility; when the winds were strong or the weather "settled in," pilots must perform. It wasn't a contest, but the necessity of demonstrating a combination of skill and common sense. And perhaps a little courage. With passengers or not, it was up to the pilot to make the right choices.

From this vantage point they could see that snows obscured large areas of the Huachucas, shuffling across them like waves passing over obstructions, scraping the ridges and sweeping down through the canyons. There were open patches, the mingling of white and blue. The sun shone on top of the thick, grayed cover and nearby over the lands of the Navajo, the Hopi and the Pima, and the descendents of the Anasazi, the Hohokam and the Mongollan.

Now Sam needed to forget everything else. He must become one with this plane, be a part of the sky, the endless space he flew through. The world of the aviator was infused with plumped clouds, havens, moisture-pots and dreams without gravity. Up here he was unnamed, born alone, without parents, perfect. He was all of it and the ground below. And he could transport himself beyond any cloud to where the sky was cleared of wet, air-blued, then black-blued, and finally all black where there was no air at all.

Because the earth offered only a few landmarks to gauge where he was, he had learned to trust the compass for the correct course. It was always accurate; in any case, he *had* to believe it because the direction it indicated was all there was to depend upon.

For a moment, Sam let his thoughts wander. He knew he would choose anywhere else to force-land but in these mountains. Majestic and beautiful as they were, they were not friendly. The ground was rarely long enough to place a plane down upon. Landing meant locating such an area, no matter what the angle or how short, and then either pancaking in or finding two trees that could break off the plane's wings in order to cushion the impact—two trees positioned exactly right so he could head straight between them. No crash: the fuselage would slowly come to a stop and then he could gently lead his passengers out. But that was ideal, a fantasy totally unrealistic. More likely in such a situation, he knew all would be killed, or hurt so badly that they couldn't walk away. Especially in deep snow.

He shivered involuntarily as he continued to envision a crash and their chances for survival. A search would be conducted, of course, but it would not be the same as on the prairie, where a landing wasn't likely to result in injury. There, probably only the landing gear would be broken. Mountains just weren't places to go down in; the longer it took rescuers to locate the crash, the worse for any survivors. And surviving, he knew, wasn't always a matter of determination. It began by not being badly injured. You couldn't do much or go very far if you were bleeding badly, or had a busted ankle. And the weather had to cooperate. It was never as dependable as the plane or as concerned as the pilot.

§

"Not so hot ahead of us," Sam told them, peering into the thick sky that had suddenly caved in on them. He turned to Johnson. "Can't pick up anything on your radio. So much static I can't hear myself transmit either."

"Damn," Johnson said nervously, "the guy I bought this plane from told me everything worked perfectly. And the mechanic gave it a complete okay." He peered through the front but failed to even glimpse the mountains they were attempting to fly above. "We going to be all right?"

"Sure as shootin'," Sam said casually, laboring to disguise his concern. "We'll work our way down through an opening to a lower altitude." He banked, heading into the opposite direction. Damn this shit, he thought to himself, it's dropping too fast. Hoped it'd stay higher, and I could fly through the passes. Better drop through that break ahead and pick my way through the canyons.

He cut the throttle, depressed the left rudder pedal and put the plane into a spiral which resulted in a rapid loss of altitude. They came out beneath the floor of the clouds, but the height above the ground was much lower than Sam had expected and hoped for. He knew they had to get out of there fast, to climb rapidly, because it was obviously impossible to find the passes or even to maneuver. All of a sudden, the area directly in front of them clouded over. He jammed the throttle forward and yanked back on the wheel, angling the plane into a rapid climb.

"Sam!" Edith screamed. The plane sliced through the tops of some tall evergreens. The tearing of the fabric sounded like a high-pitched saw. He jerked the plane up and made an instant decision.

"Brace yourselves! I'm going to pancake on that flat. Hang on!"

For a split second he thought he might manage to set the plane down in such a manner that the snow and the small evergreens would slow it down and bring it to a halt before they reached the large trees at the far end of the flat. But as they hit the snow, they bounced like an unwelcome meteor, upward instead, lurching forward too rapidly and out of control. The right wing cut an increasingly deeper path through the snow until it crushed against some boulders. That impact slammed the plane rightside up again, slowing it. It finally came to a stop under an umbrella of large trees.

And then stillness suffused the scene, as though the interruption of offensive sounds had simply been a temporary insult.

§

During sunrise and sunset along the Mexican border in Arizona, reds and lavenders and roans and sorrels mix with blues into amalgamations that demand extraordinary focus in order to distinguish one color from the other. In the middle of the day, heat rises from the arid surface of the plains, and softens and subdues the jagged features of the ridges and peaks. The impassive formations of the terrain retain without bitterness or sentimentality any part of their history. It is possible to imagine floating ever so slowly on an oscillating sea of acorn and brown leather.

This region of Arizona was unlike the northern zones, where elegant evergreens blanketed much of every valley and mountain. Here, at the higher elevations, canyons surprised, were greened in spring and punctuated by a play of flowers, by the flitting of birds and by the euphonic melodies of flowing water. In this land, fundamentals had to be encountered, the circle understood—whether something was alive or not, when it was dormant, when it would wake again. What appeared dried up and finished was not necessarily dead but might be, and those who knew it had found there was hope and promise in rain from cloudbursts, from snows drifted high through the mountains. They learned they were controlled by changing weather and capricious seasons. What occurred or did not in one particular year could devastate all things that depended on life-giving water.

In winter there were fine days of crispness when the freshness of the air was as exciting as first love. Nights were cold, water froze except when pushed by the decisive motions of streams. And there were storms.

§

When darkness settled in, John Healey called the Huachuca airport. "Not a damn thing, Major. Probably decided to stay over in Nogales."

"Did you call Nogales?" Healey asked impatiently of the lethargic voice at the other end.

"I'm not sure of their number. Besides, we're not a tracking service here, you know."

"Don't get smart with me, mister. Huachuca Airport's on Federal land. You call Nogales and then me," he bristled, his voice rising. "I expect to hear from you immediately, understand?" The last statement was bellowed.

Ten minutes later, the Healey telephone rang. "Yes, sir, they left here a while ago. Can't figure out why they didn't get there yet, Major." The airport operator sounded anxious. "Maybe they flew to some other airport or put down somewhere. Slavin's an airline captain, isn't he? Knows how to fly at night."

There was a pause before Major Healey expounded, "Unlikely in that plane. And besides, he would have phoned. They've left their two kids with us. Look, this is what I want you to do right now. Call the Civil Air Patrol. I want them to know the situation. I'll get

45

in touch with the sheriff's office. Tell them that too. I'll be down myself in twenty minutes."

Healey hung up, started towards the door, and returned to the telephone. "Tell whoever's in charge at the C.A.P. that at daybreak, they can over-fly his probable route," he told the airport manager. "The trouble is, the Huachucas are so damn vast. If we need one, we'll get a helicopter from Tucson."

Mrs. Healey told Edward his parents had to stay over in Nogales and that he'd see them the following day. "But they said they were coming back today. Daddy promised he would ride again with me," Edward said. "Can we call them on your telephone? Please, Mrs. Healey? I know my mother would want to talk to me."

"Well, perhaps. But they forgot to leave the number of the hotel. If we can find out, yes, we'll certainly telephone them," she said trying to be reassuring. Edward's baby sister began to cry again. "Edward, why don't you help me feed her? You must have watched your mother give her a bottle."

"I've done it to her all by myself," he bragged.

"Well then, *you* can feed her."

"Only I don't know how to change her smelly diapers. She stinks when she makes doody." He giggled.

"Edward, Edward," Mrs. Healey responded exasperatedly, "You just give her the bottle. I'll take care of the rest."

§

The cold front that night was accompanied by strong northwest winds that pushed away the precipitation and the clouds accumulated during the previous two days. The air was tinged with clarity and the feel of cold crystals. Early the next morning, three search planes took off from Fort Huachuca, three from Nogales, two from

Sonoita and one from Patagonia. Most were owned by ranchers familiar with the region and terrain. They were unsuccessful. The pilots concluded that any survivors of a Huachuca crash would have sustained injuries and have great difficulty in the deep snows.

"I can't figure it out, Major," said the pilot coordinating the Civil Air Patrol search. "Slavin's very experienced, and he knows what to do. He must have had engine trouble. Besides, wouldn't he have radioed a 'Mayday' if he was in trouble?"

The next morning the plane was spotted, the wreckage spread out on a small plateau near some boulders at the base of a stand of ponderosas. A helicopter landed as darkness began to infiltrate the daylight. Three people were found in the plane's cabin. In the front, a man was slumped forward, his belt fastened, his head resting against the panel. When they leaned him back, they immediately saw an ugly depression sunk into his bloodied face. His eyes and forehead were grotesquely distorted, and his mouth was open, frozen spittle mixed with the blood on his chin.

The two women in the rear were clutching each other, and for a brief moment the rescuers thought they were embracing. When they separated the lifeless bodies, they noticed the unnatural bend in the younger woman's left side and that her arm was contorted unnaturally. A man's leather flight jacket was wrapped around her, covering most of her dress. They didn't observe any injuries in her companion except for gashes and bruises about the face and hands. They assumed both had died more from shock and exposure than from injuries. A note was tied to the controls. "Heading *south,* down to ranch on map. Hurry, Slavin."

The rescuers put on snowshoes and followed his tracks. They found him sitting rigid against a boulder several hundred yards away. His eyes were open in a perpetual stare, and partially blown snow covered his legs, on one of which a makeshift splint fashioned from stripped branches had broken apart. On his lap he held his wallet and two pictures, one of a woman and a boy, the other of a baby girl. Written jaggedly on a pad: "Shit. Pilots are supposed to die flying."

§

SIX

Edward wondered why Mrs. Healey held his hand and why she looked down. They had brought him into the kitchen of the ranch and asked the others to leave. The windows were open, and Edward heard the raucous, jarring clacking of the turkeys. One in particular, close-by.

"Gobble! Gobble! Gobble!" It was a funny sound, like three double taps on the door. What was the turkey saying in turkey language? What did the Healeys want with him here in the kitchen, with its smells of bacon and coffee in the morning, bread and pies in the afternoon? His mother made great apple pies.

The kitchen floor was composed of colored stones, maroons and purples and another color close to red and brown, all positioned haphazardly. It was very hard under foot; Edward had dropped a dish the first day, and it had spattered in pieces across the entire room. The floor was cold, too. Mrs. Healey told him not to walk bare-footed because his feet might be dirty. The wool of the Indian scatter-rugs felt nicer and warmer. He tried to walk only on the scatter-rugs, taking small or large steps, even jumps. Cooky snuck him bits of food sometimes when no one was looking. All his frying pans hung in two rows over a long table where he cut things up before dumping them into pots on the stove. Sometimes Edward sat and watched him, and Cooky let him help peel potatoes, strip wrappings off the corn and do other cooking things.

"You're going to have to be a man about what I have to tell you," Major Healey pronounced almost matter-of-factly. He held Edward's hand firmly. "There's no way other than to tell you straight out." His tone was soft, not commanding, as it usually was.

Edward thought everything was eerie and sort of too quiet. What was Major Healey talking about, and where were his parents? He brought his hand towards his mouth and held the large knuckle of his thumb in his teeth. He used to suck his thumb until the kindergarten teacher made fun of him. Remembering, he dropped his hand.

"The plane crashed in the mountains. There weren't any survivors. I'm terribly sorry this happened. I always respected your father and liked your mother, too."

The Major was talking about "survivors." What did that mean? Something terrible was happening, that was sure. Edward's body jerked as if it had been shocked electrically. He heard the turkey again, then several others. A horse whinneyed. He imagined Ernesto was putting a bridle on it. Maybe it was Nellie. He'd go out and help as soon as he could get away.

He began to feel the loneliness, that terrible feeling when he wanted his father and knew no matter how much he did, he had no power to make him appear. Now he was being held on a leash and made to listen.

He stared up at the Major. Had he done something bad again? Was that what kept them away? His stomach hurt.

Major Healey glanced over at his wife, who looked away, shaking her head.

"What I'm trying to tell you is that your parents are ... they're dead." He paused. "Your aunt will be here tomorrow or the next day. There are arrangements that have to be made." He took Edward's chin and held it, making him look directly into his eyes. "Men have to handle these things. I know you're only seven, but the earlier you learn control and self-discipline, the stronger you'll become."

Major Healey was just being mean, he would tell him in a minute it was a joke and that he was sorry. "Where are my parents?" he asked again. "My family's having this vacation. We have lots of things to do."

"Edward, listen to me," Healey said, grabbing his shoulders. "They can't come back. You have to accept that. Please try to understand."

Edward shook his head rapidly back and forth. "No, no, no! They *are* coming back! You're lying!" He glanced over to Mrs. Healey, who turned away.

He didn't know whether he was going to cry or have a temper tantrum. "They *have* to come back! They have to," he said, his voice trailing off. He felt himself begin to cry, but he stopped and faced Major Healey. "You're a stink!" he yelled. As he did, he kicked at the Major's leg and made partial contact. Major Healey reached out, but Edward ducked, ran around the table and out the door into the yard.

"John," Ida Healey said quickly. "Try to understand, and don't get upset. He has to let it out some way." Healey snorted audibly. "He's not being disobedient." She went to a window and watched Edward disappear into the stable.

§

They drove slowly up a long road that went behind the fort to the cemetery on the crest of a solitary hill. From the top you saw down to the barracks, the water tower and the parade ground, bordered by the brick houses where the officers lived with their families. You could also see the little town just outside the fort, and the airport. The big ranges of the Huachucas were close, and you could watch the terrain in between rise to their foothills; the mountains looked a little like long bolsters on couches. This cemetery was different from the other one Edward had been to in Chicago, which had trees all around and grass. The ground there wasn't rocky and parched, covered with crumbling dirt.

It was weird, his being here, some exaggerated, unreal drama he was being forced to be part of, an ugly nightmare that would soon end. He was in the back seat of the Major's car, sitting between Mrs. Healey and his Aunt Sandra, his mother's sister. A very long black car without windows was driving in front of them. They were second, and after them a lot of cars and pickup trucks formed a line. The procession wound around to the fence, where they stopped. In slow motion, everyone got out. A short man wearing a black suit came over. He was the one in the front of the chapel before, who talked to them about how terrible what happened was. And other things Edward didn't understand. But he wasn't listening very much because he didn't really want to be reminded about his mother and father. The man seemed to be in charge. Edward didn't ask who he was, but now that they were up here, it seemed important; he was walking ahead, saying things in the sing-song way he'd been doing earlier. His aunt said he was speaking in Hebrew.

"I told you," she reminded him. "He's Rabbi Malev. He drove all the way down from Tucson. He wants to get to know you better." In the cemetery, rocky paths led between rows of white slabs with people's names carved on them. As he walked with his aunt, Edward made sure he didn't step on any of the stones; each foot had to be placed firmly between them. He noticed two small sticks on either side of the path, went on for a moment, and then stopped. The line behind them stopped too. He let go of his aunt's hand and put both sticks side by side so they touched. A little further on they came to where it was going to happen. The two boxes were waiting next to the holes. They were made of grained white wood, and the covers were curved and Stars of David were carved on them. When he saw them, Edward jerked his head away and looked at the mountains. What bothered him the most was that he knew his parents lay there, perfectly still inside the boxes.

Edward wished he could understand why this had to be, why God would want—why God had done this to his parents? If God was good, why *would* He do this? If Edward knew beforehand, he would have sacrificed whatever God wanted him to. Anything.

He started thinking back to that time before his father came back from the war, when he missed him so much he thought he couldn't stand it anymore. And that one time when he'd done something special to try to get him home. His mother had read him this particular letter she'd received from his father which had something in it for him.

"I can't read you all of this one, darling, because some parts are only for me. But he sent this photo for you. Why don't you show it to your friends while I read this?" She nodded her head. "Oh, wait a minute, listen to this: 'I think of you a lot, Eddie, especially when I'm high up over the clouds. We're sitting together, you and me. It sure is gorgeous, a little like being in Heaven. When I come back for good, you and I are going to have real fun. We'll go flying and go on rides. I love you, son.'"

Edward had run to the playground and found his friends. *"This* is my Daddy getting ready to fly his plane. Doesn't he look terrific wearing his special suit?" None of his friends' fathers were pilots. They looked really interested.

Back in his room, Edward had decided that his father was looking directly at him in the picture. He wished he could point his special magic ring at his plane and make it fly home. He always worried that once his father was finished with the military, he might go away again. Feelings stank because they usually mixed him up.

"You're not fair because I need you to help me learn to ride my bike, and do other stuff together, like fly with you up over all the clouds. If you come home for good, I promise I won't be a problem to Mommy any more."

Edward rolled over on his bed and gazed at the ceiling. What could he do to make it happen? An idea had come to him: I'll talk to God the way Mommy does. He covered his eyes with his hands. He remembered the Hebrew story she read him about Abraham and Isaac. God loved them, He didn't want Abraham to hurt his son. So He created a sheep that couldn't run away, and Abraham killed the sheep instead of his son. God could certainly do anything He wanted in the whole world.

His eyes filled with tears. "I want You to love Daddy and me. Mommy too. I need Daddy home because it's hard about things. I'm real lonely without him. Honest." Maybe if he gave up important things, that might help the prayer come true. He opened the bottom drawer in his dresser and removed his favorite marbles from a small glass jar. Also the plastic figures he'd saved from Wheaties boxes, and all the most valuable baseball cards he had traded with other kids.

Edward opened the door to his room as quietly as he could and peeked out. Was she in the living room or the kitchen? He stealthily took a step. He had a purpose, something he had to do. The lamps were on in the living room. Maybe she was lying down. He waited and watched for any movement, but there wasn't any. Wait, there, the bathroom, he could see light under the bottom of the door. Now he could get outside. It was quiet out and lights shone at the ground from corners of the buildings. That was okay because he needed some light.

He gazed upward into the evening sky. The moon was about half and it played in and out of the gray-creamed clouds. "Lord, God, these are my best things." He picked up his small shovel and began to dig. The sides caved in, so he widened them and placed the sandy dirt further from the edges. He stopped, looked up again. He lay the shovel down and clasped his hands together. "I know You're busy all the time because You're God." Perhaps he could do even more so God would see he wasn't holding anything back. "All right," he whispered, "I'll get them too."

He slunk back inside and carefully shut the door to his room behind him. He withdrew a small white box from the drawer and lifted the ten coins he had been saving, including the special ones from foreign places he called "country money." His mother had told him they had been his grandfather's, and that now they were his. She was nice for wanting him to have them.

Maybe God would like his giving up all his most important things forever. He had nothing more to sacrifice.

He buried the marbles and cards in the first hole, covered it carefully and dug two others, deeper than the first. Deep as I can, he thought, so no one will ever find them. He slowly and carefully placed half the coins in the first, feeling them one by one as they slipped through his fingers. He dropped the balance in the second, pushed the dirt back in and stamped down, flattening the soil so no one would know there had been a hole. He surveyed the area but didn't see anyone. He stood solemnly over the last covered-up hole. "I promise not to remember where they are. Promise forever. Please, God. Please bring my Daddy home soon."

When he re-entered the building, his mother was lying on the sofa, listening to the radio and reading a magazine. He almost made it past her, but she looked up, surprised, and asked, "What in the samhill were you doing outside?"

"Nothing. I just went to ..."

Before he could finish, she was up and her hand caught him on his hip. A second whack reverberated off his rear end.

He started to cry, less from the sting than from the unfairness of her not asking him more about what had happened before smacking him. He felt utterly helpless and alone. "I was just doing a good thing, and you *hit* me for it."

She looked at him quizzically.

"It was important and *special.*"

"What was it?" she asked with concern.

"I'm not telling you," he shouted. He ran into his room, shut the door hard and got into bed. She came in. He pretended he was sleeping. She waited and then went out and closed the door gently. He thought about how he didn't know what to do about how terrible he felt, until sleep settled in.

§

Four men lowered the coffin with tapes that came out of rolls. "Edward, come here," the rabbi said. He took a shovel and spilled dirt on the boxes. He motioned for Edward to do the same, but Edward shook his head and shrank back to his aunt. He realized he was crying, and he saw the adults watching him. Distressed, he looked up at his aunt, who handed him her handkerchief. She was sobbing and trying not to cry openly. She enfolded him in her arms. "That's all right, honey," she whispered jaggedly, "you don't have to. Just stay with me."

The rabbi said another prayer and then something in English that Edward didn't pay attention to. He was thinking how terrible it would be if you woke up somehow and couldn't get out of your grave. You'd try to breathe and shout but no one would hear you. He shuddered and pressed closer to his aunt. Then he decided his mother and father weren't really in the boxes. Didn't God remember how good they were?

The first one to come over was Ernesto. "It'll get better, you'll see," he said, trying to be convincing. Then the Healeys, and then Cooky and the other "hands." Everyone shook his hand. Shaking hands was strange, pumping up and down. It made sense when you pumped on the lever to bring up water from the well, but it was silly when two people pumped each other's hands up and down. Why only two, and not three or four people at the same time? They usually did it to congratulate someone or when they met each other. But why now?

The noise of aircraft slowly but unmistakeably penetrated the sky from the east. Everyone looked up to watch a formation of seven planes flying in a "V" toward them, only a few hundred feet above the hill on which they stood. The planes made a wide circle after they flew over, and when they returned, one of the end planes pulled out of the formation, circled around again and dropped flowers, which hit the ground close to where they stood. "It's traditional to salute a downed pilot," the Major instructed. "Civilian planes, because your father's no longer in the Service." Major Healey snapped to attention and saluted, his elbow high, his arm parallel to the ground. Edward watched him and instinctively emulated the gesture. When I get big, he thought, I'm going to be a pilot just like my Daddy was. Yes, I really will.

What had to come next? They returned to the ranch house, not all the cars, only the rabbi, some close friends of the Healeys and one other man. "Your father and I served together. Sam was one of the best instructors we had in our squadron. I never met your mother, but I'm sure she was very special." When he shook Edward's hand, he seemed about to say something else, but he didn't.

People sat on the sofas or stood in the kitchen, talking. When their eyes met his, they'd smile, trying to be friendly, he assumed. Edward smiled back but not always. He felt funny. What they talked about didn't interest him. The men drank liquor and most of the women had tea. Mrs. Healey went around with a tray of little sandwiches, but he didn't want any. "Where's Ernesto?" he asked her, loud enough for some of the others to stop talking.

"Oh, he's out back, I guess," she responded. "You can see him later." She smiled, but it wasn't all right.

After a while, almost everyone left. The rabbi, too. "I'd like to hear from you, Edward," he said. "Feel free to call me anytime at the temple in Tucson. I've given the phone number to your aunt."

Major Healey whispered something to his Aunt Sandra and then went into his bedroom at the far end of the hall. Now the living room was empty except for Edward and his aunt. She took a chair and sat opposite him. His Aunt Sandra wasn't as tall or as thin as his mother. Her cheeks were fat like a pig's, and he wondered if she and his mother were really sisters. Her hair was in bangs that looked silly, like a fake hat on someone who was bald. She walked with a kind of hook motion, starting at an angle and then coming around toward the center. Her eyebrows were thin strips and kind of looked at you like eyes, except her eyes were underneath, so you knew they weren't her eyes. She also squinted one eye a lot. It must be a nervous twitch. No wonder his mother didn't seem to like her so much.

"I know it must be terribly difficult for you to understand, Edward. Try to think they're asleep forever. When you pass on, you'll be with them again."

He tried not to indicate any astonishment. With them *where?* Under the ground? And how do you "pass on?" Oh, God, not underground. There must be another place where you're all together and can do things.

"What I mean is, we return to God because God created us. He decides how long every person's life will be." She observed his face. "You don't have to worry about it because you're very young. It's only when you're an adult and get old."

Edward decided not to agree or disagree. What she was talking about fit in with what she said earlier, God deciding who lives and for how long, because He was in charge of everything and everybody. He felt hot juices rising from his stomach, almost up into his throat.

Why did she have to talk about this stuff now? Darn it. It was bad enough, his parents were put into the boxes and then under the ground. *Under the ground.* Everybody was acting so stupid, saying idiot things he didn't want to hear—even Ernesto, sometimes. Edward decided again that he must be having a bad dream. It had to end soon.

His aunt stood up and knelt in front of him, taking both his hands. She cleared her throat. "There's something else." He jerked a little, took away one of his hands, and involuntarily held the knuckle of his thumb in his teeth. "I know this'll sound as if we don't care or want you, but it isn't true. Because Susie must come with us—I told you about your cousins—but I just can't handle more children." She pressed her lower lip against her upper. "You'll be all right here with the Healeys. They'll take care of you. Later you'll come for visits." Edward started to shake his head back and forth, fast. "I'm sorry. If there was any other way—but there isn't. You'll see, it'll work out. Probably for just a year or two." She smiled as if she wanted him to smile too.

"Please, Aunt Sandra, please take me with you," he pleaded. She didn't move a muscle. He waited a long time, then jumped up and raced out the door in the direction of the stables.

"Edward," she yelled after him, "Wait! Come back!" He was gone.

Ernesto was shodding one of the horses. Edward ran to where Nellie was, ducked under the cross rope and stood facing her. The gentle old mare didn't raise her head from the hay. Ernesto had showed him how to feed her sugar without getting bitten, and how to groom and walk her when she became sweaty after galloping.

Her coat was reddish, and she had white hair on all four feet above her hoofs. She was his horse. No one else rode her. She didn't require a Martingale like the rougher, younger horses did. Her bridle had double reins that came up from the silver-colored bit which was always hung on a hook on the wall. Edward's saddle was in the saddle room at the front of the stables, next to where Ernesto lived.

Edward put his arms around Nellie's front leg and buried his face in the shiny chestnut hair. He began to cry. It was dark, and everything in the world seemed dark brown. He smelled her horsiness. He jumped when he felt a hand on his back. Ernesto.

"I'm sorry about your father and mother," he said. "They were always decent to me. I met your father when he flew here during the war." He turned Edward around, and then pulled out his large red print handkerchief and gently wiped his eyes. Edward stood motionless, then threw his arms tightly around Ernesto's neck. Ernesto lifted him up, and Edward wrapped his arms and feet around him. He smelled of horses and leather and tobacco.

"Why did they have to ... to die?" he cried. He looked pleadingly into Ernesto's face. "Will I have to die? Where do you go when you die?"

Ernesto put him down, sat down himself against the corner of the stall, and pulled Edward onto his knees. "What happened to them, it was a tragic accident. They were not supposed to die this young. Someday every person must go like everything else alive. But for most of us, not until we get to be *viejo*, old. Like maybe your grandparents. You have them?"

Edward shook his head. "Not any more," he answered, sniffling. "I want my mother and my father, and now I can't even see them again."

"No, this is correct, you won't." Somewhere from the main building, a woman called. Neither of them stirred.

Finally Edward looked up. Ernesto pulled out his handkerchief again and nodded for him to blow his nose into it. "The Major and

Missus Healey, they're supposed to take care of me now," said Edward. "My aunt said I have to stay. I'll be all alone. Even Susie will go away."

"The Healeys mean well, but they have no experience with children. You'll have to do what they tell you. I must, too. When I was a boy in Guadalajara, my father was tough. I tried everything I knew how to please him. But I couldn't. There were some good times." He stood up, holding Edward's hand within his, and turned toward the ranchhouse. "The Major knows little but the cavalry, not like your father, who was a soldier only because of the war. He thinks everyone should live the way it was in the Army before the war. I've heard him say things about Mexicanos. Indians too. But he's getting better," he said slowly. "They're in charge, but when you will be a grown man, you won't have to follow their ways."

Edward explored Ernesto's face, hoping he would say something else, something to make it all better. "I'll help you as best I can. You can come with me sometimes when I have my day off, but of course not every time. Okay?" He smiled and squeezed Edward's arm. "It's not going to be easy to live with them. But you will become stronger. That's what you have to be to become *un hombre*." Then he added, "Like your father. He was a good man."

§

SEVEN

Ernesto was neither smiling nor grinning—it was something in between. Only the leading edges of his teeth were exposed. Whenever he observed this expression, Edward concentrated. He knew there were certain things Ernesto wanted him to remember, things that were as important as the value of a cowboy's boots and lariat, or the behavior of animals.

"The Major's got his eye on us, the big one in the center of his forehead," Ernesto half-teased. Sticking out from their normal hiding place behind his thin lips, his teeth could have been used as the "before" in a "before and after" ad. (Have to tell that kid about women sometime, he'd said to himself more than once. When he gets the itch, he won't know how to handle it, except maybe with his left hand.) He knew that Edward was only seven, but he wanted to tell him about these things before Major Healey decided to lecture him about them.

"Listen, *chico,* I told you we have to do things their way," he said to Edward. "Old tightass—a good description, no? I learned that

one and some other beauties my first year in *gringo* prep school—
anyway, the more time he sees you with me, the more chores he'll
dream up. I told you the Major's really not too bad a guy, just too
much army in him. No sense of humor." Edward let out a sigh, born
from thoughts of standing at something resembling "attention" while
the Major went on about what he wanted Edward to do. "Also
agreeing with his *senora, comprende?*" Edward nodded his consent.
What would he ever do without Ernesto's concern and interest?

With what seemed like the magic of omniscience, Ernesto turned
him to face the afternoon. "See that single saguaro? The large one
just below the ridge. Looks pretty strong, right? Notice how it man-
ages alone without help." He ran his fist lightly against Edward's
jaw. Now his face was a full grin, reddened gums included. This
close, his breath floated by Edward's nostrils, not all that dissimilar
to the mephitic smell of rotting leaves, except now it emanated from
juices mixed with the smoke of hand-rolled cigarettes made from the
contents of an Old Steer pouch. Edward had more than once thought
of swiping Ernesto's tobacco and paper, but the idea had slid away.
Once when he'd lifted and wrinkled his nose, Ernesto had charged,
"You get *that* when you get me, kiddo. The whole package."

Edward would be starting school soon. He imagined the kids he'd
have to meet, but of course *they* knew each other. He'd be the new
kid, an intruder from outside Chicago, the big *Eastern* city. He knew
they'd ask about the plane crash, and he felt nauseous, thinking
about what he'd say. If he didn't answer, they'd decide he was unfriendly. Well, he wouldn't tell about what had happened, and if it
kept him from making friends, well, he didn't have any to start with
anyway. The teacher, what would she be like? Maybe she'd feel the
same as the kids. But maybe school could be good, too: he could
travel to countries pictured in books and pretend he was actually
there. And get to know about ancient times and how the heroes
became heroes.

One day "Sergeant" Healey (that's what Ernesto called Mrs. Healey because the Major bossed her around) came up to him on the porch without warning while he was sweeping in one direction and then in the other, carefully so as not to miss anything. "Edward, I want to talk to you about your behavior and your manners. You're a child. You're supposed to be seen and not heard. It's an old saying, but we take seriously the way people act around here. It's important that each one of us understands how to handle himself properly." She sounded just like the Major, only in a woman's voice. As far as Edward was concerned, there wasn't much to talk about with her anyway. Sometimes she'd engage him in soft conversation, asking him how it was going, how he felt. But she didn't seem really interested, more like she was supposed to be trying to be friendly and kind. He couldn't really be himself with her.

"That's what we want you to do, Edward. So everyone will see what a well-behaved boy you are."

Ida Healey was a Clayton before she married the Major. Statuesque and square-faced, she had strong jaw lines that went with what she intended her behavior to signify: a high degree of intelligence, breeding and the determination to achieve her goals. When she was eighteen that goal was to be at the top of her class at the University of Arizona, which her grandfather had helped found. She almost made it. Then it was to be popular with both her professors and fellow students. She knew she was attractive, no question about that; the boys sniffed around plenty. But she couldn't waste the time to date, not if she was going to amount to someone important, someone they'd really respect, like a doctor or a lawyer. After all, she was a Clayton, someone to be reckoned with. Her dreams had died in her junior year when her father was killed in a car accident on his way home, drunker than a coyote. Her mother was rendered hopelessly crippled in the accident. She graduated, all right, but it took loans and jobs in addition to having to care for her mother.

"And you have to try to get good grades in school. If you've got what it takes—and the Major believes you have the capacity (what's *that* mean?, he thought),—it just might be possible to pull a few strings and get you into West Point. That's what you can hope and pray for: the opportunity some day to serve as an officer in the United States Army."

The Army had never meant much in particular to her, even though World War One had changed everyone's lives, especially if you were an only child and your father had been overseas for several years. She'd met John Healey at a reception at the country club in Tucson, held for her father's division shortly after the Armistice in 1918. She hadn't paid any more attention to him than to the other officers who'd flocked around her like a pack of young male hounds, sidling up with punch and asking her to dance. But John had pursued and courted her for five years. She did have reservations. He was like a ramrod, given to control and inflexibility, but his forcefulness was attractive and made her feel secure. Besides, she was nearing thirty and had the burden of supporting herself and her mother. They were married in the Fort Huachuca chapel, and they left the ceremony under the crossed swords of West Pointers from his regiment.

Ida and John Healey were childless for ten years before she gave birth to a little girl whom they named Elizabeth. The child made her feel complete in ways nothing else ever had. They talked about having another child and hoped it would be a boy. For Ida, being with the little girl and witnessing her first cognitions, sensations and pleasures was a time of intense joy.

Edward was uncertain what to do in the face of Mrs. Healey's statement. The smell of animals rose from the stables and from the yard where the turkeys pecked in the dust and shat and the males mounted the females in the thrall of some kind of secret timing. Edward knew Ernesto was down at the east pasture. Some steer was sick or something. Ernesto had taken his rifle.

Edward responded to Ida Healey with a face devoid of reaction, the best form of defense. "Otherwise," she was continuing, "you certainly won't get into the Point. We haven't the money to send you to college, and what your Aunt Sandra sends us certainly isn't enough for that, let me tell you. No sir! And as for you being Jewish," she added slowly, "well, no one has to know about it, Edward. Folks around here never see any, well maybe one or two. All they know is Jews have more money than they should. Everyone says they started the War and caused the Depression."

She stood directly in front of him, smiled and put her index finger against his chin. "Not everybody. We don't. John had a few as friends in France. Jews can't help the way they are. They just haven't been exposed to the teachings of Jesus Christ, our Lord and Savior." She smiled the kind of smile that confused him—it seemed friendly enough, but there was something that made him very uncomfortable about what she was saying, especially the slow and deliberate way she enunciated the last words.

He wanted her to stop. "Where are *your* children?" he asked. Why should anyone care that he was Jewish? Why did she make it sound that important? He remembered his mother told him their religion was about how people should be good to each other even though their beliefs were different, that the Jews believed there was only one God, and He was in charge of everything in the whole universe. Daddy would have helped him understand, only he couldn't any more. He might ask Ernesto sometime. His mind drifted. Next time he went to the cemetery, maybe he'd try to ask his parents.

"Gobble! Gobble! Gobble!" Clock-like, all the time, except when they slept. Once in a while their voices would blend with the horses in a strange chorus: a funny kind of music, language only they comprehended.

"How come you don't have any children like everybody else does?" He looked straight at her when he said it. It surprised him he'd been able to talk like that to her, to think of a way of getting back at her.

Ida Healey wiped her hands against her Levis, rubbing them on her side pockets again and again. She was unaware of her action and would have preferred not to have behaved so revealingly. But then she felt the wetness around her eyes, which she certainly was not willing to share with Edward. For that matter of fact, not with her husband either. She grabbed her Stetson, which hung from a leather cord behind her head when she wasn't wearing it, and rapidly put it on, so rapidly that she almost broke the thin loop.

Ida Healey glared at him. Then, softening, she said wistfully, "We did have a child, a precious little girl named Elizabeth. But she died of scarlet fever when she was three." She gazed in the direction of the Dragoons that revealed themselves faintly in the northeast. Edward was unprepared for her vulnerability, this side of her that was exposed now like a scar that wouldn't disappear, like the one on Ernesto's arm when he took off his shirt. The insensitivity Edward associated her with no longer seemed appropriate. Confused, he looked away when she looked back at him.

A seamless puff of air bounced off them, pulled out a wisp of her pepper-colored hair and dropped it diagonally along her forehead. This is no good, Edward thought. She's mixing me up. Now she's a person who hurts same as me.

Ida Healey was silent for a long time. Then, without warning, she took Edward's hand and held it. "We had just been transferred. The Major was only a lieutenant. He didn't think we should bring the baby to the hospital unless it was absolutely necessary. Oh, he was so wrong! We waited too long. We raced in when she began to burn up. Those doctors! Those lousy doctors at the Fort should have saved her even at that point. They couldn't. She's buried in the cemetery near your folks. My world has never been the same." Edward heard her sigh rise up and escape.

He was feeling itchy and unable to stand still any longer. He released his hand from her and made little movements with his feet, shaking them as if they had been asleep. She frowned when he pulled away, her eyes narrowing and her jaw tightening like a door locking. Why had she let herself talk this way to a boy who couldn't know what it meant? "You certainly couldn't understand what it means to lose your only child. I should never have mentioned this to a poorly disciplined boy like you!"

Edward stared back at her. Now she was acting the way she usually did. "I wish you were dead instead of my mother," he yelled. And ran across the large yard where the turkeys were talking and chasing each other around. "I'm really sorry you don't have your little girl, but I still don't like you, Mrs. Healey. You don't really care about me," he shouted, "even though you try to act like you do." He knew she couldn't hear him anymore.

He ran away as fast as he could, gasping from his effort to be free, not caring what was in his way, not being careful the way Ernesto had warned. Things whizzed by: flimsy shrubs and saplings like children told not to move. A low hanging branch whacked him across the chest when his attention was distracted by what he thought was a man standing ahead of him with some kind of weapon.

He tripped and went down into clumps of leaves and brush, ramming his knee on a stone. "Ouch!" He rolled over, hurting as much from the surprise as from the pain. It hurt a great deal. He pulled up his Levis to observe the cut. It wasn't that bad. Didn't Ernesto say you have to get used to bangs and not make too big a deal out of them?

Snatching another branch from the same enemy tree, he hoisted himself up. He was the wounded hero of a group of homesteaders trapped by Indians. He had escaped by crawling undetected from the wagon circle when the moon dipped behind a cloud. He wasn't going to let any obstacle prevent him from getting through to the cavalry.

He heard his friend, the stream, reciting its mellifluous speech, limped to it, took his shoes off and washed the wound clean. He'd rest here, and gather his strength for the balance of his mission. He climbed a boulder, found a naturally scooped out seat and plopped into it. Remembering what he'd shouted at Mrs. Healey, he began to feel sorry for himself and a little frightened.

It was so peaceful here. Somehow, in this place, he wasn't so insignificant. The Healeys weren't really nasty to him; it was just that he knew they didn't love him. He wanted them to care about how lonely and bad he felt since his parents were killed, but they didn't seem to. These weren't feelings he expressed to himself in words, but an understanding that traveled through his senses as he sat on this boulder, hearing the stream play and jabber to itself or maybe to the stones and rocks it slid against. This place was important to have; it was going to be his own special sanctuary. He could feel good alone in this place, kind of protected but still in charge. Maybe he could talk to his parents here, too—not real conversation, he knew that, but maybe listening to thoughts they might want him to have.

Things had to be figured out: how not to let the Healeys make his life so difficult. Sometimes they were all over him like the chicken pox. He felt "hog-tied" with all their rules and advice. Maybe he could figure ways to be with Ernesto more—like when Mrs. Healey kept after him about his homework, he could always say he was checking it with Ernesto. Another important thing: he had to figure out what he'd be when he grew up. If he wanted to become a pilot or a cowboy, he'd have to start practicing early.

§

The Healey's "spread," as they called it, was named the Carr Canyon Ranch. Their home and out-buildings were located at its head. Where the canyon spilled onto the prairie, their pastures spread out. Two hundred head of Herefords, the breed of beef cattle best suited for the rough conditions of the ranges, scattered over hundreds of acres, each steer foraging widely. The grasses were thinned in direct proportion to the rainfall.

Riding Nellie with Ernesto made him feel more like a grown-up than he ever could when he was down on the ground. Up high, Edward was equal and could ride at the same pace or even go on ahead. He could lasso a calf—if it would stay still. He could decide exactly where to turn Nellie, and he could fall off her and hit the earth ready to shoot, the way the Lone Ranger did. Ernesto instructed him about things a cowboy had to know and do. "Hey, *chico,* you just passed that fence post and didn't notice it was broken at the bottom. Too many of them in one section like that and down it goes. Then we'd have to chase ass over tea kettle for the steers. Good way to lose your ranch, *Eduardito.* Pay attention, you're not some 'dude' I have to play nurse-maid to."

It was exciting when they branded. You lost yourself in the speeded-up action of separating the mothers from their calves. First you roped the little ones and dragged them into a corral, pushing away the mothers if you had to. Then your horse pulled against the rope because "cow-ponies" were taught to back up and keep the rope taut. You slid off, wrestled the calf to the ground and tied his two hind legs to a front one. That kept him down while one of the men pulled the branding iron from the fire. It had to be done fast, so a couple of other guys helped hold the calf, who tried to get up and back to its mother. When the red-hot brand was pressed into its hide, it sizzled and steamed. The calf made this terrible racket, and you felt bad for it except Ernesto said they didn't feel it. And then it always had the Carr Canyon brand on it. In the old days—Ernesto said it still happened once in a while—cattle rustlers would steal as many cattle as they could get. Having your brand on your cattle made it more difficult for the bad guys to sell them. They also did something to their wee-wees, but Edward never wanted to ask Ernesto exactly what that was and why.

"Major, I did my chores. Can I go with Ernesto down to the east pasture and see about the fences?" He tried to be as polite as possible.

"That's more than I can say about Bejarano," he said, calling Ernesto by his last name. "He starts a million projects but never finishes anything," was the reply. "All right, but no galloping. Is that clear?"

"Yes, sir. I won't. Promise." He saluted, trying to do it exactly like the Major always showed him.

The Herefords weren't like those dumb Eastern milk cows that moped along, really slow with no life in them at all. Herefords were steers, not cows, and had brownish-red bodies with very white faces, crests and underlines. They were real tough; if one saw you and it was feeling ornery, watch out! Especially the bulls, who had big bags in the back and wee-wees hanging down. You had to keep them separated from each other, even the young ones.

Edward began to wish his aunt and his sister Susie, could be there with him, even for a visit. "You see," he'd tell them, "you know they're Herefords and not long- or shorthorns by the horn length. And only the Herefords are red and white, okay?" He didn't have to go into the other stuff because they'd probably be disgusted, but when you grow up on a ranch, you have to become tough. You see things live and watch them die. You get used to what really happens instead of living in Chicago where everyone dresses up and doesn't have any idea at all about what being on a ranch is all about.

"Hey, *muchacho,*" Ernesto called to him a few days later. "I believe it's time for you to see something you haven't watched before this. Get your *caballo* saddled up. We're going down to the west pasture *pronto.*" Edward rushed to put on Nellie's bridle.

"Hold still, Nellie. Ernesto's all ready. I think everyone's going."

The Healeys, Ernesto and even Cooky were already part way down the road when Edward caught up with them. "Where we headed, Ernesto?"

"You'll see soon enough. Learn a little patience," he said with a big smile on his face.

"You're mean! I'll get you back. Just wait. You won't know when I'm going to do something. You'd better watch out." When the others were ahead of them, Edward smacked Ernesto's horse on the rump with the end of his reins, which made him jump. Laughing, Ernesto wagged a finger at him.

When they arrived at the pasture, a cow was trying to birth its calf. Edward's eyes widened; he felt as if he might throw up and began to turn away. "Steady, *Eduardito*. You'll be all right. How did you think calves were born, in nice, neat packages? It happens this way."

Edward's face registered surprise and revulsion. "You'll get used to it," Ernesto said. "Kind of wonderful, yes? Soon you'll be down there helping. You're not some milquetoast who has to be treated like a girl."

That was all he needed to say. Edward moved closer. Mrs. Healey and another man had their hands at the opening under the cow's tail and seemed to be trying to pull the head out. There was blood and mucous. He could see a little white head moving. Edward thought it must hurt the mother a lot. "Is that the way it is with people?" he asked Ernesto.

"Yep. More or less."

I'm glad I'm not a girl or a woman, Edward thought. You get big and fat and have to push a huge baby out of that little place. He shuddered and shook his head from side to side. When the calf was finally born, everyone cheered. It was a boy.

§

The dirt road that wound down from the ranch house through Carr Canyon terminated in a "T" at the highway. It ran north to Fort Huachuca and south to Naco on the border. Over a small ridge in Ramsey Canyon, Mexican squatters had settled into a dilapidated shack on the part of the Healey spread that was nestled against the foothills. Edward saw a man there sometimes and once in a while two small, dark-haired children who he guessed were about his own age. When they noticed him, they would duck behind the porch post or around the side of the shack.

"Don't get too curious about the squatters," Ernesto told him. "The Major wants them out and says to leave them alone, except if they do something wrong."

"What's wrong with being curious?" Edward asked, staring intently to detect any activity in or around the shack.

"It's okay until you start snooping. Good Christ, I got a whole bunch to teach you, *chico*." Ernesto stopped his horse, dropped the reins and swung a leg over the horn of the saddle. He pulled the cloth pouch of Old Steer tobacco, with its packet of thin white paper, from his breast pocket, rolled a cigarette, lit it and glanced at Edward, who studied his actions with rapt attention. *"Bueno, amigo,* see that spot down there where the fence ends at the hill? I believe I can show you what happens when you get too curious." They trotted over and tied their horses to the low branch of a fig tree, slid off and strode to an outcropping of rocks and boulders.

Ernesto wasn't normally a man of many words, but when Edward had become a permanent resident of the ranch, he'd opened up like the father-teacher he wanted Edward to feel he was. He wanted to share as much of himself as the boy could take in. He'd get back something too, of course; his own father had been able to go to a certain point but then held back. Ernesto had become used to his silence. It wasn't until he'd realized that there was a gap in him that needed filling that he'd decided to put into language the thoughts and feelings he protected like a trapper did with his secret cache.

Ernesto crouched down on his haunches and gazed to the rocks where the shadows planted firm outlines on the sun-burnt ground. He broke off a small, thin branch-end of a dead bush so quietly that Edward wasn't quite sure he had heard the snap. He waited and waited, counting in some instinctive fashion. This was part of the mystery about Ernesto, who seemed like an animal himself, a creature of the mountains and plains who somehow understood the grand scheme. Edward wondered how Ernesto could remain so long in that position, not moving, just studying. He'd hear the slightest sound, see the smallest movement: a lizard you wouldn't notice, a jay moving somewhere in a canyon. When he was like this, he didn't make words.

Now Ernesto pointed to the outcropping, misplaced, it seemed, as if dropped there to interrupt the roll of land that spread to the foothills beyond. Edward shrugged and shook his head. Ernesto stood, unbuttoned his pants and urinated. Then he dropped his haunches again and continued to drag on his cigarette, sections of smoke dropping around him like a scarf hanging down and then disappearing. Edward waited. Ernesto dragged on the white tobacco weed in slow and measured strokes.

"What do you see?" Edward asked finally.

"Trouble with you," Ernesto said slowly and in a whisper, "is you want things to happen faster than they're going to. It's not up to you."

Edward's lips moved and he sputtered, "But I . . ."

Ernesto pointed again to the rocks. "Learn not to push before the right moment," he said. "*Comprende?* Now follow me and move slowly."

He didn't want to disappoint his mentor. I have to be more like him, Edward thought. Quiet and careful, learn from him about horses and Herefords. Not talk about things, just *know* them. And not go ordering people around or be a "big-shot" like the Major. Daddy was important, people needed him to fly. And Ernesto is important too, only not enough people know about him. I could be a cowboy some of the time and an airline pilot too.

Ernesto moved as if someone had told him he had to walk ten steps on fancy wine glasses and not break any. He glided, he advanced, but you had to watch, because he hesitated for long moments, his balance good enough to be a hundred feet above a circus floor. As he neared the rocks, he stopped, and then began to thrust the stick in his hand in and out between two large stones.

The unmistakable sound of a rattle emanated from the dark area inside. Edward recoiled. Ernesto hesitated. When his arm bent from added weight, he yanked. A snake about eighteen inches long, its fangs implanted on the stick, wiggled like something being burned and then fell to the ground.

It happened with the speed of an action that cannot be controlled, as if in a dream where the dreamer is also the spectator of something that's happening *to* him.

Edward instinctively drew himself to Ernesto for protection, moving close in against his chaps. The feel of the cowhide was the only soft part of Ernesto, except once in his room in the stable when he'd grabbed Edward with his shirt off. Edward gawked as the snake twisted in rapid motions to gain the security of the cool dark among the rocks. He was here; then he was gone.

Ernesto laughed. "See? That's something not to be too *curious* about. Right?" Edward nodded. "The same with people. You have to learn not to bother them. A lot of them aren't worth a damn, they just take up space, so associating isn't even worth it."

"But that boy and girl in the shack," Edward said, "I want to play with them." Ernesto shot him a look that meant "not a good idea."

76

"They're kids my age, Ernesto! There's no one else around." With those kids, he could explore the canyons to their very ends. He remembered how dark their hair was even from the distance and how quickly they ran. They would tell him all the places they had been and all about living in Mexico. He'd tell them about Chicago and the other cities because they probably had never been north or east. No one around here knew much about streets and playgrounds and stores that sold just lots of a single item like toys—Leo's Fruit and Vegetable Market, Lefcourt's Meat Store, the others like that. And baseball parks and escalators, fire trucks and policemen. Huge Fourth of July fireworks.

"Please, Ernesto. I won't be trouble. Promise."

Ernesto shook his head. "They're my *compadres,* but they're bums. That kind always scrounge off somebody and'll swipe you blind. They're not supposed to be living here. It's called trespassing, living in that shack without permission. They don't pay rent. Now what do you think of Mister Rattler, Edward?"

He stared at the boulders. "He had such pretty colors and marks!" Edward looked toward the rocks again. "He could bite me. I know he could, but he wasn't *bothering* us."

Ernesto laughed, reached down, swung Edward around and rolled him over in a somersault down onto the ground, then tripped him lightly. "You sure are a curious boy. That's good. I don't want you to be afraid of rattlers, just know when not to mess with them. Learn when to back off. When you're older, I'll show you how to catch them without getting bitten. If you're caught out in the desert, you can cook 'em and eat 'em. And then sell their skins." Ernesto turned and spat to the side.

Edward said urgently, "No, don't bring him out and kill him!" He put his hand on Ernesto's arm.

"Okay, *muchacho,* not this time." The sun lengthened the shadows of the rocks, pointing them so they looked like the elongated peaks of the mountains. Soon it would fall off over the horizon. Night waited. Nocturnal animals needed it for hunting, the same way daytime animals needed sunlight. Ernesto glanced at the lone fig tree that must have been at least fifty years old. He wondered about this tree. It symbolized age and symmetry and perserverence in a land where all three did not usually exist together.

"Time to ride back. You going to remember about sticking your snoot into places it doesn't belong? Yeah? Okay." He ended that with a frown. "One more thing. We gallop to the road, but after that, if you don't walk Nellie to dry her off, so help me I'm going to swat your behind good with a switch."

They mounted and started racing across the slope. "Hold up!" Ernesto yelled. He moseyed his horse between the sagebrush to the edge of a small arroyo. "See this little barrel cactus," he said serenely. "It lives on so little and makes these beautiful flowers. A little like you and what you've been through. That's what I'm going to nickname you, Edward, The Cactus Kid." He put his hand on Edward's head and stared into his eyes. "You're going to do just fine."

§

EIGHT

Edward's breakfast was always the same: bacon and dry toast, milk and sometimes an orange or juice. Once in a while there was butter and marmalade, or a "short stack" of pancakes. Eggs and thick ham were for the Major and his wife or their friends and relatives when they visited. The Major had told him often that in the cavalry enlisted men didn't eat the same as the officers. Besides, times were tough, the Major said, and money should never be wasted. While the Healeys ate in the dining room, Edward preferred eating in the kitchen with the hired help and Cooky, who had served with the Major.

The Healeys were sorry for Edward, but it was only fitting he help out a little with chores. A youngster could do many things they would have to pay an adult to do. He should understand right away about his status. Although they had taken him in and thought of him as a foster son, Edward was not a member of the family. Part of his education was to learn to treat elders and superiors properly. Later on, when some of that pampering had been worked out of him, he would have more privileges.

Certain rules could not be breeched. Whatever Edward decided to put on his plate had to be consumed before any portion of the next meal could be eaten. Edward fought it at first, but then he planned a little before deciding to take too much food. His Aunt Sandra sent Fanny Farmer candies, which were carefully rationed out; too many sweets were bad for a child's teeth. He rarely had any need to wear the "dress-up" clothes and fancy shoes she sent him: wool suits with long pants, white shirts, simple ties and Indian Walk shoes. When he did put them on, he thought of himself as Robin, Batman's nephew and helper, when he wasn't wearing his outfit with cape and mask.

The Healeys' rules and chores made him think he was in some kind of penitentiary for boys, where the freedom to make choices had been purged as if it were part of a purification rite. One morning Major Healey walked into the kitchen and began to expound. "Discipline, Edward. You might get your butt kicked once in a while, but you'll learn how to deal with any situation that seems rough the first time. After a while, after you've reached down to where your guts live, you'll find you can take it or dish it out whenever you need to. No need to be one of those disgusting, panty-waisted, honey-sopping babies." He marked punctuations in the air with his swagger-stick finger.

Ernesto was there, and ventured, "The boy will learn, Major. He just needs some time."

"This does not involve you, Ernesto. Please stay out of it," Major Healey said. "Edward, you were supposed to make sure the horses have enough hay. I didn't ask you to lug it in, just check on it and tell Ernesto. Those bins are almost empty." Tears came to Edward's eyes, more from embarrassment than about missing the rest of the breakfast he knew the Major wouldn't let him have now. He ran out. The cook looked at Ernesto and shook his head. The Major went on, "I know you think I'm too harsh with him, Ernesto, but he's better off with my being tough on him now, than later when he has to deal with strangers. It's for his own good."

After the Major left the kitchen, Ernesto said to Cooky, "If they had their own children, he wouldn't be so strict. What does he expect from a seven-year-old? The boy needs understanding, not discipline."

With all of this, there were still a few occasions with Major Healey that were pleasant and friendly. One day he asked Edward to join him on an inspection of the south pasture. "I want you to ride with me today, Edward. I'll teach you how to check on windmills and salt licks. The cattle and fences, too. A stray mountain lion has been messing around down here because of the calves, instead of staying higher up where it normally hunts deer." Edward liked the idea of feeling important enough to be asked to go with the Major. Living with this man was certainly bewildering. Most of the time he was cold and harsh, but on this ride, as in other rare instances, he was friendly and seemed interested. It was a good day.

Shortly after this ride together, the Major sent for Edward. Major Healey always thought of himself as a cavalryman, the branch he had chosen after graduating from the Point in 1916. "We routed those Heines in the Argonne, all right," he told Edward as he placed a boot on the table and began to apply polish from a can of Johnson's. "Never a match for us. Our training was superior." Edward had no idea what he was talking about. "Yes, sir, jumping trenches, bayonet charges. Bronze star—should have gotten a Silver, but that's another story—Purple Heart twice, French medal, campaign ribbons. I'll show them to you some day, young man."

Edward listened patiently, as Ernesto had instructed.

"Let me tell you something, something I learned way back that's made the difference between survival and success, Edward. I've been with a lot of men in all kinds of situations. Some make it, some don't.

Some just don't make it. And who the hell cares about those shits anyway? You can forget them. Sound tough? Your father would understand exactly what I mean."

He placed a hand on Edward's shoulder. "Discipline is your best friend and will help you succeed when other men don't. And control," he said, his voice rising a little. "When you control yourself, you can control others. That's one of the characteristics of a leader. He understands that!" The Major grabbed the boot he was working on and held it up to see it against the sky. For a moment he stared across the prairie spreading and flattening out from the bottom of the canyon like spilled sand from a jar.

Healey reached again for the polish. "All right." He reached for a cloth, the remnant of a thin handkerchief, wrapped it carefully around his middle finger and braced as he addressed Edward. "This is next. Water, just a few drops, like this, into the can. A small amount of polish on the rag, then lightly. You have to develop the right touch, that's what does it. You see a mirror. That's when you know you're getting somewhere.

"Mrs. Healey and I took you in because we admired your parents and because of the crash. We're good people. I don't know what would have happened to you. Yes I do. Orphan Home, that's what."

It couldn't be worse than here, Edward said to himself. At least there'd be other kids to play with, and I wouldn't have to do all these stupid chores.

"In a place like that your butt would really be dragging. You'd be polishing more shoes than you could imagine. And endless jobs, working in the gardens, cleaning, fixing whatever had to be done. You don't realize how lucky you are to be with us." He paced up and down, his steps exactly measured, eight of them, across the length of the porch next to the place where he kept his boots, all the pairs trooped together, always in formation. He would select the old ones for riding in rough country, where rocks and brambles scratched them. When he went to Fort Huachuca and Hereford, or on rare occasions, to Tucson, he'd wear his best dress boots.

After the Major finished his speech, Edward stepped off the porch and ambled up the road above the ranch house toward the top of the head of the canyon. The magic of early morning suffused everything. The sun was crossing the crest of the ridges to the east, transforming the deep purples into magenta, crimson and carnation. They pressed around and onto the escarpments at the canyon's head.

Near the stream, Edward inhaled the freshness of the air, trying to rid himself of all thoughts of the Major. He knelt down and splashed water on his face. Spring abounded everywhere, the gurgling sounds raced around the stones as if they were pleased just simply to exist. He tried to make the same sounds in his throat and laughed when he heard the way they came out. It all felt good and natural. Ernesto had taught him to stand silently and wait for small creatures like chipmunks and birds to move and make their sounds. He could learn what they did if he could hear them even though they could not always be seen. The howling of a coyote wasn't something to be afraid of, and the screams of a bobcat or a mountain lion didn't necessarily mean they were killing and eating another animal. They wouldn't attack little boys. Snakes wouldn't run after him and bite him. These animals, all animals, were frightened of people, Ernesto had told him over and over again, and they would only attack or bite if they were cornered.

Edward thought about this as he watched the water, deep in fantasy. Then he heard the harsh, rapid *queg queg queg* and the complaining *maag? maag?* of two magpies overhead, high in flight. He noticed their long wedge-tipped tails of iridescent green. The funny Mexican story Ernesto had told him about them helped him remember they were called magpies.

I could see everything if I were a bird, he speculated. He rose and threw his arms out like wings, circling and circling, around and around, pretending he was a hawk or an eagle resting on the wind. He wasn't quite sure which bird was which. Edward swooped and soared, filling his wings with air, feeling the rush against his arms and body like water when he swam. It felt the same as it did on his bike that first day—a long time ago it seemed, although it had only been four months. His clothes bound him, so he took off his jacket to feel freer, swooping round and round until he was dizzy and had to sit on a large boulder above the stream.

Something caught his eye, a slight movement in a clump of bushes. He stared. There it was again, not just his imagination playing out something he might want to see. Once Ernesto had told him that if he observed carefully, he could see the spirits of Indians who had traveled there.

He scrutinized the spot where the movement had taken place. There it was, a brownish animal, furry, and not large. Slowly, he crawled toward it, concerned it would see him and run away. He became a little frightened; it might be something dangerous, he thought, but it probably wasn't. He stood up and looked.

Standing absolutely still and blended perfectly against the grasses and bushes was a fawn, its spots apparent now that he could see its entire body. Its ears fluttered as he approached, but it remained motionless ("To protect themselves and not be seen, animals kind of freeze in place," Ernesto had said.)

Next to it was its mother, lying dead on the ground, a bite taken out of its neck and another out of its rump.

Edward remembered something else Ernesto had told him. "If a big cat starts to kill deer in the area, the cattle will be in danger. The Major will raise a hunting party and track it down. You'll go with us when you get a little older and can handle a rifle."

Edward inspected the scene. "Don't be afraid, I'm not going to hurt you," he said to the fawn. "I promise. You can't stay here; your mother is dead." He looked around at all the open areas and into the trees, thinking and worrying about the mountain lion. "Your father isn't here either." He walked slowly and lifted the fawn gently in his arms. Surprisingly, the fawn did not struggle. On the way down to the ranch house, he put it down twice to rest, but held it closely so it wouldn't run away.

When he got near the ranch buildings, he saw Ernesto inside the corral. He came over immediately. "Well, well, *chico,* let's see what you have there," he said with a big grin on his face. "Ah, ha, a baby. Where did you find him? What about his mother?" Edward related what he had seen, and Ernesto explained that the mother probably had "parked" the fawn in the bushes out of sight to protect it against the marauder. The baby deer could not have been more than a few days old because it was very small and wobbly. "You were right to bring him out because he's too little to have lasted very long without his mother. You saved him. We'll feed him from a bottle and put a bell around his neck." He went in and brought some thin rope from the stable. "Here, take this. You can give him a name."

"Jumper. He'll be my friend," Edward responded exuberantly. "I'll show him how to do everything."

"Wait a minute," Ernesto laughed. "As soon as he gets big enough, back up there he goes." Edward searched Ernesto's face. "If you keep him too long he won't be able to live wild. He could only survive in captivity."

"Yes, but I want to raise him and play with him. I'll take care of him, I promise." Ernesto shook his head and patted him on the back.

Ernesto built a small pen in a quiet location at the side of the stable between three cottonwood trees. Everyone came to observe, and Edward beamed as he retold the event. The Major grumbled about the food the fawn would eat, but his wife hugged it. The little fawn seemed calm and trusting in its new environment.

§

"Edward," Major Healey said one evening after dinner, more softly than Edward could ever remember, "I've decided you're ready to come to the Fort with us this Saturday afternoon for the Colonel's Weekly Review. It's quite special. Other children will be there, and we'd like our friends to see what kind of a fine young cadet we're raising." Edward looked at him almost in shock. "Now I can tell by your expression you think I've been too hard on you, but one day you'll thank me. Mark my words." The Major came over to him and placed his hand on Edward's head. "Just follow my orders, and you'll see how right I am." Edward vowed he wouldn't, and that he would certainly never tell the Major he was right about anything.

At the Fort, Edward was surprised at the way the Healeys behaved toward him. They smiled at him when they introduced him and seemed genuinely pleased to have him with them, asking him if he liked this or that event, and whether he wanted ice cream and soda. He enjoyed himself, but he remained suspicious. "This lad," Ida Healey said to another couple, "is a fine addition to our family. We think of him as our own, and we know he'll excel in all matters."

"Yes," the Major added, "he should make the Point without any problem. He conducts himself well most of the time, but I do consider myself a good teacher. He, ah, does have the makings of a fine officer, and I'm going to help him become one. And," he said, smiling at Edward, "I'm becoming very fond of him."

Edward wasn't so sure.

§

NINE

It was two miles from the ranch house down to the highway and two more across the range to the one-room schoolhouse in Hereford, but twice that far by car. From a distance, you could tell where Hereford was by the tall oaks and sycamores. When there was a cloudburst, the dried-out wash next to the dirt road filled, supplying badly needed moisture to the trees. Hereford's several square-fronted, washed-out gray buildings with their galvanized tin roofs were all located on the same side of the road. One served as Bob Parker's combination feed and supply store and had a single Tydol gas pump outside the front door. The post office was in Ted Geffner's general store. These and a few houses, their walls made of sun-baked sod, comprised the total town, except for the schoolhouse. It was situated on a rise about three hundred yards to the north.

"Why are you coughing so much?" Mrs. Healey asked Edward as she steered her black 1936 Plymouth sedan on the loosely serpentined road. The trail of dust behind them was a taken-for-granted reminder that no rain had fallen for quite some time. The tires sang with a dull drone that might have been interesting on another occasion. He wasn't aware he had been coughing, and now he stopped so he wouldn't have to answer her.

"You remember the things I told you. It's important you make a good impression," she said.

"Yes ma'am." Edward pulled up his socks again, looked toward the far mountains into air so transparent in the early morning that everything seemed much closer than it actually was. He watched turkey buzzards soar in a thermal some miles away, their wings frozen, round and round in an effortless dance of grace, rising higher and higher on unseen platforms. If he didn't know, Edward might think their wings were always extended. He coughed again.

"Edward, are you ill?" She slowed down and examined his face.

"No ma'am, just thinking about school." He turned toward the side window. How many children would there be? Would Miss Renfrew be stodgy and strict like Mrs. Healey? Maybe he'd have to stand up and answer a question he didn't know anything about. Did that happen in this school? Maybe if he coughed some more, he wouldn't have to go today. Everyone knew each other already, and the new ones who didn't meet on the first day were probably outsiders forever. And this was the second day. The Healeys had gone to Tucson yesterday on some business. Ernesto could have taken him to school, but the Major said Mrs. Healey should take him on his first day.

He wished the car wasn't making so much noise as they drove up the rise to the schoolhouse. Everyone would know, and it would be too embarrassing. He got out and walked behind Mrs. Healey and looked down. God, would they have to walk all the way to the front?

When she saw them come through the door, Margaret Renfrew stopped talking and went to greet them. She shook hands with both Mrs. Healey and Edward in a very friendly way. She looked very young, Edward thought, but not very pretty. Her fingers went all the way over his hand and weren't as soft as he had imagined they would be.

"Welcome to our school, Edward. I hope you'll like what we do out here. It's not exactly the same as where you're from, but we cover what you're supposed to learn."

He nodded, but he couldn't think of anything to say that wouldn't sound dumb. How did she know about Chicago?

"I'm sure you won't have any trouble with him, Miss Renfrew. He's here because—you know—back last February. He's eager to be in school. The Major believes he needs strong treatment. We don't ever want him to be a disciplinary problem," she concluded with a quick glance at Edward. He felt his legs weaken and he was about to cough but suppressed it. He wished they'd stop talking about him, especially in front of the others. He switched his new school bag from one hand to the other. Mrs. Healey had brought it back for him from Tucson.

The teacher looked at Mrs. Healey, gazed around the room and said in a kind of sharp accent, "We never have any of that here," in a voice a little louder than previously. "I'm from New England, Mrs. Healey. My students understand that bad behavior is unacceptable. Please don't be concerned. If one method doesn't work, I use another."

Mrs. Healey made sounds to the effect that she supposed that was so and departed without another glance at her charge. Edward hoped the teacher would hurry up and assign him a desk so he'd be out of the limelight.

"Something the matter, Edward?"

She seemed to be waiting for him, but he was waiting for *her*. She was tall, real tall, and wore a gingham dress. He had expected she'd be wearing Levis. And a white blouse with a kind of necktie, large and silky, blue like her eyes, only they were lighter, almost the color of the sky just before the sun rose, or just after it set. Her hair was different, too, shorter than the other women's, and the brown color of fall grasses. Boy, she was really tall, as tall as a lot of men. Maybe she had on very high heels in the back of her shoes. He couldn't find that out yet because he didn't want her catching him looking down at her legs. She might think he was interested in her body or something.

"Ah, no, Miss Renfrew. I just don't know what I'm supposed to do next." He really felt stupid standing there and saying that. At least he said it quietly so none of the kids heard him.

"Of course," she answered mildly. "Supposing you take that empty desk in the third row at the end, next to Carlos. No, better still, the one in the second row, between Carole and Miguel."

It'd be much better not to have to sit in between. He'd look straight ahead. "And it's *Mrs.* Renfrew. I was married. Mrs. Healey should have know that. Her habit, I guess. Some people have a problem with a single woman." It was a half-smile, with a hint of sadness in it. He wanted to make her feel better, but that was ridiculous, wasn't it? He didn't even know her. Besides, all the kids would hear and see.

"Yes, Mrs. Renfrew." He smiled up at her, his hands at his sides, his new notebook in one, the red, scotch-plaid canvas schoolbag in the other.

"And what else have you brought, a sandwich, a few pencils and, ah, a ball?" Edward's eyes widened. She must have Superman vision. "Just a minute. If you back there don't have anything to do, I can think of something. Like a test, perhaps? You had better get used to the idea that you're here to learn, and I don't mean which team is going to make the World Series. But you can bet your boots the Boston Braves will be one of them." She turned to him. "All right, Edward, please take your place." He began to make his way to the aisle.

Edward was surprised to see that some of the students seemed almost as old as grown-ups. Only a few were his age, and some were younger, but most of them seemed about twelve or thirteen, he guessed. He saw a few white kids and wondered again why the Healeys always said bad things about Indians and Mexicans—when Ernesto wasn't around—calling them lazy and stupid.

Mrs. Renfrew clapped her hands. In that flash, until he caught the meaning, Edward associated her act with praise or applause, and within that mini-second he included himself as the object. "Stop jabbering and listen to me. For those of you who don't understand that word, pretend you're listening to a bunch of magpies." She had their attention before that, but the remark halted them completely. "This is Edward Slavin who lives with the Healeys on Carr Canyon Ranch. He wasn't born around here so I expect you to make him feel especially welcome.

"A few ground rules to remember: you get one strike when I catch you talking when you're not supposed to; two when you do it twice or don't do what I tell you; then it's into the Cloakroom." She hesitated for the impact about to be enunciated. "The third strike you're out!—and particularly you older students, if you pick on anyone, especially a girl. 'Out' means what you think it means." She smacked her long ruler on the edge of her oak-grained desk. "There's a practice these days of rapping knuckles. I don't follow that method. But I do believe education is a privilege, not simply a right."

A girl about Edward's age raised her hand. Mrs. Renfrew nodded and said, "Yes, of course you may. All right, outside everyone. Camella, today's your turn. You know where the flag is kept. When we come back, Robert, you and Clarence distribute the worksheets. Edward Slavin, I'll explain what you're to do when I meet with you later." She stopped, and reviewed the faces that were lined up in her direction. Then, with a big grin, she said with slow emphasis, "This is going to be a good year, gang. We're going to have a lot of fun, and the Braves are going to win it 'hands down.'" Silence. "What, no Giant fans? All right, everyone, outside."

The morning passed quickly. Edward was completely absorbed in the multitude of activities, listening to the back and forth of remarks between his classmates and to Mrs. Renfrew explaining history and geography. Finally it was Recess. He needed his handkerchief from his jacket, and went to the Cloakroom. He thought he was alone inside this musty, windowless container and was looking up in the eaves, where spiders had created housing with beautiful symmetrical lines, their webs mysterious in the dust. Then he heard whispers from among the jackets, and a chill ran through him. He stepped carefully towards their source and came upon two slightly older kids.

"We're trading cards," one said sheepisly. "Mrs. Renfrew won't let us do it until after school." They peered at him. He knew his future was at stake.

"I won't tell, you don't have to worry." They nodded their thanks. He motioned why he had come and exited more noisily than when he'd entered.

In the yard, older boys were throwing a baseball, and the younger ones his age were running around. The girls played on their own side. He watched for a while. No one paid any attention to him. "Hi, can I play with you?"

"Guess so," came a response. He walked over, delighted with this acceptance. He'd play their way, be a bad guy or Tonto or The Lone Ranger, whatever they wanted.

A whistle pierced the atmosphere, the clarion call from the steps. "Let's go, children. Recess is over, officially and unofficially." Mrs. Renfrew had a way of making what she wanted not sound nasty.

Edward's ten minutes with her was smooth, and he felt the easy comfort of when things go well. "I'm glad your mother did some advanced work with you," she said, the soft notes of her voice soothing any concern he may have had. Then she look at him hard for a moment and stood up at her desk. "I'll be right back, everyone. Please continue with what you're doing." She turned to him. "Come outside with me a minute, Edward." What did she want with him?

He followed until they were away from the building, under the huge sycamore that spread its canopy like a gigantic leafed umbrella. She leaned back against the trunk. "I'm terribly sorry about your parents. I was one of the people who came, but I didn't stay because you didn't know me.

"Let me offer you what I can. I'll work with you so that you can advance as rapidly as you're able. I have a feeling you'll race along like a roadrunner." That sounded wonderful to him, like she meant every word. She leaned over and touched his face gently, and he saw the movement of her breasts inside her blouse. He smelled her perfume, which made him tingle. It reminded him a little of his mother, but he'd have to see what she was like over a period of time.

"How are you getting home?" Her face was bright, and her smile broad, with the two large center teeth on top pushed out a little. Yes, like a giant jackrabbit, Edward thought happily. A little, squat nose, too.

"Mrs. Healey said Ernesto—he's the foreman—is coming. But tomorrow, I'll be riding Nellie! She's my horse," he added. She smiled. Nice, Mrs. Renfrew and school, much better than he had imagined.

Mrs. Renfrew was waiting with Edward after the other children had departed when Ernesto's old black Chevy coupe with the rumble seat in the back drove up. Dust flew from behind the wheels and spread out like two streamers. Edward had seen it at least a mile away on the dirt road that wound over the hills, sometimes the car, sometimes the dust. Far away, it looked like a horizontal dust-devil. Ernesto stepped out, quite tall ("Most Mexicans are so dumpy and fat," the Healeys would say), his face groomed by wind, sun, rain and snow. He was wearing what he always did: steel-blue shirt and jacket, well-worn Levis and a wide-brimmed, tan hat with sweat stains darkening the crown in an irregular line. His boots were pointed in the front, with high heels in the back caked in manure.

He ambled over as they both stood and smiled, saying his name and putting out his hand to shake Mrs. Renfrew's. Edward beamed, proud of him.

"Seems like you have yourself a new boy, Mrs. Renfrew." Ernesto pulled his tobacco pouch from his pocket, and as he tried to tear a paper from the packet it slipped from his hands. With a clumsiness Edward couldn't understand, he gathered the ingredients for a cigarette from the ground. "This one's got more curiosity than a hound of mine chasing a mountain lion all over the Huachucas," he offered, recovering. Edward was surprised again, because he knew Ernesto didn't have a dog.

Margaret Renfrew exhaled audibly. "He certainly seems to ask a lot of questions," she said in a tone different from the one she used with Edward. She moved back. "And doesn't come on too strong," she continued with a sardonic grin. She brushed back a strand of hair that had wandered from her forehead across her eyebrow.

Ernesto advanced and rested his hand on Edward's head. "This little guy's so enthusiastic pretty soon he'll be showing *me* things about ranching and the outdoors. Tell you the truth, I'm pleased he's in your school. I hear you're the best teacher this side of the Rockies, Mrs. Renfrew."

She listened, then said flatly. "You may call me Margaret, if you wish." Her face flushed. "The children, they're wonderful to work with—except," she added, "the older ones sometimes."

"I suppose so. My mother's name is Margaret," Ernesto responded with an uplifting inflection. "From your accent, you're not from Arizona. Are you a *dude* from the East?"

Edward watched, starting to feel left out. Mrs. Renfrew seemed happy.

"If you want to put it that way," she countered. "Maine, Portland. I came out here during the war. My husband was stationed at the Fort for a while. Well," she said looking at Edward and then quickly at Ernesto, "it's time I was heading home." She smiled at them. "It was very nice meeting you, Ernesto Bejarano." She stopped talking abruptly and walked toward her car.

§

As she watched the black coupe become smaller, the size of a large beetle, Margaret Renfrew found herself bemused by her own annoyance. "What's wrong with you?" she said out loud. "An attractive man pays some attention to you, and you tell him to get lost."

A few weeks before she'd left for her first year at Middlebury College, she remembered how her mother had sat her down for a talk. "You have a right to your opinions, Margaret, but you throw people off when you come out so quickly and let them know what you think. Especially boys." Margaret had made a face, shaking her head from side to side. Then her mother had added the clincher: "You'll get married quicker if you weren't so independent and sassy. You're a nice-looking person, but you're not the very prettiest girl in town. Will you please try to behave yourself? You're getting such a reputation as a—oh I don't know what." Her mother often reached that point. All right, Margaret would think, so I'm not the beauty Alice is. So boys won't like me and I won't get married. No, that's not what's going to happen: a man will find me who's looking for more than appearance. Some really great person at college. I'm not changing for anyone.

Margaret did care about her looks, but there wasn't much she could do about them. "Are you sure you're my real parents?" she would ask them. "You're both so good-looking! Maybe you bought me from one of those baby merchants for five ninety-five." She would peer closely into her mother's face and wrinkle her nose.

"You're impossible with that talk, do you hear me? Where do you get those ideas? You think it's funny! You treat everything as if it was a joke, except your books." She grabbed her daughter. "Now look at me, Meg, I'm serious. If you'd only wear a little makeup the way the other girls do, you'd be very attractive. And your hair."

"Well, if you call attractive having a face that looks like the football team ran over it. I *like* my hair short. But how about these perfect teeth? They really sparkle, don't they?" Then Margaret would pull her mother's face to hers and give her a kiss on the cheek, at which point her mother covered her eyes with one hand and shook her head.

§

TEN

U nable to sleep any longer, Edward got up and went out to the stable long before light created the new day. He was terribly excited about the ride to school on Nellie. For the first time, he'd be alone for such a long distance. "Nellie, are you ready?" he asked her. If there was an answer in her head it wasn't anything he was able to discern. "Because we're just about to go, you know." Was he ready? He rechecked his possessions and accoutrements: school books and notebook placed in the left saddle-bag, sandwich, orange, canteen in the right one. Yes, the rope was secured to the saddle (every cowboy has to be ready). What else in case of emergencies? He had matches in his pocket but no penknife. He'd lost it somewhere. The next time he went to the Fort with Ernesto or maybe the Healeys, he'd buy a two-bladed job with his savings. A kid in school back in Chicago had had a new kind—the black handle was made from hard plastic, but it was chipped out to feel and look like wood.

Was he dressed right? Seemed okay: hat, chaps and boots, of

course. Nothing would stand in his way between the stable and the schoolhouse down on the plain. His father would have been pleased with him and how he had prepared. He'd handle whatever might happen all right, no matter what it took.

Edward got onto the little stand they had put out for him and placed the toe of his left boot in the stirrup. (Everyone knows you always mount from the left side; that was another thing he'd tell Aunt Sandra and Susie if they ever visited.) But then he looked up for a minute and slipped, crashing down right next to Nellie's leg. He couldn't help looking to see if anyone had witnessed the misstep. Only dudes messed up like that.

The Healeys didn't come out to see him off, but Edward knew they were probably watching from a window. The Major had told him last night that even though he was starting school, he still had to complete the daily chores he had been assigned. But he had wished Edward good luck, and so did Mrs. Healey. Ernesto stopped pitching manure and strolled over to him.

"Okay, *chico*?" He pulled the tobacco pouch from his pocket and started to roll a cigarette. "Mrs. Renfrew is one smart teacher who can help you learn. And something else. Sooner or later you will have some kind of incident."

"An incident?" Edward asked.

"In this case, a problem. No one will be there to help you. One of your schoolmates will say or do something you won't like. Later on, things much more serious. You must stand up for what you believe. You'll be worse off if you back down." He struck the match against the bottom of his boot. "Do that, you lose respect for yourself. You even may have to get into a fight. There were times I didn't, and I'm sorry about them now."

"Okay, but I don't like fighting except with you, when it's just fooling around stuff." Edward slapped dust off his chaps as he remembered Ernesto doing.

"Don't worry about it. You'll find out when the time comes." He reached out and they shook hands. "Good luck, *Eduardito*."

As he rode off on Nellie, he felt the comforting, rocking motion of her gait. He liked feeling the quiet, seeing the timeless set of canyon spotted with boulders and cacti, the vastness of the plains in front, knowing that it had been always been this way and always would be. His route required leaving the road, a much shorter way than following it would be. He would pass the "squatters" shack.

As he got up to it, he saw the little girl carrying a heavy pail of water. This time she put it down and looked at him. He waved, but she stood as if she had been frozen into a piece of sculpture. He waved again, this time with his hat, and she slowly raised one hand shoulder high. "See, Nellie, she's not so weird." He started to gallop, aware that the girl was watching. "Maybe we could really be friends," he thought.

The trail required him to cross the highway. He looked in both directions, even though he knew he would have heard any cars or trucks. He stopped at the trough underneath the windmill and the horse put her mouth into the water, breathing through her enlarged nostrils. This was great, riding to school by himself.

He surveyed the broad expanse of the plains. The mountains to the south were in Mexico; Ernesto had told him that when they went to Naco several months before. It was surprising to Edward that a foreign country could look exactly the same as his. Now he turned behind to see the Huachucas brightening in the light of the sun, its warmth holding his back. He removed his denim jacket and lashed it with the leather cords behind the seat of the saddle. Nellie finished drinking at the same moment he heard the clanging of the bell from the top of the schoolhouse. It was still far out of sight. "Oh, no, now we're late!"

Edward decided to race straight to the schoolhouse. Nellie printed her hoofs in the sand on the bottom of the wash as they tore along the dry stream bed. He was a Pony Express rider who had to get through; bad guys hid behind the suguaro cacti, waiting to ambush him, and he couldn't be sure where and when they would attack. They're not going to get me, he thought.

When he rose onto the plain, he saw that the schoolhouse was still about a mile away. He'd ridden in the wrong direction. The bell was silent. Now he was really late.

When he arrived, he tied up Nellie quickly, dashed up the three steps and then slowly opened the door. Mrs. Renfrew stopped talking. There was complete silence. Everyone was in their seats and turned to look at him. He wished he was anywhere but there.

"It seems you didn't plan your time very well, Mr. Slavin." The students giggled. "Since you're late, suppose you just wait outside for a while. And tie your horse in the shade with the others. You don't want him to cook, do you?"

Edward's mouth opened. "But Mrs. Renfrew, I, I got lost on the way here and—"

"You are required to be in your seat at bell-time," she said in measured tones. "That's called being responsible, Edward. I think you will learn something valuable from this experience." She turned to the blackboard and then faced him again. "Look, I'm not angry with you. Perhaps a little disappointed. Responsibility. Yours is to be here on time. Mine too. And if I can be, so can you. There are other responsibilities, children. You'll learn about those as well. Now outside, Edward. You think about what I've said."

He sat on the steps after walking Nellie to the rear and tying her to the branch of the large cottonwood tree. Boy, he thought, his elbows on his thighs, both hands under his jaw, she doesn't care! Just like my mother when something embarrassing or bad happened to me. She started out nice and interested, but then she changed. And in front of all the kids. They'll make fun of me, I know they will. She should know I really care about school. I don't want to be out here.

100

But when Recess came, the others didn't mention his being late, or say anything about what she'd said to him. They didn't seem to care, and that bothered him even more than if they'd said something. Everything was going wrong. All he could think of was that he'd displeased her. At the end of the school day, as he climbed onto Nellie, Mrs. Renfrew appeared at the rear door. "See you tomorrow, Edward. Be sure to complete the arithmetic and spelling assignments."

"Yes Ma'am, I will."

"Don't be so glum. Tomorrow will be much better. You'll see."

"Yes Ma'am," he answered, happy for her words. He wound his way through the arroyos, up across the main road and past the shack. The two kids came out and stood on the steps of the porch, stock-still, watching him, their hands at their sides. Edward heard a shout, and they scampered back inside, caught in a place they shouldn't be.

When he got back to the ranch, he searched at once for Ernesto and found him in the middle of shoeing one of the horses.

"How'd it go in school, *chico?*"

"Terrible. I got there late. Mrs. Renfrew scolded me, like Mrs. Healey does. I won't ever be late again. The kids are okay. No one did anything bad to me." He sighed. "I made friends with Carlos and Johnny. On the ride home I thought about 'incidents.' I remembered some things that happened when Mommy and I lived on the Army bases."

Ernesto took the horseshoe nails he was holding between his lips and lined them up beside the stool he sat on. "Yes? Which ones?"

"I don't know. I guess when the other kids went to their churches on Sundays. I was left out. They'd treat me differently. When they found out we were, I was Jewish. Nothing terrible, well maybe around Christmas, one or two times, one of the kids said something about how the Jews killed their Lord, as if that was my fault and all that." He gazed out the stable door to where the turkeys had become excited by something. "What's happening out there, Ernesto?"

101

"Stop changing the subject. What'd you learn from that?"

"When I told Mom, she said it wasn't true, that I should tell them it was the Romans. But even if it was, why would anyone want to kill God? And you can't even see God, so why—I mean how would anyone be *able* to kill Him?"

Ernesto paced the stable floor. "It's complicated, but for now just accept what I tell you. Christians believe that Christ was God's son, and He died for man's sake, to teach man about goodness, dedication and conviction. Most of all, about sacrifice for a cause far greater than Himself."

"I don't understand what you're saying and your big words," Edward said, almost ready to cry with frustration.

"I'm sorry. I'm not explaining it too well."

"Well, the kids at that base made me feel lousy, like I was some sort of horrible person." He hesitated. "That Jews were terrible. One called me a 'kike.' Everyone heard him. No one stuck up for me. I didn't know what to do," he said sadly.

"That's what I was referring to this morning." Ernesto pulled the tobacco pouch and paper from his breast pocket for the inevitable cigarette, but then he stopped as if he had heard some call of an animal he had been waiting for. There was no sound or movement. He said nothing, for what seemed like the longest time. Then he asked, "You think that was a rotten thing they did?" He lit the cigarette.

Edward nodded.

"Well, that's just too bad," said Ernesto grimly. "Better get used to it, it's not going to be the last time." He took a drag and smacked a fly against the wall of the stall. Edward glared at him wide-eyed and made a move to run in the direction of the corral.

"Hold it," Ernesto shouted, grabbing one of Edward's hands. He stood up, stuck the cigarette in his mouth and gripped Edward's shoulders. "You'd better understand there's a lot of people who feel the way that kid did, so-called nice people. In Guadalajara, they said things about Jews and Orientals that weren't nice or accurate. And here, *I'm* different. I don't want you ever feeling sorry for yourself. Learn to take it and—this is what I meant—to give it back."

Edward nodded slowly.

"You look like you're staring into the next county," Ernesto said.

"I was remembering what my mother told me." Ernesto waited. "She said we had to be careful not to *seem* different." He ran the toe of his boot in the dirt, making an "E."

Ernesto leaned against the wall. "Listen, we only have a few minutes. I'm going to finish up this horse." He slid his stool next to the horse's rear leg and bent the leg so that the bottom of the hoof lay in his lap. He talked as he set four nails through the U-shaped shoe into the horse's hoof. "I'll give it to you quick. Some Christian people are jealous because Jews are more successful than they are."

"Doesn't everybody believe in God?"

"That's not what I'm talking about. Remember what you told me Mrs. Healey said? Try not to listen to too much of that crap."

Edward handed him the square-edged nails for the next hoof, one at a time. "Daddy told me about the Nazis killing Jewish people. Could that happen again? Will they come and take us away?" he asked.

"No, you don't have to worry." Ernesto put the hammer down and looked up at Edward. "Wars have been fought over religion for thousands of years."

"I hope it doesn't happen again." Edward drew closer, leaning in and touching Ernesto a little.

"Me too. That's why you have to fight back when it's necessary, understand?"

Edward nodded and braced himself with his back against the post. "Yeah," he said, "if one of the kids says anything, I'm going to give him one."

"I'll do the last two tomorrow," Ernesto said. "Come on, it's chow-time. I could eat a steer." He grabbed Edward's collar and tugged him forward. Edward sprinted ahead.

§

ELEVEN

"I don't mind his correcting your homework," Mrs. Renfrew said one morning during recess. "Well, yes, I do," she added with a frown. "It's better if you let me see it without his help. You'll learn more." Then she said, "Here, Edward, please take this note to Ernesto. By the way, your handwriting could be neater. Practice and do it more slowly. This way." He stood next to her at her desk, watching and listening to the slow scraping noise she made with her pen as she moved it into flowing, graceful curves and careful, straight lines. Pretty, like the work of an artist. It only added to how perfect she seemed to him, being able to do whatever it was she tried. He'd have to practice in his notebook and not rush the way he usually did. He'd have to get better at one more thing that would make him stand out from the others.

Because anybody could be ordinary, just all the same, like Herefords. But he felt so unsure about everything, especially about his life in the future. What would happen to him? What could he do about it? Not too much was clear except wanting to be a pilot and a cowboy. When his father had taken him flying, it was special, not only being with him, but being so high in the air. Houses and cars and people were like little toys in a game where they were the giants. They were airborne of course, but he marvelled at how they could actually be above the whole world with "nothing" in between. His father had explained it, but it was still dreamy. And the power and control the pilot had, moving the airplane in this direction or that, banking, going straight, rising or gliding, slipping to the ground at the end of the flight, like the birds he constantly watched coming in for landings, especially ducks on ponds. There was nothing in the world like flying.

Being a cowboy was also something he wanted a lot. He was sure that if he learned about roping and horses and could lead others, he'd become a foreman. Ernesto was a successful leader. Everyone knew him and liked him, but they would have liked him anyway because he was such a nice person. Being an Army officer, well, that was definitely one thing he *didn't* want to be when he grew up, except if he were a fighter-plane pilot. He wouldn't go to West Point ever. No sir, they'd have to force him.

Thinking about what he wanted to become helped eliminate Edward's gnawing realization that he was alone. He was sure that except for Ernesto and Mrs. Renfrew, no one really cared any more whether he existed or not. And no matter how he secretly wished or imagined that he and his mother and his father could all be together again, he knew it could never, never be like it was before.

He watched Mrs. Renfrew. She seemed to glow. He closed his eyes for a moment, making believe she was his mother. He missed his mother right now and regretted ever thinking she hadn't been good to him. She took care of him when he was small, and made sure he had clothes and food when he could hardly do anything for himself. He remembered her staying with him and putting stuff on his sores when he had measles and chicken pox. Even sleeping in his room a few times. He remembered her humming and singing. No one will ever sing to me again, he thought.

Edward felt himself shaking and brought himself out of his daydreaming. Mrs. Renfrew was inspecting his face, her expression gentle and caring.

"Are you all right, Edward? Sit down, I'll get you a glass of water."

"No Ma'am, I'm okay. Really," he answered.

"Perhaps there's something bothering you. Want to talk about it?"

He decided he could trust her. "I was thinking about my mother. I miss her a lot."

"I miss mine too, even though she's still here." She patted his hand for a moment and held it in the large, soft mitten of her own hand. "You're not going to understand this, Edward, but what I miss is how it was when I was small. My Mom and I were close then. Things changed when I became a teenager. We were never again like we were before." She smiled, not as if she was happy, but as if she was sharing a secret with a friend.

"I think I know what you mean, Mrs. Renfrew."

"That's all right. I want you to know I understand."

"Yes Ma'am." She really cared, Edward thought. He felt peaceful.

§

More and more frequently, Ernesto offered to drive Edward to school on his way to or from picking up supplies in Hereford. On some days Mrs. Renfrew drove Edward back to the ranch. The second time it happened, Major Healey turned to his wife as he watched from the house and said, "Beats the hell out of me why she wants to have anything to do with Ernesto. She starts messing with him, she's going to be sorry. Aren't our own boys good enough for her?"

"For God's sake," Ida retorted, "when are you going to realize that outside the military, people decide things for themselves? The war's changed the way people go about their lives."

"Not some things," he said. "I can understand if a woman has no one else around—she gets sort of, you know. But we've lots of good men at the Fort."

"You carry on too much about Mexicans, John. Ernesto's never given you any cause to talk so ill of him." She was watching the animated conversation going on outside.

"I can't help the way I feel, especially about bright ones like him. Look what they did in Texas in 'sixteen. They're all right as ranch hands, provided they stay in their place." He closed his hand into a fist. "Ida, I'd appreciate it if you wouldn't interfere about the way I handle the men."

She glared at him and walked out of the room.

§

Margaret's house in Hereford was at the edge of town. It was singled out like she was, at the point where the road turned south some fifteen miles toward Mexico, following the bed of the Rio Pedro River. A black coupe was parked along the side of the two-room bungalow, to the rear of a sedan given to her three years before by her father, who had driven it from the Northeast in ten days with her mother: "The Big Trip," he had called it. "We'll get a chance to see something of our country," he'd said. "You know, Meg, your mother and I have never been west of, oh I guess, Harrisburg, Pennsylvania, when we visited one of my cousins. We'll call you when we're a day away or so." He revered the AAA as if it were the source of all knowledge and light, like a surgeon who plotted the direction of his scalpel through the maze of the unknown that a simple citizen like her father would never understand but would have to accept if it were he on the table.

Inside on this Saturday morning, several cups of black coffee had already been consumed and the sun was pounding down on the roof

108

with angry intensity, as if it focused on this one building to vent its force upon. The windows were opened, and the breeze fluffed the white linen curtains on whose folded bottoms Margaret had sewn red and blue flowers, following a pattern she remembered from the room she'd lived in as a child. The door to the bedroom was also open, to permit cooling. The two people inside were oblivious to the intermittent breeze or, for that matter, to anything else.

Some weeks earlier Ernesto had surprised her when he knocked on the front door and called out who he was. "Just a minute." When she'd opened the door, her hair was wet and she was shoeless. "Oh, Ernesto. Something on your mind? I'm a little surprised to see you." She closed the lapel of her robe more tightly over her chest and waited, looking straight into his eyes. "I wasn't planning on company," she said in her abrupt way. "You here to talk about Edward?"

Ernesto had chuckled, finding the hint of sassiness a little offensive, but it was one of the things about her that attracted him. That, together with her manner of talking. It had gotten his attention right at the beginning, and it did now, too.

"You don't have a telephone. I would have called." He fidgeted, then said, "I've been hoping to get the chance to know you a little better. The boy's in town with Mrs. Healey." He handed her a bag. "Here, this is for you, Margaret. Mexican coffee, the best there is. And this Indian arrowhead I found." He waited.

She nodded and observed his freshly shaven face, clean shirt, the fresh Levis and the lotion she smelled when he leaned close. "Since you've got yourself all dressed up, I guess it's only right I ask you in."

"I can leave if you're busy." Ernesto stood uncomfortably, jittering and trying to glance inside the door.

"Oh, come in for goodness sake. You're about as subtle as a newly released inmate. I'll put up some coffee and put on some clothes."

Over eggs made into an omelette filled with pieces of ham, onions, parsley, and red and green peppers, and browned toast marked with parallel lines that were almost black, they talked about inconsequential things. Then he confided, "I don't expect to work at the Healey spread a helluva lot longer. I've got my eye on some *terrano* up in Ramsey Canyon. As soon as I've got more put away, I'm going to see about buying it." He hoped that would impress her. But from the way she regarded him, he couldn't tell.

"That's most interesting," she said with a touch of sarcasm in her voice. "It's amazing how important cattle are to you." She rose from the kitchen table and brought back the coffee pot. The outline of her breasts against her blouse was marked by the flow of the breeze.

Ernesto got up and went towards her. She turned to face him, her lips separated, breathing faster. Now they were almost touching. He took the coffee pot from her, then put it down and gently held her hands. Their eyes engaged. She edged closer, her nipples burning into his chest.

There, that first time in her home, he could stand it no longer and ran his hands up along the flat of her stomach, firming them on her breasts. He lifted her off the floor, his hands on her rear and let her slide down slowly against his body. "Yes," she said jaggedly. She probed his mouth and moved her tongue first around his, then to the corners and the furthest places she could reach. He swept her up in his arms and kicked open the door to the bedroom, rolling them both onto her bed. "Yes," she repeated. He quickly opened her blouse and brassiere, exposing twin mounds, soft and silky except for her firmed nipples. He brought his mouth over the nearest, absorbing as much of it as he could, his hand on the other. He began acting like a concupiscent demon.

After a few minutes, she rolled over, stood up and rapidly took off her Levis and underpants. He gazed at her navel but concentrated at the light brown swatch beneath it. He pushed her back onto the bed, his mouth on the slot between her legs. She shivered more and more,

110

moaning with the kind of unique sounds that lovers often make to their own surprise.

Involuntarily, Margaret arched her back, and then she and Ernesto lost themselves in one another. Afterward she floated as in a half-dream, and when she thought about her fantasy later, it would be almost comical.

She had become the central character in an extravagant illusion that had been lurking in her mind for a very long time: Margaret was a princess at the very top of the sacrificial pyramid, being prepared for this greatest of all the annual rituals of Attutapepityl, the young glorious man-god, leader and champion of all the pre-Columbian nations.

She wasn't a victim, but the one who had been honored and chosen for this great event. Down below, the cry from the hordes increased in crescendo around the two of them, the excitement of the moment inviolable. It was coming, her unique role in this greatest of religious events. Everyone clamored for it, and she writhed towards the finality until, losing consciousness, the burst came, the central power of the heavens manifested and focused upon her, light and time and all reality inconsequential, the fusing with the rippling explosions inside her the only truth that would ever matter.

And then Attutapepityl himself, prepared for this singular moment, hovered above her, his magnificent muscles gleaming in light she could barely endure, the repeating electrical surges seemingly inexorable. He lowered himself upon her—no, into her, his strength pointed in front, raised powerfully, not a lance, but a ramrod she craved. She received him, the fullness completing whatever there was she had been without, her world completely fulfilled, her existence comprehended, the meaning of why she had been born fully fathomed.

Margaret slept peacefully for a short while, intertwined with her lover. The second time they coupled was slower and tempered by the first. She nibbled Ernesto's ear, stroked him everywhere, examined his body. In return he ran his tongue aross her back, down her spine, and slowly, ever so slowly, around each firm cheek, finally exploring the mysteries hidden between the rounded sweep that ended in the canyon between her legs. Whatever they learned about each other only stimulated a desire to know more, to experiment and play.

"I don't care," she whispered in his ear as she tried unsuccessfully to comb his black hairs with the end of her tongue, "we're going to stay in bed all day. Let them do without you."

He propped himself up on his elbows, turned a smiling face to hers, placed a soft kiss on her cheek and said, "Got any beer? All this exercise has made me thirstier than a camel."

"Sorry, I don't keep any, but I will in the future. How about a soft drink?" He nodded and lightly slapped her fanny as she bolted out of bed.

"You were beginning to tell me about your husband," he called to her in the kitchen. "His name was Eugene?"

She came back and stretched out, face down, her face against his leg, and held his foot, fondling his toes. "Yes, a really nice guy, but I hardly knew him." She shook her head. "We met when I was half-finished getting my Master's at Columbia, living in New York and working part-time. A friend introduced us at a party. He had just graduated from flight school, and the war was invading everyone's lives. We eloped, went to see my folks, spent a rainy weekend at Bar Harbour, and then flashed through a whirlwind of different bases. Then he flew off to England with his squadron." She punched the mattress.

"Good God, the stupidity of it all. Eugene was killed in Italy in 'forty-three. The fact we hardly got to know each other is even more of a shame than getting married so quickly." She bunched her shoulders, and lifted herself onto her elbows.

Ernesto focused on her breasts that had been flattened under her, delighting in the resumption of their normal shape. He reached under and raised his palm against the softness of one. "I am truly sorry, Meg, it must have been terrible for you." He brushed her arm with his lips.

"He said he wasn't afraid of dying because he was fighting for his country. I told him he shouldn't be so damned romantic. Wars are idiotic except if you believe it's a clever way to hold down the world's population. They rarely achieve anything for the people. And the best of a generation gets decimated."

She felt the swell of self-pity within her, stopped it, and peered instead into the face of her new lover, where she found what she was looking for. "Enough about me, my Mexican jumping bean, tell me more about how a handsome latino cowboy develops such an excellent vocabulary. And behaves as if he could step into high society without a moment's hesitation."

Anger flashed into Ernesto's face, a look she was unprepared for. "Don't say that. It makes me feel the same subtle prejudice I hate." He waited, gazing into her sturdy face and noting the Anglo-Saxon lineage, from the line of her jawbone and nose, balanced by thousands of years in the British Isles, touched a bit by the Norman involvement.

"I'm sorry," she said, "I didn't mean it the way it came out. My mouth always gets me in trouble." She brought her fingers gently across and kissed his lips.

He nodded. "I told you my father sent me off to the States to prep school. It was fun except for studying. He's a good man, but old-world. Anyway, I was in my fifth semester at the University of Arizona and I got booted out. Fooling around too much. People say I don't finish what I start, but that's not so. He didn't forgive me for that, said it was an insult to our family name, to his standing in Guadalajara. I liked ranching better than school anyway. Stuffy

113

classrooms don't have the action of the outdoors, *claro?*" He grinned, then added, "That's the whole, sad story of one Ernesto Castellano de Umberto Bejarano, fourth and youngest son of Don Miguel, all of them with the same distinguished names. Look, he wasn't altogether wrong. I found that out." He finished the soda.

And continued. "In Guadalajara they don't have much to do with the outside world. Not yet, anyway. One can live graciously, but that way of life is no longer possible for me. I can't bridge both. Here I'm on my own, not Don Miguel's son. And the Major Healeys don't trouble me. I get along well, and I'm free, happy."

"We all have a place we think of as home," she said, "where we feel best. Where's yours?" She had that incisive way of cutting through to the pith. Ernesto shrugged.

"Where you are," he said. "I know it's early for us, but I need to be with you, Meg, more than I can say."

That first day of intimacy was unlike any other, as it had to be: the extended length of their sexual joining, the sharing of their pasts, the disclosure of some—but not all—of their sequestered thoughts and feelings. Later, even when they had become far more familiar with each other, their desire did not dissipate. There were nuances that came with what they learned, but the force of the magnetism that pulled them together was undiminished, the invisible lines just as strong.

For Ernesto, in whom generations of Bejaranos had mixed at rare times with the blood of the *indianos,* it was the locking magnetism of the poles, the Mexican south and the American north. Margaret was his, and by his penetration into the sweet warmth of everything she was, they balanced the forces of the physical world that was beyond him to analyze—his function only to act within it, his thrusting in the rhythm they both created. Then, time unmeasured at the wellspring of his totality, the generic substance of him throbbed from the dammed waters in which it had waited and poured into her, seeking every available place.

This morning Ernesto had brought some Mexican sweets and placed them on a plate next to the coffee pot. He had left the entrance door slightly ajar, and a thin line of light was penetrating inside. The breeze entered through the bedroom windows, cooling the kitchen and living room and slipping out the front door.

"Why is it I can't be around you for very long, schoolteacher, before I want to do all the things to you I've been thinking about since last Sunday?" He put down his cup and pulled off his boots, a grin widening his mouth like a sliver moon on its back.

"Because you're a sex maniac, that's why. And it's my responsibility not to let you starve. Very dangerous around these parts. You'd better come with me for a mutual and thorough examination. You've gotten me all wet with your depraved talk. Now come with me before we end up on the floor."

She took his hand and led him into the bedroom. The gentleness of the warm breeze encircled them like the mystery of a fading dust devil on the prairie, enclosing them in its magic. Like most lovers, they presumed they were unique, that the oneness they created could not be duplicated, that no other two people could ever have experienced or comprehended it.

Soon they were transported by a pull they did not deny, and they did not hear Edward's quiet "hello" when he entered. He watched them with an expression so shocked that it might have made the front cover of *Life* magazine, his disbelieving eyes witnessing his two impeccably immaculate mentors "doing something like *that*" (clad in his underwear, Ernesto was bent down, his head buried in Margaret's breasts, while she, standing, was holding his head tightly to her with both hands).

Edward gaped at them until the words surged out of him like

uncontrollable vomit: "I hate you, I hate you!," he yelled, then raced from the living room and leaped off the steps onto the road.

"That's marvelous," Margaret laughed. "Just what we need. He's just received a graphic introduction to sex. The only thing now is to try to explain to him about the facts of life. What the heck was he doing here anyway?"

"Jesus, I don't know," Ernesto said. He put on his pants and grabbed his shirt off the floor. "I might have heard him, except you're the only one I was paying attention to," he shouted, scrambling out the door with his shirttails flying.

He found Edward propped up against a large oak tree a short distance away, motionless and transfixed, like a statue of Puck. Well, Puck would certainly be easier to talk to, Ernesto decided, than this little boy who must be trying to figure out what he had just witnessed.

"Where the blazes did you come from and what were you doing in the house?" Edward turned his face away. "Oh, stop pouting, I want to explain something to you, something important."

"I don't want to hear it! You and Missus ... you were—you weren't wearing clothes!" Edward's thoughts and questions crowded in like cattle at a salt lick. What *were* they doing when they stood like that? "I wasn't spying on you! I saw your car next to her house, and I just wanted to say hello."

"Yes, all right. You didn't do anything wrong." Some reception, Ernesto thought. Edward should have brought Mrs. Healey and her cronies along too. He held Edward's face and turned it to him. "But we didn't, either. Your snooping got you more than you bargained for." Edward started to get up, but Ernesto pulled him down again. "Hold on a minute. Now listen to me. Margaret and I feel deeply about each other, very. And when a man and woman feel that, and they are attracted physically, they want to make love."

("*Make* love?") Edward snorted and stood up, this time without being restrained.

116

"Go ahead, run away. I was going to explain something to you in a year or two, but later seems like now." Ernesto ran his hand across his chin and reached inside his breast pocket for the tobacco and cigarette paper. He stopped talking.

"Well, what is it?" Edward fumed, his voice whiney, both hands on his hips.

"People are animals, you may not think of us that way, but men and women get together sometimes. We have to make love, have sex, in order to have babies. It's complicated because animals don't love, but people animals do. All animals have sex, don't ask me about that word right now. I'll explain more another time." He laughed. "Eddie, now don't get angry, I wasn't laughing at you, just at myself trying to handle this. It's enough right now to say that all animals put their bodies together, it's normal and natural. You know, like turkeys and cattle."

Ernesto stood. "But sex and love-making is complicated and private, it's not that simple to explain. Or understand." Was it working?

"Are you going to marry Mrs. Renfrew and then be a mother and father?"

The answer came slowly. "Probably, but it's a little early."

Edward jerked loose and ran as fast as he could. He looked back once to see if Ernesto was chasing him, but he was walking instead toward the house. Edward quickly located Mrs. Healey's car, climbed in the rear seat and waited for her to come. When she asked him if he had seen anything interesting, he said no.

§

In school Mrs. Renfrew acted as if nothing had happened, and once or twice Edward even wondered if he had imagined what he had seen. Ernesto and Mrs. Renfrew had betrayed him in some way. The something between them obviously did not include him.

"Where you going?" he asked Ernesto the following Sunday after he had polished several pairs of the Major's boots for a total of twenty-five cents. He hadn't been able to stop thinking about them, and he'd hoped Ernesto would talk more about their marriage, but he hadn't.

"Oh, I thought I'd go get Mrs. Renfrew, climb up Biscuit Mountain and have us a little picnic. Should be real pretty up there today."

"I guess so." Edward poked his foot in the dirt, the picture of dejection. He started to trudge toward the stable, and reached into his pocket for sugar lumps.

"And," Ernesto continued, "if you thought you might be able to spare some of your precious time, you could come with us." Edward stopped abruptly and turned, his face beaming. "But I'm sure you probably have better things to do."

"No, no, I don't. I don't. Are you teasing me?"

"Okay then, get your stuff, *chico*, time's walking by," Ernesto said. "Mrs. Healey told me you could go," he added, pointing his finger at Edward. "I'll pick up Margaret and meet you down on the Ramsey Canyon Road. You can take the short cut."

Edward began to walk, his thoughts on the picnic. He passed the shack and saw the two kids on the road a short distance from the driveway that led to their place. They were carrying bags he figured were from Tom Jenkins's, the gas station and dry goods market that was located at the juncture of Carr Canyon Road and the main highway.

As they passed one another, Edward stopped, and they did too. Their clothes were torn and patched and their faces were dirty, as if they had been playing and rolling in the dirt. They didn't wear shoes. Edward noticed a red mark on the right side of the boy's face, and that his cheek was swollen. The girl was very pretty, her features balanced and delicate. "Hi," he said. "I'm Edward, and I live up there with the Major and his wife, only they're not my parents. I don't have any." They stared and didn't answer. "Maybe we could play together sometime. I could come down here and see you if you want me to, and bring my games."

They looked at him without expression, then looked at each other. Suddenly they started to run. Why don't they want to, he wondered? As he watched them, the girl stopped and then turned and waved. "Good-bye, Edward." She turned again and caught up with her brother.

"No, please, wait!" he yelled, running toward them. "I really want to be friends," he said. "It's very lonely, specially now that Ernesto's busy all the time with the schoolteacher." He looked past the road toward the cliffs beyond the ranch. "Up there, I could show you lots of things. About animals and stuff."

"No, we must stay here," the boy said deliberately.

"Our father, he says it is that we have to be careful, because of the Major." The girl smiled weakly, her eyes directed on Edward's. "We would like to play with you, but we are not able."

"Wouldn't your mother let me come over your house?" he asked eagerly. There must be a way, he thought.

"Our mother is dead, and our father, he isn't really our father. The man our mother was living with." It was said matter-of-factly but with an acceptance and resignation that eliminated any other possibility.

"Oh. I guess we're all orphans. That means we're alike." The Healeys had used that word several times.

"*Orphans?*" the girl asked. He would share with them his feelings of being helpless in the tangled skein of the web he'd fallen into. They could tell him how to get used to not having your own mother and father. The door of the shack opened, and a man yelled, "*Venga! Venga!*," the second time more angrily than the first. The boy and girl ran quickly. Edward peered at them until they disappeared inside.

A few minutes later, the car drove up the road. He waved and climbed in next to Mrs. Renfrew. "Good morning," she said with a lilt in her voice. "I'm very pleased you're joining us. I've got a dandy lunch. Let's see what this *caballero* can teach us about Biscuit Mountain. I'll bet he doesn't know very much about the geological history of this prairie. He probably thinks it was ordered from Sears, Roebuck."

"What's 'geogical history?'"

Ernesto responded, "Geological. The way the valleys and mountains formed over time. All right, *Señora* Renfrew, how do you get water from the desert when there isn't any?"

She laughed, throwing up her arms as if she had been held up. "Okay, cowboy, you got me." Then she poked him. "I know what I'd do: find a spigot and turn the blasted thing on." Ernesto covered his eyes with his arm.

Soon they stopped at the end of a dirt road. Margaret gazed up at Biscuit. "It's going to be nice up on top, escaping from everything down here," she said dolefully. "I'm planning to fantasize about all the things I want."

"Yes Ma'am," Edward responded. He wished they weren't behaving so silly with each other. They were playing like they were kids, and the only real kid there was *him*. But he was happy to be with them.

§

"Boy, oh boy," Edward exclaimed when he reached the summit, running up the last small escarpment slightly ahead of the other two. "I can see the whole world! And I'm bigger than anybody!"

"Shh, stop cackling and listen," Ernesto said. "Don't speak until I tell you." He took Margaret's hand, then moved to Edward and held his. The silence was absolute; not even a breeze brushed across their faces. It was as if time had paused, without any requirement to mark the moment. The stillness they shared made Edward feel good but a little uncomfortable. They stayed that way for what seemed a very long time.

"Being here is like nothing else," Ernesto said. "When I'm in places like this, all the bullshit and nonsense disappears." He turned to Margaret and smiled. "The only thing really important is the three of us." Then he said to Edward, "Look there. No, this way. What direction is that?"

"I don't know."

"East. The sun moves across the sky from east to west. Here, let me show you." He located a straight stick and stuck it into the ground, then carefully pushed two stones on either side so that the stick's lined shadow fell exactly between them. "Soon the line will move. By watching, you can determine which way the sun is moving so you'll know the directions."

"Edward, tell this boob that you can save a lot of time with a fifty-cent compass. 'Ernesto Of The Mountains' hasn't been introduced to modern devices. He's trying to get me to give up matches and light bulbs."

"Don't listen to that New England talk," Ernesto said. "All right, *chico,* one last thing to learn today. Take a look to the *east,* yes, over there, on the horizon. How far away do you think that mountain range is?"

"I don't know," Edward said, frustrated he couldn't answer.

"Well over a hundred miles. It's in New Mexico. The Animas and Hatchet Mountains. The Continental Divide runs through it." He peered at Edward. The history of the planet was in front of him, its mysteries and secrets, the blood of ancestors devoted to acts of courage, then bleached out onto the earth. It was all there, to be probed and studied and understood.

"I know, I know that. That's where the water goes one way, no, that's where, uh, it's very high and the water from the rivers go, this way on this side, and uh, uh, the other way on the other." Edward looked at them with the anticipation of a young hound that's brought home his first rabbit.

"Right! Good thinking. Margaret will teach you book learning, and I'll learn you the important stuff." Ernesto pushed Edward's hat forward over his eyes.

That was what Edward wanted, but not just in small isolated pieces and glimpses. He wanted the dependability and firmness to continue. He turned to them, his face unsmiling, and looked down.

"What's the matter?" Margaret asked.

"When I'm with you and Ernesto everything is so good." They gazed at each other, saying nothing. Ernesto drew Edward in between them. Edward looked from one of them to the other and let the tears run down his cheeks.

The next few hours were consumed happily, as were the food and beverages, beer for them, soda for him. Ernesto and Margaret lay on the blanket, close, talking and holding hands. "I've been wanting to ask you something, my dear," Margaret whispered, making sure Edward couldn't hear her. "Besides wanting to make out, why are you trying to have me believe you're really interested in me?" Edward was becoming annoyed that they were whispering and playing again.

"Beats the hell out of me," Ernesto said and rolled over. "Hey, stop poking me, Meg, I was just teasing." He became serious. "I can never be sure what's going to come out of your mouth. You're a mystery, you really are, different from anyone I've ever met. You're smart as anything and I know I can be sure you're never going to bullshit me. You're also a helluva challenge, that's for sure." He squeezed her to him.

"You're talking too loudly," she said. "I was thinking last night that if anybody ever said I would get involved with someone like you, from a different country, wowee. Back in Maine, we all seemed cut from the same mold." She stroked his face. "I'm not sorry you find me to your liking."

Edward became itchy and decided to explore whatever was below. It was boring watching the way they were acting, like dumb animals poking around that didn't have anything more interesting to do.

The trail danced in front as he walked, and he strained to hear its whispers: of the other times Ernesto had told him about, when olive-skinned black-eyed Indians had scampered up to celebrate the full moon in daytime, to raise their arms to a dried cobalt sky in homage to the Great Spirit, who gave his red children a land that offered browned bison and yellow maize, the thick sweet honey of the bee and water from streams as distinctly clear and simple as the vision of a brave on a victorious hunt. Why couldn't they have stayed, the tribes who belonged to this land as none other? Why were they violently forced like wild, free horses into pens of land no one else would live on, land so bleak and desolate you might believe God made it that way as a hell for those He wanted to punish?

All that remained now were the spirits from that other time. A disguised lizard was on guard, lying in the sun on a rock of no consequence, and the incredible panorama spread out before him made Edward believe he was being permitted to see it because he would, from then on, carry in his head and heart the responsibility to tell others—not as a boy, but when he became a man who would be listened to—of this place, Biscuit Mountain, that rose up alone, strangely, from the flat plate underneath. "Why is it called 'Biscuit?'" he called, but they were too far away to answer.

§

A month later, Ernesto informed him that he and Mrs. Renfrew were going to be married. They would start out living in her home in Hereford. He had purchased land in Ramsey Canyon, but building a house on it would have to wait until he earned enough money. "We want very much for you to be at our wedding. It's not going to be very big as these things go." They had walked up to the stream and sat on Edward's favorite rock. "I have to tell you it's become complicated. Margaret is a Protestant. I'm a Catholic. Both our families are having fits about that."

Edward looked at him. "Do you have 'fits' at weddings?"

"No," Ernesto laughed, "I mean the families are all riled up, upset. So, no church. That means my mother's not coming. And my father's not talking to me anyway. Silly, isn't it, you'd think the actual ceremony would be less important than the fact that their youngest son was in love and had found himself a wonderful *mujer*." He sighed and skipped a stone on the water. "My brother Juan will be the best man, and a few of our friends and other relatives will be there. Margaret's very special, Edward. I am indeed one lucky man." His smile was met by a long face. "What's the matter, aren't you happy for us?"

"You won't live here anymore," Edward answered glumly.

"Well, I have some ideas about that." He brought his face in front of Edward's. "We're not deserting you. That is a promise you can count on."

§

TWELVE

When John Healey heard about the marriage, he became enraged. Edward heard him through the bedroom door. "What did I tell you, Ida? Give them an opportunity to work, a decent place to sleep and food. That Ernesto, especially. Doesn't know his place. I never did go for that phony, superior demeanor of his." Edward heard a noise that sounded like something being hit. "Now he's planning to marry a white teacher. If I had him in my command for just a week, you'd see how fast I'd run those funny ideas out of his head!"

"John, for goodness sakes, it's their lives, not ours. Margaret and Ernesto have the right to choose their own mates. No one could have told *me* who to marry. Some of my friends had plenty of misgivings about you. I made that decision for myself."

"C'mon, Ida, it's not the same. He's not American, you understand that. We don't need them marrying our women. You want more squatters around?" Edward imagined him pacing from one end of the room to the other, swagger stick in hand, smacking the chair as he swung around in the opposite direction. "In the old days, he'd be lucky not to get strung up or run out of town with tar and feathers up his behind. That man's looking for trouble."

Edward was careful to do exactly what he was told that day and stayed out of the Major's sight as much as possible. Several times he thought about different kinds of sabotage, but he couldn't translate them into realities. He also noticed over the next few weeks that Ernesto was becoming more and more hostile. "One of these days, that tin-horn is going to get what's coming to him. He's beginning to push me too far."

"Yeah and he's getting to be a real sourpuss," Edward joined in. "When I asked about going with you and Mrs. Renfrew to the museum in Tucson, he said Mrs. Healey would take me when I was older."

§

After the wedding, the months went by and the seasons drifted past. A pattern was established: school, chores, homework and some free time. Ernesto was living on Ramsey Canyon Road with Margaret, but he came to work at dawn every morning. During the summer Edward helped him and the other hands with the cattle and horses, fixing fences and making sure the windmills operated properly. He enjoyed being a part of their group. In the evenings when the light lingered longer, he would walk the road above the ranch, stopping to watch an animal or improving his secret place near the stream. It wasn't a structure that could keep out the rain, or anything you could live in, just a hut to hide in and use as a retreat.

Tension continued to elevate, and the strain between the Major and Ernesto was now obvious to everyone. Edward worried. He wanted Ernesto to stand up to the Major, but he didn't want them actually fighting. In his hideaway he kept thinking of all the things he would like to do to the Major: place burrs, spiney ones, under his horse's saddle in a way he wouldn't notice until he was on the trail somewhere; then his horse would rear up and chuck him into the brambles. Or cut the stitching in his breeches so when he was being a big shot at the Fort, his pants'd come apart and everyone'd laugh and make fun of him.

Secretly, Edward wanted to be with Ernesto and Margaret, and he had long fantasies about living with them. Why should the Healeys care if he did? He only seemed to be causing them trouble. Then he wouldn't have to listen to all the Major's complaints: "It would be more appropriate if you expressed your gratitude a little bit more than you have, Edward. We're putting ourselves out to help you, and you act so discontent. I don't really understand you."

The passions festering between the Major and Ernesto were like a storm, developing strength as it approached from a great distance. It broke in the last hour at the end of a work week, beginning with silence, as if both men were dumb and unable to communicate. But Edward knew, as did the others, that the calm was just part of the gathered rage.

"Bejarano," Major Healey yelled, "get out here on the double!" He wore his old cavalry breeches, high-calfed boots and khaki shirt. Even a tie. His arms were rigid, held straight down at his sides. "Are you coming out, or do I have to come in and get you?" His voice cracked like electrical bolts splitting the air. It was still except for the idiotic claims being made by the lamebrained turkeys, who were always ignorant of everything except their need to expurge their insistent cluck-gaggles.

A moment of restiveness preceeded Ernesto's appearance from the stable. Then he was there in a slow deliberate motion, his eyes fixed on Major Healey the way an angered mountain lion approaches. Ernesto had once told Edward that you can actually watch it spit, observe its tail weaving, its body slinking lower, its forward progress slow, but ready at any second to spring with incredible speed.

"You got something on your mind?" Ernesto hissed. He was still about fifteen yards from where Major Healey stood like a ramrod. "Now's the time to say it."

"Your work leaves a lot to be desired, Bejarano. You're a trouble-maker and way out of line filling that boy's head with your cockeyed ideas. You're finished here!" To Edward, who'd taken shelter just inside the stable, it sounded rehearsed, like part of a radio program.

"Yeah, what kind of ideas? Somebody's got to have plans and think ahead." Ernesto said this softly, but in a measured cadence.

Major Healey stood with legs apart, swatting his right arm against his breeches. Ernesto came within two feet of him. "You're fired, Bejarano."

Ernesto flung his hat. It skidded on its side into the dirt. He clenched his right fist, his entire arm trembling, and glanced quickly back, at Edward. "You're a damn fool, Major," he said. "No, I take that back." He hesitated. "You're completely without any sensitivity. Control is the only thing that counts with you. You're excessive and stupid. You remind me of my father." He stepped back. "Wasn't it all that rigidity that prevented you from being promoted? I'm wise to you. So's everyone else around here!"

Major Healey's face grew into a shade of bright red, and sweat beads formed on his forehead. He was about to speak, but Ernesto continued, "Fire me? That's a laugh! Give me my pay. I'm out of here for good. And then you can see how easy it's going to be to get someone to manage your spread the way I did." He started toward the stable.

"Wait a minute!" Major Healey yelled to his back. "I haven't finished with you yet!" He grabbed Ernesto by the arm, and Ernesto swung around and pushed him away. "Off my ranch, before I have the sheriff arrest you."

"As soon as I get my stuff," Ernesto sneered. "And one last thing, *cabron*. Edward. He's only nine. You'd better treat that boy right. Or you're going to account to me, get it?"

Ernesto must have decided that the one thing he wouldn't do was hit Major Healey, because Edward could see how hard he was working to stay in control, flexing his hands tightly back and forth as he kept them at his sides.

"If you're not off this ranch in ten minutes, I'm going to have the sheriff arrest you for trespassing! How dare you talk to me like that." Major Healey spun around in a perfect military turn and stomped— no marched—to the ranch house.

When Ernesto came inside the stables, Edward was leaning against Nellie, his face against a front leg. Ernesto stood facing him. "I'm glad you told him, Ernesto," he said a little weakly. "Only," he struggled not to cry, "what am I going to do when you're not here?" He felt the tingling run through his arm.

"You're going to do what you have to. I told you back the day of your parents' funeral, remember? Life's no goddamn pony ride. I know that dumb sonufabitch runs this place like a drill sergeant." He eyed Edward, and a grin opened on his face. "But I believe you can handle it. I'm counting on you to be strong when you have to. You know what I mean?"

"I'm going to be smarter than that *dummy*," Edward answered. "And one day he's going to get so mad he'll turn into a puddle of butter. Or wee-wee." Both of them laughed at that.

"You said it, *chico*. He can't beat us, right?"

And Ernesto was gone.

For Edward the void created by his departure reminded him too much of the utter and final sense of abandonment he had felt after his parents' deaths. He knew Ernesto and Margaret weren't dead, but he knew too that soon they wouldn't be able to be with him at all. In the future, emptiness would be his only companion.

When he could, he retreated to the stream and the woods, where he imagined he saw the Indian Spirits. They were of the earth, Ernesto had told him, the canopy of light and air. They were able to be at peace with their place in existence. They knew the entire scheme. They embodied all of it, and they would befriend him because he believed in them and because they knew he loved the land and the water and the animals. The earth was Mother to everyone. Indians believed that. In the woods he was free, safe and in control. His mother and father were dead. They were gone, never to be seen or talked to again. But the things of nature would never leave. And it was all right they never talked to him. They weren't supposed to.

§

These days nothing he did at the ranch seemed good enough. Almost everything seemed to draw criticism, as if he were the provocation and justification for Ernesto's having been cashiered out. Edward had fantasies of setting out alone, but only until he pictured being by himself in strange places. He began to hide more and more of his possessions in a cache he built behind some rocks near his hut. At least he'd be ready to leave. Maybe, just maybe, he could live with Ernesto and Margaret.

Even though he knew he couldn't leave yet, on a Sunday when the Major and his wife went to the Fort for a social gathering, Edward put his watch and what little money he had saved in a small package with a note to the Major. "I will buy Nellie and get enough money and give it to you. This is for now. She is old and not important to you but she is to me. Edward Slavin." The next morning Mrs. Healey returned it to him and said she was sorry he wasn't happy and would try to do what she could to make things better.

§

130

THIRTEEN

"I need to speak to you," Margaret said to Edward during one of the first days of school that Fall. "At lunchtime. It won't take long." Whatever she had to tell him, he knew it wouldn't make much difference. Things had been piling up, and he felt like he was suffocating at the bottom of a stack of manure.

She must have sensed his dejection. "I told you we've contacted the Healeys about adopting you. Unfortunately, they turned us down." He pictured himself blindfolded, or maybe it was at night: he had to continue alone on this slippery trail, high up the side of a steep canyon. Sounds he had never heard before, bad ones, slinked out from many locations. He was completely by himself, and absolutely no one was the least interested in helping him get through.

"I don't want you to become discouraged, Edward." She reached for his hand. "Something will happen, it always does. And even if it doesn't, don't forget how much Ernie and I care about you. You'll see us as much as we can make it possible."

"What if—maybe I could go to Chicago to Aunt Sandra's." Not that he wanted to, but it'd be better than staying on the ranch.

Her usual smile was replaced with a face akin to a doctor's when he has to give "it" to you. "I did write her," Margaret said, and shook her head. "And she wrote back she'd like to, but right now she has her hands full. She sent a little money for games and toys."

He refused to look at her. "I don't want it. Tell her to give it to Susie." He didn't wait for an answer. Outside, he mounted Nellie and galloped over the rise and out of sight.

It was late afternoon by the time Edward returned to the ranch. He put Nellie in her stall, removed his saddle and reins and wiped her down, every part of the procedure performed with a deliberateness that indicated he might not be sure of just what he could think of to do after he was finished. He ambled past the turkeys, hardly hearing their squeaks. He went into the kitchen and sat watching Cooky preparing a casserole, answering his questions only with grunts. Mrs. Healey came in and asked him to come with her into the living room. The Major was standing next to the fireplace, packing his pipe.

Ida Healey sighed and spoke first. "Edward, the Major and I are very distressed at how you are. I mean, you seem to be very unhappy in spite of everything we've tried." What was she leading up to, Edward wondered?

She turned and looked at her husband, who cleared his throat. "I really don't understand why it's not working out better, Edward. I assured Mrs. Healey that it's not because of how we're treating you. I don't want her feeling bad or anything like that." He lit the pipe and drew deeply on it until the blue-gray smoke rose up, serpent-like. "Let's all sit down," he said matter-of-factly.

"We've thought a lot about this, and it seems the only thing to do is for you to, ah, live with the schoolteacher. She seems to understand you better. She's younger and has more experience dealing with children."

Edward's eyes widened, but his face remained a blank. "As far as Ernesto is concerned," the Major continued, "it is regrettable we parted on bad terms. Perhaps it had to come to that. In any event, your continuing to stay with us doesn't appear wise any longer. Margaret and Ernesto made a request to us for custody. I didn't agree then, but I've changed my mind. I suppose you were aware of all this. I assume the solution is acceptable to you."

"Yes Sir," Edward said quickly. He felt sorry when he looked at Mrs. Healey. He wished he could remove the sadness and sorrow on her face. Edward remembered what she had told him, and he felt sorry again that her baby had died.

§

The Healeys signed the papers giving up their legal guardianship of Edward. He greeted the change about to take place in his life with a mixture of serenity and verve. They did not seem to be in conflict with one another.

The night before he was scheduled to leave the ranch, he packed all his belongings and then walked up the road toward the towering cliffs at the head of the canyon. The moon, halved and angled, rose above the ridge and seemed to concentrate its light on the escarpments, creating an eerie, tattooed pattern. The light was bright enough so that Edward could see the rocked rubble, the cacti and the hills and cliffs enclosing the ranch.

As he walked, the refreshing crispness of the night washed through his thoughts. He was almost able to put aside his leaving the Healeys, but not quite. He felt a touch of regret that it hadn't been better, and felt a little sorry that they hadn't been able to understand how difficult it was for him now that he was an orphan. He knew they were the way they were, but, much to his surprise right then, he found himself wishing that his relationship with them had gotten better. When he reached his favorite boulder, he hugged and petted it in a sort of farewell. Then he surveyed the dark woods and open places that were fired up in the light of the Arizona moon. He observed that his friend, the stream, didn't distinguish between day or night.

Edward began to think of his parents, but mostly his father. He knew answers were available if he could figure out how everything worked—the way animals and plants behaved, why people did what they did and how he could respond the right way—that is, if he only *knew* and understood what the best course of action was. He remembered how a mother horse on a neighbor's ranch had tended to her foal in just the right way. Even those stupid turkeys, making sure their babies stayed right in line when they were taking them someplace they decided in turkey world they were better off going to. One spot in the area they lived on seemed to Edward exactly the same as any other.

He closed his eyes, rubbing his head and deeply inhaling the air that carried in its arms the scents of brush and plants, of the animal droppings that time had not yet divided down into parts so small they were lost, to be blended in the fabric of earth and ground. He wanted to understand all these things, and most of all about people, but he was keenly aware he didn't have the sharp insights men like his father had. His mother had them too, different ones. He had to become smarter so he could make out better, no matter what situation he found himself in. So he would be able to take charge when he should. He hoped he would know when that would be.

Edward lifted his eyes into the sky until they settled on the Milky Way. He remembered his father telling him that there were so many stars they could never be counted; one could only guess as to their number. And the people who studied stars, astronomers, watched throughout the night until the Milky Way moved on, like everything did. Things repeated themselves, most things anyway. There was always a beginning and an end.

He became aware of another feeling about his parents: his anger because they had left him, and the terrible sense of unfairness that it wasn't his fault they were gone.

Hearing something, he looked around, his senses primed. There was nothing. He listened for another moment, then whispered, "We didn't even say good-bye. If only I could have been a little bit ready! How do you expect me to grow up? Ernesto's good to me, but he's not my father, you are. No," he snorted, "you *were*."

Edward rose, surveying the scene again and settling his gaze on the moon. This would probably be the last time he'd look at these surroundings. He was aware he still loved his father and his mother, and still tried to reach them in his thoughts. But he knew too that they had now become part of the earth.

Back in his room, he slept very little that night. He arose before daybreak, dressed quietly, and went to the stable where he spent a long time with Nellie. Then he moved to the porch. For a few minutes he stood looking at the boots, *the Major's boots*. They were without a mark and stood up at attention, like stiff, shiney wooden soldiers who never did anything but remain rigid. Zombies. Nothing would ever make them different. He glanced around, picked up a few stones, put them inside one of the boots and quickly walked to Nellie's stall to say good-bye again. He hugged and kissed her, took one of her horseshoes, and told her he'd never forget her. He thanked her for being so good to him.

A short while later Edward sauntered down the canyon road. At the point when day replaces night, the sky began to lighten even though a few stars still shone. He gazed for a long time at the ranch house, then brushed off his Levis, sucked in the air like fresh water, and began to hum as he skipped. He wondered whether the two kids in the squatter's shack were still sleeping.

Soon he saw Ernesto's pickup truck. He had traded in the coupe. "Do I know you?" Ernesto asked, without a trace of recognition. "I've seen you around, but I just can't remember your name. Happy to give you a ride, though, cowboy. Where you heading?"

"With you, with you!" Edward said excitedly. "Stop fooling." He threw his arms around Ernesto's neck for several moments, moments both would remember always.

"Okay, I suppose I'm stuck with you. Hey, *chico*, Margaret's been fixing a helluva feed for us when we get home. You hungry? You better be. Just wait and see. I'm not planning to put all that grub away by myself, got it?" He made wide S-turns across both sides of the road.

"Yeah." Edward's grin was spread out and free. "I could eat a steer, even with the hair on. Oh, I brought this," he said. Beaming, he reached into his sack and pulled out the horseshoe.

"So now I have a *bandito* on my hands," Ernesto observed, chortling. "You'd better hope Healey doesn't miss it." He poked Edward.

"Mister Sourpuss will have to get another one."

"All right, so now that you have it, what are you going to do with it?

Edward grinned but didn't answer.

"Okay, *señor*, your business. I'm not messing into *this* one, no sir."

The truck dropped down past Tom Jenkins's store at the bottom of the canyon, from the cool early morning darkness into the sun's candescence laying itself out on the open prairie. Ernesto turned left toward the next canyon, Ramsey. "Nice to be away from there, huh? Now I can tell you how bad I felt when I couldn't take you with me. But that's all behind us, *chico*."

136

They reached the point where the trail from the ranch crossed the highway and slipped into the arroyo through which Edward rode to school. "Ernesto, could you please stop a minute?" Ernesto pulled over, and Edward sat for some moments, absolutely quiet, peering at the horseshoe he had taken. Then he turned in the direction of the Healey ranch. "I'll be back in just a little, okay?" Ernesto nodded and folded his arms. He watched Edward slowly open the door and get out, holding the horseshoe in his hands as if it were a religious object.

"Got something in mind?" Ernesto asked, reaching for his tobacco pouch.

"Yeah. I'm going to bury it like I used to do with my most important things when I was little." Getting a shovel from the back of the pickup, he walked to the top of the arroyo.

Several minutes later, he came back and stepped to the middle of the highway. "Wheeee!" he exclaimed, circling and circling, his head back and his arms spread all the way out. "I feel like digging it up and burying it every day. Only I'd forget the spot."

"I guess you did what you had to, *Eduardito*. And no one could stop you, could they?"

"No, they couldn't," he responded, grinning.

§

FOURTEEN

Edward slipped down from the truck in front of the Bejarano house, holding the sack with his possessions, clothes mostly. He'd also brought a carton filled with toys, games and boots, and now he strapped on his white pistol belt with the two identical guns. He could wear them here without anyone making fun of him.

Ernest came up behind him. "Hey, Meg, look what I found meandering down Carr Canyon Road," he yelled out. She came out the front door, wearing a long dress, the kind ladies did at parties. She's real pretty, Edward thought as his new mother ran to him and hugged him. He held her tightly. She was nice and soft, like her hand was that time, and she smelled of bath soap and toilet water.

He stood motionless and gazed at both of them. Ernesto broke the silence and swatted him on the behind. Margaret grabbed his hand as they walked to the front door. "No more just visiting," she said. He wasn't ready for the large sign inside leaning against a chair.

"Welcome Home, Edward." He caught his breath, remembering the one he and his mother had made for his father.

Oh, the wonderful smells of corn bread and coffee. And what else? He focused on the dining table to the right. A chocolate cake? Yes, at one end on a large doily between two brass candle holders. The table was set with three places, on a fancy white embroidered Mexican tablecloth with ornate forks, spoons and knives. Red cut-glass goblets were filled with water, and in front of one place there was a second goblet and a pitcher of milk. Napkins that had the same embroidering as the tablecloth were folded like hats.

"We're beginning with steak and eggs," she announced. "We figured we'd fatten you up a little."

He didn't say anything, just took it all in and waited for them.

"I told Margaret your favorite was chocolate cake with chocolate filling. She spent the whole of last evening on it." The cake was very high, probably three layers. The dark brown icing was thick and spilled off the sides onto the cake plate that had a raised pattern of blue birds all flying in the same direction. On the top was a circle of chopped walnuts. And on top of them, thick whipped cream spelled out "Edward."

At the other end of the table were two silver plates. His favorite candy, Mounds, were unwrapped and set in two's like building blocks. Around them were multi-colored Jujubes and licorice sticks.

He looked again at the table and then at them, his mouth slightly ajar.

Ernesto chortled. "Well, let's get at it. Steak and eggs and then flapjacks if you're still hungry. Okay? We thought you'd like the idea of a real breakfast."

"You guys get settled," Margaret said. "Ernie, show Edward where to put his things. I'll start cooking. Eggs over or straight up?"

Edward smiled before putting his head close to his plate, eating as if he were afraid someone would take it away. He broke the yolk and dipped pieces of steak in it. Then the flapjacks, soaked in butter and syrup. When he finished, his eyes wandered to the chocolate cake. They looked at one another and smiled as he nodded "yes."

Margaret leaned over and kissed him on the cheek. "We've looked forward for a very long time to your being here and to giving you the home you deserve and should have." Then she said, "But just so you don't get the wrong idea, men, the dishes are yours. That's the deal: I cook and you cowpokes do the rest. Sharing the load, the modern way," she finished, with a glance at Ernesto.

"Okay, tyrant," Ernesto answered, "in a little while. Let's just set our rears on the couch and relax. Eddie, it's a little nippy. Suppose you make us a fire." Edward went to where the wood was stacked and arranged it in the way Ernesto had taught him made the best blaze: first plenty of newspaper or bark, then kindling either cross-hatched or in a pyramid (when you're up in the mountains and it's windy, you do it that way to shelter the arrangement before putting on heavier wood). He put a match to it, and soon warmth filled the room. Edward sat down between Ernesto and Margaret, enjoying the touch of a hand on his shoulder and the feel of a leg against his.

"Got some plans," Ernesto said after a long silence. "You're in them, Eddie. But we have plenty of time to get into that. In a little while, supposing we go down to the Fort for the movie? It's an Abbot and Costello—what do you say? And some ice cream after that."

"Yeah, yeah!"

"*Yes,*" Margaret corrected.

"Yes Ma'am."

"Margaret. Please call me that, except when we're in school, of course. Later on, perhaps, Mom if you want."

"Okay, Margaret," he said, relishing the way it sounded.

§

141

FIFTEEN

One Sunday morning a few months later, Edward was deeply engrossed in the model airplane he was building. His Aunt Sandra and Susie had sent it to him for his birthday. The cover of the cardboard box displayed a photograph of a P-41 Mustang fighter plane, chasing and shooting at a German Messerschmidt 109. That fired up his imagination: he was the American pilot downing some louse who'd strafed our soldiers at Dunkirk, El Alemein and The Battle of the Bulge. You had to coordinate and manipulate properly when you flew, and the parts of the model had to be fitted precisely. It took patience while you held the right two pieces together until the glue took hold. The wings were finally assembled, and now he was attaching the stabilizers to the fuselage.

But he wasn't so preoccupied that he failed to hear Ernesto's pickup turning rapidly into the driveway. That was unusual, because Ernesto never returned from his foreman's job at the Butler ranch before dinnertime. He ran out to greet him. Something important must be happening.

"I just saw Mel Martin down in Hereford," said Ernesto from the truck's window. "He needs some help. Lost seven heifers up in the mountains. I told him I'd meet him as soon as I could saddle up." He tousled Edward's hair and walked quickly to the small barn.

"Papa, let me come with you. I can help." He tugged on Ernesto's shirt. "Okay?"

"Stop that, Edward! You're acting like a two-year-old when you do that." He grabbed a bridle off a long wood peg and swung his other hand into the opening in his saddle between the horn and pommel, as if he were sweeping up the parts of a costume he needed to wear. Edward watched the motions and the speed with which Ernesto saddled his horse.

"Look," Ernesto said after a moment, "it could be rough up there. There's no telling where those critters are. If it gets difficult we may not be able to get out that easily. Maybe you'd better stay here," he said gently. The dejection on Edward's face caused him to reconsider. "Well, all right, son, but don't complain later. I really *would* like to have you along." Edward yipped like a hound on his first hunt. "Get your gear, your lariat, your—oh, hell, you know what to bring. And your chaps, the new ones. Tell your mother us men will be back later, most likely well after dark." He finished just as Margaret appeared from the house. She wasn't smiling. For a quick moment Edward even wished he and Ernesto were back at the Healey ranch without her.

Margaret folded her arms and said, "It's not smart for him to go up there with you and the other men, Ernie. He's too young. He hasn't had enough experience. And you don't know what you'll run into. I'm right, aren't I?" Edward peered at Ernesto, who frowned at Margaret.

"He has to learn about these things, Margaret. Part of his *education*," he said with a hint of a smile. "He'll do just fine. He's coming with me, Meg. I'll be watching him." He turned to Edward. "Let's move, *chico*!"

Margaret threw her dish towel into the air and stared hard for a moment at Ernesto. "I'm concerned," she said.

He dropped the reins of his horse and walked to where she stood. "Don't be," he said, planting a fast peck on one cheek, another on the other and a long kiss fully on her mouth.

Edward yipped again and ran for his gear.

§

They rode for nearly three hours before they reached the place where they were to meet Martin. The trail crisscrossed the wall up the head of the canyon, over a ridge, across a small depression, and then straight up the incline. The horses were experienced and sure-footed, and the riders gave them free rein, their weight forward against the horns of their saddles. At times the trail was blocked by brush, and Edward was glad his chaps protected his legs. Ernesto whistled as they rode, pointing out animal droppings, once some hair the edge of a boulder had claimed, and the way growth on the bark of a tree was fuller on the side facing north.

On the southwest side of Carr Peak, in a small area where the incline and decline were not as steep, they found Mel Martin. He greeted them with a tip of his fingers to his hat. "Howdo, gents." He rode a big chestnut mare, one he had trained particularly for rough work and long rides. Now he slipped off his saddle and shook hands with Ernesto. "Thanks for coming up," he said. Martin limped as he walked, the result of a bad compound fracture that had never been set properly after a fall. He was in his forties, lean with a ruddy complexion that went with his fiery red hair. Edward had seen his three sons and his daughter, all with the same color hair as his. The twang in his speech made it difficult for Edward to understand all his words.

"Found three of them buggers. Damned if I know'd how they got themselves out." He motioned to Ernesto to help himself to the pot of coffee he had set between two rocks over a small fire.

"Pretty good, Martin," Ernesto said as he poured a cup. "All the fixings of home. Any apple pie to go with the coffee?"

"You ain't gettin' that until we gets us back them calves. But my missus is cooking up a mess for when we're done. Said to tell you bring your new bride if'n you like." His face cracked into a smile. "But them calves. Second time this year. The only place I'd know is by the corner by Healey's, by that well we share out to the west end." He spat, the brown juice from his chewing tobacco slapping a rock and splattering. "Glad you brought your boy. If'n you're hungry, some tack's in the saddle bags."

"We're here to find heifers. Later'll be fine. Where are Cal and Len?"

"T'other side of the ridge, over to the Reef Mine way. Seeing if any of 'em are by there."

"Okay," Ernesto chimed in, "Eddie and I'll start to the north where the trail splits the other side of Carr Peak. Ted here too?"

Martin shook his head, then turned as two men came into view. "Them is back for lunch. Guess t'ain't seen nothing."

The new arrivals dismounted and shook hands with Ernesto and Edward. It made Edward feel good, and he broke a twig from a tree and dangled it from his mouth, walking with a slight swagger. Martin passed around hardtack and cans of beer. As Edward was about to take a swig, Ernesto grabbed it from him. "Hey, time enough for this stuff later."

"There's no soda. What am I supposed to drink?"

"Good old water from your canteen. That's what you brought it for, remember?" Edward gave him one of those "aw, dammit" looks.

Ernesto shrugged. Afterward, while the men talked and smoked, Edward wandered down the trail and watched two turkey vultures rising up in a spiral, their wings fixed as if they were kites. They looked like fake birds. When he returned, the men stood and urinated. He stepped next to Ernesto and did the same, but made sure the other men couldn't see his penis.

"Mel," Ernesto offered, "Eddie and I'll start looking for them over where I said. We'll meet you back here, say, four or four-thirty. We can cover that whole side. You're looking for four, right?"

"Yeah, four of 'em little bastards," Martin responded. "If there's light enough, if'n we find 'em, we'll bring 'em down. Otherwise, rig something for tonight and come up tomorrow. See you 'bout four, then."

§

At the point where the trail became too rough and narrow for riding, Edward and Ernesto dismounted and walked their horses. Edward led the way. "I want *you* to see everything, not me," Ernesto said. "Let's play a game: for anything special you see, you get a point. If I see it first, I get one. Ten wins. I want all the little details. Did the calves come through? You should be able to tell. What other animals have been here? And when?"

Edward scrutinized the boulders for hairs, and searched the ground for prints, broken twigs, displaced stones, branches torn off (which Ernesto told him didn't always mean an animal or person had been through, but could have) and, of course, all droppings.

"Papa, look! Down there, past those rocks. Isn't that—I think I see calves, there're two of them," he said. He hoped Ernesto would tell the others that he and not Ernesto had spotted them first.

"Yeah, sharp eyes, you got them. That one lower down looks like he's busted a leg." They dismounted and drew closer. "See any others?" Edward didn't. One calf startled from surprise and fear. "Eddie," Ernesto said quietly, "go around the other side of those boulders and send him toward me. Move slowly. Talk to him so he doesn't spook again, to where I can rope him."

He carefully followed the instructions, and when the heifer retraced his steps, Ernesto lassoed it, rising rapidly from a crouched position. He led it up to the trail and tied it with one rope around a boulder. "Here, tie this rope to that tree to keep him from roaming around."

They climbed down to the second calf, which was in a sitting position. Ernesto inspected its front right leg. He shook his head several times and sighed deeply. "Bad," he said, glancing at Edward, who bent down next to him. The calf tried to stand but was unable to. It bellowed in an instinctive reaction, hoping to bring its mother.

"We can fix a splint so we can get him down," Edward said quickly. "You know, like they do for skiers." The distant cries of magpies made their way up from the canyon below, and then the muted hush of the mountains reinstated itself.

"It wouldn't work. It's much too far. And obviously, we can't carry him." Ernesto walked to his horse and lifted his 30–30 rifle from its battered and shoddy leather scabbard. Edward's jaw dropped, a look of torment on his face. "I'm sorry," said Ernesto, "but I have to put him out of his misery. You don't want him to suffer."

There must be a better answer, Edward thought. There must! "No, wait! We can get the others, and—"

"C'mon, you know this is the only way. He's in pain and he would die a terrible death. It's his time. That's the way it is." Ernesto lifted his head. "Go stand by the horses," he ordered. He didn't move until Edward was up on the trail. "And don't turn away," he yelled up. "Watch this."

A single shot. It was over, the calf caving in onto its front feet and then, with life quickly spilling out of it, tumbling onto its back. Ernesto moved into position over it, lifted the rifle again and shot it a second time between its eyes, its nervous system producing a few shudders and a partial raising of one of its rear legs.

Ernesto untied the other calf and mounted. He rolled a cigarette, lit it, drew in the smoke and exhaled slowly, not looking at Edward. Silently, they started down the trail, towing the calf. After a few minutes Ernesto stopped and dismounted, dropping the reins of his horse and walking over to Edward. "You all right? About the heifer?"

Edward stared at him, then brought his eyes to the ranges of the Huachucas that were slipping into darker tans and purples in the aging light of the afternoon. He didn't answer immediately, but then let out a deep sigh. He nodded. "I guess so. I know you had to do it." He looked again out over the canyons below them and into the distance of the prairie, its horizon obscured in the haze.

Ernesto waited, but Edward said no more. They rode for some fifteen or twenty minutes in silence until Ernesto stopped again. "You struggling with this?"

Edward glanced straight up, tears beginning to roll down his cheeks. He wiped his sleeve against his face. "The little calf never even had a chance to grow up. I was thinking about things dying or getting killed, never knowing it's going to happen, like that mother deer whose baby I found. I can save it, but I can't be its mother or father. And all the others everywhere.

"I remember what you always told me, I haven't forgotten." Edward straightened up in his saddle. "Sometimes I feel what happened to my parents could have happened to me instead. Or if I was with them. Only I don't want to be dead. But I don't want them to be either."

Ernesto dismounted and looked into Edward's eyes. "You're a good, decent person," he said. He turned, and remounted his horse. "I love you, Edward. Remember that."

"I know. I love you too. An awful lot," Edward replied.

§

SIXTEEN

"He's progressing very rapidly in school," Margaret said brightly one night over dinner. "Devours advanced readers and math books. And figures out the answers to most of the questions. I'm so proud of him. He must have Maine blood in him." Edward liked hearing her say that. It made him feel acceptable. School came easy, anyway. And Ernesto was always talking about how important school was, and going to college. But *he* had dropped out, hadn't he? That was because he'd had problems Edward didn't have, he told him.

Margaret turned to him. "You understand that no matter how important you are to me, I grade you the same as the others."

"I know that," Edward answered with a smile. "But you make it fun to learn, even though you're strict a lot." That just blurted out. He hadn't meant it to sound like he was trying to—what did one of the kids say?—"polish the old apple."

"Meg, the boy started out being smart. Never hurts." Ernesto raised up from hunching over his plate. The tiger cat they'd found

151

looked the same way when he ate. "Want to pass me the potatoes, Eddie? Thanks." Really nice, both of them talking like that about me, Edward thought. "Yeah, *muchacho,* you pour it on. One day you could be governor or the biggest rancher in all Arizona. Maybe both. What's that guy's name? The one up in Phoenix who's getting so much publicity. Goldwater, Barry Goldwater." Ernesto took another bite. "I hear they're testing all kinds of new feed grains using chemical nutrients." He let those last two words come out as if he just created them. "I've been reading some of the Ag School literature about research and new methods," he said with a grin.

He cleared his throat and made his fist into the shape of a gun, pointing it at Edward, winked an eye and said, "Pshoo, pshoo!" But Edward's response was a long face. Ernesto rose from the table, put his arm around him and squeezed him. "Hey, son, I'm feeling terrific. Why such a hang-dog face? I told you a long time ago I wouldn't let you down, even during those black days at Healey's."

"I don't know what would have happened to me if it hadn't been for you. And Mom. I don't want things to ever change."

Margaret reached for one of Edward's hands. Then the three of them embraced without anything more being said. After several moments, Ernesto began to sing, "The whole fam-ily, the whole fam-ily, hi ho the jerio, the whole fam-ily." He clasped them on either side and began to do a kick-step. "Theee daddy takes the mommy, the mommy takes the boy, the boy takes the daddy, hi ho the jerio, the whole fam-ileee ..." He sang it a second time. It was silly, Edward thought, but he soaked it in like the redolent aroma from the flower of the barrel cactus.

"Ernie, you sound like a sick, flat Mother Hubbard. Edward and I are too old for your nonsense. I can just see you running a nursery school, you'd be perfect at it. Why don't you hire yourself out as a professional mother? We'll dress you up, bonnet and everything." Now *that* made Edward laugh.

"Okay," Ernesto shot back, slightly surprised and a little hurt, "after being with me for fun and affection, they'll go on to your Renfrew School For Reality. I teach them fun, then you turn them into adults." He smiled, wrapped his arms around her waist and lifted her off her feet. "Children are terrific, Meg, don't you think so?" That kind of annoyed Edward, the mushy stuff.

"Wouldn't know, *señor*, never was one myself. Went from babyhood right into full-blown woman. Skipped the whole thing. You'll have to tell me what it's like growing up, in a big family, dozens of siblings. And *you* the baby." She thumbed her nose at him. "I have papers to correct and material to get ready for tomorrow. Dishes, men. Remember?"

"Getting back to babies . . ." He had that same silly look on his face, Edward thought.

"You're too impatient, Ernesto Bejarano." Edward wished they'd talk about something else. He carried a plate in each hand to the sink, but he listened carefully to them. "Your brothers told me you always were. I can just see you, clamoring for attention, chasing after them, stamping your foot and yelling, 'I want it *right now*!' You even got them to send you to college, the only one of them." She glanced at his face, which was suddenly joyless. "I'm sorry," she said, "I didn't mean to bring that up."

"What does she mean?" Edward asked.

"She's reminding me I snafued it."

"I didn't say that at all," Margaret protested.

"But you were thinking it," Ernesto shot back. "You're saying if I'd been more serious I'd have graduated. I had the talent. I made Dean's List. But I snafued it."

"Those words," said Margaret, "did not come out of *my* mouth."

"Look, Meg, I don't regret leaving the university. As smart as you are, you don't understand." He pulled out a chair from the table and straddled it, his arms folded around its back. "There's nothing wrong with ranching. College isn't the real world anyway."

"Then how can you encourage Edward?" Margaret asked. Edward was very interested in what his answer would be.

Ernesto tapped a Camel from his pack and lit it. "Things aren't the same when you come from another country. You certainly understand what I mean." What *did* he mean? Edward wondered.

"Forgive me," Margaret retorted, "but America has a long history of successful people who were born somewhere else. Besides, the war's changed things even more."

"Maybe if I was an American G.I.," Ernesto said. "They told me raising beef was the most important contribution I could make." Edward sat down at the table. He'd never heard them talk like this. Ernesto made a move toward the door.

"Where are you going?" she asked, in a tone that meant the conversation wasn't over. Ernesto stopped but didn't turn around, as if she had lassoed him with an invisible lariat.

"Perhaps you didn't want it badly enough," she said sharply. "To finish what you start." Then she added, "I'm not trying to hurt you by saying that."

"You really dig in, don't you?" he demanded. Then, more mildly, "I'm a rancher, that's my line of work. But you changed the subject. We were talking about children and babies, how nice and adorable they are. And—"

"And nothing!" she broke in. "This is not the place for such a discussion. Nor the time, which there is plenty of." Edward brought more dishes to the sink. Mom was right this time, he thought. Ernesto didn't have to keep talking about babies.

"Yes Ma'am, Mrs. Renfrew, Ma'am," Ernesto answered. "Only I have my eyes on you, if you know what I mean." She closed her eyes and smiled. He put his arms around her, and she buried her head against his shoulder.

Edward expelled air in disgust, and went to his room and shut his door, almost slamming it. He threw himself on his bed and stared at the ceiling. One good thing back at the Healeys, he thought, was that Ernesto would spend his free time with me and not act so silly with *her*. We'd do lots of things. Out behind the ranch, up by the stream, he'd show me things I didn't see even though I'd look at the same things he did: being right next to something and studying it, like a plant or a tree, seeing the patterns tiny animals made in a piece of bark. Learn about those things, what went on, what was *really* happening. Not like in school. The important stuff was out "in the world."

Edward turned over, put his face into the pillow, and took a deep breath to see how long he could hold it. Johnny Weismuller, in the Tarzan movie they saw, had to really hold his breath for minutes while he was battling a giant crocodile. The way he swam! Like a racing boat. And swinging through the trees, across the open areas on those vines, he was fantastic!

He thought about yesterday and when he was irked about what one of the big kids had asked in the cloak room. "Hey, Slavin, what kind of a name is that?" Edward pretty much knew what he was talking about because he had pronounced it slowly with a big accent on the "a." Margaret had just finished the last class of the morning, about the different people who were now Americans and where they had come from, and about their different names and religions. They'd talked about the Chinese, and even the Japanese who everyone still hated for what they did, and the people in Africa, the Mexicans and ones from further south who were mostly Catholics and a litttle about Jewish people who lived in just about every country, she had said. She'd mentioned that she was a Protestant whose *ancestry* (she took out her dictionary and read them the meaning and made sure they all knew it) was Anglo-Saxon. Her ancestors had migrated from England to Massachusetts and then to Maine.

"I don't know. It's the name my parents had." They all knew he wasn't born around there like they were. Certain kids, the lousy ones, always held that against him. He remembered a long time ago on a base when a couple of them had teased him and yelled out, "Hey, *Slavitsky.*" Edward didn't see any need to continue the conversation, and he put on his jacket and left the cloak room. He wasn't different from them. Why'd they need to try to make him *feel* different? He began to understand what Ernesto meant. It was always there, the stuff about not being accepted. Especially just when you'd forget about it.

§

"We've been thinking, Edward," Margaret said one evening after he'd told her about that incident in school. "You'll be twelve soon, and since you were born Jewish, you should know about your religion." He waited for her to continue. "But more than that, Papa and I believe your parents, your original ones, would have wanted you to be Bar Mitzvahed. That takes place when boys are thirteen."

She explained the ceremony. "It's a confirmation, sort of. When a Jewish boy comes of age. We've called Rabbi Malev in the temple in Tucson. It's also called a synagogue. He remembered your parents' funeral, of course, and then we explained to him who we were. We told him how we'd adopted you, that your father's a Mexican Catholic and your mother's a Protestant from New England. When he got over his shock, he invited us to come in and attend services some Saturday."

Being Jewish was only a concept for Edward, but now he was confronted with stepping into the path of his heritage. He began to worry that it was going to separate him from them and everyone else, from this time forward. It weighed on him as few things had. "Maybe it'd be better if I wasn't Jewish. I mean, what if I was like you and was Christian?"

Margaret let out a deep sigh and looked into her husband's face. "We'd better go inside and talk about this," she answered. The kitchen table was the place where serious sit-down discussions took place. Ernesto sat at the head of the table and lit a cigarette.

"I listened carefully to the way you expressed yourself, Edward." Margaret continued, "The point is you were born Jewish." She held his hand and spoke earnestly. "Everyone should have a right to choose what they believe. No, that's badly stated. If, in this case, you, Edward, really find yourself compatible—comfortable—in another religion, then okay, but only after you've had proper exposure to both your original faith and the new one. Then conversion is possible, if that's what you want."

He concentrated on the meaning of her words. Then Ernesto said, "Look, it'll be your choice. But are you sure you don't want to be what you aready are? Think about it. We'll back you any way you decide."

Edward looked from one of them to the other. A few moments elapsed and then Margaret suggested, "What about checking out Tucson? If you like what you hear, stay with Judaism. Okay?"

He nodded and said slowly, "My first Mom and Dad, I think they'd probably want me to be what they were. I just don't want it to be hard for you."

The Saturday they drove to Tucson, they dressed up in their best clothes. "I guess I'm a little nervous," Ernesto said in the truck. "They'll take one look at me and know I'm not Jewish."

"C'mon, " Margaret said. "You know there's no such thing as 'looking' Jewish or Mexican or anything else." She directed her comment more to Edward than to Ernesto. "They'll sure know something when you don't participate in the service, but I don't think they much care. Stop believing our presence is that important."

"Are you kidding, Margaret? You sound like Pollyanna. When do you see a bunch like us? Or maybe just me. You have this unrealis-

tic attitude sometimes that everyone is tolerant and compassionate."
She didn't respond, and for the next ten minutes or so nothing was
said.

When they reached Benson, Ernesto turned left onto the straight
black ribbon of Route 10. The Santa Catalinas appeared to their right
in the distance. "There's snow up on Mount Lemmon, Eddie, even
this time of year."

"The caps the men wear in temple are called 'yarlmukas' and the
shawls around their necks are 'talleisim,' " Margaret said. "I learned
that from my roommate when I lived in New York. Your nervous-
ness will go away once we get involved, so don't become paranoid
like your father."

Judiciously, Edward decided not to ask what *that* meant. Not
now, anyway.

"Look," Margaret went on. "This is new for all three of us. The
language they speak is Hebrew. They've used it for over three thousand years. And don't worry—the rabbi will instruct us, I'm sure.
He's the one who would supervise your religious education. Let's
just see how it goes, okay?" She looked at Ernesto. "Maybe your
father should convert and be Bar Mitzvahed too."

"I'm afraid not," said Ernesto. "They didn't do to me what they
do to little Jewish boys when they're born."

"What's that?" Edward asked quickly.

"Remember when you asked me about my penis when you first
saw me peeing? I told you about circumcision." Edward nodded, not
wanting to hear any more about that being done. He forgot why it
was necessary.

The temple was about the same size as churches were, maybe a
little smaller. The Healeys had taken him to the non-denominational
chapel at the Fort, and he had seen other structures almost identical
to this one in Bisbee and Sierra Vista with Margaret and Ernesto.
The inside wasn't so different either, except in this place they had

this large cabinet behind the platform which they ceremoniously opened once in a while and withdrew a large pair of velvet-covered scrolls capped with two silver crowns that clunked when they carried them to the table. A red light hung over the cabinet. The windows were different, made up of pretty colored stained glass showing scenes of animals. Besides these things, everything looked pretty much the same, except of course the others had a large cross, either in front or on the roof. Here a six-pointed star was on the sign that told about the sermon and other events.

Edward began to feel a lot better. Maybe this was where and what he was supposed to be.

"Boruch shem kevod malchuso l'olom vo'ed." When they said that, the men were swaying as if the were transfixed. It sounded like moaning. Edward wondered if they were taught that as young boys. "Praised be His name, whose glorious kingdom is for ever and ever." They all sat down after the second man on the platform sang and the leader said a few more things. Edward had heard Hebrew spoken only a few times and couldn't understand what was happening. Margaret pointed in the prayerbook to the Hebrew on one side and the English translation on the other. They stood when the leader gave them the signal or when they got to a certain point in the service they all seemed to know. The men wore long, white talleisim with fringed corners, some draped over their shoulders, some not. And small yarlmukas toward the backs of their heads, mostly black ones. The few women in the congregation wore hats or kerchiefs on their heads. Edward tried not to gape during the proceedings. Everyone was serious except the little children. They made noise, and some of them fooled around until their mothers took them outside.

"You'll learn to read it," Margaret said after they were seated. He just looked at her, his mouth open, an expression that meant, "I will?" Ernesto smiled and closed it, one hand grabbing Edward's nose and the other pushing up his chin.

After the service, Rabbi Malev introduced them to the other people there, at a little party they called the Oneg Shabbat. Food was on plates on the tables and there were also paper cups of wine for the adults and soda for the children. "It's too far for Sunday School, Rabbi, but I'll work with him on his lessons and send them on to you," Margaret said. Edward was proud because he knew the rabbi knew his mother was a teacher. "His father will help him practice saying what he's supposed to out loud."

Rabbi Malev smiled and said to Ernesto, "How would you like to be my assistant rabbi?"

"We'll make sure he keeps up," Ernesto responded nervously. "My wife will wear a kerchief and light candles every Friday night. She'll say the *Shabbos* blessings." They all shook hands. "We'll be back in a few weeks," said Ernesto. He had his arms around Margaret and Edward.

The idea of training for his Bar Mitzvah had seemed strange, but now after being in the temple and with everyone wanting to help him do it, Edward felt excited. It would tie him more to his first parents even though they were dead. To all four of his parents. Nothing wrong with that.

§

SEVENTEEN

The highest spine of the Huachucas was perpendicular to all the ridges and canyons that descended from it. Two of the canyons, Carr and Ramsey, were twinned and parallel, following the turns and twists of the small mountain that separated them. Edward often rode along the trail on top of the ridge with Ernesto and Margaret. From there you could see the squatter's shack, located on the other side of the ridge, and several times Edward saw the girl hanging wash on a line that ran between the corner of the shack and a nearby mesquite tree. Or sometimes he would see the boy chopping wood. He wondered what went on inside the cabin.

Ernesto had talked to him a lot about growing up in Hermosillo, the capital of Sonora province, to the south. Margaret gave Edward old picture books and stories to read about colonial Mexico, and they both told him how the war had brought great changes in the peasants' lives. Electricity, better sanitation and new schools were beginning to bring modern conditions into rural areas and small towns. Edward grasped the general meaning of this, but when he

161

rode near the shack he still imagined that the girl ground corn in a large terra cotta bowl, that she wove thread into cloth, and that they made everything they had more or less by themselves. Because they possessed so very little, Edward fantasized, the girl had to become the little mother, taking care of her brother and her father because there was no other choice. But they were happy, anyway, he liked to think, making do, working together, loving each other and solving all their problems. When he remembered the man yelling angrily at the kids, he had to revise the fantasy and conclude that maybe it wasn't so good all the time.

Just before dinner one night, Ernesto was washing his hands at the sink while Margaret spooned meatballs and sauce made of tomatoes, onions and garlic plus crushed, dried, hot peppers onto a steaming pile of spaghetti. Edward was setting the table. "Know those squatters up the road?" Ernesto asked. "I saw the man in town today, coming out of the liquor store. Grungy-looking guy. No wonder people won't have much to do with him."

"Exactly why are you telling this to us?" Margaret asked. Edward was struck again by her ability to get right to the point.

"I don't know," said Ernesto, drying his hands and face. "I suppose it's because I'm ashamed he's Mexican. The sonufabitch lives like a bum. I tried speaking with him, but he slurs his words. His name's Alberto. From Guymas."

Edward poured water into their glasses. "You're not responsible for him just because you're Mexican, Ernesto. You know that, don't you?" Margaret said. She patted his hand and leveled a solid look at him.

"I guess so. It's just that those two kids with him deserve better. Healey wants them thrown out because he stopped paying rent. It seems *el stupido* drinks up whatever little money he earns."

Margaret shook her head. "I know," Ernesto said, "you can't 'drink up' money. But if I always used good language, *I* could become the schoolteacher around here. One know-it-all in the family is enough. Besides, somebody has to show Edward what really counts."

Margaret thumbed her nose at him.

§

These days Edward was feeling very good. He was happier than he had ever imagined he would be with his new family, and he was also getting along well most of the time with the other kids. And he was growing taller. His body was changing into a man's; hair was developing under his arms and around his genitalia.

Sometimes he and Margaret would saddle their horses and ride together after school, but usually he went alone because she was busy with schoolwork. One of his favorite places to ride was on the ridge, to a few commanding spots where he could look out over the entire plains, and one special place where a fig tree grew beside a large rock. He loved lying on the rock in the sun, with his horse tied to a branch.

A week or so after Ernesto had talked about the squatter father, Edward was up on that flat rock thinking about things, remembering how pretty the girl in the shack was and wondering what she looked like without any clothes. His "thing" was becoming stiff just by thinking. That was happening more and more. The most surprising part was that it would get hard for no reason, and worst of all, sometimes it happened in school, or in the house. The problem was keeping anyone from seeing. He could walk a little hunched over, except then they'd want to know what was wrong with him. Or he could put a hand in his pocket to keep it from pushing out against his pants, but that wasn't good either, because then they'd think he was playing with himself. He'd seen some of the boys doing just that. The best way to act when it stiffened was to put his books in front, or even better, his jacket. That usually would be okay until it behaved and went down again.

Now, up so very high in the sky, the sun was unquestionably the center of everything, the source which, if he could understand its incredible energy, he thought might provide him with the insights he needed to achieve what he wanted. This afternoon it poured its strength down, warming him in a way that made him feel he was being lifted off the rock to float free of gravity, like a god. Margaret had read to him about the Greek and Roman gods, and the gods of the Navajos and the Apachees. Now his penis was hard, pushing to break out of his Levis. Almost without being conscious, he let it find the sun. It felt good exposed to the freshness of the air. He thought about the girl then, and he was barely able to keep from jerking off. It wasn't that he hadn't done it plenty of other times, but somehow it didn't seem right at this particular moment. Everything was okay without doing it.

Edward kept his eyes closed, permitting his mind to relax. The breeze that moved in a wave across the rock continued to carry him up into the sky, where anything was possible. Before long, it was as if he was lying on a pillow of sleep. When he awoke, he had no idea how long he had slept.

He started home by way of the path near the shack, hesitating near it, hoping for signs of activity. But it was silent.

"The squatters?" Ernesto answered Edward's question later on. "They high-tailed it. Healey got the sheriff to throw them out. I kind of think they're living in that run-down pickup of his."

Several days later, when Margaret was returning from a teachers' meeting in Bisbee, she crossed the bridge over the San Pedro and stopped as usual to look for birds and other wildlife. Something caught her eye: a reflection in the willows just above the gravel flats. She left the car and walked down the small dirt road that began at the end of the bridge. The sun flashed off the window of a truck. A man squatted next to a fire, and two children stood next to it. Small shirts and underwear were spread out, drying on bushes.

"Hello!" They froze but raised their heads to see who had intruded upon them. The boy and girl, on command from the man, scampered into the truck. He rose and put his hand on a rifle which was leaning against a rock. Margaret didn't move. He left the rifle where it was and walked toward her. "Hello," she said again. The man didn't respond but continued staring at her as if she should understand that there wouldn't be any conversation. "I'm Margaret Renfrew, the schoolteacher." She waited; there was no response. She was sure he had heard her. "We live on Ramsey Canyon Road. Weren't you up past us? My husband is Ernesto. He said the two of you talked."

The man ran the back of a hand across his unshaven face. He glanced over to the children inside the cab, and then back to Margaret. Then he spat out some tobacco juice, aiming it uncomfortably close to her; she couldn't tell whether he was simply getting rid of it or whether he meant it as a contemptuous gesture. "Maybe. So what?" he asked. She saw that everything about him was filthy. His pants were greasy, and the shirt he was wearing seemed as if it had never been washed.

Margaret advanced closer and waved to the children. "They yours?" she asked brightly. She desperately wanted something to talk about, but as soon as she spoke, she realized that it was hopeless. She wasn't surprised when he didn't answer.

"What do you want, lady?," he demanded then. "I'm trying to do something," he said, slurring the words together. She noticed some bunched and bloody fur next to the fire—a jackrabbit's, she guessed. A pot was slung across. Now the boy and girl stepped gingerly from the truck. They were both very thin, almost emaciated. Their clothes were ashen and torn.

"We heard Healey made you leave your place," Margaret continued gamely. "Your children should be in school. These are such important years for them, and ...." The look on his face caused her to abruptly change the subject. " ... Ernesto and I have an adopted

165

son with us." She didn't know what to say next. She glanced at the two children and turned to leave, but turned back after taking a few paces. Reaching into her pocket, she took out a five-dollar bill. "I'd like to leave this for, for the children," she said, putting it on a stone. She walked rapidly toward her car. After she started the motor, she looked out the side window and saw the man pick up the money.

§

"Ernie, I can't stand knowing that children are living like that," Margaret said. Edward had found what she reported fascinating until he realized that the Mexican family weren't simply camping out for a day or two, but really living in the truck.

"You didn't see what went on in that shack. No different than all the others, Meg, I've known hundreds like them. If he wouldn't spend whatever little he makes on booze, maybe they'd be all right. Damn him," he said, his voice rising, "I'd like to boot him square in the ass. That bum just doesn't want to understand he has to work like the rest of us."

"Maybe we can do something for the boy and girl," Margaret said.

Ernesto ruffled Edward's hair. "Maybe. I was thinking that too. There's that other shack not far from us, up there about a mile or so. We'd have to board up the sides some and the roof. I think he'll listen to me because I'm a *compadre*. You and Eddie put some things together. We have those old mattresses in the barn. And maybe he and I can make a table—that is, if I can get him to do anything."

Margaret smiled broadly and kissed him with a loud smack. "Ernie," she said, "get good at this, and we'll make you a county welfare worker."

"Very funny, Renfrew," he responded, shaking his head. "All right, there's still some light left. I'll run down and talk to him."

Edward made a move towards his jacket. "No, son, better I go alone. Give your mother a hand." He rose from the table. "Just so you two don't get the wrong idea, we're helping them, but it's not the same as with new neighbors. If there was a woman, maybe that'd be different," Ernesto continued. "But I'm not having that bum in my house, *compadre* or not."

"You going to prevent the children from playing with Eddie? I hope not, because that's up to them. And that girl and boy are definitely going to go to school," Margaret insisted. "I'll see to it." Ernesto shrugged as she handed him his jacket, and started clearing the dishes from the table. "I mean it. Even if I have to get the authorities and take those children away from him."

"I don't think you've considered what that means," Ernesto said. "They're probably better off with him than they'd be in some institution. He's probably impossible, but they're used to him. Besides, they don't know anything different." Edward remembered what the Major had said about the Orphan Home. He didn't want them taken away from their father, even if he wasn't sending them to school. You could learn at home, he remembered. Abraham Lincoln did.

§

Early the next morning, Margaret and Edward brought food, blankets, and some clothing to the shack that Ernesto and the man, Alberto, were in the process of making habitable. "May I talk to you for a minute?" she called up to Alberto. He climbed down from the roof and walked over to where she and Edward stood. Even though he wasn't very close to them, Edward could smell liquor. Edward glanced over at the boy and girl, who had stopped what they were doing and were standing with blank expressions on their faces. He decided they were eager to be friendly—he could play ball and ride with the boy, he thought, but then he realized they didn't have a horse. He wanted to do things with the girl too, but couldn't think of exactly what.

"Your children should really be in school," Margaret said matter-of-factly. "As you may know, I'm the schoolteacher in Hereford. They're probably far behind the others their age, but I'd be willing to work hard with them." She waited for a reply.

Alberto lit a cigarette and scratched his head. He moved some dirt with his boot, and spat behind him. "I don't like someone telling me what rule to follow. You and your man give me these things, but that means nothing." He took a drag on the cigarette. "School is where they do *nada,* only sit, think things that mix 'em up."

"Don't you want them to amount to something?"

He glared at her. "*Que viene?* Get fancy and forget who they are. The people, they don't let you forget." He inhaled again, and spat again.

"*Es tiempo por nuevas cosas,*" Ernesto said, joining in. He was looking down at them through the opening he was about to board up.

"*Bueno, entonces* they go for now," Alberto said. "But they do the same work around here as before. For now, but—*quién sabe* how long?"

Edward was very excited. Margaret gave the boy, whose name was Roberto, a few of Edward's clothes to wear and told the girl she'd see if she could find some things for her. Perhaps they'd make a dress. Her name was Francesca. She was striking, with exceptionally beautiful skin, except Edward could see she didn't wash much. She was tall and thin-waisted, with a solid hint of developing breasts. Her eyes were large and round, very dark and set below long black eyebrows. Only the slight slanting of her mouth detracted from her remarkably lovely face.

§

On school days the three youngsters walked for about two miles to the main road where the bus picked them up. School buses were new in Cochise County, and Ramsey Canyon Road had no other children. The three of them enjoyed themselves during the rides. Margaret had told them she believed she should not take them with her; besides, she arrived at school earlier and left later than they did.

Edward introduced Roberto to the other kids on his first day in school. It didn't go very well because Roberto spoke such poor English and Edward knew only a few words of Spanish. Roberto seemed very uncomfortable, so Edward stayed with him as much as he could. They watched the other kids play, but pretended they were involved with a game of their own; at least that's what Edward wanted it to look like. Francesca mixed with the girls, although Edward noticed several times that she was staying close to Margaret. By the time a week or ten days had elapsed, Roberto was beginning to fit in better. Roberto didn't always respond to what Edward said, which was frustrating. He could communicate better with Francesca and often sat next to her on the school bus. How her mouth changed positions fascinated him. He liked the bouncing of the bus because it pushed them together, although he sensed she tried to avoid contact.

Edward couldn't help showing off a little to her. "Of course I could become a cowboy and have a ranch like my Dad. One day, a big spread, maybe *thousands* of cattle, a place with plenty of water, up north near Springerville somewhere. Or," he went on, "I could be a pilot like my *real* father was." He watched her expressions. "I could be both, have a big ranch and be a pilot, too." He liked the way Francesca smelled. He tried to decide exactly why but couldn't. She listened, and she was pretty besides.

"Well, well, it looks like our young man here has found himself a girlfriend," Ernesto said gleefully one day after letting Francesca out in front of the shack. He had met them walking up their road. "One day she will grow up to be a very beautiful woman. Who knows, my Jewish son might marry a Mexican *muchacha,* and I'll be the grandfather of Jewish Mexicans," he said, laughing.

Edward poked him. "You're not very funny. And don't tease me when Mom is around. She'll start asking me a lot of stupid questions and everything."

"All right, I won't," he promised as they turned into their driveway. "But I really am glad you made new friends. I think the experience with them will be an important one for you. You're bound to learn what having it rough is."

"It hasn't been so easy for *me,* you know," Edward countered.

"Yes, but it's different. I just don't ever want you feeling sorry for yourself."

§

On a day when the students were let out for the day at noon, Edward left school as usual with Francesca and Roberto. At their stop they jumped down from the bus and started the two mile walk up the canyon road.

"Want to come over?" Edward asked. "I have two new rabbits and you can feed them. Mom made a pie yesterday."

They looked at each other. Roberto was the one who answered, "Maybe *uno poquito,* but I must soon be back to Alberto for the chores. If not, *muy malo.*"

After they devoured three helpings of pie, Edward conducted them to the rabbit cage in the barn. "Alberto, if he get his hands on these, dead very quick and in the pot," Roberto said, laughing. But Edward didn't like the idea. Roberto noticed. "I was making a joke. I will not tell him, please." Roberto sighed. "I must go. She can stay a little. Tomorrow I see you. *Adios.*"

Edward brought some rabbit pellets and put them in Francesca's hand. They crouched as she fed the gentle little animals. He was acutely aware of her next to him. "You smell real nice, Francesca," he said awkwardly, looking quickly at the rabbits. She didn't respond.

After fumbling with closing the door to the cage, he said, "Want to see our horses? One for each of us except Dad has two. I'll get some grain." She nodded. As they walked to the grain bin, they brushed against each other. Edward turned toward her and stepped on a rake, which smacked him in the face faster than he could put out a hand to protect himself. A red welt appeared on his jaw. He remained motionless, his surprise and embarrassment greater than any pain.

Francesca placed her fingers on his face and Edward sat up opposite her, his hand brushing unintentionally against her chest. Then he kissed her, a quick peck on her mouth. He kissed her again, and then drew back, breathing rapidly, his eyes looking straight into hers.

"You're real pretty," he said. "And I like you very much," he added, smiling.

She looked at him passively. "I've never touched a girl before," he said. "Is it all right?"

Francesca did not respond but put her hands over her face. "Honest, Francesca, I didn't want to make you feel bad." He put his arm around her, the way he had seen Ernesto do when Margaret was upset about something. A small smile appeared in the corners of her mouth, which made him feel easier.

He summoned into words what he had been thinking about. "Could I see you, see what you look like? I wouldn't do anything, I promise." She peered at him. "And you could see me."

She knelt and removed her blouse. Her small breasts pushed against her white underwear top, the kind made for boys. Edward stood up and took off his shirt, listening for any sound from outside the barn. They took off their jeans. His eyes centered on her panties and all that might lie underneath. "Could I touch you? Please." She looked at him without speaking. He put his hand on the place where her legs came together. She turned her head and started sobbing.

Edward recoiled. What was the matter? The boys bragged about doing this. One older guy even said the girls he "did it with" told him they liked it as much as he did. Why was Francesca crying? He was in trouble, all right. He sure as hell wanted to "get something." But how? He really liked Francesca.

"I—did I hurt you? Honest, I didn't mean to, Francesca; please don't cry. I won't do it again." He felt like one of those cads in the movies. Why was this so complicated? What if she told? He didn't know what he could say or do to make her feel better.

"In the house, what Alberto does to me. He would give me a beating if I told." She sounded more composed.

Edward wondered exactly what it was. She began to put on her shirt and jeans. "Can't Roberto help you?" he asked.

"Once he tried, but he got slapped around bad and made to go without food for one day." As he walked her to the road, she said, "Please, Edward, do not tell your parents, no one. Promise me." He quickly agreed, and she began to hurry away.

"Francesca, wait." He ran to her. "Ernesto told me this once at the Healeys, when it was bad. He said someday I would be away from them." She shrugged her shoulders and moved off in the direction of the shack.

§

In the one-room schoolhouse in Hereford, Edward raced through the texts and the other work Margaret gave him. One afternoon, after class, she walked him to the school bus. "I think," she said, "you'd be better off in the new high school in Sierra Vista."

"Sierra Vista?" he exclaimed. "That's a dude town, all the retired army people and trailer parks. Uglysville. I mean, Mom, if I go anywhere, it should be Bisbee. Their baseball and basketball team is almost the best in southern Arizona." Edward waited for her reaction.

"That's terrible grammar. '*Teams are among the best.*' Your interest in your school work lately is 'stinko,' young man. Sports and girls are okay, but I want to see more time spent with your books. No son of mine is going to 'goof off,' to use one of your expressions. Sierra Vista has enlightened teachers from other parts of the country. New ideas, just right to stimulate a curious mind." She looked at him. "You *are* curious, aren't you? If not, there's no point in pushing you. College would just be a waste."

He knew she had him. "You know I want to go to college! But all my friends will be in Bisbee High next year, and Sierra Vista is full of all those Easterner dudes."

"I've laid it out for you, Edward. You select which school. I'm not kidding. You decide, right now, this minute. But once you start, you're not switching."

"I'll think it over. Promise."

"No, right now."

"Okay, okay," he replied in a tone that he knew made him sound like a little boy. "Sierra Vista. But I don't like your forcing me."

"A wise decision. I'm glad you're acting so maturely." Margaret began to walk away but turned and said with a grin, "I'm proud of you, Eddie."

§

173

EIGHTEEN

Edward walked along the highway, Route 2, toward Sierra Vista and the Fort, turning around every so often to scrutinize the cars and trucks coming up the long rise. He gazed out across the prairie, imagining the behavior of the animals he knew were there but couldn't be observed unless you were right with them, downwind and stock still.

A small dust devil jumped out of nowhere and playfully scooped up the soil, making the swirling air tan and cloudy. Then it faded into nothing, as mysterious in its disappearance as it had been in its birth. Good thing they weren't big, like tornadoes. The sagebrush off to the side were pushed together in clumps. He thought of the homesteaders crossing the plains, gathering in their Conestogas at the end of a day for mutual protection. What happened if a wheel broke, and you couldn't catch up to the wagon train before the Apaches got you? Scalping was horrendous to imagine, and so was being tortured.

A black sedan drove toward him, and he recognized it as Mel Martin's. When it slowed down, Edward took on his John Wayne saunter, which he had practiced a good deal after seeing him in a great cowboy picture. Wayne had come through the swirling barroom doors, arms loose, hands ready by his pistols, and said in that drawl of his, "I'm callin' your bluff." Martin waved, asked how he was doing and said to tell Ernesto he wanted to talk to him about some steers. Edward said okay and resumed his movie fantasy.

It was 1955, and at almost sixteen, the flabbiness of the youngster had been transformed into the pronounced muscles and agility of an active youth. His clear, dark brown eyes and long black brows looked like the ones in the photos of his father. He relished the way his arms and shoulders felt when he flexed them. When he studied himself in the mirror with his shirt off, he liked to grip his hands together to watch his pectorals and biceps firm; turning, he watched his muscles flow over his back and move on either side of his spine. So why didn't seeing his good-looking face and body eliminate his doubts about his looks? It just didn't.

One of the girls in his class, Ellie, told him in front of some other kids that he was one of the cutest boys in school. Actually, she wasn't so bad herself—especially when she pulled her shoulders back. He decided to sit next to her in history class. The only part of him he wished were better were his thighs. They were thick, but since he never had to appear in a bathing suit at a country club or anything, he tried not to worry about them. He got up the nerve to tell the barber not to cut his curly hair too short, to keep his large wave where it seemed to want to lie, on the wide side of his part. It looked much more grown-up, much better than the old crew cuts; they were now definitely out.

He recalled Ernesto coming into his room a day or two earlier. "You planning to run in a beauty contest? Keep that up and you can go to acting school with the rest of the sissies."

"You should knock when you come in," said Edward. "I don't sneak into your room."

"Your door wasn't closed." A grin cut across Ernesto's face. "And what's this noise about shaving? All you have to do is stick your face in the breeze. When you get older, I'll show you how to shave like a man."

"Yeah, well I know how already. One of these days you're going to find a real powerhouse on your hands. I'll pin *you* down, and you'll have to scream for mercy," Edward said.

"Tell you what, Tarzan. You blindfold me and tie one, no, both hands behind my back." Edward made a "tsk" sound, threw his head back and walked by in a huff. Ernesto grabbed him around the waist and kissed him loudly on the neck. With that, Edward wheeled around, slipped loose and pushed him backward onto the bed. Ernesto landed on his back, and the surprise of Edward's elbow in his solar plexus caused him to emit an "oof." Quickly Edward was over him, trying to pin him, pressing down on each of his wrists. He seemed about to succeed when Ernesto yanked his right arm out and pushed him over and off the bed onto the floor with a thud, landing squarely on top of him. That was okay, Edward thought; of course Ernesto was stronger. They rolled over, with Ernesto flashing his hands like tentacles clutching for an object to grab. But Edward moved fast, slipping away just when Ernesto might get him. They both got up, and Edward lunged forward like a tackler, shoving Ernesto back onto the bed again.

Now it wasn't funny any more. They weren't fooling around the way they had in the past. Serious purpose was apparent in their grunts. Edward was exerting all his strength and challenging Ernesto at a level neither of them had previously imagined. Warily, each noted the hostility on the other's face, and it was Ernesto who decided to stop.

"Hey, look," he said, a little out of breath, "you're getting too strong for me. I give up."

For a moment Edward didn't know what to do. Why had he felt

that rage, even for those few seconds? "Yeah, okay. But you let me," he said. He would have liked to be the sure victor if he could have been, but Ernesto had broken the charged atmosphere of combatants.

Sweating a little, they sat down, winded. The change that had occurred rang like a fire whistle. Both knew that things between them would never be quite the same again.

"Sam Slavin's little boy is growing up fast," mused Ernesto.

Why'd he call me "Sam Slavin's," Edward wondered? Doesn't he think of me as *his* son any more?

His recollections and dreams about his father had diminished in a slow fade, like passion does, leaving him with less and less memory. He hadn't forgotten his father, he knew that would never happen, but his dependence and loyalty had shifted. Ernesto had been there for him, and on some preconscious level, his father not only wasn't around, but had also deserted him, while Ernesto was with him every day. Ernesto approved of him, too—not that his original father hadn't, but that seemed so long ago now.

§

A few days later, as Edward was hitchhiking on Route 92, he heard a car coming and immediately recognized it as Major Healey's DeSoto. Swinging his arms, he walked rapidly ahead, trying not to display any indication that he might be interested in a ride. He didn't need the past to catch up with him like a truant officer, he thought. Who wanted the Major yakking at him? The farther the Healeys were out of his life, the better.

Maybe the Major would ride past and not bother him. Way the hell away.

"Hello there!" Healey called from his rolled-down window. "Want a lift? It'd give us a chance to talk." His voice was friendly. "Hop in." He leaned over and opened the door.

178

Edward turned to face him with an absolutely blank expression on his face. "Thank you, *sir,* but I need the exercise," he said, as flat as a gravestone. He continued to stride up the incline, glancing out on the prairie to his right.

It must have looked strange to see a person walking and the driver of a car right next to him moving at the walker's rate of speed. Healey raised his arm, then dropped it. "It's up to you. I can't make you get in, and I certainly wouldn't want to." That didn't sound like the same person who had controlled Edward's life for so long with so little real feeling for him. This person seemed to be practically begging. "I'm trying to be your friend, Edward," he said.

So what if you are, Edward thought. He avoided looking at Healey's face, and an unsettling quiet ensued.

He tried to walk faster and then slower in an effort not to be next to Major Healey's window. Finally the Major said, "Riding with me won't kill you, you know." Edward turned to him and shook his head firmly and emphatically from side to side, very slowly. In a moment, he was watching Healey's car diminish down to the size of a toy. I guess I wasn't very nice to him, he thought. Well, so what? He kicked the road.

Ten minutes later he got a ride into town, getting out where the highway intersected with the main street of Sierra Vista. He knew that Ernesto and Margaret were somewhere around town that day, but didn't realize they were in the attorney's office until he passed the window and saw them shaking hands. He saw Ernesto catch a glimpse of him and then disappear to run outside. A second later, Ernesto flashed an arm around his neck from the rear. "You're also supposed to know what's behind you!" He held the grip and pressed his fingers into Edward's ribs.

Edward threw them off. "That's not funny. I'm not in the mood for fooling around."

"You sound like an old crank." Ernesto faced him with a big grin.

179

"Today's an important day for us. Go on down to The Egg Pan and get a table. I'll get Mom and see you in a few minutes, all right?"

"Stop beaming so much," said Margaret after they had left the building. "You look silly, like a dumb farm boy all 'ga-ga', seeing the big sights for the first time." He stopped and kissed her flush on the mouth.

"Buying the property makes me feel great. Almost as much as doing you know what." He kissed her again.

"Me too," she said to his surprise. "But you might try being a little more subtle."

"Why should I be?"

"I suppose you're right. A New England upbringing crossed with a fiery, emotional Latin one," she said, widening her eyes. "You're really not exactly the way they advertise, but you're better at not keeping things inside than I am." She looked down the street. "Hey, I can just taste a hot fudge sundae. With nuts and whipped cream." She put her arm around his waist.

They found Edward seated at a window table, and after the waitress had taken their orders, he related his encounter with Major Healey.

"He did write you that letter of kind-of apology last year, Edward," Margaret said. "That couldn't have been easy for him."

Edward glared. "Whose side are you on? Dad understands, don't you? I will *never* have anything to do with him. The other night I dreamed he was begging for my help."

Edward looked askance at the hot fudge sundae the waitress put down in front of Margaret and said, "Your baby's hungry like maybe it's a colt." He was trying to be funny, but his tone was a bit sarcastic.

"What do you say we go out for dinner?" Ernesto proposed. "That new fancy place. We'll get all spiffed up and drink wine, like rich people do." He beamed. "Gotta celebrate. Eddie," he said grinning,

180

"guess what. I've gone to contract on that hundred acres with the well on it across the road."

Before he could continue, Margaret asked, "Where are you getting the money for the cattle? Planning to rob the bank?"

"Poker, Meg." He glanced from one to the other. "I knew you'd be challenging me. It will take our savings plus a loan. I talked to a guy down at the Bank of Bisbee."

" 'Neither a borrower nor a lender be.' Willie Shakespeare. When they chase you for payments, I'll take on extra tutoring." Margaret smiled and raised her spoon to him in salute.

"The hell you will," he said. "You won't have time." She made a face but didn't answer.

Edward didn't seem to catch the exact meaning of his remark. "And I can work after school," he added. "We'll have our own spread, right?"

"You bet. Prices are zooming, the economy's taking off like a bat out of hell. It'll take a couple of years. I'm tired of working for other people. Our time has a-rrived." He stood. "To us. The best there is. 'Salud.' 'L'chaim'!" They clicked their spoons together. Edward wished Ernesto would sit down, because people were watching.

§

NINETEEN

The military and political authorities in Washington decided that Fort Huachuca would become an elaborate and advanced electronics base. The Fort and the entire area around it were expanding enormously. Sierra Vista had been created from nothing, and now it encroached on and surrounded Fry, the unincorporated town at the Fort's gates. Fry was old army, replete with down-at-the-heel trailer parks, assorted shacks, shabby stores and a whorehouse or two, a crowded settlement of hangers-on, squalling babies and dirt.

Sierra Vista had needed a new high school to accommodate the burgeoning number of children who came with the servicemen and civilians attached to the expanded base. The site selected was next to the airfield, which had been enlarged to accommodate the kind of aircraft required by the expansion. Edward loved to go there to watch the planes and talk to the pilots. He was intent now on learning to fly, and broached the subject with Ernesto.

"Maybe I could use the money from my father's insurance," he suggested. "Aviation's a terrific career, and I know I'm a natural," he said, trying to sound convincing.

"First of all, there wasn't that much insurance, plus you know half of it's for Susie," Ernesto responded. "I believe your parents would want it saved for your college education."

"If I go to West Point or Annapolis, I wouldn't need money."

Ernesto was prepared. "But you haven't finally decided, Edward, and you certainly shouldn't. It's too early for that. You don't know if you could get in, even though your grades are good. Anyway," he continued, "it would be irresponsible for your mother and me to permit you to use that money for anything but your education."

"But Dad, learning to fly is part of my education!"

"No, Edward, I'm sorry. It's natural to be attracted to the thing your father did. He was a good pilot, and undoubtedly you can become one too. I'm not trying to discourage you."

Ernesto put his hand on Edward's shoulder. "Tell you what, *amigo,* you want to fly badly enough, you pay for half, and I'll contribute the other. From now on you get a dollar an hour when you work on our place. Hey, why such a sad face? I never got paid for working on my family's ranch."

"They have a job open for a 'line boy' at the airport," Edward said. "They told me they would charge me only half for lessons. That way I could learn about planes and engines. Okay, Dad? I'll still do stuff around the house, I promise." Ernesto shook his head but smiled. Edward knew it meant yes.

§

The airfield was very different since Sam Slavin had taken off from it on that fateful day. But the mountains and prairie were unchanged.

Edward had long ago persuaded Ernesto to bring him to the crash site in the Huachucas, although Ernesto had made him wait until he

184

turned twelve. They had spent a few days on the trip, and had camped in places of uncommon beauty. When they reached the site, they had found that the plane's engine, the wheels, wings, rudder and stabilizer had been stripped over the years and taken for salvage. The crumbled fuselage was still there, bent and torn like a smashed erector set. Ernesto had told him that he hadn't wanted to bring him to the crash site, but had changed his mind when he'd heard Edward romanticizing the crash to a friend.

"I want to take this piece back with me," Edward said matter-of-factly. He held a piece of a strut with the cream-colored fabric showing two chocolate brown stripes. "And one of these seats to sit on." Ernesto had said no to that, that if he was going to learn to fly, he shouldn't get to thinking about how it felt to sit in that seat. "I really want this," Edward had insisted. "It'll remind me to be careful." He kept it in his room, under the window.

He wanted to conclude the past and move ahead with his life, but sometimes he still felt a need to visit the cemetery. He still felt a little of the old pull, and wanted somehow to be near where their bodies were buried, as if he could connect with them again. Margaret encouraged him to go as often as he wished.

One afternoon after school, before he headed to the airport, he traveled to the graves of his parents. A fall chill covered the plains, and he raised his collar against the wind as it plummeted down from the mountains. He had learned a number of Jewish customs and practices during the year he had studied for his Bar Mitzvah, and one was to place a small stone on the grave of a loved one during each visit. Today he found two stones that were almost the same shape and size. Placing one on each grave made him feel linked to his parents in a way he couldn't explain to himself.

He stood, thinking: I don't know why I come here so much. They're not here. Their dead bodies are, but so what?

A gust splashed his face, ruffling his hair so that for a moment he

185

couldn't see clearly. He sat down on the path in front of the graves and stared at the two headstones. I miss you, he thought again, I do more than anything. You shouldn't have crashed. Why did you have to? I know I have to get over wanting you back so much.

"Ernesto and Margaret are great," he whispered. "I don't understand what I'm complaining about. She's gotten big as a house. She'll have to take care of the baby." Maybe then, he thought, Ernesto will have time for things with me.

"I took my first flying lesson this week. Told them I was sixteen—didn't let on to Ernesto, not yet."

The sky was woven with grays, some creamy, and in the grooved clouds the color of slate and charcoal. The ground was crisp; when brushed or pushed by his steps, every stone created little movements of dirt and dust. He froze, staring at the dinosaur face and fat, ugly body of a Gila monster. He was impressed with its black and pink blotches and the bands wrapped around its beadlike scales. Poisonous, Ernesto had warned, its venom capable of hitting the respiratory system, sometimes causing death. He'd also said they became agile when they were annoyed. Edward waited until it decided to secrete itself out of view— probably to lie in wait for some poor creature, he thought. God, all kinds of things can get you! You just can never relax, even outdoors. How could Ernesto and the other men be so nonchalant?

It stank, being alone. Just when your life seemed solid, something changed. He wished he'd brought some chocolate. Mounds. Hershey candy kisses. Even gum would be better than nothing. He bit on one of his nails, tearing it down. Then he covered his face with his hands, surprised that he felt so emotional. If only his parents—they're gone. *Gone*! Can't you get it through your thick head?

He swung around in a circle, his eyes closed. Something to connect. A prayer. The basic one of his people, say it out loud. *"Sh'ma, Yisroyale, Adonai Elohanu, Adonai Echod."* And then in English:

"Hear, O Israel: The Lord Our God, the Lord Is One." He felt steadier.

Edward remained, fingers spread over his face. Several moments passed. He stared at the two graves, pressed his fingers to his mouth in a kiss and tried not to choke up. "Good-bye, Dad. Good-bye, Mom. I hope—" He didn't finish, but turned instead and ran rapidly down the hill.

§

TWENTY

The yellow bus, Number 23, shimmied down Route 92, picking up speed like an old runner heading home. Edward stared out the window. After a long time, Francesca said, "You're very quiet, Edward. Was school bad for you today?"

He sighed deeply. "Yeah, lousy. Stupid, dumb kids."

Francesca shrugged. She and Roberto didn't have much interaction with the other kids at Sierra Vista.

"They shouldn't have started talking about their fraternity. All that gab about parties and stuff, fooling around with sorority girls. They can shit in their hats, and they can shove their fraternity right up their you-know-what. Their asses," he added. This kind of language was new for him. It had a two-fisted ring about it, he thought.

"We're the 'creepy ones' from way out at Ramsey Canyon," Roberto said. They were the last three people on the bus, as they always were. "I know they say that about us. But who cares about them dummies?"

The bus lumbered to a stop, and the three teenagers dropped down

189

off the last step. They waited until the churned-up dust settled down onto the road, and then began ambling up their road.

After a few moments, Edward turned to Francesca. "Yeah, we're different because we don't have our own parents. We're orphans. They don't understand what it means to grow up without your own parents."

"At least you are with kind people, nice, like real parents. Not with an animal who pretends to be a man." Now she reminded Edward of a seething female mountain lion, about to deal effectively with something she didn't like. You want to be out of their way when they get angry, he thought. But Francesca sure was sexy, and he wasn't the only one who thought so—not by a long shot. A lot of the junior and senior guys hung around her, just trying to get her attention. They sneaked looks at her boobs— not that Edward didn't; they stood straight up and were just the right size. He tried to guess where— exactly where—her nipples were when she wore certain sweaters or blouses. Once or twice when she was chilly, he saw where. That was something to remember. And he loved when a breeze flowed through her jet black hair. Sometimes she'd run her part down the center and let it fall straight at the sides, and sometimes she'd wear it tight with a barrette, or bunched low near her neckline in the back.

Francesca was aware of her looks, all right. Her terrific white skin and long neck were like some sculpture. She curved nicely, her hips rounding like musical rhythms, offering legs that Edward thought were as exciting as any he'd seen in a girlie magazine (the barber kept a few in his shop so the men wouldn't mind waiting). All of her had that elongated look, and she was flat from just below those gorgeous breasts down her stomach to that wonderful place between her legs. She could pose for Varga, the illustrator for *Esquire*. Those clowns in school, in that fraternity—if anybody was going to make time with her, Edward sure as hell was going to try to be the one.

190

What drove him wild was when she would tie the ends of her blouse together and expose some of that chamois-smooth skin above the belt of her Levis. He would have loved to run his fingers across that area, up and down, making circles, feeling her goose bumps, getting her hot as a firecracker. He'd think about her getting undressed, imagine her taking off each garment. Or maybe when she washed: the thought of water running down her body in rivulets. Or his washing her slowly from top to bottom. Wow! That resulted in his doing it to himself, right away before he could decide whether he wanted to or not.

Roberto mostly listened. It wasn't that he was dumb, just that he didn't have a whole lot to say. And it also had something to do with the fact that his poor English still limited him, Edward thought. Francesca's was much better.

Francesca was still talking, "One day someone will care for me the way *I* need." She had told Edward she hardly remembered her parents. Her father had left when she was three. Soon Alberto had moved in, and a couple of years later her mother had died.

Edward hoped Francesca was about to explain all the details of those intimate feelings you reserve for your best friend, the one who'd be there for you, who you could count on no matter what. But she became silent.

"It's terrible being scared when you're little," he said. She looked at him, and though she didn't respond, she edged next to him. "I like being with you a lot, Francesca, you and Roberto. (He was right there so he couldn't be excluded, could he?) I feel a lot more—I don't know—comfortable. Sharing things and sticking together. Because we're orphans." He held her hand. She squeezed it. He was delighted.

"*Amigos,*" Roberto agreed, "friends who do good for each other because they know."

Edward said, "The trouble with Ernesto and Margaret is they're adults, interested in their own stuff, mostly. Like right now, they're

191

all wrapped up in a baby that's not even born yet. Ernesto's not nearly as much fun as he used to be." He kicked a stone, hard. "Besides, they wouldn't understand us." He ran his fingers through Francesca's, touching as much of her hand as he could.

She stopped walking. "It is a nice feeling I have with you because you do not care we are Mexican. And because like us, you have no parents too." She looked across the sky; it was wide open except for some high, thin clouds, usually an indication that the weather would be changing. "I would do anything to be in a home where the man and his wife love each other, and the baby they have made is from love they want to give it and to each other. A wonderful gift." She turned to him. "You are very lucky, Edward."

More and more, Edward realized that she was very smart, someone who could make him feel very good. "Yeah," he said, "you're right, except when they get mad at each other, or at me."

"How would you like to live with a so-called father who beats and kicks you when you don't please him? Like you were a dog." Her voice deepened into sort of a growl. "I dream, no, I pray he will get a leg caught in one of the traps he sets. I see myself watch him from a distance. He is screaming with pain and I would do nothing.

"All the time he is drunk and grabs me. He smells like a porcupine dead three days. Oh, I hate him! I am starting to plan how to get away." Roberto let out a deep sigh. "But if I got out, he would beat Roberto more," she said. Her brother added that they both must leave, but his voice had no conviction.

Now it was Edward who was silent. He had always understood that they were poor, but he hadn't realized it was as bad as Francesca had just described. He really could thank his lucky stars about how he'd ended up. He'd talk to Ernesto about trying to help them more.

Edward wanted his two friends to do better in school. Both did poorly, as though neither they nor the teachers expected anything more from them. It was hinted that they would probably have to be "left back," and Margaret had suggested they stop off at their ranch one or two afternoons a week. "Francesca, you and Roberto are both intelligent. You must be patient and ask questions when something doesn't make sense to you. There's nothing in your work that you can't learn."

"The teachers go too fast," said Francesca. "They really don't want questions from us the way you do. They stink!" Edward had nodded his head in agreement. He had noticed that except for one or two, the teachers really did make it clear that they didn't want to be bothered. "Mrs. Renfrew, you are real nice to help us. That's the only reason why we are not in a lower class," Francesca said.

Edward invited Francesca to the big spring dance in May and was delighted when she accepted and said Alberto would permit her to go. This would demonstrate to everyone at school that she was his; the others could get their own. Sure, he wanted to belong at school, but the other guys were treating him as if he had some kind of disease. He didn't want to feel that being an orphan was what made a difference. Some of the kids knew about his parents and what had happened, but they'd ask him about it anyway. He told them about the plane crash, but he stretched out the part where his father took care of his mother and the other couple even though he was in great pain from his broken leg, and then made himself that crutch and headed out in the deep snow into the storm for help. He played it for all it was worth. He felt a little guilty, because he knew his motivation was solely for sympathy and acceptance, and he knew that wasn't right.

After the dance, Edward planned to park with Francesca in the family car, down the lane and off to the side of the bridge over the San Pedro. He had already made out with Francesca. She had let him "feel her up." Sometimes he'd hold his hand over a breast and feel her nipple harden against his palm. It felt like a poker, but different from one that was red hot and burning. And he'd run his hand on her jeans along her thighs and unbutton a couple of buttons—once *she* did it, but she hadn't gone as far as taking them all the way off. He wished she'd wear skirts. It'd be easier, but he certainly wasn't complaining. She seemed to enjoy getting him hot, especially when he came in his pants. Good thing Levis were dark blue; if he wore army chinos, you'd be able to see the wet. He'd die if anyone saw that.

The night of the dance, several boys huddled together as soon as they entered the gym, elbows poking and faces making note that Francesca was Eddie Slavin's date. They cut in on him so quickly during dances that he finally said no, and someone yelled, "Hey, Slavin, what's she, your own private stuff?" He turned and glared at the speaker, but he noticed that Francesca smiled at everyone who looked at her.

"Eddie," she said, "you're not being fair. You can't keep me all to yourself." He didn't answer. When the next dance started, a senior cut in, the tall Mexican-American who was Sierra Vista's star half-back. Edward walked off, watched them for a minute, and then went out to the car and grabbed a beer from his six-pack. When he got back, Francesca was gone. He looked at the group of senior boys, but they just made search-me faces and shrugged their shoulders.

In a little while, Francesca returned alone. Edward felt defeated, a fool without power, cut down without even a fight. She came over to him, took a mirror from her purse, and checked her lipstick. He waited for her to say something, and when she didn't, he grabbed her hand, jerking her along behind him. "You really stink, Francesca," he told her.

In the car, after a few minutes, she said, "I'm not yours, you know, Eddie. No one owns me. I do what I want. I see a lot of guys." She was humming.

They kept driving south on Route 92. He was still furious. "Eddie," she whispered, reaching over for his hand, "why don't we find

194

a quiet little spot? If you want to," she said, "we can go all the way." She cuddled next to him. He raced to the turnoff and parked in the cottonwood grove. They moved into the back seat and he grabbed for her, his hands on her breasts like clamps. She rolled on top of him, sliding up and down.

"I don't have a rubber," he said breathlessly.

"Don't worry, I won't get pregnant. It's not my time of the month. I know about that."

"What? What do you mean?"

She looked straight at him. "You some kind of jerk?" she asked angrily. "What do you think's been happening in that shack of ours? That man hasn't let me alone since I was ten or eleven. Tell you what, though, it's not going to be too long before I'm hightailing my ass out of there. You know I'm not planning to stick around."

The thought that Alberto had been having sex with Francesca seemed completely disgusting and impossible. It was crazy! Men didn't do that with little kids, especially not with their own. He felt very scared, and angry too. He didn't want to envision Alberto putting his rotten penis in Francesca. And when she was *ten*? If she wasn't so definite about it, he would have been sure she was making it up.

"Francesca! How terrible. But if you leave, what would you do? What about school?"

"School stinks. I'll find something. A pretty girl can always get along. You see it all the time in the movies." She kissed him wetly on his neck, and then licked the inside of his ear, but he was distracted by his fear that she seemed so determined to leave.

He struggled to put into words what he was thinking. "Couldn't you wait a while? I'll do anything to help you. Then you and Roberto could move to some new place, get jobs and be on your own," he implored. She reached down and began to unbutton his Levis.

"Hey, I love my brother, but he's all screwed up. It's going to take him a while before he can get away. Me, I won't wait that long." She moved both hands to his penis, which was erect. "Oh, aren't you big? Wouldn't you like to do it? I'll show you everything. Don't worry, it'll be good, 'specially your first time," she giggled. "Just do what I tell you."

§

Over the next few months Margaret watched the growing animosity between Edward and Ernesto. She told Ernesto that it probably was because Edward needed to rebel. "It's very natural," she had said one night in their room. "In order to become his own man, he's got to do battle against you. You understand that. Don't get upset; it's better he's doing it now." She took off her robe, stood in front of the mirror and patted her belly.

"I suppose you're right," he said. "But it's damn distressing. I want so much for us to be close, but he flashes out. Maybe he's reacting to the baby."

"Have you talked with him about that?" She slid into bed, pulled on the quilted bedcover, and took a book from the side table—*Gentlemen's Agreement*.

"I tried to, but he changed the subject. Something else is bothering him, but I'm not sure what."

A few nights later, Margaret waited intently for Ernesto to come home, moving back and forth from the kitchen to one of the front windows. "What's the matter, Mom? You feeling okay?" Edward had set the table and was studying. He wanted to nail the math exam the next day. "Can I do anything?"

"There's something I have to tell you and Ernesto, but I'll wait until he's home." She saw that he looked scared. "No, nothing like that," she said. "I'm fine."

When Ernesto arrived, he kissed her, greeted Edward, and headed to the kitchen sink. "Ernie," she said, "I'm worried about Francesca.

196

I haven't seen her for three days, so I stopped in at their place. She's run away. Roberto didn't want to tell me at first, but he did when he was sure we weren't being watched." Her voice dropped. "Francesca found out she was pregnant, and she left on a bus to Nogales. Roberto said when he couldn't talk her out of it, he helped her find Alberto's money. I asked him who made her pregnant, but he said he didn't know."

Edward remained motionless. Ernesto wiped his hands with a towel and peered at him. He stood next to the table. "You were seeing her pretty often, weren't you? On the sly, sometimes?"

Edward said nothing. Then: "Yeah, I was. So what? I wasn't the only one." He glanced away as they exchanged looks.

"You don't seem to understand, Edward," Margaret said urgently. "That poor girl's in a lot of trouble. Where is she going to go? Have you thought how she's going to manage?"

Ernesto walked to the window. He stood there for a moment and then whipped around. "Well, were you sleeping with her?" he demanded.

Edward didn't reply. "Look, young man," Ernesto said, his voice rising, "I want a straight answer. Were you or were you not?"

"I don't have to tell you," Edward answered. "It's none of your business. Leave me alone!" He started to move to the front door, but Ernesto grabbed his arm and wheeled him around.

"Hey, you, where the hell do you think you're going? You want to play grownup, then you don't run when what you do comes home to roost. Damn it, Edward, you slept with her. Now be man enough to take responsibility for it. If I wasn't your father, maybe I wouldn't care so much."

Edward glared at him. "You're not my real father, so you can't say that! Why are you blaming me? And what about all that stuff you used to tell me about how the animals 'get together' because they have to?"

197

"All right, you two," Margaret broke in, "you're not accomplishing anything this way. Calm down."

Ernesto and Edward glared at each other. Margaret pulled out a chair and sat down. "It's very delicate and not easy to talk about, but we have to. Edward, you did have sex with her, right? The simple fact is that *she's* the one with the problem." Edward snorted and turned his face away. "All right, no one's accusing you of being evil. Just that you're too young to be sleeping around. You certainly should have talked to your father about protection. And you, cowboy, what *about* the birds and the bees?"

"It may not have been me," Edward said quickly. "I mean, Francesca was having sex with other guys besides me, she told me that. But I wish I could help her, honest I do." He was about to burst out crying.

Ernesto put his arm around him. "Okay, but there's another problem. Did it occur to you that she might have syphillis or gonorrhea? How do you know she didn't sleep with some vet?" Edward's face appeared frozen. "I'm taking you to the doctor tomorrow. But what's worrying me more is what's going to happen to her. She'll probably get an abortion, and I just hope it's not done by some filthy butcher."

"Ernesto, please. Sometimes your need to be realistic is a bit too much. Edward knows what's going on."

"He does now." He lit a Camel. "I'll talk to Alberto and Roberto. If she gets in touch, I want her to know we'll help. Sixteen or fifteen is awfully young. Why is she so loose? Down in Guadalajara, there were girls who were wild, but that's a different world."

"Not that different, *señor,*" Margaret commented dryly.

Edward sat limply in a chair. "Alberto had a lot to do with it. She told me what he did to her. God, I feel terrible. She's had it so bad."

After a few moments of silence, Ernesto asked, "Do you mean *he* had sex with her?" Edward nodded, and told them it had started when she was ten. Ernesto and Margaret looked at him incredulously, and then at each other. "That bastard," Ernesto said.

"If there was something I could do, honest, I'd do anything. I wish I knew where she was. I'd try to take care of her somehow." Edward gazed at both of them, struggling to figure out what he would answer if they asked, "How?"

§

TWENTY-ONE

Margaret was slowly walking down the hall from the hospital bathroom and stopped inside her room. Now that the baby was here, the Potters of Maine could brag to friends that their daughter (referred to by some as "that homely Meg Potter") had provided them with a grandson. The local D.A.R. would be advised, of course, but not that the Potters' son-in-law was Mexican.

Ernesto and Edward celebrated with a huge breakfast of steak and eggs in the dining room of the Copper Queen Hotel. Later, when she and Ernesto were alone in her room, Margaret suggested, "How about naming him 'No-Name Bejarano'? Isn't he gorgeous? So pink, and a head full of black, Mexican hair." She was smiling, but she coughed and looked haggard, her face drawn and her eyes hollowed as if she had a fever.

Ernesto found Edward, and the three of them ambled down the hall to view the baby behind a large picture window. He was held up by a pretty nurse with strawberry hair, blue eyes and a mask clamped over her mouth and nose. When Edward saw her shape under her white nurse's uniform, he had a flash fantasy of how she might appear naked. Ernesto gestured excessively when the nurse waved one of the baby's little hands at them. Stupid, Edward thought.

Watching the baby with them didn't make Edward feel very good either. He didn't think he had expressed it, but in the past month or so he had become more and more annoyed with the increasing focus being afforded to the coming addition. Oh, sure, Margaret had to prepare herself for giving birth (though exactly what was happening to her was sort of a mystery), and naturally they had to fix up a crib and all the stuff the baby would need. But Ernesto, why did he have to fuss so much over Margaret? It seemed every time *he* asked Ernesto to do something or go somewhere, he always had some excuse why he couldn't.

"You've been a wonderful help, Edward," Margaret said one night after dinner.

"Yes, Eddie, you're really a fantastic kid," Ernesto added. "No, actually you're behaving like a real grown-up." If he was all that marvelous, why didn't they respond to him more? Was the new baby going to change everything? No, it would be all right. The baby would require their time, but he would be just as important to them as he always had been. They had told him that, hadn't they?

After Margaret had been home for about a week, visitors arrived late on a Sunday afternoon. The Healeys were among them, and they shook hands with Ernesto, who greeted them politely. As soon as Edward realized they were there, he slipped into his room and watched through the crack behind the door. The Major wore a tan leather vest and his best dress-up boots.

Fucking goat, Edward thought, dressing like a big rancher. He doesn't fool anyone. The stuffed shirt's never been a cowboy! And look at *her*. Like the witch in Hansel and Gretel. Why the hell did *you* have to come? I'm staying put until you leave.

Margaret's parents had flown in from Maine. Her father, Olin, was very easy-going and made himself useful around the house. Margaret's mother was holding the baby. "He reminds me of Olin except he has such dark hair. Oh, my," she said sheepishly as she looked at Ernesto and quickly added, "what have you decided you want to name him, Ernesto?"

He gazed at her and then at Edward. Everyone waited. Finally he said, grinning, "His name will be Miguel Umberto Lenardo Ernesto Bejarano. North of the border, Mike." He rose and walked toward his bedroom. He poked his head out, held a hand to the side of his mouth and said, "That is, provided it's all right with his mother. I'd better make sure or I'm in big trouble."

It was all very nice for *them,* Edward decided. Margaret needed to rest and couldn't completely care for the baby by herself yet. Mrs. Jenkins, who lived with her husband behind their store, came every day to help out. All of a sudden their home had become too crowded, Edward decided. The four of them at meals *plus* the baby. And often visitors like the Potters and others.

Edward began to feel more and more left out. It really stank, just like when Susie was born. He understood that he was jealous, and he knew he had no right to tell Ernesto and Margaret how having their baby made him feel like he had when he was five. What could he do? The answer was nothing, absolutely nothing. What kind of a rat was he, anyway? Just the idea that he might resent the new baby made him feel lousy. Everyone had a right to have children of their own.

But it would be years until "Baby Mike" wouldn't need their help. Well, at least he slept most of the time. But the first little cry and Ernesto was by his crib, as if the whole place was burning down. Didn't he know babies cry a lot? The two of them fussed so damn much. The Potters told him it was because little Michael was their first child, and that's what new parents did. It seemed to amuse them.

"Dad," Edward asked on one occasion when Ernesto was holding the baby after he had finished his bottle, "it's the four of us now, isn't it? I mean, 'the whole family.'"

"Of course it is," Ernesto answered, swinging around to study Edward's face. "But remember that for quite a while this big blob of fat will need us constantly. I mean, look at him, Edward. He's absolutely helpless. He doesn't even know when he's shitting or not. Completely unconscious!"

"Except that someone who loves him is holding him and taking good care of him," Margaret added, coming out from the bedroom. "That will be very important to him when he eventually leaves the nest."

"Meg, get back in bed," Ernesto ordered gently.

"Oh, stop. I'm stronger every day. Besides, my son needs his mother, not some big, burly cowhand with rough hands on his dainty tender skin." Edward listened disapprovingly to their interchange.

"Now, don't give me that look, *Daddy*. I love to see you with him. You're a wonderful father. Sensitive, involved, just perfect. Now let me have him. He hasn't burped enough."

"How do you know, Mom? He did just a couple of minutes ago."

"Mothers know. Besides, his face tells you. It gets all screwed up," she said laughing. "Gas. He makes it by the ton. Now hand him to me, Ernie. Mommy knows how to help her baby monster with his problem. Didn't you feel his bottom? You could have changed him. Smells like he's made a big load." Ernesto handed her the baby. "P.U. I don't love his doodies." She hummed as she put him over her shoulder. "The new washing machine is worth every penny. Eddie, get some fresh diapers for me, would you, please?"

Edward brought a bundle back from the bedroom and held them out. He liked the way they felt and smelled. He tried to imagine how his mother must have changed him when he was that little. "Here, Mom." She nodded and took two. Edward turned to Ernesto. "Want to go riding? I think I spotted a new hawk's nest up the canyon. Want to see it?"

"Not today, kiddo. Have to take Mom and big, fat *Miguelito* to the doc's. Come with us and we'll drown ourselves afterwards in ice cream sundaes."

That didn't sound very exciting. He wished Francesca hadn't left. Fooling around with her always made him feel good afterward, as if he were on top of the world. "Well, I want to go riding. I haven't been all week, and later I have an exam to study for." Maybe they would insist that he join them. They didn't. After they left, he fumed some more. They care about me, he thought, but I'm not *theirs*. That's never going to change.

He knew Ernesto had specifically warned him never to take out any of his rifles. A man's guns are very personal, he'd said. He had given Edward a .22 caliber target rifle as one of his Bar Mitzvah presents, and had instructed him carefully over the years about weapons and safety. They practiced behind the house, up against a hill, where it wasn't dangerous, using tin cans, even a few bottles. Margaret wasn't happy about the idea of guns, but she didn't interfere any more than making it clear she didn't want Ernesto encouraging Edward to hunt. "There are just too many accidents you read about. Some trigger-happy cave man stalking a giant squirrel and shooting his partner. Or some frustrated guy who's been drinking."

"Meg, there's nothing wrong with guns in the right hands," Ernesto always said. "Wouldn't you rather me make sure Edward is well trained? I know what I'm doing, okay? You're wrong about this." Ernesto had taken him through the basics: never carry a cartridge or clip in the gun unless you're actually ready to shoot. Count the number of bullets in a clip or a rifle when you're loading. Never point even an unloaded gun at anyone. If you're leading your horse, keep the rifle in the scabbard so if you trip, you won't have a rifle going off. Stuff like that. And of course how to sight, keeping your left elbow high if you're a "righty," and how to balance yourself.

My .22 can't do much, Edward thought. It's a kid's gun. Ernesto's 30–30 Winchester packs some power. Maybe I'll see a coyote, one of the ones that's been killing the chickens. He won't find out, because I know exactly how he has it put away. And I have extra bullets, he'll never be able to tell.

He carefully removed Ernesto's rifle from the gun closet, tied the leather scabbard to his saddle and saddled his horse. He put the rifle in the scabbard and checked to see if the single bullets were in his pocket. No clip. Safer and smarter. He led his horse out of the small corral. The morning breeze rose up through the canyon; he would have liked someone to share it with, but if he couldn't, he decided, maybe he could have some fun by himself.

As he rode the trail up to the ridge where he could look down into both Carr and Ramsey canyons, he began imagining he was a bounty hunter charged with ridding the area of dangerous animals. That was his job. He'd do it because they hired him. He pulled his wide-brimmed hat a little further down over his forehead—a "tough guy," like in the movies. It was better by himself. Grow up, kid. You want them taking care of you for the rest of your life?

He swung one leg over the horn of the saddle and pulled out a pack of cigarettes. Lucky Strike. Ernesto and Margaret had made him promise he wouldn't smoke until he was at least eighteen. He didn't actually enjoy smoking; it made him cough, and the taste afterwards wasn't great, but he'd get used to it.

He lit a cigarette and let it dangle from his lips. When the trail reached the ridge, he drew in the reins and stopped. He gazed across the canyons and watched the last vestiges of the shadows before they succumbed to the advancing sun. He peered towards Tombstone and thought about what it would have been like living there so many years ago, when your life was limited to how fast you could draw and get off a shot before some other guy "plugged" you. Now *that* was exciting stuff. He pretended he was in a bar. Some outlaw had challenged him. They'd settle it right there, or maybe out on the street. But only one of them would live to tell about it, and that would be him, Ed Slavin, the fastest "gun" in Cochise County.

He rubbed the lit end of the cigarette out against his chaps and exhaled very slowly, the smoke curling up in the still air. Time to do what he came for, keep a sharp eye open for some marauder whose hour had come. He loosened the reins and urged the horse forward, inspecting the terrain and glancing down both sides, watching for signs.

Nothing seemed out of place, no movements or indications. He continued for twenty minutes or so and came to a familiar flat area. Slipping off his horse, he tied it to a branch and leaned his body against a large boulder. He pushed the brim of his hat way over his eyes, daydreaming. Wouldn't it be nice if Francesca was here with him? He'd unroll his tarp and sleeping bag, lay it out under the tree and invite her to have a little "rest" with him. She'd want to, of course, and it wouldn't be long until they became all hot and excited. Edward was just at the point of his fantasy where he'd be taking off her clothes when he heard a small rush of sound behind the boulder. Careful, he said to himself. Slowly, very slowly. No noise. Where's the damn rifle? Damn, in the scabbard. Maybe I can just sneak up quietly.

He crept carefully, retrieved the rifle and made his way the short distance back to the boulder. Good, he still heard it. What the hell was it? He loaded a bullet into the chamber, raised the rifle and walked gingerly toward the place where the noise emanated. Then he saw it—a fat porcupine, waddling near a hole which was obviously the entrance to its home. Damn, it could have been something bigger.

Edward aimed carefully and fired. He was at close range. What looked like a combination of brains and all kinds of other stuff poured out from the other side of the animal's head. Amazingly it continued to walk, jerky and stupid-looking, but it didn't keel over the way it was supposed to. Ridiculous, he thought, I hit it square in the head. Don't want to waste another bullet. How do I kill the damn thing?

He spotted a broken branch and clubbed the animal until it finally stopped moving. He threw the stick away and gazed down on the bloody mess, his stomach churning. The porcupine's mouth was open, its pink tongue lying out against one corner. Its ear was almost ripped off, and steam rose from the wetness; blood and reddened flesh were mixed with pieces of its fur. The needles that had been so uniform were bent or broken, some sticking backward into the carcass that Edward thought for a second was going to move again. He turned his eyes and began to vomit. After a few minutes, he placed stones over the carcass and walked quietly away, looking all around to make sure no one saw him.

Some hunter you are, Slavin, he thought. A lousy porcupine. Stupid, real stupid. You're a real asshole, Slavin. If you can't do better than that, you're nothing. It was supposed to be fun. Some fun! Nothing I try makes me feel better. God, is this the way it's always going to be?

An agonized cry rose up without warning from his depths, a raw, broken, bloody sound that covered him so completely that he dropped to the ground from its weight. He rolled over and over, trying to get away from it, but its strength was overwhelming. At last he lay silent, resigned to its power and control. There was no place to go, no person, no refuge. At that moment he felt that living was unbearable. I'll throw myself over a cliff, he thought, or I'll learn to fly and put the plane into a spin and won't pull out. Slavin, you jerk-off, you wouldn't even do *that* right.

After a period of empty whiteness in which time had no dimension, he opened his eyes. He became conscious of the breeze, which was light with the odor of the dry grasses close to where he lay. "The whole thing stinks!" he yelled. He took the pack of Lucky Strikes and kicked them as far as he could. Normally he'd be careful to pick up anything left on the trail, but now he spat toward the scattered cigarettes. Then he mounted his horse and rode slowly back to the corral, hunched down, hardly aware of anything around him.

"Have a good time?" Ernesto asked him later. Edward tightened the muscles in his jaw but didn't respond. When he was in his room, the word "shit" was said once and then again. He flopped down on his bed.

In that moment, he remembered the terrible howl on the base in Oklahoma. Those invisible sounds. He'd always wondered exactly where they came from, what actually caused them. And that sense of non-existence. Why was it there? Your eyes go blank, held and caught by something weird and supernatural. You can't see the wind, that's the problem. And they'd think you were crazy if you talked about not seeing the wind. Why wasn't it like other phenomena, like electricity, or sound, or even thoughts? It was a funny thing about the wind—how it moved and controlled the sky, bringing storms, and the way it pushed clouds. And made trees dance or shudder. And look what it did to oceans, stirring them into crazy killers.

He tried thinking about Francesca. Christ, anything other than the lousy way he was feeling. His hands found their way to his penis, but even that wasn't going to happen.

§

TWENTY-TWO

Afew days later Edward was hitchhiking home from school, on the highway from Sierra Vista to Hereford: "Hup, two, three, four. Hup, two, three, four." He didn't feel like continuing to count cadence, so he stuck out his thumb for a ride. When he saw Major Healey drive past and slow down, he dropped his hand and turned, started walking, the same as the previous time.

The car stopped and backed up, and Healey rolled down the window. "Hello there, Edward! I want to talk to you a minute." Go to hell, Edward thought. He stared angrily and walked on.

"Wait, will you please?" Major Healey got out of the car, which took Edward by surprise. It seemed almost like an attempt to be equal. "Now look, Edward, it's about time you stopped thinking of me as such a bad guy. Please get in the car a minute. I have a few things to say to you." His tone was friendly and almost beseeching.

"I can hear you just fine from here."

"Suit yourself." Major Healey sighed. "Well, this isn't easy for me. What I wanted to tell you is this: when a man becomes older, he begins to review his life. Maybe he thinks about the things he's done, things that were right. But also the things that weren't. Plus, I suppose, if his wife keeps whispering in his ear, he starts to hear a little better. All I'm trying to say is that I regret certain ... parts." He waited for Edward to respond, but saw a face without expression. "I'd like to put whatever was bad between us in the past."

"I have absolutely nothing to discuss with you, Major Healey. Z-E-R-O." Edward turned away to look toward the Huachucas and at the wisps of cirrus strung out high above them. "Why don't you get lost?" he asked. He closed his hands to keep them from shaking.

"What did you say to me?"

"You heard me," Edward said, backing up. "You're an old man and you'd be better off in an old soldier's home." He spat to one side and kept walking.

Major Healey caught up with him and grabbed him by the shoulder. "No one talks to me that way, young man," he said, almost shouting. "Especially some snot-nosed kid without any manners."

Edward pulled away. "Yeah, well, I just did. Now why don't you stop bothering me and just go fuck off?" The expression was one he'd heard in school, and it seemed to fit exactly.

Healey reached for him, but Edward bobbed to one side. "You're coming to no good, do you hear me? Your parents would be ashamed of you!"

"Well, you should have known better, should have talked my father out of going," Edward said, his voice rising and wavering. "It's your fault! You're the one who lived around here!"

Healey stood like a ramrod, motionless. "You're a little confused, Edward. I am deeply sorry about your parents. But I'm also disturbed by what's happened to you." He moved toward his car but turned back. "It hardly requires an answer, but if you distort things like whose responsibility it was to make the decision to fly that day, then you never learned one of the things I tried so hard to teach you: to understand what the truth is and in this case, the responsibility that goes with it." He spoke calmly, with no trace of the pompous, condescending tone of the past.

Edward stared coldly at him and turned his back, then ran down the road. Major Healey returned quickly to his car and drove off.

Puzzled that he wasn't feeling more satisfied, Edward looked up, as if there he might find some comfort. He noticed a funny-looking cloud, a finger of darkness with smooth, polished edges. What made it stranger was that it had retained its exact position since he had first viewed it several hours before. What permitted it to remain stationary? It was weird and a little scary.

At dinner that night, he was unusually taciturn. "Hey, *amigo*," Ernesto said joshingly, "you look like you had a bad day at the office. I heard you lost a hundred million. But for a big *typhoon* like you that's chicken feed." He waited for a response. Edward glanced up but put his head down again, close to his soup bowl. "What's bothering you, Eddie? We're getting a little concerned."

"Everything's okay. Really." He said it quietly. "I don't want to give you and Mom any trouble."

"Hey, son, you don't. I mean, besides the fact that we love you and you're part of this family, nobody's kid helps out more than you do. Every time I look around, you've done something I hadn't even thought of asking."

"You wouldn't be troubled because of the baby, would you, Edward?" Margaret asked. "It's normal for an older child to be upset when the balance changes, you know." She passed him the potatoes. "I made them crisp, the way you like them," she said. The baby was in his crib next to her, and now he gave a little cry. She got up immediately and picked him up.

"Little Mike doesn't bother me, honest. I know how important he is. I mean, I know having children is great." Edward smiled faintly.

"Sure is," Margaret said, "but we want you to remember that no one will ever replace you. We're a family with two sons." She beamed and looked from Edward to Ernesto. Edward joined in their good feelings, but somewhere he knew there was a difference. Despite their reassurances, the immutable fact was that he was still an orphan. And that would never change.

§

Only sex and flying provided Edward relief, and he found sex confusing and only temporarily satisfying. It seemed so complicated. Jerking off relieved his tensions, but sometimes he didn't feel better afterwards. Much more exciting was going to a particular "house" in Frye with Roberto. He'd only been there twice because it cost ten dollars. Manuela, the girl he had sex with, was alluring; her body was beautifully formed, with small but firm breasts and a rear end that drove him crazy. She knew it, too.

Edward was nervous the first time he was with her and rushed the experience. After "Madame" introduced him to her, he paid the money and they went into a small room, which contained a bed, a dresser, a chair and an ottoman. Manuela was wearing very little. He scrutinized her, with his mouth slightly ajar. She reached for his hand and they embraced, his erection pressing against her. When he didn't make any moves, she brushed her lips against his chest, letting her hands pass to his crotch. Edward moaned and she led him to the bed. He breathed rapidly as she removed her lacy underwear. She lay on her back, her legs apart, and reached her arms up. Edward penetrated into her, and in just a few moments he ejaculated. Too fast, he thought afterward.

This third time, on an afternoon that he and Roberto had decided to cut school, Manuela let him know that it would be much better, more pleasurable, if he could hold off. "Stay over there," she said seductively, "and watch." First he stood watching her, but then he sat down on the edge of the ottoman. Slowly and very provocatively, Manuela undressed, hesitating as she stripped down to her underwear. "Would *you* like to take them off?" she asked in a whisper. Edward nodded immediately. "Yes, I want you to do that. Come." He rose and unhooked her brassiere. As he did, she took one of his hands and placed it over her breast. She put the other between her legs. "You make me all wet." Edward didn't understand what she meant, but he knew from the way she said it she must be feeling sexy, like he was.

She pushed him back on the ottoman, swung her hips across and sat on him, moving against his erection. "Your panties," he gasped, "are still on. And ..." He didn't finish. She licked his nostrils and then moved her tongue into his ear, circling slowly and finally putting it as far in the opening as possible. He shivered. "Oh, oh, oh," he moaned.

She rose and slipped off her panties with one hand and with the other reached down, stoking his penis. "Manuela, oh, I ..."

"Shhh. Try not to move." She went to the other side of the ottoman, behind him, but did not remove her hand from his full erection. She let only the pointed nipples of her breasts move in circles against his back. "You enjoy this, I think." He nodded, and became more and more excited. "Try to wait as long as you are able, I want you to do that," she whispered in his other ear, her tongue again probing there. Now she took both her hands and rubbed his back on both sides of his spine. Edward turned his head and saw her smooth skin in the dampened light. She kissed his mouth tenderly and moved her tongue inside his lips. She came around to the front of him and stood. "Put your fingers here," she ordered gently, directing them between her legs. He smelled the strong odor of sex and felt the viscosity inside her vulva. "Rub this part slowly." He did as she commanded. He would have agreed to do anything she asked. Ernesto had talked to him about prostitutes, but Edward thought Manuela must be as wonderful a sex partner as he'd ever find.

Manuela rocked against his fingers. "Now, you have really made me ready. Now we shall make love." Still standing, she straddled his legs, reached down and guided his penis deep inside her. "Wait, please. I want to feel you big in me as long as possible." But as she began to move in a kind of circle, he could no longer restrain himself. He pulled her against himself, jabbing up, his head thrust back, his moans now becoming small screams. She cradled his head in her bent arm. "Yes, yes. All of it. Let it come. As much as there is." He shook his head involuntarily, his sighs becoming calmer as his thrusts slowed. When he had completely stopped, she rose, one hand over her crotch. "Lie on the bed and rest," she said. "I need to clean up. I have so much of you in me."

When he regained his senses, Edward called to her, "You're good to me, Manuela. You're really fantastic. God, that was great. I wish I could spend the whole day with you."

"You could, *Eduardito*. You have more money?" she asked coyly, her hand on a breast as she moved her hips rhythmically.

"Gee, I don't. I hate to see you in a place like this. You're even younger than me. How old are you?" He sat up on the bed and began to put on his socks.

"This place is okay," she answered, looking into her mirror as she redid her hair and put on new makeup. "It's dreamland here, you know? Where I was in Naco, no, before that, in Hermasillo, *muy malo*. I don't even want to think about that." She turned to him and blew him a kiss. "You are very nice, I thank you for caring a little. Most of the men, boom, all they want is a fuck. That's okay. They pay for me. I don't mind. But someday, yes, I will find someone.

Some good man finds me, then I'm finished with here. You know, get married and have nice babies."

"Yeah. I sure hope you do. Well, I have to go to work—at the airport. I'm learning to fly! My father was an airline captain. He's dead now. I sort of want to be a pilot, maybe fly passengers." He grabbed his jacket. "I might join the Air Force and become a fighter pilot. I'm good." He turned away from her and pulled out his wallet. "Here, Manuela, I want you to have this." He put a five-dollar bill on top of the ten.

"You don't have to do that, but thank you. When you return, I will give you a very special time." She laughed. "I'm not going to tell you. You'll see. Come back soon, yes?" Edward nodded and closed the door behind him.

Roberto was waiting in the living room. "Good thing you came out," he said. "The madame was going to knock on your door, but I asked her to wait. I told her you were always slow." Roberto winked. "My *muchacha* was *fantastica*! *Bueno, hombre,* let's *vamanos.*"

"Hey, don't say anything about this to Ernesto," Edward warned. "I don't know how, but I think he's suspicious." Roberto nodded in agreement. Edward gazed into a high cirrus sky, the freshness of the air sharp on his face. "Same sky as in Mexico, right, Roberto?" He dwelled on what he saw.

"Same for both, my friend. Why? You thinking about something?"

"This place is starting to stink just like the baby's diapers. Know what I mean?" Roberto didn't reply.

§

Toward the end of the following week, Edward met Roberto on the corner of Carr Canyon Road as he was stepping from a car at almost the same moment Roberto was being left off by the school bus. "Didn't make it any faster than you," Edward greeted him. "But at least I didn't have to sit with all you birdbrains."

Roberto began to punch him lightly on the arm, but as he did, Edward grabbed his hand firmly, his face somber. Roberto didn't understand. "Nothing's good for me," Edward said. "I can't stand it anymore, Robby. I'm hightailing it out of here. I figure I'll head south."

"Ah, Eddie, you don't want to leave from here. Nothing better down there. I know you ain't been feeling so good, but how would you like to have to live with the cocksucker I got to? An animal, a goddamn fucking animal. All of the time." Edward shrugged his shoulders. "I mean bad, rotten like the devil himself." Roberto crossed himself. *"Mi madre."*

"It used to be okay with Francesca around," Edward said morosely, "but not anymore. Except for you, you know what I mean." He drew a line in the dirt with his shoe. "You heard from her or anything about her?"

Roberto patted his jacket pocket. "Yeah, today! This letter! She sent it to school. Said she took care of why she had to leave. A nice woman took her in. She left that place with a guy and went to Durango, but it was terrible. Then she went to another town, made money, and got lots of nice clothes and her own place." Edward's attention was absolute. "But it's not good what she does, Eddie. She said I could come one day. She'd have a place. But later. The letter is from Hermasillo, that's where we are from. Oh yeah, she said say nothing to Alberto. Also *abrazos* to you, you shouldn't feel bad about anything, tell you she is okay."

Edward nodded. "I'm glad about that. I'm getting out of here too. I've just got to leave before I go crazy. Hey, when they ask you, just tell them you don't know anything about it. Okay?"

Roberto placed his hand on Edward's arm. "You're real sure?"

"Yeah," Edward said, "I'm going to head up to Chicago first to see my sister Susie. You know, family. Like Francesca for you. I'll come back before I leave for good."

"*Bueno*," Roberto said dejectedly. "But if you go, Eddie, I have no friend left."

"I have to, Robby. I feel so God-awful. No matter what I try, I'm at the bottom of a deep well. I don't even care about feeling good any more—I just want to stop feeling so miserable. Maybe Mexico will do something for me."

§

Ernesto and Margaret always had encouraged Edward to visit Susie, and a week later they drove him to the train station in Tucson. "Here's *dinero* for your trip," Ernesto said, handing him some folded money and the ticket. They embraced. Edward thanked him, kissed Margaret and the baby, and walked through the station doors.

Inside, he went to the reservations window and exchanged the sleeper ticket Ernesto had bought him for a coach seat, pocketing the difference. The old man who sat next to him in the coach car tried to engage him in conversation, but Edward hardly replied. He peered instead out onto the prairie. March would pull spring behind it, he knew, but now it was still held firmly by the heavy hands of winter. The sun was becoming higher and stronger in the annual contest which it always won. But spring was just not in Edward's head. Winter's ingredients, the bunched grasses, browned his world. The time of renewal, once a magic show that he would watch, clapping excitedly because he knew "it" would be coming, all fresh and green and alive, seemed never to have existed. The ugliness of winter was never final, but now there was nothing else he could conceive of. In the flash that memory provides, he saw the grass tufts bent over and seemingly dead, the same way he remembered seeing them years earlier during the train trip with his mother, leaving Fort Sill for yet another Army base. But then at least his father had been waiting for them.

§

"It's great being with you, Eddie," Susie said. "You look so different from last time. I guess I do, too." Edward had grown to six feet and a half an inch, and weighed one hundred and seventy pounds. His hair was thick and black, and quite often his expression was that of interest mixed with caution and a kind of sadness, as if disappointment was never a surprise. By most standards, he was handsome. The red birthmark on his forehead didn't bother him the way it had when he was a boy. His nose wasn't straight—the result of a fall off his horse on a rough trail in the Huachucas—and Margaret and Ernesto had suggested that one day he might want to have plastic surgery performed. But he'd rejected the idea because a girl in his class had said his nose gave him "character."

They were scuffing in the light snow that had fallen in Highland Park, a suburb in northwest Chicago. Edward had arrived at his aunt's home earlier that day. Their greeting made him feel they were glad he had come, but he still felt like an intruder, and that the unit Susie was an integral part of did not include him. In some ways his sister was a stranger. Her smile was just right for a Pepsodent toothpaste ad, he thought. Looking at her, he recognized family features— his mother's expressions, his father's eyes. And he hurt again, remembering.

Edward had looked at the photos Susie had sent him, but he hadn't been able to imagine what she'd really looked like. And would she be spoiled, or somebody he'd like and be proud of? He felt the gnawing of their having grown up separated, and caught himself feeling guilty once or twice, as if it was his fault.

"Yeah." He pulled his collar up to break the rawness of the wind, and reached out to grab her hand. "I've missed you, Sooz. It's been good with Ernesto and Margaret, a helluva lot better than with the Healeys. Only now that the baby's here, they're busy with him all the time." He exhaled and dropped his head slightly.

"A new baby must be very exciting," Susie bubbled. "Is he cute?"

"I remember when you were born," he said. "I was five, and I expected you to get big right away so you'd be able to play with me. Boy, what I didn't know about anything. I've meant to apologize if I was mean and stuff." He managed a small smile. "Mom was so happy with you. Dad, too."

"I can't remember much. You were always running around with your friends. Sometimes I wanted to go with you, but you used to hide on me. I guess it wasn't so bad."

Edward wanted to tell her how important she was to him. "We're the only ones left," he said. "I mean, from our original family." If he was only closer to her, he thought, he might be able to discuss his confusion about women. But probably she wasn't old enough, and wouldn't be able to understand why women didn't make sense to him. They were mysterious, they sure the hell were. Margaret, Francesca, even Mrs. Healey. With men like Ernesto or a friend like Roberto, the Major for sure, you damn well knew what to expect. He would have liked Susie to tell him why it seemed girls always changed their minds, said one thing and did another. He thought Francesca probably would be the best to learn from. She'd been around and knew the ropes. And he knew she was very smart. "You're a good kid," he said to his sister.

"Everyone tells me that. But I'm not a kid, I'm almost thirteen, you know." She put her hand over his. "Please take care of yourself, Edward." They hugged.

"I wish we were all together again," he said. "Their not being here hurts a lot."

Susie squeezed his hand. "I think of them, too. Also, how you couldn't come with us. Aunt Sandra still feels terrible, but she says she didn't have any choice."

Edward glanced sharply at her. "Somehow I would have found room. She should try living with the Healeys. When you're small and your parents have been killed, and you're put with strangers."

"She didn't realize how bad it would be for you. I know she didn't. Besides, that's over." He shook his head, but Susie didn't notice.

§

His Aunt Sandra found an opportunity that afternoon to talk to him. "I didn't want to speak with you while the girls were around," she began. Edward waited. She gazed into his eyes, hoping for some help. "This gives me a chance to tell you how terrible I've felt ever since I learned how the Healeys treated you. I'm so sorry I didn't take you with us." She looked away and waited for his response. Edward thought, what does she want me to say, that it was okay to slug me in the guts?

She continued, "I wish there was something I could do to help."

"There is," he said. "I need some money. I'm going to Mexico." He explained briefly that he had to get away, and didn't want to hurt Ernesto and Margaret by telling them.

She looked concerned. "I read the other day about some American tourists there who stopped for a bite and when they got back to their car, they were robbed and badly beaten, one of them seriously. You've never been in a strange place on your own, have you, Edward?"

His neck tingled, the hairs lifting up, speaking their own special language. Another adult was challenging him. Sure, he was worried. He had tried to think it all through in the last few days: searching deeply about the future, what might happen. But he knew he had to leave. And he hoped to find Francesca.

"I'm pretty experienced. I've been with Ernesto in Naco and Nogales, on the Mexican side. Besides, I speak pretty good Spanish." He turned to her. "Will you help me?"

"Maybe I can," she said. She looked at him. "Yes, I will. But promise me you'll take good care of yourself. Promise you won't do anything foolish." They walked back toward the house together. When they reached the rear door, she turned to him and hugged him warmly.

Edward stayed with them for several days. They went to the art museum, a concert and saw a John Wayne movie. Afterward they ate Chinese food. But his cloud of sadness didn't dissipate, even with the warmth and acceptance they offered. His aunt had left him, he kept thinking. At times, especially at night when it became completely quiet, he alternated between wanting to cry and scream.

He left a day early, telling them that he had to return to help Ernesto with some new cattle. "Here, take this with you," his aunt said. She had given him money earlier, and now she handed him a large bag, tied carefully. "Cheese, bread, dried fruit, a salami. We made these cookies, too—rugulahs and schnekens. Your grandmother taught me. This way you'll carry a little Jewishness with you. As she used to say, 'It can't hurt.'"

"Write and call me, Eddie, please" was the last thing Susie said as he boarded the train. He nodded and told her he would.

§

223

TWENTY-THREE

Edward knew little about the process of creating himself. He was not equipped to deal with the truth, and was unable to tell his story properly to anyone, least of all to himself. The unresolved fears and loneliness he had suffered had been like a march to the place in which he now found himself, where to remain seemed like a continued reminder of being perpetually lost in the desert. Every direction seemed deadly. Mexico, a new and different world, had to be better than Hereford. There, he hoped, he could involve himself with new things and not have to look back at what he considered the wreckage of his life. Besides, he might find Francesca.

Back on Ramsey Canyon Road, he carefully concealed any indication of his plan to slip away, as well as the extent of his emotional state. Engrossed in *Miguelito,* Ernesto and Margaret didn't detect the code that was subtly displayed on his face. In one more day, he would gather his painstakenly assembled cache of provisions, grab his rucksack and begin his journey in the battered old Plymouth coupe

Ernesto had helped him buy. If he had thought it through more thoroughly, he would have realized his cherished auto would probably not be able to stand a trip of that dimension.

"Your brother's eating as much as you do, " Margaret said at dinner that night. The baby looked happy—he was plump and the color of cherry blossoms.

"What's the deal with you, *hombre?*" Ernesto asked sloppily through a mouthful of food. "Your grades are nothing to write home about. Too late to bring them up this year. For Christ's sake, do a little more concentrating in the fall, will you? College is only a year away." He pointed a finger at Edward. "Pass the spuds, please."

There isn't going to be any school in the fall, Edward thought. Not this year.

He fell asleep that night in the semi-peace of emotional exhaustion but startled awake in the chill of midnight air that had gathered into his room. In his dream he had been lost in the mountains, the Dragoons or the Huachucas, and did not believe he would survive. He found the images terrifying: alone, having only himself to rely upon, not sensing the monstrous, great black widow spider that bit him. He was helpless, dying an ugly, painful death.

§

The next afternoon after school, Edward went to work as usual at the airport next to Fort Huachuca. His boss there was Richard Banks, a flying instructor and the majority owner of a small trunk airline that he'd started in order to take advantage of the growing number of military and civilian personnel who traveled to and from Tucson and Phoenix.

Banks always wore his old Air Force twill pants, highly shined shoes and a flight jacket, except when he donned a captain's uniform for his recently commenced commercial operations. He was tall and

226

lanky and moved with the grace of the male lead in a ballet. To tell him that would have incurred a smack in the mouth, if it was said in a bar, or a charming smile, if it was whispered in bed by a recent conquest. His only apparent blemish was a scar on his forehead, partially hidden by a curl he encouraged to slide down over it. Banks seemed very sure of himself, and Edward was pleased that he usually paid him a great deal of attention.

"You make me look bad every time my partner sees how hard you're working," he said to Edward late that last afternoon. "I tell him you're trying to be a hotshot like me. But the war didn't get you and deflower your youth and beauty." He tipped Edward's cowboy hat forward from the back so that it covered his eyes, the way Ernesto used to do.

"Kid, let me tell you something," he said as if he was confiding a great secret. "I knew guys like you who didn't know the difference between sleeping with women and marrying them. I thought I did, but as you can see, I ended up like all the rest. I had quite a few broads in England, even a couple at the same time. The uniform got 'em every time."

Edward surveyed Banks and his grin. "The guys told me not to believe anything you say. Next you'll tell me how you charmed the Nazis into letting you date their women after you were shot down. Someday I hope to meet a terrific girl, and we'll both know it right away." He shifted his weight to his other leg.

"You've got some romantic imagination, kid," Banks responded. "As far as you ever getting married," he said, "it sounds as if I gotta teach you about women as much as teach you how to fly. Unless, of course, you'd be content with a steer. Hey, that'd be okay for you." He ran out of range of a small stone Edward threw at him. Edward liked Richard Banks; though he fooled around a lot, Edward felt his genuine interest. He would miss the persiflage as well as the good feelings he experienced while flying with him.

The sun that late afternoon painted the plains the colors it had saved for the occasion, shadows from the mountains growing in a jagged fashion and lengthening awkwardly on the prairie. It quickly became cool in the shade.

Edward spent a long time that day watching the light fade. At home later, he told Ernesto and Margaret he was tired and kissed them good-night. At his desk, he carefully composed a letter. He didn't want them to worry, he wrote, because he knew how to take care of himself. He read what he had written and added a P.S. "I know you really care about me. It's not your doing that I'm such a mess. Don't worry, I'll be all right." He signed it "Love, Edward."

§

A couple of hours later he quietly filled his rucksack with shirts, socks, pants, underwear, a windbreaker, two canteens, a pair of sneakers, an aluminum Boy Scout combination plate and soup dish, a knife, fork and spoon and some other gear. He would have liked to bring along Ernesto's .38 pistol, to have just in case. He loaded the gear into the car without any noise, together with a five-gallon can filled with fresh water.

The motor had been overheating recently as if fevered with a respiratory virus. He kicked the tire, then a second time. He and Roberto had removed the thermostats, but it still overheated. They had also plugged the leaks in the radiator, but the water hoses were so worn that they were like old horses, hanging on because they'd been drafted to continue enduring the hard chores of ranch work.

He had parked the car where it would be almost impossible for Margaret and Ernesto to hear when he pushed it down the incline of the driveway. He started it up on Ramsey Canyon Road, turning south on Route 92 for the crossing into Naco. Begin in Naco, he thought. Catan's Cantina's on the way. Then Cananea. Ernesto always talked about it. "One hot Mexican *tamale* I used to go with. *Fantastico*." He'd stop there too. He'd have to pass through Magdelena even if he went down by way of Nogales. Then Hermosillo, and Francesca, he hoped.

To reach Naco he decided to drive through Hereford and not Palominas, a small settlement inhabited by crazy "Fundamentalists," as Margaret called them. The San Pedro was particularly pretty where it crossed through Hereford. It was here, along its banks, that Ernesto had first taught him about animals. And there was the small grove of cottonwoods the three of them used to picnic in, the same spot where he'd liked to park and make out with Francesca.

He eased the car down the dirt road and parked among the trees. Some ground doves scurried, their colors so deceptive he didn't spot them until they bounded into flight. He took off his boots and sat on a rock, dangling his feet in the gently flowing water. The sky was spotless except for the high flashes of cirrus that took the form of a half arrow, with a sweep of long line for the shaft and another for half the head.

Everyone said seventeen was a great age, but how could it be when life seemed so terrible? His ideas of being somebody important were fading like smoke. Now Edward thought he would be lucky even to finish high school and be able to make ends meet afterwards — probably become a cow-puncher, just like all the other slobs, he mused.

He gazed about: two rabbits jumped out from sagebrush, young ones, chasing each other. He washed his face in the stream, then leaned over and drank. Though he'd decided the year of his Bar Mitzvah, when he'd learned all about his religion, that he wouldn't pray unless it was very important, he did it now. "Help me, God. I won't ask You to make things great. Just so I don't feel I can't do anything. I promise to go to temple on the High Holy Days." He realized that the pact he was making would be difficult to fulfill, but it was too late. He was not going to renege. He would keep his end of the bargain if God kept His. There were Jews in Mexico, he knew, and a city like Hermosillo had to have at least one synagogue, didn't it?

He pressed the starter; the car reacted as he'd hoped, and he drove it up the bank onto the road. But when he depressed the accelerator to cross the bridge to Hereford, an ugly noise belched out from under the hood, a wet bleat, apparently the serious affliction from which it had never recovered. The car jerked as if it was attempting to break out of shackles. He put the gear in neutral and rolled to a stop. Opening the hood, he saw that several hoses were torn. Oil oozed from the top of the cylinders. "Damn," he exclaimed. "Now the rings too!" He slammed the hood and sat down on the running board. "Sonufabitch!" Okay, take it easy, he thought. Walk back to "Nicksville," Nick Gregovitch's place. He'll help me.

He decided to carry his essential gear, but because there was too much of it, he consolidated it into the rucksack, leaving the saddle bags and some of the food he'd brought in the car. It took more than two hours to walk back to "Nicksville," which was nothing more than Nick Gregovitch's spread: his combination house, store, bar, and gas station.

One could always get a cold beer from Nick's refrigerator, and thirsty cow men gravitated there at the end of a long, hot day. A pool table had been installed and hours were wiled away there, to the consternation and complaints of wives and girlfriends. Nick had put up a bulletin board so that used cars and trucks could be sold or traded, and it carried communications of all kinds: everything from windmill repair services to available puppies and kittens. He also owned an Ercoupe, a low-winged, two-seater airplane which he kept in the back and used to deliver chain saws and other goods to distant miners and ranchers. Taking his customers for a ride over their land and mines contributed substantially to the business they gave him, he found. Nick's customary drinking made him look a little grisly most of the time, and sometimes he became hostile and aggressive. He knew enough to drink less before he used the plane.

When Edward entered, he was sitting at a table with two other men, a bottle of Seagrams in the center. "Well, what the hell do *you* want?" he asked, his voice slurred and a little belligerant.

"I'm Ed Slavin, Mister Gregovitch. You know me, Ernesto's son, from Ramsey Canyon. On my way to Naco. My car gave out. Right on the bridge before Hereford. The hoses are shot. I think the rings are too. I was wondering—"

"Yeah, I know you. Look, I'm no fucking nursemaid. You got a father, haven't you? Get *him* to help you." Edward retreated, surprised.

"But Mister Gregovitch, my car broke down and I'm stuck."

"I *used* to be his friend until he stiffed me. Got along real good. Long talks and all that shit. Even had him up in my plane a couple of times. Ran up a bill, then he doesn't pay. That shit doesn't go around here. So just take your ass and get the hell out of my place. I ain't doing a goddamn thing for you."

It didn't sound like Ernesto, but Edward knew better than to question Nick. "I have to get my car fixed," he said instead. "It's gotta be pushed or towed to your shop. I'll pay you. Please, Mister Gregovitch," he pleaded.

Nick leaned back in his chair and shakily poured himself a Seagrams. Slugging it down, he stood up and pointed at Edward. "You don't seem to hear so good. Goddamn it, out!" he bellowed. "Fool me once, but that's it!" He made a sweeping motion with his hand. Edward went out, letting the screen door slam behind him. He picked up his pack and walked a short distance away.

Now what, he thought. Go back home? I've already left.

He gazed over the brown plains which swept down from about thirty miles to the north, and past the border five miles to the south.

Finally he scanned the horizon, outlined by the distant mountain ranges. Besides the Huachucas behind him and the Mule Mountains to the east, single humps rose several thousand feet over the enormous prairie, their heights varying, in colors of purple and brown. He took them in, thinking about how simple it was for inanimate objects.

Gotta hitchhike, he thought. Maybe it's better if the Mexicans don't think I'm some rich Gringo kid with a car. I'll tell them my father's Mexican. Put some money in one boot, some more folded inside my hat band, in my canteen cover, a little in my wallet. He remembered Ernesto's always warning him about where he bedded down, and not to venture opinions or say very much. Be respectful and friendly. He'd sleep in the car tonight, he decided, and then start tomorrow early.

§

The next morning in Naco, he walked into Emilio Catan's cantina. Catan was short and very round, his shirt straining the buttons. He was dark-complexioned, with a thick handle-bar mustache, and he smiled frequently as he talked. After they had greeted one another, he said in English, "How is my friend Ernesto? I have not seen him in weeks. How come you're here? Down with anyone?" Edward told him he was on a little vacation and wanted to see some of Mexico on his own.

Catan opened a Pepsi and handed it to him. "Ah, becoming a man. I know."

Edward nodded and looked down at the floor. "Si, *Señor* Catan."

"Here, have something to eat. Then you will go." Catan stepped behind the counter, and soon they were feasting on tacos and enchilados. When Edward tried to pay, Catan refused. *"No, no, por favor. Tienes bastante dinero?"* Edward nodded. *"Adios, Eduardito,* have

232

good luck." They embraced, and Edward stepped onto the dirt street. Catan followed him. "*Momentito. Créo que mi amigo va a Cananea esta tarde.* You can ride with him. Take care of yourself."

Edward sat in the back of Catan's friend's truck with two dogs. The driver was transporting small machinery parts from the train yard in Naco to the mines outside Cananea. The war's end had reduced mining activity, but the increased demand for farm produce and beef had created other jobs. Mexicans who had worked in the factories in Douglas and Agua Prieta needed to find other work now that U.S. servicemen had returned to reclaim their jobs.

The prairie to the south was the same as in Arizona, Edward saw. Mesquite trees studded the hills, and the grasses were colored tan and cream, with darker tans and browns mixed in. Some of the weeds were thin, in shades of green. White and yellow wildflowers played among them, but the land was parched. Edward remembered learning from Ernesto about the ocotillo, the spidery bush that grows both leaves and prickly needles of the cactus. "You must know which cactus you can get water from," Ernesto had said.

He thought about Francesca, wanting to see her but at the same time apprehensive about it. After all, she was a prostitute, tarnished and stained, like Manuela. Margaret had told him women often carried venereal diseases, that it was a tragedy for them to have to sell themselves. Ernesto's point of view was different: women became prostitutes for a variety of reasons. Many who did were good people, generous, decent, intelligent, sometimes far better than certain "respectable" wives and girlfriends, who controlled their men through sex. He told Edward not to judge a person quickly, because one never knew about their pasts and what they had had to do to survive.

Now he was in the desert, and the hum of the tires sounded like music. Margaret had taught him, with records played on the victrola—Beethoven, Brahms, sometimes Gershwin—listen carefully Edward! *Hear* the music, their genius, touching something we can't relate in words, not exactly, but filling us in a special way. Listen hard, Edward, be patient.

Sleep drifted in. Edward dreamed he was on Nellie, going up to the top of Miller Peak. Then Nellie disappeared, and he was on foot and very thirsty. No water anywhere. Someone was with him, he wasn't sure who, some adult who was in charge. And whoever it was talked about where the water was, but Edward couldn't hear the rest because different sounds kept intervening. Suddenly the other person was gone and so were the sounds, and he walked on the trail higher and higher, the sun brighter, hotter. He almost couldn't see where he was going until he came to the edge of the cliffs that looked down over the valley. He wasn't thirsty any longer and he could almost see forever, into New Mexico as he had that time from the top of Biscuit Mountain. He looked around, and then the adult reappeared, but his hat was large and a shadow covered his face. Was it his original father? It was so strange not to be able to tell. Maybe it was Ernesto. The man nodded his head up and down.

Then, all of a sudden, Edward was flying, but not in a plane. His arms were wings, his fingers feathers that pulled him through silken air. It was wonderful, flying loops and rolls, sitting on clouds momentarily until he slipped through the cotton fluff and soared in wide figure-eight sweeps over the plains. He was free and unafraid. Down below, the Healeys and Ernesto and Margaret clapped and cheered. Behind them, not quite in the full light, were his Slavin parents. They were smiling and their arms were wide open. His father gave him the thumbs-up sign.

He woke from the lurching of the truck as it came to a stop at a small lake a few miles northeast of Cananea. This was as far as his ride could take him. The lake was fed by the San Pedro, their river, the old river from the north draining the huge valley between the Mules and Huachucas. It was no larger than a stream, but it moved through rocks and stones and almost never ran dry, water coursing through the surface, coming down from the mountains in the north. The San Pedro flowed into this lake, and then into another a few miles the other side of Cananea; it began again, united with other streams and became the Rio Sonora, winding its way through the desert to Lake Presa Abelardo Rodriquez at Hermosillo; then it was channeled for irrigation before finally dissipating into the swamp areas along the Gulf of California.

At one point, Edward knew, this road, Route 2, converged with the railroad. Maybe, he thought, I'll wait for a train to slow down and climb into a freight car.

The truck's driver stepped out, yawned, stretched, and yelled for his barking dogs. They bounded into the water, looking like porpoises until their legs no longer touched the bottom. He leaned over and removed his *sombrero*, his face submerged for a moment. *"El agua es bueño"* he said, then stood and urinated near the edge. The dogs were called, and shook themselves off too close to him before he shooed them away. Edward jumped down from the rear of the truck and pumped the driver's hand. Saying *"adios"* to him, the driver climbed into his truck and turned onto a small dirt road toward the mountains.

When he reached Cananea, he saw abandoned railroad cars being inhabited by squatters and railroad workers, their white wash hung from the windows. They waved at him. Nearby was a small grocery store, *"Abarrotes"* on the sign. A few people sat in chairs near the door, talking and viewing the activity. It was late afternoon.

He walked to the edge of town. Five men huddled around their truck, heads under the hood as if they were doctors attending a dying patient. Smoke in the form of water vapor billowed from the radiator, rising as their voices merged with the invisible frustration that filtered into the emptiness of the sky. It seemed to Edward they were more concerned with who was right than with the motor's repair. He waited, and then offered his opinion that if they removed the thermostats from the water hoses it might prevent the engine from overheating. At first they looked at him suspiciously, but then one of the men gingerly unfastened the steaming hoses, waiting until he could remove two small metal coils from inside. Edward handed them his large canteen, but they refused.

When water had been poured into the radiator and the motor returned to a happier state, he asked one of the men if they'd give him a ride. As far as Cocospera, they responded, that's where they lived. The forty-kilometer drive was made under a canopy of ashen sky. He peered into the desert. The saguaro cacti seemed like the gray-green skeletons of medieval chessmen, their eerie arms holed by birds. Edward noticed a flicker above its needle-protected nest.

Mesmerized by the unlimited expanse of the desert and the towering presence of the mountains, he thought: you know everything that happens out here. What the hell's going to happen to me? What do I do? Please. You know why a man travels, you notice exactly how he walks and moves. Tell me, desert, mountains, even though I have nothing to give you in return. He surmised that they had more important things to do, these mountains that crouched on top of the desert floor, their faces sharpened, peering into the sky, watching and waiting for the wind or the rain, animals and people.

Cocospera turned out to be a tiny village with a single gas station, a cantina, a store, several houses, and a dilapidated part-time auto repair shop. He walked to the end of town, where the road split, going left to Magdalena, and right to Nogales. It grew dark; shadows advanced and spilled into the mountains, making them three-dimensional again. Edward selected a spot to camp, next to a small stream. He shivered at the prospect of having to camp alone, even though he knew he would have to get used to it. He built a fire and placed a can of beans over it, chewing on slices of his aunt's salami and bread while he waited. Later he laid his bedroll under a large oak and slept in ragged spurts. Again and again, distant coyotes jarred him awake with their howls, but he reassured himself that they weren't after him.

The next morning he decided to swing by Nogales rather than travel directly to Magdalena. After he walked for an hour on the unpaved road, a truck picked him up. It took him only as far as where the rail line crossed the road; then he trudged a grueling three more hours to the edge of the city. He was tired and hungry, and he ate at a small restaurant for sixty cents American. Then he drifted into a bar and downed a beer. It was a Friday, and the *vaqueros*— cowboys—had come in; their laughter mixed with the smell of the beer, and mariachi music wove through the cream and gray smoke. The next cantina was on Obregon, as seedy as the first one, but the bartender, Jorge, was pleasant and told Edward he knew Ernesto Bejarano because years ago he, too, had been a *vaquero,* and their girlfriends were sisters.

Edward told him about Ernesto, Margaret and little Miguel. That night Edward slept in Jorge's room. In the morning, he bid him *"Adios, muchacho,"* and invited him to stop there on his way back. The easy invitation crystallized thoughts that Edward had not been willing to formulate: that eventually he would probably want to return to Hereford. But not until he was ready, he told himself. He shook hands with Jorge and stepped out into the sun of a crisp morning. It didn't help him feel warmer inside.

He walked several blocks toward Al Central. A couple, obviously American, asked him if he could recommend a store to buy silver and leather. A little boy was with them, his moppy dark hair almost covering both eyes. He reminded Edward of the way he looked in a picture his parents had taken of him shortly before they were killed. The little boy grimaced, his toy guns in their holsters hanging from a white gun belt, a cowboy hat set too far back on his head. His high-heeled boots were also white, their sides intricately crafted.

Edward bent over and placed his face close to the little boy's.
"You're some cowboy, all right. I'd be afraid of how tough you look.
I'll bet you're pretty good with those guns."

"I shoot bad guys. And some of my friends, when we play." He
peered up at Edward. "This is my Daddy," he said, reaching for his
father's hand. "It's his birthday." Edward nodded. He crossed the
street to the park and sat down on a bench. Women carried or
dragged their babies along the walks, their bundles and other possessions toted by their older children. He stared at the small fountain
and the water spilling over into the circular basin. Several small birds
sat on the edge. Some drank, and one stood inside, splattering water
with its wings.

What the hell *am* I doing here? he thought. Maybe I should turn
around and go home. His thoughts went to the little boy, and then
to how Ernesto had been there for him during those lousy years with
the Healeys. He remembered how Ernesto had helped him when he
was so confused, afraid and despondent. He'd been only a child then,
but now the problems that confronted him loomed larger than any
he had ever faced before. He seemed to have lost whatever confidence
he'd ever had about his capability to deal with them. Whatever it had
been that permitted him to feel good about himself was gone. Even
his feelings of love seemed to have vanished. He was a real rat-
bastard, all right. Ernesto and Margaret were better off without him.
And so was Francesca, probably.

He sighed deeply, unconscious of everything until the sounds of
passing sparrows crossed his senses, like the good feel of cold water
on his face in the mornings. Then he rose and walked back to the
commercial section of Nogales. He bought matches, batteries, beans,
sweet bread, tortillas, canned spam and sardines. Then he turned
south on Route 15 where it sliced through the city. Near the outskirts
of Nogales, the houses thinned like hummocks on a flattening plain.
The chill from the barren hills settled in like cold, hard reality. A

truck stopped, and he climbed into the cab. Speaking rapidly, the driver immediately started discussing the coming presidential elections. Edward didn't understand most of what he said, and soon he drifted off into a sleep where he would have to confront no one, most of all himself.

§

TWENTY-FOUR

Three more rides brought Edward to the edge of Magdalena. He hesitated, standing on the heights above the town, peering down at the main thoroughfare. To the right were some mission buildings and a large church, its rounded top sitting like a half globe with a huge cross on the top, the golden surface reflecting the bold afternoon sun.

If Francesca's here, he asked himself, what happens if I find her? What will I say to her? Maybe she's changed and won't have any interest in me. Maybe she's got all she can do to take care of herself. He kicked a stone and ambled down the road, dragging his feet in the dust.

Magdalena was a prosperous small city, the center for ranching in this part of Sonora. The waters of the Rio Magdalena flowed fully, generous enough for crops and cattle. On Sundays the *peons* came into town to visit the mission founded by Father Kino in 1711 and the church built later by the Franciscans. Some *peons* swam and bathed in the river, carrying their screaming and giggling babies. A

241

rusting suspension bridge hung over the water, from which one could observe the activity below and also watch drivers test themselves in their pickup trucks as they attempted to cross—a contest of sorts, with the men trying to demonstrate they had what it took, wanting to succeed in front of their families, friends and even unknown spectators like Edward.

In the plaza next to the church, the stores in the arcades sold handicrafts, ice cream, and sodas. Edward was thirsty. He walked down to the river, removed his denim jacket and shirt and patted water on his chest and shoulders. The water was brown from its run-off through the Sonoran soil. He scooped it up with his hands and splashed it on his face, bubbling into it as he did.

It was time to look for Francesca. He figured that "those women" probably hung out in the section of town where several cantinas congregated like cousins gathering for a party. Edward entered what seemed the most active one and was about to inquire about Francesca when he actually saw her on a bar stool not far away. She saw him at the same moment, and he felt her gauging him. She beamed as she made her way toward him. Oh Lord, he thought, she is so gorgeous. How can she look so good after being a whore?

Francesca said nothing, but placed her arms around his neck. "*Qué pasa, Eduardo?*" she whispered. Her embrace was firm, and her body pressed tightly against his. He felt all her femininity, as well as a poignant softness and affection that made him want to stay in her arms. Only when he became aware of others watching and felt uncomfortable did he reluctantly pull away.

"My God, look at you, Edward. No longer *el chico*." She smiled. "I'm so very glad to see you, but I am not surprised you have come here. Sooner or later I knew you would." She took his hand and pulled him to a quiet table in one of the corners. "Stay. I'll be right back." She returned with a beer for him and some kind of drink for herself.

242

"Well," she said. "Say something." She threw back her head, her raven hair sweeping across her face. He was intensely aware of her perfume.

"Francesca, you're—you're more beautiful than anybody," he blurted out. "It hasn't been so good for me, but *you* sure look like things are okay."

She examined his face, smiling. "Listen, *amigo,* for me, whatever's down here is a helluva lot better than with that bastard, Alberto. How I ever let that so-called father of mine do what he did to me all those years!" She drank from her glass. "But even though I was so young when it began, Edward, he controlled my body, but he couldn't control my mind. *'Remember who you are, remember who you are.'* When it was the worst I said that to myself. It helped."

Her smile was gone. "I'd like to kill him!" Silence, and then she said very deliberately, "One day, I think I will."

They left the bar and walked through the square that surrounded the San Ignacio church. Edward was keenly aware of being next to her, and his strong physical excitement was mixed with longing to be close in some other way, too. It was unlike anything he had ever felt.

Francesca was explaining something to him. "This is his mausoleum, here in this small place, just the same now as it was more than two hundred years ago, when he was buried. Father Kino. He was the missionary, he explored this whole place. Arizona too," she said. She held Edward's hand.

She brought him along Callé Cinco de Mayo, chatting about the people of the town and their acceptance of her. Though she talked lightly, he realized that her words contained a real measure of maturity. "I know how terrible it is in your mind I'm a whore, Edward" she said, "and my being only seventeen. Well, I was when I first came—that is, after I recovered from the abortion. But only for a few weeks. Then this man saw me and I went with him. What he had in

243

mind was," she laughed, "you know, he didn't want me to be with anyone else. He's from Monterrey and has homes in Guadalajara and Mexico City." Edward's eyebrows rose. "You're so innocent," she said, brushing her fingers across his lips. "He comes here only every three or four weeks for a few days. Business. He says his wife isn't nice. He's pretty old, forty-six. But he likes me very much, he's gotten me this place. You'll see, we'll be there in a few minutes." Edward said nothing.

They stepped into an *abarotte*, and she bought some coffee, bread, sweet rolls and a few other provisions. When he was silent, she said sternly, "Edward, you're judging me, what I am. I don't like that."

"I'm sorry, Francesca. It's just that I always thought you and Roberto would get away from Alberto when you got older, find new lives in Tucson or maybe California. Mom said you were smart. She said you could go on to college."

"*Pobrecito,* you're so romantic. Let me remind you of a few things. You received my letter?"

"No," he said, petulantly.

"You must have! I wrote you." Edward said nothing. He was feeling rejected and angry.

"Listen," she continued, "you grow up the way I did, you never think you can have what other people do. You only know the horrible way you must live. You simply want enough food and a decent place without someone forcing you to do terrible things." Her face became contorted. "Then you grow up a little. When you are a young girl, you think about a decent man to take care of you one day. In my case, because of *him,* you believe that sex is, well, rotten and horrible. I have had many confusing feelings." She paused. "Don't be a goddamn judge, Edward. You have not been so perfect either. Besides, your life's been much easier than mine."

"Francesca," he said, "please don't think of me that way. I'm not judging you. I don't know what to think, only that I'm like you, that you and I are just the same."

"No," she said firmly. "We are not the same."

He looked away restlessly.

"Okay," she laughed. Then she poked him. "We are both orphans with bad stories. In that way we are alike."

When they arrived at her small, bleached-adobe building, Edward heard two people shouting at each other from inside the ground-floor apartment. Francesca opened a door that led up two flights to her flat. She said, "I am very happy to have this life. You have to understand how much better it is now for me. This man treats me well and gives me money which I save. He knows one day I will leave. Or maybe he will tire of me. *Quien sabe?*" She placed the groceries on a small table in the kitchen.

"He was here a few days ago and he will not return until next month," she said. She put some water to boil on the stove. "You, Edward, need a bath. We even have a shower in the tub!" She kissed him on the cheek. "I am so glad to see you, *Eduardito!* Why such a sad face?"

"I can't seem to feel good about anything, Francesca. I don't know what's the matter with me. Everything's so rotten. I thought if I got away from Hereford then maybe I'd find something, work it all out." He slumped over. "Ernesto and Margaret, I didn't tell them I was leaving. I told you about the baby, didn't I?" He gazed imploringly at her.

Francesca pushed her rear end against him as she sat on the edge of his chair. "I am sorry for you about that." She kissed him tenderly on the cheek. "Maybe later you will talk to me about the things that bother you. You know, sometimes when you let yourself feel and talk, it comes out, what it is that troubles you."

She moved to the sink and filled the coffee pot with water. "You are feeling sorry for yourself and that, that never will help you." She observed the expression on his face. "Look, *Eduardito,* I am not your friend unless I tell you the truth," she said in the manner of a mother. "I think you feel sorry for yourself because of your parents, the plane crash. It was for me something like that, my not having a mother or father I needed so much. What was I supposed to do, carry the cross for all my life? *Mi madre,*" she said in a whisper. "Jesus, I believe He wants me to be happy now. Yes, I know He does not like me doing what I do, but when I had nothing, not even myself, He forgives me. Later, maybe soon, I will change my life again."

Francesca laid her fingers softly around the back of Edward's neck. He gazed up into her face. What she said made sense, but he couldn't believe he had the strength to come to the same conclusions she had, to have direction. And he didn't feel he was capable of changing.

"Stay and rest here for a day or so. That will make you feel better. I promise to make sure you will," she said. "Now, go wash off the dust you have brought. I'll finish making the coffee."

The apartment was on the top floor of a three-story walk-up. As he undressed in the bedroom, he looked down across the street at a small factory and a row of one-story buildings. He turned to examine Francesca's bedroom. White lace curtains covered the sides of the windows, and a large sombrero and serape hung on one of the walls together with several pictures of Mexican peasants weaving, fishing and farming. A cut-glass decanter with delicate wine glasses was on a tray on top of the dresser. An opening that served as a closet was faced with a multi-colored cloth. Lamps were set on either side of the double bed. A fan hung from the ceiling in the center. There were flowers in a vase on the top of an old table, and a radio.

Edward stepped into the tub and adjusted the shower hose. The warm water soothed him. He found himself wishing that Francesca were his for keeps. He began to hum and didn't hear her come in.

"Francesca! I'm taking a shower."

"Really. I thought you were making *tortillas,*" she laughed. "Now, how are you going to clean your back? Ah, that's for me to do. Besides, I can see you are helpless when it comes to some things." She pulled the curtain to one side. Edward brought his hands down to cover his genitals.

"Oh, stop that! Turn around, I'll do your back." He obeyed. She washed his shoulders, using both hands in a strong, circular motion. "Just a minute, there's a better way to do this." She slipped her dress over her head, and placing it on the toilet cover, kicked off her shoes. Without removing her brassiere and panties, she stepped inside with him. Then she stood, pressed against him from the rear. He lowered his arms in submission, feeling her breasts flatten against his back, enjoying the outline of her legs on his. She reached around and washed his chest and stomach, then moved her hand down among his genitals.

"Francesca—"

"Edward, your thing has become very big," she said with a laugh. "Don't you want to do me too? Why should you be the only one?" She turned him around, put her arms around his neck and pulled him closer. He almost fell over, but caught himself in time.

"Sure, yes, I will," he stammered. "But you're wearing under-wear."

"My goodness," she teased, "then it will have to come off, won't it?" Francesca took his hands and placed them behind her back on the hook of her brassiere. "That's right, now the bottom." He followed her instructions and slid his hands down her legs. She turned the shower head on them both, smoothing his skin until the soap ran off. They faced each other, his gaze on her breasts, then tracing the flatness of her stomach as it ended in the gracious curves of her hips and the dark wet nest where her legs joined.

She heard his excited breathing and whispered, "Yes, yes, whatever you want." He placed his hand on her breasts, their nipples firm and pointing. His fingers spread as he moved his palms over them. She wrapped her thighs over his penis. His excitement was so great that he ejaculated almost immediately.

Edward throbbed, the well of his sperm very deep, its fullness apparent in the duration of his orgasm. "I'm sorry, Francesca," he gasped. "I didn't mean that to happen so soon."

She patted his face, kissing him tenderly through the shower spray. "It is never a bad thing, *mi amor*. You are hungry. I will teach you how to hold yourself back when you want to. It is even better when you do." He remembered Manuela.

"And it's more than the sex, isn't it, *mi precioso*? You have not had much affection, have you, enough touching of your heart? I will give you some. You do not have enough loving and caring." Edward almost cried. He didn't remember when he had ever felt so good and filled and expansive. It was like being thrown a life preserver. Francesca dried them both with a towel and moved to the bed. They lay next to each other, with Edward absorbing her warmth and smells until her softness aroused him again. He turned and kissed her, deeply, penetratingly, his tongue searching the inside of her mouth. Francesca rolled over on top of him, straddling him and placing her vagina over his erect penis. Then she lifted up and sat on him, placing her fingers over his penis and sliding it inside her, controlling the action. He sighed deeply and closed his eyes.

Afterwards, she brought in the coffee and rolls, and they quickly showered again. When they were dry, she led him back to the bed and drew the sheet over them both.

"You're the most wonderful person I have ever known, Francesca. Not just because we made love. You're kind, and you really know me." She placed her second finger lightly on his lips.

"Your heart is good, Edward," she said. "And big, like your thing." She held his chin in her hand.

"Francesca, I need to talk to you. It's so difficult for me. I can't talk about real private things with Ernesto, even though we're close. Or with Roberto. I guess it's because they're men. But with you . . ."

She stroked his face gently. Then she took his hand and said, "Touch me. I feel excited." This time she told him exactly what to do. As he moved his fingers in the way she guided him, her body became rigid until it jerked; her first scream accompanyied a long series of rhythmic oscillations that diminished with delicious slowness.

Francesca opened her eyes to his wondering face. "You look as if you thought I was in pain, Edward. No, no, my lover," she said, a contented look on her face. "I see there is much I must teach you." She rolled on top of him. He was erect again. She laughed. "Edward, you *are* very hungry. I promise that you will have eaten fully before you leave here."

§

TWENTY-FIVE

He woke slowly to the cool rays of the late spring morning, to light reminding him of uncertainty, of questions without answers.

He stirred in the warmth against Francesca's coal-black hair and searched her serene face. She had a look that he decided was blissful. He remembered their lovemaking, savoring it. And the inexpressable pleasure of release during his orgasms. But what he treasured most was the closeness, the rich, fat, luxuriant abundance of having been given the most precious gift she could give him: the specialness of her intimacy and sharing.

He thought again about his choices. If I continue to travel, what's next? I can't run around all over Mexico. I'd like to stay here. He closed his eyes, rolled over, and faced Francesca, enjoying the odors of her sleep and her femininity.

He moved closer, and nuzzled against her satiny body. *"Buenos dias,"* he whispered. She half-opened her eyes and smiled at him. They kissed deeply and kissed again. Then they made love. It was

251

not like the quick sex of the day before or the way it had been in the car with her next to the San Pedro. It was different, fuller, with meaning.

"I have been thinking how I can help you, Edward," she said as she dressed. "You will go south, yes, travel through Santa Ana and Benjamin Hill and a place called El Oasis, and then you will come to Hermosillo, the big city, the capital of the state of Sonora. We can get you a map and learn how far are the distances." It surprised him that she was already talking about his leaving. He didn't relish thinking about being back on the road. She left the bedroom and he trailed behind. "There are problems. One is that up here on the high desert—it looks the same as in Arizona, it is in many ways—but the little towns, they are very far apart, practically nothing. What I am trying to say is that there are only a few places to get water. You can get stuck; I am worried about you."

He was pleased she was concerned and answered her with a touch of fake bravado. "Hey, I've got my big canteen, and Ernesto showed me all about getting water from a cactus if I have to. I'll be okay," he said. He sat down at the table as she opened the door of the icebox.

"*Huevos*? I'll make you a big omelet. You," she laughed, "use much energy. We have to keep you strong. Like *un toro*." Then she said seriously, "The other thing that worries me is you in Hermosillo. In smaller places like this one, you would not get into trouble. But there," she shook her head, "the people are not *campesinos* like here. That is one big city with many bums, and bad people in the bars, the flophouses. Railroad yards. You forget the differences, perhaps, some good, some not. How do I explain? It is rougher in Mexico. The people are so much poorer, they have no time to care about anyone or anything except surviving."

He got up and poured the pot of boiling water onto the fresh-smelling ground coffee.

252

"Most Mexicans are good people, Eddie, accepting and kind. But the *peons* are uneducated, and," she added, "their ways are, oh, superstitious. They think about saints and stories the priests tell them.

"That's changing, the war has made them at least aware of the rest of the world. Not in small places, in *barrios* and villages, in the back country. The changes are in the cities, Guadalajara, Mexico City, where Americans travel." She brought the frying pan to the table. Edward buttered the good bread and poured coffee into their cups. "Here," she said, handing him a newspaper, "read this. Your Spanish is good enough to get an idea of what the world is like around here." She bit into a slice of bread. "When you talk to people, you must pretend you are one of them." He remembered what Ernesto had said about when you are with animals or with people: Think and act like they do.

Later, when it was time, she kissed him sweetly and affirmatively. "Take care of yourself. You know I am here," she said. Francesca had changed. He wished, as he walked away, that he was more like her, that he had the confidence she radiated.

§

The rain rummaged across the desert, sweeping through like dark, heavy curtains. Sheets of water drenched the rough land, the dirt filtered by eons of wind and blanched by the incessant sun. Edward couldn't see the mountains clearly, but it made little difference where they were as he walked, head down, trying to forget the ceaseless sting and bite of the rain. He thought about how good it had been with Francesca, but now that was over. He had moved still further away from everything he was familiar with, and there was no one to help him. Sing or hum or whistle to feel better, he thought. Don't stop, keep singing and whatever is happening won't bother you so much. "Don't sit under the apple tree with anyone else but me, no, no anyone else but me—peg of my heart, your glances make my heart sing ..." It's not working. Damn, nobody's driving, and I need a hitch. It has to let up; it can't stay this heavy.

He walked the shoulders of the road until it became too mushy. Ernesto had warned him that fast drivers couldn't always be depended upon to swing around a hitchhiker. For a time he imagined he was a zombie who didn't feel anything. Okay, c'mon—Santa Ana can't be more than another hour. But now the rain was so thick that he had difficulty seeing even immediately in front of him. He'd take a ride either way, he vowed, either ahead or back to Magdalena.

After what seemed like hours, he saw a car chug up the rise toward him, filled to capacity. The occupants waved at him and smiled. He lifted a wet arm. Then a truck and a car came from the other direction. The truck slowed, but he motioned it onward. Somehow he seemed destined to complete the walk into town, as if he had to be punished or tested.

When he got to Santa Ana, he was still thoroughly soaked, and dead tired. He thought only about finding a dry bed, taking a long bath, and eating something hot. He would try talking, but knew they wouldn't tell him anything about anything until he said his father was Mexican. And then they'd just say men drift in and out, *señor,* how can one keep track unless he is someone from our area, we watch out for him, take him home, he has friends here, *amigo.* You say your father traveled through here? Maybe. But who remembers?

In Santa Ana that night, he decided to buy a bus ticket to Hermasillo.

§

TWENTY-SIX

The bus was fat, swathed in travelers, their children, and their belongings, including a few chickens. For Edward the three-hour trip was disquieting. They were together again, he, Ernesto, Margaret, little Michael. They were eating, and there was laughter and teasing, warmth, good feelings, and there were no problems, none. He was shaken from this reverie by the driver's quick, lurching maneuver to avoid an errant automobile. *"Santa María! Stúpido! Qué pasa, stúpido!,"* the driver yelled. The passengers rearranged themselves amid the confusion and shouting.

The bus slowed as it passed through El Oasis, where the mountains to the east were a uniform cocoa-brown with patches of tan. Only in the spring, Edward thought, will green return and water be easier to find. The cacti will flower, octillos and saguaros. The birds will become active, fighting, nesting. He noticed the large mesquite trees that were sometimes settled down on the plains and bottom slopes of the mountains; at the higher elevations the vertical bluffs would permit little if any vegetation. The redness of the bluffs made them seem angry, and he thought how difficult it would be to scale them.

He noticed the town's single gas station and a small repair shop. A truck waited in front of the garage door, its hood open. Three men peered into its mouth. Produce was piled high behind the cab. A car was being gassed by an attendant from the single pump. Two *vaqueros* on horses were about to dismount in front of the Restaurante del Bronco. A sign said "59 kilometers to Hermosillo."

Two hours later they entered the outskirts of Hermosillo. As they approached from the northeast, Edward saw a great lake, much larger than he had imagined from looking at the map he had on his lap. Small adobe buildings were set along the highway. Hermasillo bustled as they traveled closer to the downtown, where numbers of people were walking in and out of stores and crossing the streets with apparently little concern for traffic lights. He focused on the green and red signals, remembering the recent talk about constructing one or two in Bisbee and in Sierra Vista. The bus terminal was an agitated nest, the comings and goings of people and vehicles a droned rumble interrupted by the blast of horns and the cries of mothers, shouting at their children to remain with them, for the older ones to grab the hands of their younger siblings. Edward took his pack from the rack above his seat and jumped down into the clean air. He plunged himself into it, exhaling the voyage.

In the Mercado Central on this Saturday, the day was soft and without the anger of winter. Edward decided to bring himself to the center of the city, wanting to feel it, to understand its heart, perhaps to comprehend better the forces that would enable him to act out his self-assigned role and to find—oh God, he thought, please help me find something, please, help me.

Hermosillo's central market was buzzing; the *campensinos* had come by bus from their *barrios,* from the ranches, from the wheat and cotton farms. They crowded around the tables upon which vendors had placed their wares. Amid the talking and shuffling, children ran through the alleys and streets, temporarily liberated from their parents. As Edward lingered in front of a fruit stand, a man bumped hard against him, almost causing them both to fall. His hand came to Edward's wallet pocket, but the unintentional hardness of the shove had thrown off his timing. Edward recoiled automatically, noting his assailant's anger as he quickly disappeared in the crowds.

A thin young man sat on the pavement, leaning against the front wall of a store, shirtless and shoeless. A pile of old orange peels was laid next to him, together with other scraps of food and bits of paper and wrappers, all jumbled into refuse, small pieces of dirty material in the mess of him and what he sat in. People passed around and over his legs. Every so often he looked up at someone as if he was about to speak, but did not; he seemed to be in a trance. Edward offered him some coins but the young man only stared at his face and did not put out his hand. Shaken, Edward put one of his shirts over the man's shoulders and walked on. The pitiful sight of the abandoned man not much older than he had frightened him.

He kept maneuvering through the bustle until he arrived at a small square, presided over by a statue of a distinguished general enshrined in a pose neither the man nor his faithful horse had ever contemplated. Why pretend that he was there when he wasn't, Edward wondered? Well, it was time for a beer. Several blocks away, not far from El Coloso Amusement Park, Hermosillo's stores were replaced by bars. Edward sensed where they were located, their congregation as sure to exist as the Mercado Central. He was becoming practiced.

He opened the battered door of the Gandara Bar. The cantina was full. Some of the men wore *sombreros;* he had noticed that in the small towns, almost all the patrons wore their hats, but everyone did in the cities. Posters of old bullfights hung on the painted walls. At the L-shaped bar, two bartenders served and chatted with the customers. Men also sat and drank at tables on the side. The floor was tiled, far more sophisticated than the dirt or mud floors of the country cantinas. The place smelled of stale beer, urine, disinfectant, smoke and sweat. Pictures of old Carta Blanca and Montezuma bottles decorated the metal serving trays.

Everyone looked up when he came in, and he felt uneasy being watched and judged. He slipped into an open spot at the bar, remembering to put money down and let it lie as a signal that he intended to remain.

"*Mandé,*" he said in his deepest voice to the bartender, "*cerveza.*" A man ambled over and asked him for a cigarette. "*No tengo,*" he responded, and received a sneer. A second man came over and told him not to pay attention to the first. His eyes were better focused, and when he asked, Edward told him in Spanish that yes, he was an American, but his father was Mexican.

A third man replaced the first, who retreated to his table. The new arrival was Edward's age, spoke English, and said he had lived in the States for two years. He introduced himself as Tomás. He talked with assurance, and after a little more conversation told the others nearby that Edward was okay. Tomás invited him to his table for another beer. There another man came and sat with them, placing a bottle of tequila on the table, his other hand holding a lemon. He slugged from the bottle, squeezed the lemon over his mouth and placed the bottle in front of Edward. "*Usted!*" Edward shook his head. The tequila drinker angrily grabbed his arm, but Tomás pulled it off with a sharp pronouncement that he was to leave Edward alone. They began to argue. Heads turned, and Tomás shoved the other man away.

"He gets nasty when he drinks," Tomás said. "He is my brother-in-law. I know exactly what he will do. This is not the first time. Please forgive us, we are not, how do you say, unwelcoming or unfriendly."

Edward thanked him and shook hands, and the other drinkers settled back to bar and table, like buzzards who had been disturbed at a feast. After a few more beers, Edward walked to an area at the side of the room, an aperture behind which was a urinal that ran along the floor for the length of the wall, almost as long as the room itself. He joined one or two others who stood in front of it; one was singing off-key, while the other farted loudly. Edward was feeling the effects of the beers. Careful, he thought, you're drunk, Slavin.

He finished urinating, stepped around the wall and surveyed the room. Someone was strumming a guitar, and its notes floated between the tables. In the corner were two men, one with his head on his folded arms, and the other, a cowboy, peering deeply at the ceiling. Through the smoke and haze that permeated like pessimism for the condemned, Edward thought he recognized the face of his dead father. He walked closer, staring, his eyes wide, but his face otherwise controlled, flat and motionless. The tears he had not known were waiting there welled in his eyes.

"Dad, Dad, I'm here. It's me, Edward, your son." The seated man Edward had approached waved a hand limply, as if trying to brush away the confusion. His face tilted up in the direction of the words he was not sure he had heard. "Yes, it's me," said Edward. "I'm here with you."

Edward caught himself, frozen for these moments as he examined the man's face and eyes. Finally, it penetrated through his mind that the man was not his father. He wanted to turn away, but he had to be sure. No, he thought: this cowboy has no smile, no interest, no involvement with anyone around him. The stranger peered upward, worked on a smile as he stared through his haze. Edward saw him ask: Who is it who wants something? I know nothing. Please leave me alone.

Now the sounds of the guitar ceased. Some applause was heard, and "ole" was shouted. The room filled again with the din that settled on it. The cowboy rose unsteadily and pushed Edward away. He called to the bartender, who came over, sized up the situation and conducted Edward to the door. "*Gringo,* you had too many drinks. When you start to make trouble, out," he said unceremoniously.

259

Edward tried to collect himself, surprised that he was having difficulty standing. Then fresh air replaced the malodor inside the Gandara. He inhaled it, caught somewhere between nausea and self-
disgust.

As his head cleared a bit, it registered that he was hungry. He
noticed a small restaurant across the street and started for it. The
walk seemed to take forever; people and things weaved and bobbed.
He picked a table in the corner, where dishes were set upon a brightly
colored oilcloth. Edward asked for *carne y frijoles refritos,* focusing
on food he remembered Ernesto ate, and *café con leche caliente,* with
flan for dessert.

In a rundown hotel only slightly better than a flophouse, he rented
a room for $1.50 American. A couple laughed as they passed in the
hall, and the door next to his kept opening and closing. His room
contained two single beds, a straight-back chair, a dresser with a
basin on top, a pitcher of water and two spotted towels. He laid
down, his hands folded behind his head, but did not remove his
boots. "You won't have to worry about me anymore, Dad," he said,
his voice filled with self-pity. He stood up, shook himself and gazed
into the mirror, where, only after a moment, he discerned his face,
pulled down from the weight of his despair. Feeling just as frightened
and helpless as he had during those ugly days after his parents were
killed, he vomited into the sink.

When he awoke, he had difficulty remembering where he was, and
the hours since he'd entered the bar were a total blank. Shaking with
a hangover that made him feel absurdly weak, he left the hotel.

After a good breakfast with strong coffee, he saw in front of him
La Campana Hill, from which, Francesca had told him, you could
see great distances in every direction. He walked to the bottom of the
slope and began to climb. The fog in his head was lifting at last. At
the top of the hill, he surveyed the city, its buildings and streets now
miniature houses, the people Lilliputians.

He was surprised to see a man standing nearby, holding the hand of a child and pointing with his finger to something below. Opening the map Francesca had given him, his eye fell on Guymas, on the coast. What the hell's the difference? he thought.

The sun was gaining strength now, and to the east, the higher peaks of the Sierra Madres penetrated through the morning haze. He felt the sharp, tingling sensation running down one arm.

He trudged down the path, bought what he needed in the Mercado Central and hitched a ride that took him to an intersection at the edge of the city. He waited a few minutes on Route 15, the road that turned north to Nogales. When no cars stopped, he began to walk, ready to stick out his thumb. An old Ford pickup chugged from the other direction, rattling and complaining from under the hood. The driver slid out; his family waited inside. He opened the hood, and Edward joined him. The man smiled, then cursed the engine, saying that it had to have problems on this of all days—this day, Sunday, when his family and he were dressed in their best clothes, this important day on which he would ask his brother-in-law, a big official, his wife's oldest brother, for money so he could buy the house and farm he was renting, not much, just a beginning, but a start, and over the years he would pay off the amount that was still owing. "Tell me, *amigo,* where do you travel?" he asked Edward.

Edward described Ernesto, explaining that he was Mexican, and being as vague as he felt about his journey. Then he tried to figure out why the engine was missing and reset the points under the distributor cap, which still didn't improve the engine's sound. But the man thanked him, and they shook hands; he continued to walk, hoping for a ride. No cars or trucks came in his direction, and in about forty-five minutes he came to a small rectangular adobe building, its roof fallen in, the grass grown high around its perimeter.

Smoke rose from inside, and he moved to where the front door had been and peeked inside. A disheveled man was squatting against the corner, a bottle next to him, and the contents of a can was being heated over a fire set between two large stones. He motioned to Edward to come in and have a drink.

Edward backed off a few paces, then came forward, grabbed the bottle, and slugged some of the sweet, burning stuff inside. He peered up where the roof had been; high wispy clouds were pasted against the blue-white canopy of the sky. Then he kicked the ground with his boot, stepped toward the opening and yelled in English, "I don't want to be like you!" He turned, sobbing until snot streamed from his nose. As he'd assumed, the man didn't understand what he had cried out. But then, after a long silence, he said in Spanish, "Go home, youngster, where you belong."

Edward ran out of the building just as a truck lumbered up the rise. He waved it down and climbed in, averting his face from the driver. The man was right. He had to go back. But back to what?

§

TWENTY-SEVEN

He sat at the edge of the San Pedro, his head sunk into his hands. It had taken him three arduous days and almost sleepless nights to return to the familiar surroundings he knew he needed. He tried for a moment to pretend he had been shot down over enemy territory. It didn't work. Fear and loneliness strapped themselves to him once again.

Now, in late summer, the river's trickle was reduced to a stream, supplied by the ever-diminishing run-off from the mountain snows far to the north. In a few more weeks the flow would stop completely, until it began again when spring returned.

What the hell did I accomplish, he wondered? Except for those days with Francesca, the trip was a complete disaster. The pain of his thoughts crushed like a weight he couldn't budge, and he felt a gripping sensation in his stomach. He took a deep breath, as if by exhaling he might unloosen its grasp. He speculated briefly about living with Francesca: fantasizing first that they could be their own family, and then wondering what he could offer her after all the men she had been with.

He lay back on the hard stones, staring into the vaulted sky. "Please, God, please help me," he sobbed. "Show me what to do. I'm so alone."

Edward wiped his eyes with the back of his sleeve. The sun warmed him, and he was grateful for that. A hawk swung across above the cottonwoods, flashing in the sun as it executed its quick, graceful turns, spinning and plummeting to the earth with its talons extended, more than likely about to sink them into the fur of a jackrabbit.

He couldn't live with Ernesto and Margaret, he thought. Should he get a room in town? Go to Tucson or San Francisco? Not without a decent job, he decided. Was he really going to end up like all the other stiffs?

He walked in the mottled light as the sun threw its rays among the leaves and branches of the trees, and was surprised and pleased to come upon his car. Nothing had happened to it since he had left, but it would have to be towed back to the house, and he sighed again as he contemplated the cost.

§

Edward had telephoned them when he had reached Naco. Margaret had answered, expressing both relief that he was all right and concern about him. "My gosh, we've missed you! Hurry home, Eddie. I'll find Dad. He'll be ecstatic about seeing you." Edward decided not to say just then that he couldn't live with them. Better to reassure them that the trip had been good and had helped him sort things out. It was a lie. The one thing he was sure of was that flying was what he wanted to do.

They welcomed him lovingly, but during dinner, Margaret announced in a chilly tone, "I do have to say to you, Edward, that I was very disappointed that you left without discussing your trip with us. You know, being close means being able to talk things over." Her voice mellowed. "I guess I'm a possessive mother, but I didn't sleep well worrying about you." Edward nodded in agreement.

"You're getting to be old enough to make your own decisions," Ernesto said to him after dinner when the two of them took a walk. Edward confided that he thought it would be best if he rented a room in town for the rest of the summer. "Well, try it, son. We'll make sure to see plenty of you." He put out his cigarette. "I'll take care of it with Mom."

The mornings were crisped now, sharpened enough so that his senses began to focus on autumn. Grays clung more to each other and became clustered in longer shadows. The sun pursued its daily course of inspection, marking the clear molding of the mountains and canyons, the boulders and thickets of snakeweed. The morning after he returned, Edward asked to take Mikey on a walk. As he pushed the baby's carriage up Carr Canyon Road, a chill rose from the soil. His eyes settled on the shack where Francesca had lived with Alberto and Roberto. Margaret and Ernesto had told him that both had left one day, with no good-byes.

He came to the shanty which looked to him like a corpse slowly collapsing in the scorch of the sun.

When you get bigger, Mikey, I'll tell you about all of them. What it was like in the beginning with the Healeys. About my horse Nellie and the fawn I found and the schoolhouse. "See, way over down there," he said, pointing. "Of course about Mom, how wonderful she was to me when I started school. And Dad, how he saved me." But maybe not about the Major and his wife, he thought; the less you learn about people like that, the better.

With the baby snug in the carriage, Edward continued higher into the canyon, pointing out buzzards floating high in the thermals borne by the rising heat. "Buzzards," Edward said, "birds."

"G, gg," the baby answered back as Edward pretended to take

265

flight, clamping his hands over his eyes. He lifted the baby and held him up facing him.

"I'm going to fly and be a pilot," he said. "You'll come with me sometimes." He said it for fun, just to talk, but the words seemed to crystallize in the air. No matter what else happened, no matter who came, who went, who loved him, who abandoned him, Edward was going to fly.

§

Southern Arizona Airways had increased its flights, scheduling new ones to Douglas and Nogales. Tourists were vacationing year-round now, and more businessmen and military personnel needed to get quickly to and from Tucson and Phoenix. Edward was rehired by Richard Banks. "Listen, kid, this isn't a nursery," Banks admonished him. "You work for me, you work steady—none of this taking off traveling crap. Get my meaning?"

"Yes, sir. I'm real serious about flying, Mr. Banks. And I can do all kinds of things for you." A rare smile unfolded on Edward's face. "Before you put that ad in for an assistant dispatcher, will you give me a crack at it?"

Banks made a mock grimace and surveyed the young man standing in front of him. "Call me Richard, kid. Okay, I'll give you a shot. I guess I'm better off with what I know than with what I don't. As for paying back that loan, you can baby-sit a little for us. By the way, in front of customers it's 'Captain' or 'Mister Banks,' okay? Now, get your ass out of the office and fuel those planes." He threw his hat at Edward.

All Edward wanted now was to get his "ticket," the precious license that would allow him to fly passengers. He decided to try to make himself indispensible to Banks. He'd remind the pilots about revisions in their schedules—something Banks had been doing—set up a billing system, and keep the files better organized for all the records of how much time each of their three planes had been flown. And he'd clean and sweep perfectly and make the passsengers feel as comfortable as possible.

"Okay," Banks said a few weeks later, "pull out the Cub. No charge for this hour, you've earned it. But if you're ready to make a commitment towards a ticket, you'll have to come up with the money." He frowned at Edward, who said nothing. "All right, I'll work it out against your time." Banks shook his head. "Why do I always get wet-nosed kids to teach? I suppose I have to keep a permanent supply of diapers."

Edward walked away with his shoulders back, like in the movie he'd seen of Pappy Boyington, the hero and fighter pilot. Except, perhaps, for those days of intoxication with Francesca in Magdalena, he couldn't remember the last time he'd felt this good.

§

TWENTY-EIGHT

That fall Edward entered his senior year. In those first few weeks after school began, he had great difficulty concentrating in class. He also withdrew from all his extra-curricular activities.

One night in the room he had rented in town, he turned to his visitor. "We have to be quiet, really we do," he pleaded. He placed his hand on the beer bottle the young woman was holding, spilling some as he put it down on the night table. The people in whose house he had a room had requested that he not have any company.

Sex meant twists and tumbles with someone you wanted to be drawn to like a magnet. When the two of you joined, you were suspended as if you had defied the laws of physics; you couldn't see or talk about what you felt in the wonder of that emotion. You were free from everything else, you lost your mind and pushed against gravity as in no other way, suspended in ecstasy. The sphere of euphoria that suffused you became an escape from pain—at least for the time being.

Except for flying, everything seemed to be going downhill. His grades were bringing warnings from his teachers. And he couldn't seem to focus, to stay with the scheduling and planning his job required. He was screwing up too many things.

Only when he was in the air did things seem really right. Standing next to the 65 h.p. Piper Cub at the airport, the smell of prairie grasses and the moisture and dew in the early mornings made him feel joy at simply being alive. He felt revived. And in the air, with the window and door open, the thickness of wind against his face was like splashed stream water.

Above the ground he was unbound and free, in charge of himself, not burdened by his history and pain. But back on land, he coudln't sustain the feeling; he couldn't either escape or be easy with the actions and choices of others, the decisions and events that turned him in the wind like a weathercock.

"Eddie," the girl said, "you're acting so nervous, like a kid his first time. A person has to make noise. That's part of the fun. I didn't come all the way out here to be *good*. I could have stayed home." She grabbed a pillow and hit him with it, pushing him off balance. Then she gave him a loud whack on his rear, accompanied by a yell.

"What's going on up there? Edward?"

He slid over to the other side and slipped on his pants. "Be right back," he said, closing the door quietly.

When he returned, after giving his landlady what he knew was a lame explanation for the rumpus, the young woman was dressing. "Why are you doing that?" he asked. "It'll be all right if we don't make noise."

"I can see what's important around here. All your talk about how much you want to be with me. I have to be free to have fun! You ruined the mood."

"Please don't leave. I'm sorry I yelled at you."

"No, Eddie, you ruined the spell. Tell you what," she said, "M-a-y-b-e, I'll come tomorrow. I can be lots quieter if I want to. But now I'm leaving, so good-bye." She turned and added, "You'll just have to wait for my special 'Delights of The Night.'" She threw him a kiss, and he wished again that he could figure out how to prevent her from leaving.

Once he saw her drive away, he opened his refrigerator door, poured himself a glass of milk, and got back into bed. He tossed for what seemed a long time until his hands closed over his genitals. As he touched his erect penis, he thought of the young woman and how sexy she had looked naked in the dimmed light. Would she really come back tomorrow night? She'd probably change her mind, he thought.

Masturbating was often reassuring, like sucking his thumb had been in the old days at the Healeys. Edward swung out of bed to his window and stuck his face out into the night, surveying for a while the quarter moon that looked a little like the base of a rocking horse.

§

Richard Banks was becoming worried about Edward's work: he was falling down on coordinating the flights and pilots and scheduling the arrangements for maintenance, fuel and parts. "What the hell's with you?" he demanded. "You're beginning to make one mistake after another, kid. Or else you just don't finish what you begin. And you're starting to get pushy."

Edward frowned. "What do you mean?"

"And you're doing new things without checking with me. Take it easy, kid, you've got plenty of time. I want you to do a better job on what you're already supposed to be doing." Edward returned to filling in information on his clipboard. He enjoyed watching the passengers look at him and loved answering their questions. But Banks continued, "About your flying, you have natural ability. You *feel* the plane. Your air work is good, I like your seven-twenties and your rectangular courses. But your landings could be much smoother. Think about air speed in relation to your approach. Your last landings were like riding on an out-of-control roller coaster." He spread his fingers, thumbs touching and moved them, undulating, in the motion of a porpoise. Then he contrasted this with a slow smooth landing, his fingers raised and his palms down. "Remember, set the plane down at the right air speed in the classic stall landing. You'll get better with practice."

"I think I'm ready to solo," Edward said, a little impatience in his voice. "I've had eight hours."

"I'll let you know when you're ready, Mister Hotshot. By the way, there's a couple of nice young girls at our church. Why don't you come Sunday morning? My wife will introduce you to them."

Edward was unsure how to respond. Religion again! And he wasn't in the mood to meet new people. "Maybe I can come after the service," he said. "That would be better." He hoped this would end the conversation.

"Come at the beginning," Banks said. "You probably haven't been to church in a dog's age, and I can see you don't want to go even when someone presses you. I don't feel all that strong about it myself, but my wife does. Her father was a minister."

"No, you don't understand." Edward waited and then added, "I'm Jewish."

"You're *what*? I don't believe you. You're kidding me."

Edward's jaw tightened. "No, I am. Anything wrong with that?" He began to fidget. Once Mrs. Healey had made a remark about city Jews moving into Sierra Vista. She didn't go any further, but Edward had felt prejudice in the way she said it.

"No, of course not. Just that I never expected *you* to be. Kind of unusual. I mean, nothing wrong with it. In England, I flew all the time with Jewish guys. Damn good pilots, most of them." Banks ran his fingers through his hair. "Converted?"

"No," Edward said with an edge to his voice. "Both my original parents were Jewish. Look, if it gives you a problem—"

"Don't be an asshole," Banks said, cutting him off. "It's different here than in a city." There was a silence. Yes, Edward thought, you mean hardly any temples and hardly any Jews.

Edward looked at Banks and wondered what he would say next.

"What about your parents? I mean the ones you have now?" he asked.

"What about them? Ernesto, Dad's a Catholic and Mom's Protestant."

"Just curious. Anyway, come Sunday at eleven in time for the service, kid. We don't kneel, so you won't be that uncomfortable," Banks said with a grin.

Edward didn't think the remark was funny. "Maybe. We'll see," he said flatly.

Just then the phone rang in the office, and Edward ran in and answered it. He recognized the voice immediately. *"Qué tal, amigo?"*

"Francesca! Where are you?" Her voice stirred him in a way that made him immediately picture himself with her. "It's been months. How come you didn't write?"

"A lot has happened, Edward. I've been moving around. I called to say hello and tell you something." There was a delay before she continued. "Actually, two things: I left Magdalena a while back with a guy I met, a salesman. I had to get out of there. He's okay, a cute gringo like you," she said with a laugh. "And we got married. We traveled all over and now we are settled here in Phoenix. Much better than in Magdalena. We are even talking about having kids. Would you believe we even have a little spread in the outskirts?"

The shock was like a wallop to his mid-section, as if she had slugged him with a club. Edward hated surprises: they brought pain and hurt and endings, usually terrible ones. He sank into the chair next to the telephone. He had thought about Francesca often, how wonderful and safe he had felt with her. Now that, too was shattered.

"Congratulations, Francesca, I hope you'll be very happy," he said stiffly, as if quoting a memorized statement. He was aware that he also sounded sad and bitter, and he decided to change the subject. "Where's Roberto?"

"Albuquerque. He's a mechanic. I just talked to him a little while ago, and he told me to say hello to you. He misses you, Edward."

"Can I have his address and phone number?" he asked. "You said there was a second thing."

"Yes," she said. "I wanted to know how you're doing. I was concerned about you in Magdalena."

Edward felt shame, and after a brief silence he said, "If you really want to know, lousy, Francesca. I can't seem to be able to care about anything except flying."

"No girlfriend? That's what you need, you know. Listen to your old friend, Mama Francesca." He imagined the smile on her face.

"I'll be all right," he said with a touch of bravado in his voice. "I really don't need anyone. It's better that way." That would show her how much he cared about her getting married.

"Look, Eddie, you don't fool me. We all need someone or some-ones. You damn well know what I mean." Her tone smoothed into the one he remembered from Magdalena. "Eddie, are you really all right? You don't sound good." She could always tell, he thought.

"There's no one left," he said. "I guess I'm pretty messed up." He detested the way he sounded.

"Eddie, you remember I told you what got me through? 'Remember who you are, no matter what?' It made all the difference for me."

"I tried that. Nothing works, Francesca. Nobody cares. I don't either, any more."

"C'mon, Eddie, things change. A lot of us care about you. Don't you feel that? What about Ernesto and Margaret?"

"Yeah, they're around, I suppose. But being alone seems all I'm good for."

"You have a lot to learn, kiddo. Stop feeling so sorry for yourself. Don't tell *me* about how it feels to be out there."

"Women are better at being alone," he said. "All I know is that it hurts too much."

"I want you to come up for a visit," Francaesca said warmly.

"You're married now, Francesca."

"You're talking like a child, Eddie. I'll see you around. Good-bye." There was a quick, sharp click.

§

In Sierra Vista, Edward entered The Egg Pan and sat down at the table with the pilots from Southern Arizona Airways. It had been weeks since the day he'd spoken with Francesca. On this warm late August Friday, the fans over the oil-clothed tables were spinning the aromas of food and smoke. The room was noisy, with groups of men in conversation, most of them from the Fort.

"What's the matter, Slavin? Your head seems to be up in thunderstorms today," one of the pilots asked as he sat down. "If you're thinking about our cute waitress, don't. Jim has her all tied up. But you won't have to wait long because he'll mess up sooner or later. He always does. At least he flies straight."

This morning Edward added nothing to the badinage. He stayed behind, sitting and staring off into space when the others left, and was oblivious when a man with a cane walked to his table and stood there erect for a few moments. Then he looked up and recognized Major Healey. He had heard about the car crash, and knew Mrs. Healey had died a few weeks later from a stroke, but his expression didn't change. He had gone to the funeral at the urging of Ernesto and Margaret. Wasn't that enough?

"May I sit down?"

"I was just leaving. I have to get to work," Edward responded in a monotone.

"All right. I just wanted to see how you were doing. I was hoping you'd have stopped over after the accident. You know about Mrs. Healey, I'm sure."

Edward couldn't look at him. "I was at the funeral," he said. "I'm sorry. I was going to send you a card, only I misplaced it." I hope you hurt a lot, Major Healey, he thought. Now you know how it feels, how you used to make *me* feel.

"I'd like it very much if you'd come up to the ranch some time, Edward. We could do some riding, and the stream's running pretty good."

Edward put change down on the table and rose. "I have to go," he answered, and left quickly, before the Major could say anything more.

Driving to the airport, he passed a cowboy in a pasture; from a distance he looked like Ernesto. He sat in the saddle the same way, loosely, as if he were one with the horse. A cigarette dangled from his mouth, and he wore his black Stetson in the same easy way Ernesto did. Edward pulled the car off the road. The cowboy gazed at him but continued riding. Edward beeped his horn twice, and the rider approached. He got out of the car slowly and walked to the barbed wire fence. When the cowboy came near, Edward waved to him and said, "Sorry. Thought you were someone else."

In the office, he checked on the day's schedules. Then he found

Richard Banks and announced that he was ready for the dual cross-country flight they had scheduled for that afternoon.

"You are, huh? Okay, let me see your courses to Douglas and Deming—and weather reports, the fuel you expect to consume, time enroute, estimated time of arrival, all that stuff. If you make just a single mistake, we don't go." He grinned. "Don't stare at me like a baboon, get your ass moving."

For Edward the trip was charged with excitement; for Banks, it was a matter of amusement and pleasure. He was firm about what Edward must be aware of: the potential drift of the plane as effected by cross, tail or head winds; his attitude and altitude in relation to the horizon; the necessity for safe margins over mountains; keeping aware of engine temperature and pressure; and the visual objects on the ground that ascertain a pilot's location in terms of the charted course lined on his map. But Banks also shared Edward's enjoyment at seeing the land from the air, feeling the wind and skirting loose clouds, the puffs of cotton fabricated by giants.

The flight was exhilarating for Edward, as it usually was. They landed back at the Fort Huachuca Airport and climbed out of the Piper Cub. "Not bad, kid," Banks said. "You know I'd let you have it if you goofed up, but your flying and navigation were right on the mark." He put out his hand. "What's the matter, you don't seem so happy about it."

"Yeah, I know I can fly," Edward said. It was the one thing he was confident about, but he didn't seem able to sustain his pride in it for even a few minutes after he had gotten back on the ground.

The next step was his solo cross-country. At last he would be able to be up there alone, free to go anywhere. And do anything. He'd be able to fly over the place where his parents had crashed. Yes, over and over it if he wanted to, round and round like a spinning wheel. He could spin right in. Poof. Right down in the exact spot they did.

Just like them. Why not? Yeah, why not? No one could tell him anything. He was Edward Slavin, almost eighteen years old, son of Major and Missus Sam Slavin.

Banks said, "I want you to remember at all times that planes and people aren't perfect machines. Things go wrong. They shouldn't, but they do. Never be a wise guy. When trouble happens, the best manuever is a 'one-eighty.' "

"Uh, huh," Edward added in a sing-song manner, " 'and there are old pilots and bold pilots, but no old bold ones.' "

He stopped in to have dinner with Margaret and Ernesto. Margaret studied his face. "Do a good job this semester and you'll still have no trouble getting into UA for next year, Edward. Decided what you want to study?" she aksed, trying to be light.

He glanced from her to Ernesto, who didn't offer any help. "Oh, that's a long way off." He squirmed in his seat. "I don't know. I can always decide later." He was uncomfortable, but he was glad she had this interest in him. He never wanted to disappoint her, not if he could help it.

§

TWENTY-NINE

At last it was time—the time to fly alone to airports he had never seen before: the triangulated solo cross-country flight over new territory that tested proficiency, navigation and most important of all, common sense, the combination of instinct and unreflective judgment that could keep him alive. It had to be done right.

Edward was to take off in the Piper Cub, fly northwest to Casa Grande, southeast to the Nogales airport on the Mexican side and finally northeast, returning to Fort Huachuca. The amount of time for each leg between the airports had to be carefully calculated, as did the fuel he consumed and the adjustments necessary for wind drift. He also had to spot crucial checkpoints enroute. He wouldn't use a radio except for landings and take-offs; besides, the smaller airports didn't have them, and even if they did, they usually wouldn't acknowledge the pilot of a small plane—no one just sat around next to the radio. To qualify, he had to demonstrate that he could fly in unfamiliar areas, then pass the written and flight examinations. If he passed them all, he would receive the treasured "ticket."

Though Edward was sure that he had been ready for weeks, Richard Banks still found his landings less than acceptable and his overall flying not precise enough. "Damn it, Slavin! Where the hell's your mind? *Carburetor heat*! You want the engine to die when you reduce power? And you're not watching the altitude! The pattern is eight hundred feet downwind and five hundred on base. You're not paying attention. Tell me," Banks asked when they were down on the ground, "what happens if you don't have enough fuel left after you land in Nogales?"

"Fill the tank before continuing," he answered matter-of-factly.

"You would, huh? Wrong, dummy! You forgot. I told you gas in Mexico is most likely contaminated, and anything but what you want to use. No, Mister, you'd top off in Casa Grande, even though you had only consumed a theoretical one-third of your total." He grimaced and shook his head. "I'm going to quiz you on other things, and you damn well better give me the right answers. Or no go."

"Oh, Richard, don't give me such a hard time. You know I can fly! You told me I did really well on my dual cross-country over the mountains and everything." I'm going to fly, he thought, to where *they* are. I will. Screw all the bullshit down here. Bullshit Valley, home of Bullcrap Hereford, Bullcrap Fort Huachuca, Bullshit Major Healey, Bullshit school.

"Yes," Banks retorted, "because I was with you. It's the unexpected that I'm concerned you won't know how to handle."

But a week or so later, after Edward's technical landings and take-offs had improved, Banks agreed that he seemed reasonably well prepared; he scheduled the flight for the following Saturday.

That morning Banks fluttered like a mother bird, carefully instructing her fledgling that was about to leave the nest. "You have any trouble whatsoever with the plane or your navigation, call me collect from wherever you are, you hear me? Don't be a smart-ass." He slapped Edward on his rear. "It's getting late, so get going," he said. "Good luck. I don't have any doubts you'll do fine. But I want you to pay attention, okay?" He put his arm around Edward and gave him a little shove in the direction of the plane.

Edward's take-off was smooth, the climb-out by the book. He circled over the field and rocked his wings in the traditional farewell gesture to a miniature Banks, who waved and gave him the thumbs-up signal.

All right, he thought, I'm finally on my way. Compass three-thirty degrees, altimeter fifty-one hundred feet. Richard said a hundred feet either side is acceptable. Air speed seventy, wind supposed to be right into my nose at ten. First leg should take one hour and fifty-two minutes. Four twenty-eight-minute checkpoints. Pick up the Santa Ritas over on the left with big, old Mount Wrightson sticking up at nine thousand four hundred.

Hey, you babies, there you are, just where you're supposed to be. Okay, Route 80, Tucson and Route 93, sta-raight to Casa Grande. Land, get my log signed, fill the tank, check the oil, *fill the tank full,* enough to Nogales and the last leg over the Huachucas. A cinch.

Keep looking around all the time, Richard said: clouds, weather, other planes; nothing here, maybe some near Tucson and Phoenix. Watch the gauges, temperature and pressure, maintain altitude, make small compass corrections if you start to drift, write down times for each section of every leg. Remember. Remember to remember.

Nothing stopped me from learning to fly, he thought. Hey, look at me! I'm up here, in charge of myself. No one can tell me what I can and can't do. Flying's the answer, just like it was for Dad. He was the best, they said. So how come you crashed? I saw where you came down, Dad. Ernesto took me there. And Richard and I flew over, remember? When he was teaching me about mountain downdrafts. Why did everyone get killed, even you? What about a flat enough place, or just two trees to fly through? Break the wings off and slow down the impact. But Richard said that only happens in the movies. If anyone could have found a way, couldn't you? Why didn't you? Why didn't you do a one-eighty? It's been real bad without you. You were supposed to help me grow up.

He glanced at the gauges and the altimeter. All were operating properly. Then he thought: you and Mom, you're at the crash site right now, aren't you? I fly close coming back from Nogales, right here, next to the line I drew. You'll hear me, I'll make sure. The weather's a little hazy, but you'll definitely see me this afternoon.

The heat rose off the tawny desert that stretched for what seemed unending distances, interrupted only by the rumpled mountain ranges that looked today like gargantuan ocean waves rolling in. The Catalinas, the Chiricahuas to the east and the Huachucas—fists with knuckles like rocky stubs. Coyotes hunted throughout the territory, mountain lions and even the Mexican wolf and jaguar. The desert was rock-strewn, as if giants had pitched them.

Although the prairie was generally level, a safe landing on it would be uncertain at best. Edward concentrated on what he was supposed to do and peered forward when a land feature, a road or town was due to present itself. Then, unaccountably, he began to feel angry, and his mind wandered to thoughts of the Major.

I hate that man. He caught me when I was a little kid. The bastard crippled me. I'm not good for anything, beaten down like a helpless hound dog that can only watch the other dogs chase after their prey. At least Mrs. Healey tried sometimes, but he was too much for her—the bully, strutting around, scaring the life out of me.

Oh, what I wouldn't do to be in charge when he kicks off. Send him straight to hell without stopping. I'd march him up and back across red-hot coals a foot thick. Make him salute every two seconds. Make him smile at me and say "thank you." That'd be for starters. Then I'd jam that goddamn riding crop up his ass, and he'd have to go around wearing it everywhere. And we'd throw him on the rack, pull him apart until he became twelve inches longer. That face of his would lose its high and mighty grin. At every inch I'd remind him of what he did to me.

An image of the vulnerable Major Healey who had approached him in The Egg Pan rushed in, but he brushed it away.

Edward searched the sky, trailing his eyes from the left wing tip across the horizon and everything below, then moving to and past the right wing tip. The visibility was deteriorating, objects were getting hazier than in their usual sharpened and delineated forms, but his over-all line of sight was a clear fifteen miles. After twenty minutes more had elapsed, he landed at the small Casa Grande airport several miles south and west of Phoenix. To his surprise, he found no one to sign his log book, and he waited for more than an hour before the owner arrived. Edward fueled the tank, and ate half his sandwich and apple, deciding to save the rest for Nogales. He urinated behind the old hangar. "No coffee," Banks had advised him, "it'll make you have to piss. That can be a problem, let me tell you. Just drink a little water."

On the second leg between Casa Grande and Nogales, additional thoughts slipped in and settled onto his consciousness: Edward flew over a long expanse of desert given to the Papago Indian Reservation. Except for a rare ranch or road, he had trouble locating any landmarks. He was not aware that he had slipped fifteen degrees off course, and the checkpoint he was supposed to see didn't show up. "Damn! I wasn't paying attention. Where the hell am I? Damn it to hell!" He began to sweat as he banked left to turn easterly. I'll pick up Route 93 if I keep heading this way and cut off the angle. Jesus, I hope so.

After about twenty minutes that dragged like a ride home in the dark, he located the highway from Phoenix to Tucson. "All right, you sonufabitch highway," he shouted to the road, "don't move!"

He adjusted his heading to 150 degrees, but he knew he had lost valuable time and had wasted gas. You dummy, he said to himself, shape up.

He busied himself trying to replot the course. Okay, okay, stay steady, he thought. He crossed Route 86, but not at the intended checkpoint. The landmarks he had pencil-marked on his map were not visible. Over this area of the desert, which had been delegated to the San Xavier Indians, he understood that the only success seemed to be the saguaro cacti. The ranches below were pitiful, with few if any cattle on them. The windmills stood like sad and rusted beacons, old sentinels waiting for a wind that rarely passed through. Edward looked carefully at one that was slowly turning, working in the wind. He imagined someone fashioning warm, gentle breezes that would make him feel good, wash him completely in that special way when he'd so rarely felt happy and loved. Oh, how sweet it was in Magdalena with Francesca. In the shower. In bed, talking, drinking coffee, her cooking. But she's gone for good. What do I have? Nothing to look forward to. Nothing makes any difference anymore.

He continued the heading of 150 degrees and remembered Banks's warning to trust the compass: waiting for what's supposed to be ahead requires concentration and patience, he had said. Isn't it like following someone on a trail in the clouds high up in the Huachucas? No, not the same, Edward thought. At least there I'd know that the trail would eventually lead me out. But any kind of trusting or expecting usually ends up with me being the loser.

Where the hell was the route from Tucson? It's got to show up, he thought. C'mon, where are you? He pulled out a can of soda from his sack on the front seat and drank its contents, spilling some in his haste.

Now the wind shifted to the south and slowed the plane's progress even more. It took longer than he had planned to reach Nogales. At last he located the airfield on the Mexican side of the border and landed on the dusty runway. A corrugated metal hangar with a torn windsock on its roof were the only objects he saw; they seemed to be baking in the arid, listless air. He pulled the mixture control to shut down the engine, opened the two half-door panels and sat waiting for someone to come out from the hangar. He swallowed, aware of how parched and thirsty he was.

He stepped out of the Cub and noticed a dripping spigot at the corner of the hangar. He leaned into the plane, removed the sandwich from his sack and ate the half that remained as he walked to the spigot. He forgot about the water until he had finished drinking. Oh, Jesus, that was stupid, he thought. I hope I won't have any problem.

Inside the small office, a pilot, or someone he assumed was a flier, was dozing, his feet propped up on a dilapidated old desk. When he stirred, Edward handed him his logbook. He was middle-aged, unshaven and grungy.

Edward wasn't sure if he would speak English or Spanish. It was English. "Cross-country, huh? Yeah, remember mine. Thousand years ago. Flying down here's not what the bastards promised. Mechanics are lousy. I got to do my own. Names's Cleary, Patrick Cleary. What's yours?" he asked, extending his hand.

Edward began to feel cramps in his stomach. When he told the pilot he had forgotten about the water, he said, "Nothing you can do about it now except try to get it out of your system before you take off again. Bathroom's in the back." He made a motion with one hand toward the rear of the office. "I have some bottled stuff. Help yourself if you're thirsty." He smiled, then looked out the window at a car approaching the building. "That's my wife. See you kid. Have a good flight."

They shook hands. The pilot departed and Edward raced to the toilet. Sitting on the seat, he thought again how stupid he'd been about the water. His insides felt like barbed wire. He waited until he felt nothing more coming.

When he walked outside, he saw a man screwing the cap on the fuel tank of his plane. "Hey! What are you doing? I didn't ask for fuel!"

"Sorry, *señor*. I always fill the gas. The boss, he has always told me to do this." He smiled, then added, "Eight gallons you only needed, so that is less than five American dollars."

Edward demanded, "The gas, does it have impurities? Bad stuff?"

"I do not think so. I come back after the lunch, but the boss, he always knows the gas." Edward paid him, slid into the rear seat and taxied to the end of the runway. He decided to run a full mag check in order to test the fuel and its flow. At 1700 r.p.m.'s, each mag dropped off no more than the acceptable 100 points.

Sounds okay, he thought. Last leg. My stomach feels all right. I want to get to the Huachucas.

The afternoon advanced, but he had fallen further and further behind schedule. Twenty minutes into the third and final segment, the stomach cramps were increasingly painful. He tried to fight diarrhea by concentrating on flying and on the terrain below. His course over the high range of the Huachucas required an elevation of approximately 9,000 feet. Miller, Carr and Ramsey peaks were higher, but he could cross between them. The mountains were still about thirty miles away. There was no way around, and he wanted to be in them anyway. The crash site was at around 8,000 feet, near Scott Canyon.

I came all this way, didn't I? See, Dad, I fly pretty damn good.

Edward searched the land below, absolutely desolate from the Mexican border to the Huachucas— no ranches, no signs of life on the ungracious plains. When the cramps were at their strongest, he tightened his sphincter muscles. Jesus, he thought, I can't let go now.

He looked down at his hand on the control stick. Was it his imagination? Was the vibration coming from the plane or from him? No, the Cub trembled, but perhaps it was from leaning out the fuel too much. The engine had performed well so far. If there was going to be a problem from the gas, it should have occured earlier.

I have to stop getting excited when it's important to stay calm and relaxed, he thought. It's taking longer, but so what?

He checked the instrument panel. The oil pressure and temperature gauges read normal. A smell? He sniffed, his nose raised like an animal sensing danger. No, nothing. He shook as if chilled.

The afternoon sun lowered, creating a rich texture on the plain and on the serrated walls of the ranges which loomed larger as he approached the Santa Ritas on the left and the Huachucas dead ahead. Other mountains drifted all the way to the horizon on his right. The air had purpled, a magenta separating the deepness of color at the bottom from the pinks and pale powder blue of the canopy above.

The high-pitched roar of the engine remained almost steady, but, yes, he was sure he felt the vibrations now. And they were increasing. His body tensed and the cramps became worse.

Not much further, he thought. Have to climb higher. If the fuel's contaminated, she'll struggle, but if I get enough power, I can get up there.

The Cub complained, then strained, unable to respond to its pilot's commands.

He briefly considered the classic one-eighty, but the problem now wasn't the weather. His father wouldn't have turned back in this situation. There was only about a half-hour of daylight. Time, he needed time.

He was forced to make a shallow turn and eased back on the throttle as he did. Can't put this plane down in that rocky mess, he decided. There's nothing flat enough. Plunk it down in those oaks? Maybe I could walk away, but getting out is a whole different matter. Ease the power down as low as possible, take the strain off. Oh, if these cramps would only stop.

He began to sweat and tremble, both from his thoughts and from the roughness of the engine reverberating through the plane.

§

Richard Banks had grown increasingly concerned and was pacing up and down in his office like an expectant father. He consoled himself with the fact that he was confident Edward flew well enough and that the weather was good.

Where the hell are you, kid? What the blazes are you thinking about? Damn it, Edward, concentrate! You're more than two hours overdue, maybe three. The Cub was just top overhauled. Not much that could go wrong with that simple engine. And I know you wouldn't be stupid enough to fuel up in Nogales.

Banks telephoned the airport in Nogales and was told that Edward had departed much earlier. "By the way, you didn't fuel the plane, did you? You what! You dumb-bell. I'm going to file a formal complaint with your government. Where the hell do you guys get off gassing up planes? You'd better pray there's no problem. That kid's on his first cross-country. If anything happens, I will personally fly over and beat the shit out of whoever's responsible! Get me?"

§

"Come on, damn it, just a little more!" Edward pleaded. "The ridge is just a little higher. Please, we're past where I can turn around." His parents' crash site was just ahead. He'd pass directly over it.

Now the enriched flow of an oranging sun splattered the granite formations. Shadows filled the crevices, the canyons readying themselves for night. The small yellow plane neared the craggy masses which seemed to rise higher and higher as the plane labored unsuccessfully for altitude. The engine coughed, missing more and more. His cramps intensified. He knew that both he and his plane had been poisoned. The power the motor was supposed to supply no longer maintained the nose in the previous climb attitude.

He was sweating profusely and felt the sharp flashing of adrenalin. If he had to crash, he decided, he would try to do it exactly where his father had. In his fantasies, he had pictured circling over the site, in control, and then, when he was ready, jamming the throttle and tearing into the same spot. But this wasn't how it was supposed to go, this was all wrong. "God, please help me out of this," Edward begged. "I'll do anything! I promise!" The motor coughed one last time and became silent. The hours of steady drone were replaced by frightening quiet.

He remembered practicing forced landings. Richard Banks had instructed something like, "The first thing: Put the nose *down, opposite* to what your instinct tells you. You'll stall if you don't keep up your air speed. Next, pick a spot. Don't rush, select the best one. You won't believe you have time, but you do. And for Christ's sake, stay calm."

Edward's eyes widened, trying not to believe he had no choice but to come down into this mountainous morass that would destroy whatever invaded its privacy. He quickly reached for the magnetos and turned the master switch off, cutting the fuel flow and reducing the risk of fire on impact.

Instinctively, he pressed the left rudder, bringing the plane away from the steepest of the ridges. A recollection shot into his mind: playing with his toy airplanes and models when he was seven, imagining he had to crash-land after a dogfight in which he had disposed of Baron von Richtoven and his heinous henchmen. His plane, smoking badly, and he himself wounded, needed expert flying ability to make it down alive. In those days, Edward would expertly bring the stricken plane over the edge of the couch, and pancake it onto an incredibly short, bumpy kitchen table mat, over a plate or bowl. Only the very skilled pilots could pull it off.

The maneuver he executed now added time and permitted higher altitude over the lowering slopes. The best glide ratio and angle was fifty miles per hour. There's time, there's time, he reminded himself. Pick a spot. Damn this! Goddammit this to hell!! He search frantically, wanting to call out to his father's spirit.

The darkening haze from the sun made it difficult to see except straight down. He decided to spiral in a shallow circle. He hoped the Cub might start up and that whatever it was in the gas would be blown out. Then he remembered that the plane didn't have an electric starter.

All right, bird-brain, he thought, quickly directing his frustration at himself, do like you used to do with model planes—execute a forced landing. But a place, where's the spot? Sonufabitch, sonufabitch! Why is everything going wrong?

The altitude unwound like time running out. He had to make an immediate decision, but he saw nothing but rocks, trees and ground that was anything but flat. "Come on, come on!" he yelled. "A place!" He tightened the belt across his lap and pressed his shoulders back against the hard upright of his seat.

A minute later the land below revealed itself in more detail: ridges and canyons, outcroppings and boulders. But this terrrain wasn't as steep as what he'd been flying over a minute ago. There! It was a single space that he might slip into, not nearly long enough for a normal landing, but all there was. Maybe he could get in. It was on the edge of a rise. If he approached from below, he could bring the nose way up, slow the plane's forward speed and then just before stalling, pancake onto the area at about forty miles an hour. It might work.

He banked and lined up his approach under the rise. As he came closer, he saw that he didn't have enough altitude to accomplish the dead-stick landing he'd planned. He banked sharply and reversed direction, away from the rise. He was about 300 feet above a small canyon, filled with tall ponderosa pines and oaks. The canyon floor was the only place possible. He aimed down the center and pulled back on the control stick as far as he could with his right hand, bracing his left against the instrument panel.

Large green branches, as if hurled, flashed toward him. Quickly the slam of metal and fabric shrieked against the trees, their arms and bodies hacked off, parts sheared to accommodate an object that didn't fit. "Damn! Damn! Damn!" he screamed. He closed his eyes as he hit, hearing the terrible ferocity of the impact. There was some give as the wings tore, slowing the forward motion.

Edward smacked his head on one of the struts. He felt more pain as his right leg was gashed by the severed edge of the lower entry panel, which had torn off. The fuselage penetrated through the branches and came to rest at a thirty-degree angle to the ground. The last jolt was hard enough to push the engine off its mount and through the fire panel in front of him. Its rear portion looked bizarre inside the cabin, the wires hanging and the oil line spilling its life-supporting juices. The engine halted just inches in front of where he sat belted into his seat, but it remained smoking serenely in the cool mountain air.

Edward was shaking, and waiting for more. His terror was soon replaced by the realization that he wasn't dead, but then he became aware that he had defecated, the ooze apparent in his crotch. He laughed. Then he unbuckled his seat belt, raised the upper entry panel and squirmed through the opening. As he worked his way out, gas spilled down on him. He gasped. Oh, please, he thought, no fire, not now. One wing was folded back awkwardly against the fuselage. He glanced up at the other, caught above him in the branches.

He crawled laboriously onto the needle-covered ground and set-tled against the large, textured trunk of an evergreen. Then he surveyed the wreckage and himself. The right thigh area of his pants was bloody and wet. He crept back to the plane and grabbed the emergency kit. He slid his pants down and wrapped the wound he found with surgical gauze, binding it with the Ace bandage. The light was fading.

They'll never find me, he thought. I'm going to die here, right near Mom and Dad, but not with them. He scanned the small clearing.

His thoughts jammed like railroad cars about to smash, and he began to talk to his father: What were you thinking when you crashed? Probably the same as me, only you had to worry about Mom and the other two. You must have talked to them, but Mom died on impact or shortly after, didn't she? That must have broken your heart. You must have felt you were the world's biggest failure, you, a professional airline captain. And you had to look at the other husband and wife too, see what you did in their eyes. Oh, how horrible for you. I never really figured out how terrible. If only your leg wasn't busted!

You didn't want to leave her, but she was dead. For the first time, he let himself imagine how his mother had looked, her body distorted and bloody, with a look of frozen terror on her face, or what remained of it. He shuddered. You fixed the others up the best you could. The snow was deep and it was freezing, wasn't it? You rigged a splint and dragged yourself as far as you could.

He pictured his father fighting to pull himself through the snow drifts, cursing, hurting, knowing that it was only a question of time before he wouldn't be able to continue. Then having to give up, propping himself against the tree, knowing he'd never move from the spot alive. And his last gesture, writing that note. Even then he hadn't lost his sense of humor.

Edward began to sob, wailing loudly to an indifferent audience of trees and boulders. You weren't afraid to die. But you didn't *want* to die. You didn't want to leave me. You loved Mom and me and

Susie. And all the things you did. Flying, sports and just being alive. Mom loved living, too.

He wrapped his arms around his head, ducking down into his grief. He could hear the whistling melody of the wind through the pine needles above him.

I guess I never realized. Oh, Dad, all these years, underneath I decided in some crazy way that you left me because you didn't want to be with me, that I wasn't good enough. "Not good enough," he whispered slowly. "And I was so little."

Looking up, he noticed how the branches of the pines were like arms swaying in a rhythm, acting in concert with the wind. He was intent on their motion. He had not observed this before, how they appeared to swim and float in the air. I was so stupid and selfish not to understand. You didn't *want* to hurt me. I miss you so much.

He raised his arms straight up, his fingers outstretched. Please, wherever you are, hear me. I know it's too late, but I'd do anything to bring you back. You should have lived.

Mom, you loved me too. I always thought you didn't care about me and what I needed, but now I know you did. He heard his own deep breathing. I love you, I still do. It hurts that I can't tell you both how much I still love you. But I'll be with you soon. I'm not getting out of here, that's certain. Funny, to die here—not where you are, the way I almost planned. But you had it so much worse than me, the way you crashed in the dead of winter.

He had the sudden, thunderous thought that dying was only what he deserved, but then he rose up on his knees, sank back on his heels and covered his eyes. I was so angry, he understood at last. I didn't figure it out the way I should have. But I know it now. Please forgive me.

He listened. The only sound was the wind, singing a single note as it cried through the pine needles. He returned to his sitting place against the tree trunk.

The plane's tail had snapped and tilted backward, but otherwise the fuselage was intact. The wheels were still fastened, although the wing strut on the left side had slashed through the fabric above the wheel. He decided that there wasn't going to be a fire, but he felt dizzy and rested for a few minutes. Then he reentered the plane. For tonight anyway, he thought, inside. Safer. And warmer. Hope they start looking in the morning. The trouble is it'll be tough to spot the plane under these trees even though it's bright yellow. It's all over, he thought. But then he almost smiled. You sound like you're dead already! But you're not, jerk.

He was about to take water from the thermos and try to clean himself, but he decided it had to be saved instead. He remembered that he'd refrained from filling it with the water at the Nogales Airport, so what he had with him was drinkable. He wiped himself as well as possible with his large handkerchief. All right, Edward, you baby, you don't need to be so angry: check the rest of your emergency gear.

He inspected the pines in the diminishing light. Some reached a hundred feet or more. His vision pierced in and out until he noticed a larger clearing not far away. He decided to pull pieces of the yellow fabric into it, as many parts as he could, so that they would be visible from the air. That's what they do in the movies, he thought. But no one can land and take off here! They'd better find me quickly.

Slowly and arduously, he managed to pull off a large section of the wing. He used the last vestiges of light to drag it and other parts from the plane into the clearing. They should see that, he thought. They'd better. Ouch, my head hurts. Nothing to do but sit in the fuselage and get some sleep.

Inside, he reflected on the flight. Dummy! This didn't have to happen. You could have turned back when you had the chance. Or not left Nogales and called Richard. Stayed over and flown back the next morning. And especially after that jerk filled the tank—you should have called and told Richard.

But then, instead of blaming his fate on others or being angry at himself, as he'd always done in the past, sweet calmness came over him. One of the Psalms he'd memorized for his bar mitzvah began to run through his mind, and he closed his eyes, remembering how it looked on the page:

> I lift mine eyes unto
> the hills; whence cometh
> my help? My help com-
> eth from the Lord, who
> made heaven and earth.
> He will not suffer thy
> foot to stumble;
> Behold, the guard-
> ian of Israel, He
> sleepeth not. The sun shall
> not smite thee by day,
> nor the moon by night.
> The Lord shall preserve
> thee from all evil; He
> will preserve thy soul.
> The Lord will watch
> over thy going out, and
> thy coming in, from this
> time forth and for evermore.

The waiting tears moved slowly down his cheeks, and he felt a strange sense of serenity, that everything was all right. At least for these moments, he was still alive. And being alive had an almost unbearable sense of joy and sweetness. He heard the piercing shrill of a jay, and in the distance, an answering call. Then he slept.

§

THIRTY

Richard Banks was fuming. "What the hell do you mean, you can't get more planes? What do you guys in the C.A.P. do, dress up in your Boy Scout uniforms and march around playing with yourselves? We have a plane down. *Repeat*! *A plane is down*! Don't give me any of your bullshit! Two searching aren't enough."

"Now keep your hat on," the voice at the other end of the phone said, "we're doing all we can. Some of the guys just aren't available. I can't help that. This isn't the Army. The war's over, you know."

"You listen to me, buster, and listen good!" Banks shouted. He tapped on the desk top in a staccato pattern. "If you haven't lined up at least *six* planes by noon, I am personally going to call your C.O. in Phoenix, and then I'm contacting the governor's office. Your ass is going to be in more trouble than you ever dreamed of. You get me?"

"All right, let me see what I can do." The Civil Air Patrol official was about to hang up, but added, "What were you, a drill sergeant?

Take it easy, Banks, we're doing the best we can. I'll call you later."

"Just a minute," Banks snapped, his voice bristling, "you'd better understnd something. The pilot's an eighteen-year old kid who's like my own. We're taking off from here with three planes in one-half an hour. I've got a rancher from Patagonia and maybe an Ercoupe from Nicksville. We're searching on a line fanning out both sides from a direct Nogales to Fort Huachuca route. Get those other planes! *I'll* call *you* when we get back."

He put down the receiver and gazed at the thunderstorms crossing the peaks of the Huachucas to the southwest. He failed to notice Ernesto, who had entered quietly. "Not good," the Mexican said, gesturing at the sky.

Banks turned. "You're Ernesto Bejarano, aren't you?" Banks put out his hand.

Ernesto nodded, reached for a pack of cigarettes, and offered one to Banks. His face was weathered and lined, but Banks noticed that his eyes were a shade of blue not easily forgotten. He had thought all Mexicans' eyes were brown. Silently, the two men studied the mountains for a moment. Then Ernesto spoke, calmly but with an edge of great concern. "The Cub's yellow, isn't it?" He turned toward Banks. "I'd like to join you." The eyes were piercing.

"I was going to call you right away," Banks responded. "I know you know these mountains as well as anyone." He motioned to the other men who were arriving that he wanted to get started. "Bejarano and I will fly the new Cessna. I've marked these maps for each of you." Then to the others, "Look, the weather will keep you from flying everywhere, but obviously whatever areas you can cover can make all the difference. Thanks, guys."

As they taxied to the end of the runway, Ernesto leaned over and advised, "When you make your passes, try to do it up and down the canyons instead of across. The chances are he's not on a ridge but down *in* one of them. If the canyon's narrow or the trees're real tall, we'll pass over too quickly. He could be difficult to spot, yellow or no yellow."

Soon they were airborne, sweeping up in a short ascent above the high desert floor. Cumulus and cumulonimbus began to gather over the mountains. They climbed and turned west, over hills that were bathed in early morning light, the old purples transformed into the beiges and tans of a new day. It was bumpy as they plowed through invisible currents of air. Banks peered at Ernesto, whose bushy eyebrows were raised at the turbulence, and shouted through the noise, "Think of it as water flowing over boulders. It's the same with air over ridges and mountains. Where do you want to begin?"

"Montezuma Pass," Ernesto responded without hesitation, "then Copper Canyon and Bear Creek. Granite Peak, too. His father crashed near there. The best I can figure is that Edward had to fly next to Granite to get between Carr and Ramsey." Banks pointed his finger first to the right side, then motioned to the left. Ernesto nodded. They started scanning, flying a random pattern up one canyon, over a ridge and down another, like eager hunting dogs after a scent.

After an hour of arduous probing, they completed a run over the Bear Creek pack trail. "When we finish Lone Mountain Canyon," Ernesto said, "fly the other side of Granite." As Banks headed the Cessna there, the floor of the canyon rose swiftly, and they proceeded toward the 8,000-foot peak that loomed ahead.

A rain squall edged across their path, an unwelcome adversary. "Damn," Banks shouted, "where the hell could he be? Thunderstorms all over the place. We can't stay. Hell, it's like looking for a needle in a haystack."

Several miles and a few canyons away, Edward thought he heard the noise of a plane engine, but he wasn't sure it couldn't have been his imagination. He had awoken earlier, cold, stiff and hungry. The same rain squalls had kept him inside the fuselage, which he had managed to level by moving aside branches and lowering the high tail portion. The gash in his thigh throbbed. He rewound the bandage over the wound, hoping it would prevent additional bleeding.

I guess I wanted to be killed, he marveled. But now I'm not so sure. Not that sure of anything.

The rule when you're down, Richard had said, is to stay put. But how can they spot me? It's so quiet and lonely. Damn the weather. Which way is out of here? Canyons can be like rabbit mazes. It's already the second day. I'm hungry. I'm scared, too.

Hungry as blazes, he continued to think. If that *was* a plane, it was too far away. They must be looking. Damn all this rain. Lousy visibility. Maybe I can trap some animal, but how? At the next break in the rain, I'll see.

He peered at the edges of the clearing. Tall ponderosas, their bark as rough as if someone had taken a knife and chiseled indentations into them, went straight up, like a wall guarding a penitentiary. Grasses bunched in small islands of green and tan, separated by large stones and rough boulders. I can't possibly bring down birds, he thought. But maybe in those rocks, a chipmunk—if I stand frozen, throw my jacket over one.

He maneuvered himself to the side where the breeze was blowing at him so his smell couldn't be detected, and raised his jacket very slowly over his head. As he'd hoped, the squeaking sounds of small animals abounded in the rocks, and after several minutes a chipmunk popped out about three feet away. He flung his jacket, but it escaped. "You're supposed to let me catch you," he said aloud.

Just as he was about to vacate the rocks, a small snake wiggled hear him. He saw that it was a diamondback rattler, and carefully, as Ernesto had showed him, he picked up two stones. He shifted position and threw the first, which arrested the snake's movements. Then he moved closer and hit its head with the other. The snake writhed and lay motionless.

Edward waited a moment and bent down. He was completely

unprepared for what happened next: the snake struck his left arm so rapidly that he was hardly aware of its motion. He stood and stomped its head until he was sure it was dead.

Don't panic, he thought, you know what to do! Ernesto showed you.

He raced to the plane and took out the emergency kit and snake bite packet. The fangs had punctured the soft area above his left wrist, between the two bones that formed the forearm. He tightly wrapped a tourniquet above the bite, then removed the triangular blade fashioned into a round piece of wood from the kit.

This is me and this is real! Pretend it's a movie, he thought. Cut "X's," suck out the venom. The snake was little, maybe the poison's not that strong. Ready? No!

C'mon, Edward, don't delay. Do it! Make cuts one-quarter inch deep and a quarter long, in "X's" or "V's." You've got to, it's the only way. You know it is.

He grabbed a smooth stick, broke a piece off, and placed it between his back teeth. Then he untied the tourniquet, inhaled deeply, bit down hard into the stick and firmly held the round wooden holder with the triangularly shaped razor.

He breathed deeply again and noticed his right hand shaking. Steadying it with his left, he made the first crude "V" above the reddening holes. He was astonished how much more it hurt than he had expected, and how loud the moan he emitted through his clenched teeth was. He'd make all the cuts quickly, he decided, because he was sure that if he stopped, he would lose his nerve. Soon he had cut three "V's" into his flesh, and he put the razor down. His forearm was bathed in flowing blood, wine-colored and running like spilled gravy.

He sucked blood and spat it from each of the "V's," repeating the procedure several times and then retying the tourniquet. After a few minutes he loosened it. The blood flowed and he sucked again, spitting out the blood and saliva. Again. And again. After a while the flow slowed. He felt a strange satisfaction, the pride that he had done something difficult and necessary.

When he had calmed down, he crawled over to the snake. If I can cut into myself like that, I can cook and eat this goddamned thing, he thought. Keeping out of the intermittent rain, he carefully built a small fire under the stabilizer of the plane. Then he severed the snake's head, peeled the skin and sliced the snake into chunks. He held these over the flame, one by one, each pierced by the sharpened end of a stick. The flesh was chewy and the taste was strange, but he swallowed the chunks with sips of water. Better than nothing, he thought. It'll keep me going.

He climbed back into the fuselage and huddled as much as he could, wrapping the towels from the back of the plane aound his shoulders and over his head. He fell into a deep sleep, but he was awakened when it was still dark by the bleating calls of two magpies that had settled in the pines above. He had been dreaming. Both sets of parents stood across from his bed. They spoke, first individually, then as a chorus. It was baffling not to be able to make out what they were saying. The way they looked at him he knew it was important, as if everything they had ever learned was summed up in what they were trying to tell him. Then Sam Slavin stepped in front of the others. It was all so eerie; it reminded him of a soloist or a statesman speaking from a podium. His father smiled, the same smile he'd had that time he was still in the Air Force when he threw his arms out and pretended to be an airplane. He motioned, as if he wanted Edward to either follow him or come closer, but the gesture wasn't clear.

Waking, Edward was quickly slapped with the realization of where he was. He felt groggy, and couldn't tell whether it was from the snakebite or general exhaustion. It was still night. All he could do was try to keep warm, and try to sleep. Just before losing consciousness again, he thought how frightened he was being alone in that remoteness. He knew there were bobcats and mountain lions, even jaguars that came through once in a while. And certainly coyotes. He could hear them off somewhere. If they're going to get me, okay let them, he thought. Baloney, jerk! They always run except when they're cornered. Don't you remember that Ernesto told you that over and over?

He was jarred from sleep several times during the night and glanced at his watch. Now dawn was still an hour or so away. On the horizon, behind the dark silhouette on the east, the blackness was not yet prepared to relinquish its grasp on the canopy of sky. What did that dream mean?

Light would come, wouldn't it? Of course, it always does. You can count on the light. Everythng is better then. But you're still stuck, Edward. There's no one to run to for help, and no one to help you unless you're spotted.

To the north, where the sun was about to rise, the Big Dipper seemed to be falling, the bottom of the bucket dropping over the furthest range. The air was absolutely still and fresh. As the light began, the outlines of the Huachucas became more visible again.

He remembered other things Ernesto had told him, not the exact words, but the ideas: How a man has to make a place for himself, that nothing or no one can do it for him because each person has to struggle and solve his own problems. Some make it, some don't. Even the Major had said something like that. That's the way it is. You're born, you live, you die. You never know when, so you'd better keep living the best you can. Margaret had said another thing: The difference between us and animals is that we love. Edward lifted his head. A small crisp breeze washed hs face. It was all so silent. And lonely, yet he seemed able to think calmly.

I want to see them all again, Mom and Dad, little Mikey and Susie, Aunt Sandra. Even Francesca. Not Mom and Dad Slavin, they can't.

I want to get out of here! If only I can. The snakebite's not going to make it easier.

Edward rolled himself out of the fuselage, stood and unbuttoned his cuff. He had bound his forearm with a piece of torn towel, and now it was colored the roan red of dried blood. He felt woozy and sat down. When he heard the distant sound of a motor again, he listened, pulling in the sounds as if someone was calling him. But it was too far away and faded into the wind. He sipped the last of the water from the canteen and gazed at the scene surrounding him. He imagined riding with Ernesto. "Figure it out, Eddie. Like I taught you."

"You'd say it's up to me. You'd tell me I have to be with myself no matter what happens—don't let anything or any one destroy me. And Francesca said 'Always remember who you are.'"

Edward clenched his fist and walked as quickly as he could to the Cub, where he perused the wreckage. He inspected both the gash in his thigh and his wounded forearm, and he rewound the bindings. Then he formed some of the yellow pieces into the shape of an arrow. I'm not just sticking around and waiting in case someone flies over to save me, he thought. I'm getting out of here while I still can. Just take it easy, buddy. Think, for a change. Let's see: what will I need to take?

At the fuselage, he filled his small hiking pack with the empty canteen, the first aid kit, some rope, what was left of the towel, and his wool hat. His knife was in his pocket. He selected the piece of the wing fabric with the large "N," part of the Cub's identification number. Maybe one day it would hang on his wall at home. He would have liked to have one of the seats, to place next to the one he still had in his room.

I'll come back for it, he mused. That is, if I survive. Cut that out! *You'll make it.* You will because—because you're going to.

When he reached the edge of the crash site, he looked back at it. "Good-bye plane. Thanks. You did your job. The rest is up to me." He inhaled deeply, took a last look and set off.

§

THIRTY-ONE

Deciding that he couldn't climb the steep pass ahead of him to the north, Edward navigated through the large clearing to the south end of the canyon. North would have been better because it was in the direction of Fort Huachuca, but he'd be lucky to have enough strength to get out to the trail he remembered to the south. Unfortunately, this was a box canyon, and he would have to ascend at least two hundred feet in order to descend into the one adjacent.

The sun became hotter, draining and slowing any animal in its sight. Edward found that he needed to stop more often than he wanted to. He came to a spring and sank his face into the tiny runoff, then filled the canteen. That's a help, he thought. But how long will it take me? And where's the damn trail?

He shuffled between stands of large pines, cottonwoods and oaks, trying not to think about the snake bite and concentrating on listening for plane engines. He kept trying to picture a rescue party on its way up.

When he rested, he took small sips of water. Nausea was becoming a constant companion, but he vowed not to vomit. Concentrate, he told himself and keep moving. Yes, okay. Find the trail. He pitched ahead.

Major Healey. Ernesto, Dad. Francesca. Richard. Dad. You didn't get far from the wreck, did you, Dad? Snow too high.

Thirty minutes later he found the terminus of the trail, which began at the bottom end of a small mountain pasture, where the grasses ran to an edge of a cliff. The trail wound tightly against a rock face with a dropoff of about fifty feet. Edward lassoed an outcropping so that he could hold onto the rope while he crossed. The sun beat down on him with real fury now.

Slowly, slowly, he made his way across. Then he sagged in the shade against a tree. He knew now that his mind was affected by the venom injected into him by the snake. He was in a kind of trance, with little dreams grabbing him like a pack of coyotes, snatching small pieces of his consciousness. Francesca was with him, laughing. She's so free, he decided, not troubled by an arm amputated right below her shoulder. "Edward," she whispered, "what's wrong with you? You're wasting too much time."

He shook himself into reality. Loosen and retighten the tourniquet, he thought. Slow down the poison. C'mon, keep moving. You can't spend another night here.

He struggled to pull himself up and leaned for a moment against the tree. He imagined being in conversation with Ernesto: "You know how to survive, damn you, now move your ass! You're young, you're going to make it. Not just for me, for yourself."

Francesca reappeared: *"Remember who you are!"* Edward nodded.

The venom was succeeding, afflicting him with the sureness that nature had designed. What he hated most as he stumbled on and forced himself down the trail was that it was winning control of his mind, not permitting him to really think. He resolved to be stronger than it.

Going to do it, can't be far, he thought. See them soon. Maybe just a little rest, then go on. Sip some water, yeah, over there, in the shade, just off the trail.

He leaned against the thick bark of an evergreen and quickly fell into a deep sleep. When he woke, the beams of sunlight filtered by the trees had shifted many feet from where they had shone earlier. He realized that he had slept far longer than he should have.

He went on, staggering the distance down the trail until it emptied into a large meadow. A deserted mine was off to the left, its entrance seated into the side of a hill. He knew he could not go on, at least not right away, and sat down on a boulder near the mine. He was just about to open the canteen when he saw dust rise from a vehicle coming up the road. Once he decided it wasn't an illusion, he sped toward it as a truck came into view. Mel Martin waved and drove up to him.

"I thought I'd head up the trail a bit, in case you'd be coming out. Glad to see you, boy. We were a touch worried." He stepped out. "Your Dad and Richard Banks been flying around up all over. You sure look done in." He put a hand on Edward's shoulder.

Edward looked back toward the mountains. He inhaled deeply, throwing his shoulders back like a new recruit who had completed basic training. Mel helped him gently into the truck.

§

THIRTY-TWO

Of all the mental vignettes Edward retained since arriving at the hospital twenty hours earlier, the one he remembered most was how soft the cot in the Emergency Room felt when he'd collapsed onto it. What he saw when he woke were the curtains billowing in the afternoon breeze and the grinning face of Richard Banks.

Edward raised himself up on his elbows, only to be battered down by a headache whose intensity might as well as have been coming from a blacksmith pounding a metal clamp around his head.

"So," Banks began, "you just couldn't restrain yourself, could you?" Edward wondered what he was referring to specifically. "Talking to you is like pissing in the wind. Didn't I make it a point to warn you not to gas up in Nogales?" His tone ranged somewhere between annoyance and razzing; Edward wasn't sure which it was. "And you decide to give the Mexicans business! I'm not paying for *that*, buster. It's coming out of your pocket, not mine."

What the hell was he talking about, Edward wondered?

"And if you think you're getting any compliments from me about your forced landing, forget it. I'm not even sure I won't have them confiscate your license for keeps." Banks seemed delighted with his choice of words.

Edward realized at last that Richard was elated to see him. "Cut that out, will you please?" he asked. "You should say something nice about the fantastic way I plunked old Betsy down into that mess of trees." His arm throbbed where he had made the cuts. He must have looked at it, because Richard told him the doctors had stitched them with some difficulty and added that Edward's skill as a surgeon would never get him into medical school.

"You're full of it," Edward bantered back. "Under those circumstances? I did fantastic, all around," he said with assurance. "Let me see *you* do half as well. You'd probably be too squeamish, and die of snake poisoning. Besides, no self-respecting snake would even bother to bite you." Then he became serious. "Was it you flying over where I was?" He shut his eyes, remembering the terrible frustration of not being seen.

"Yeah, I think so. Ernesto guessed you'd be near there. We were together. He wouldn't give up." Banks rose from the chair. "You did damn well, kid. Now I'm not kidding. You didn't fall apart. What you did wasn't easy, not for anyone." He placed a hand on the form made by one of Edward's legs under the bed sheet.

"Where is he, where's Dad?" Edward asked. The question was delivered firmly, not with the ring of a little boy's voice, or even a teenager's.

Banks cleared his throat. "He stayed here all night, sat in the chair next to your bed. Your mother was here for a while too. They told the nurse they'd be back soon. You'll be out tomorrow, the doctor said so."

"Good," Edward said rapidly. "Are they okay?" He tried to con-

312

jure up their faces. Before Banks could answer, he asked, "What day is today? I lost count."

"Friday. All day." A nurse came in and took Edward's temperature. "I see you're going to get fussed over. I have to get out of here anyway. There's a *huge* airline to run." He reached the door, then looked back and said, "Since you've been away on vacation, I've had to do all the paperwork and scheduling." He braced, his hands on his hips like an indignant business executive preparing himself to mouth clichés: "I'm much too important for that type of activity. I need some poor dumb jerk to do the donkey work. And I had one before he decided to go camping in the Huachucas. He's not very bright, but it's tough to get the right help these days." His expression became serious. "You've been very important to the operation, Eddie," he said. "And you're very important to me, too." Then he added a characteristic parting shot: "I wouldn't fool around with these nurses. They're familiar with your kind. You'd wind up in big trouble, and I'd have to come to your rescue. Like always." He headed swiftly out the door.

The nurse declared his fever down, and said the doctor would be coming soon to check his arm. He was responding rapidly to the penicillin and teramycin, she added.

Then she checked his blood pressure and advised him to finish his apple juice. When she touched him, Edward focused on the sensations: soothing and agreeable. She had him turn over on his stomach in order to administer an alcohol rub to his back. The sensation of her fingers required him to concentrate on the fact that it was simply a procedure any patient would receive, but he couldn't help imagining her hands traveling further in a lingering and provocative manner. When she told him to turn over again, the sheet rose as if a pole was lifting a tent. He brought his hands rapidly to his penis. She laughed and kissed him lightly on the mouth.

"Yum," Edward said, "more of that." He reached for her hand, but she pulled away, saying something about all the nurses and attendants who were around and that as a newly commissioned lieutenant, the last thing she needed was anything in her record to hurt her career. "How about when you get off?" She responded with a smile and a noncommital "maybe."

This *is* really nice, Edward thought. Kind of light, a lightness. That garbage I carried around, what happened to it? It's gone, finished. I'm rid of it. Strange and nice, I feel great. What died up there was that old part of me. I hope.

The phone next to his bed jangled, and he swept his thoughts into suspension. The voice was familiar. The lilt, the sassiness, the direct manner could only belong to Francesca. Like vines competing for the same tree to latch onto, his mixed feelings wove around each other.

"You had me up all night," she began, as if they talked every day. "It was all over the radio. I just heard you were okay and in the Fort hospital. I would have driven down right away, but that bastard, *mi esposo,* took my car and hid it so I couldn't use it. When—how did—oh, tell me everything when I see you, all right?" She talked so fast Edward couldn't find an opportunity to respond. "The announcer said a rancher found you near an old mine."

"Mel Martin. Ernesto searched for me from a plane with Richard Banks. Francesca, I thought about you." He added, "I remembered the days and nights in Magdalena."

"Yes," she responded softly. "I prayed for you, Edward, as much as I ever prayed for anything." Her voice slowed down. "Were you hurt, I mean, do you have any bad injuries?"

"No, I'm fine, Francesca. I stupidly let a snake bite me. It made me crazy, like being on a drunk. The worst part was having to make cuts in my arm to get the poison out." He wasn't going to miss the chance to share that piece of drama with her.

"Oh." She became quiet. . . .

314

"But everything's fine, the doctors here stitched them all up, the fever's gone, and the gash in my leg—"

"Your leg?"

"When I crashed. A piece of the plane sliced into me." He hesitated. "But I'm fine, really." His was the voice of the hero, John Wayne or Robert Ryan playing the part of a Marine fighter pilot. He couldn't have been more pleased with himself.

"Edward. Tomorrow, I *will* see you. I'm going to borrow my girlfriend's car." He advised her to call the hospital first because he most probably would have been released, but he'd expect her, he said. He'd be at Ernesto and Margaret's.

"I'm glad you're coming, Francesca. So much has happened. Not just the crash. I think I've changed." The sound of a plane taking off filled the room. He looked through the window and saw the flashing lights of an ambulance racing up the driveway.

"We will talk, Edward, like we always do." When she said that, he hoped there would be more. "I've missed you, *hombre*." A moment, then, *"mañana."*

§

Margaret and Ernesto greeted him with yips and shouts, so loud that the nurse shut the door. Then they were on his bed, laughing, talking. The baby was somewhere among them. "Banks told me you made a helluva landing. Don't do that again, will you please? I'm too young for heart failure," Ernesto cautioned.

Margaret brought his hand to her mouth and kissed it three times. "We were so relieved when Mel called us. There's nothing worse than feeling helpless." She mussed his hair. "You look terrible," she said. "And thin. We'll get you back to normal with some good home cooking." Edward was delighted. He hadn't even waited to be invited back before he'd told Francesca he'd be there.

315

"Jesus, we just couldn't locate your plane. We tried so hard."

"Dad, I want to go back there."

Ernesto gazed deeply into Edward's eyes. "You sure? All right, when you're up to it. We got a release for you, so let's vamoose. We brought you some clothes. Francesca called, she'll be down tomorrow. We invited her to stay over."

"Do we have to pay or anything?" Edward asked as he got out of bed.

"They said they'd send us the bill."

"I'll take care of it. I want to," Edward said. Ernesto looked at Margaret, and then he nodded.

§

"*Buenas tardes, amigo,*" Francesca sang out. She smiled and hugged Edward tightly. Her hair was shorter, and although she no longer looked like the very young woman of a year or two earlier, Edward still found her breathtaking.

She'd be sexy no matter how she dressed, he thought. Her looks could stop a train. All the trains.

"You're as gorgeous as ever," he told her. "But I shouldn't say that to a married woman, should I?" He hoped she would disagree.

"Well, I'm not really sure. He's away this week, so I don't have to deal with him." She looked away for a moment. "He *was* nice, really he was, Edward, until we got married. After that he thought he owned me." The inflection and the hiss in her voice reminded him of the way she used to talk about Alberto. He kicked himself mentally for feeling a surge of hope.

For the next hour they talked about the crash, and he spoke haltingly to her of his new lightness. Then Francesca related what had happened to her since they were last together. "I like the way you sound, *hombre*. You're a survivor, like me. It makes you strong, yes?

316

Yes. And you are much more attractive now you are a man. Before, also, but only as a boy." That pleased him.

They drove to their favorite place along the San Pedro. Edward had bought a large T-bone and other groceries for the occasion, and Francesca made a concoction she called *"arroz con legumes Mexicanos."* They cooked and ate luxuriously, and talked about their early experiences. A few hours of daylight remained.

"Eddie, I want to go back to the place I used to live and see what's left of that shack. I've been thinking a lot about those years, even dreaming about them." She stopped for a moment. "I'd still like to get my hands on that bastard Alberto. Oh, would I like that! Thirty seconds would be enough, Edward." She breathed audibly. "But first I need to take a shower and change. I have been in these clothes all day and the drive down was sticky." They returned to the Ramsey Canyon house. Margaret had given Francesca Edward's room, and he was to sleep on the living room couch.

Edward lay on the living room floor and waited. He piled the baby's blocks one on top of another, remembering his own when he was small. His father would ask, "Ready?" and then would slowly topple them. And Edward would laugh, enjoying the fun, and then put the blocks in his father's hand and beg to repeat the game. He listened to the shower and imagined how Francesca looked naked as the water splashed off her splendid body.

A few minutes later, they drove further up Ramsey Canyon. Edward watched Francesca's face as they passed the bend where the two oaks marked a gate in the fence. "Stop here," she ordered. "If you don't mind, I want to walk the rest alone." There was a strange look on her face, as if she was almost oblivious to the present. He saw her open the door, step down, and gaze for a long time at the ruins of the shack. Then she moved slowly to the gate, leaving it ajar as she stepped through.

It seemed to Edward that the daylight diminished rapidly as he waited. A breeze swayed the grasses, and then tops swirled like the wind blowing across the surface on the water of a lake. He buttoned his denim jacket. Francesca turned and motioned for him to come to where she stood. "So many memories. I was so ignorant at the beginning. Some men should be exterminated. Everyone would be better off without them." She hesitated, then snarled, "They should have their balls cut off."

"And I never had any idea until you left about just how bad it was for you." He knew he should have understood better, but he'd been far too devoted to his own pain.

"I called Roberto," Francesca said. "He must not have gotten my message. I miss him. Maybe in a couple of weeks he will come from Albuquerque. We can have a reunion." Edward was close enough to her to smell the odor of her soap. It made him catch his breath. They walked back to the truck.

An orange moon climbed up from the horizon, slowly turned white, and stood on one of its crescent ends. The night was balmy and peaceful. When they got back to the house, Francesca lingered in the doorway. "It's much nicer here than in Phoenix. The nights there are not as cool or quiet. And there are too many people."

The rest of the household was asleep. Edward made a fire and Francesca prepared a pot of coffee. "Having you here is great. I can share how I feel, about things that happen." He meant every word. "You're as strong a person as I've ever met." It sounded corny, he thought, but he knew it was true.

"Christ, you and I had to do without so much, didn't we?" she asked. "Sometimes I'm surprised I'm not in the looney bin." She laughed, indicating how close she thought she'd come to it.

Edward stared into the fire. "I never realized before all the things you showed me, Francesca. I mean, I thought men were the only ones you learn from." He turned from the fire and looked at her seriously. "But women are very strong in their way, even stronger

318

than men." He held her hand. "It's taken me a while to understand things, hasn't it?"

She smiled. "You're fine," she said. She rose, watching his face. "It's time for bed." He had a certain expression that caused her to say, "No, Edward, that is not a good idea. Sleep well."

He trudged reluctantly to the couch in the living room. Lying down, he listened to the sounds in the night outside.

Some time much later he was surprised when Francesca came out from his bedroom and sat down on the couch where he slept. "I don't want to be alone tonight," she whispered. "I need you to hold me. Come inside." They went in to the bedroom, and Edward carefully closed the door. Francesca slipped under the covers and put her arms around him. "This feels very good, Edward. I have had a very sad time with my husband. But I think I am finally rid of him. I made a terrible mistake. I was so anxious to get out of Magdelena that I let him just take me away. Unfortunately, I got to know him only too late. It really was not even his fault." She held Edward tightly, and wrapped her legs around him.

"I could stay like this forever, foo-foo," he whispered.

"How come that's my name?" Francesca asked. She sniffed the skin of his lower neck and made a sound of approval.

"I don't know, I just thought of it. It's the way I think of you."

She took his head in her hands and kissed him gently on the mouth. "I need you tonight as much as you need me." She held him very close and kissed him on his neck, his ears, his cheeks and again on his mouth. She took his hand and placed it on her breast. "Yes," she said, breathing faster. "It's all right. Let yourself go."

Edward lost all sense of consciousness. He was able to abandon his recollections, here with her, without time, drifting, floating above everything, without the gravity that held him on the ground. He was aware of nothing except how good it was and how intimate he felt with her.

After breakfast the next morning, Francesca declared it was time for her to leave. "I have things to do in Phoenix. My job in that real estate office, for example." Outside, the disappointment on his face reminded her of a little boy's. "Oh, Eddie, stop looking that way. We will be in touch. I am not staying in that house, so don't worry if you cannot call me. I'll let you know when I get settled again." She waited for him to say something.

"We're going to miss you."

"I know you will. I'll miss you too." Francesca threw her arm around his neck and leaned her head against his shoulder. "You know," she said, "there was a time when things were so bad life seemed like a never-ending horror movie."

"When you first went to Mexico?" he asked.

"Yes," she said. "Earlier too. Much earlier. But with you, Eddie, sex was always more than just pacifying or getting approval. Besides, I knew you almost from the beginning. I used to watch you when you rode by our shack. And all the years growing up. No, it was always different with you."

Edward stared at her. "You seem to be able to survive everything, Francesca. You really know what you want, and you're determined. You're very fortunate." He felt his new confidence slipping.

She knew what he was thinking. "Edward," she answered carefully, "we cannot live together, you know." She had always been like that: direct, with no fooling around.

"Okay, okay, okay!" he said angrily. "Go find your Prince Charming! I'll be just fine without you. You've got it all wrong. I don't *need* you, I really don't." He stormed toward the corral.

Soon Francesca came out carrying a small valise. She put it in her car and then came over to where he was. "Edward, sometimes you really give me a swift pain in the ass." He kicked into the dirt several times. "Hey, I'm not going anywhere, except to Phoenix right now." She kissed him on the mouth.

He watched her drive away, and once her car disappeared around the turn he hit the fence post. Then he slumped along the fence, out of view from the house. "Go to hell, Francesca!" he yelled. He picked up one of Ernesto's half-smoked cigarettes and held it up. "You're not getting the best of me, no one is," he muttered defiantly. He sat down again and chucked the cigarette away.

"You know, Francesca, the trouble with you is that you've become a goddamn know-it-all. Trying to impress your old pal, Eddie Slavin, with how smart and wise you are? Well Francesca, my dear, you can go fly a kite. I'm going to look around for someone who wants me more than just a visit once in a while." He stood up and brushed off his Levis.

But after a minute or two he thought some more. He'd gotten caught up in the old self-pity again. She's not wrong, you know she's not, Slavin. That's just the way she feels.

He inhaled, trying to remember the way she'd smelled the night before.

Suddenly, he hoped it wasn't too late to see Major Healey.

Edward moved away from the corral and headed up the road. High cirrus strung out across the center of the sky, creating a sense of white motion. He brought his eyes around in a complete circle: the Huachucas first, then to the north toward the Fort and Sierra Vista, continuing onto the prairie in the direction of the Dragoons and Tombstone, then to Hereford and Naco, somewhere beyond, then Mexico and finally back again to the Huachucas.

Without knowing why, Edward began to smile. The smile developed into a wide grin, and then he laughed. "You are really a funny duck, Edward," he said out loud. "But I do like you. You're coming along pretty good. Don't mess up, because that can ruin everything. It takes time. And you have things to do."

Edward swung himself around in a wide circle as if he were a dancer. "You damn well do." He clapped his hands for what seemed like a long time.